# YOU CALL THIS

# 'PEACE'?

Eric Brady

The Jackson story
Part 3

# COPYRIGHT

## You call this 'Peace'?

# Table of Contents

# Chapter 1
## Start ups

"Do you deal in cruisers, Mrs. Jackson?" Terry asked. "Only father is thinking of getting one."

It was a warm spring Sunday afternoon and he was sitting with Kathleen and Anne in the garden, the remains of tea on tables nearby. Ron had just left to collect Tim from Wingmore Airfield where Tim was now working in the Control Tower.

Three years had passed since he had joined his father, Anne and Kathleen in Folkestone.

It had been a hard decision for him as May, his mother, had been so against it but as a 14 year old he hadn't liked the jobs his step-father, Des Ackroyd, had talked of getting for him. The lure of working with 'planes, though that had just been in the Stores as the Junior to start with, had proved much stronger than working in an architect's or shipping office in London.

He had worked solidly in the Spares Department, learned all he could of the way the Airfield operated and spent every moment he could in the Control Tower where it was his ambition to work. Six months ago he had achieved that ambition.

Still seriously disabled, often in pain from his semi-paralysed arm and fractured ankle, he was as determined as Kathleen to live a 'normal' life despite the injuries.

"Only very small boats – more dinghies than proper boats really. But that is an idea," she added thoughtfully. "We'd need to find the right kind of premises of course with a slipway first. But I wonder ...."

Kathleen looked sharply at her.

That was how the Carruthers Group of Companies had expanded over the years. From Anne's Chandlery firm of four shops scattered in towns along the South East coast of England, then a tiny Transport arm of a lorry and a van when her father Ron had joined her which had grown into a biggish transport company, then as WW2 came to an end they had met a bomber pilot by chance and because of what was almost a throwaway comment by him her father had bought a couple of war-surplus Dakotas and had built that up into what was now a fairly large air cargo firm.

Now it looked as though Mum was doing the same kind of thing with her Chandlery business – picking up an idea and developing it hugely.

Anne Carruthers was not really Kathleen's mother, though she now called her 'Mum'.

At the beginning of WW2 Kathleen and Maralyn (her best friend) had been fostered by her as Evacuees, and she and Anne had become close. The girls, and Kathleen's brother Tim, together with the other Evacuees (and other children from Folkestone), had been re-Evacuated to South Wales eight months later with the realisation that Folkestone was bound to be on a German invasion route, but the relationship between Anne and Kathleen had continued to develop.

Taken back to London in 1942, Kathleen and Tim had both been seriously injured when their school was hit in a daylight raid in January 1943, Kathleen losing both legs, Tim suffering injuries that resulted in a semi-paralysed left arm, deformed left leg, spinal injuries and severe concussion that had had lasting effects.

Anne looked up at the sound of a car on the gravel drive. A few minutes later Ron and Tim came through the side gate to the side lawn that stretched round to the back of the house.

"I'll get you some drinks while Mum tells you her latest idea, Dad," Kathleen called.

She locked the artificial knee joint of her left 'leg' with a quick flick through her slacks and stood up.

"I'll carry the tray," Terry said quickly, standing up as well.

Everyone treated Kathleen as though she was not disabled though 'lee-way' was given. From the time she'd been first injured she had insisted she was 'normal but just had a couple of bits missing'.

"So what's this idea Anne?" Ron asked, flopping down into an empty chair by her.

Tim pulled over another one as Kathleen and Terry, her fiance, went to the house, Terry carrying the big tray.

"Jason is thinking of buying a boat and Terry asked if we did them. He's looking for something bigger than our kind of dinghies, not just a converted small fishing boat but a real cruiser. So it occurred to me that we could move into that market because with the number of ex-navy people about it could be big."

"Boats? Cor!!" enthused Tim.

"Mmm." Ron knew nothing about boats and little about Chandlery. His forte was transport and over the last few years, aircraft transport, but Chandlery was Anne's business as it been her father's and grandfather's before her. "Sounds interesting." He glanced at Tim. "And do you see yourself as our first sea-going Captain, Tim? As you've done a couple of trips on The Sea Queen which is more than any of us have?"

The Sea Queen was a Cross-Channel Ferry that Uncle Wilf, Tim's first foster-father, had been First Mate on. Having met up again towards the war's end, they had stayed friends.

"And you have even been on the Bridge with the Captain, haven't you?" Anne added smiling. "And visited the engine room."

Tim grinned back. He had now got used to the family practice here of gentle teasing. They all did it to each other and no one took offence. But it had not been an easy lesson for Tim to learn and accept because Mum (his 'London Mum') and Des, his step-father had never acted like that.

"Great idea! I'll be him and keel-haul any of you motley crew that disobeys my slightest order."

"Bags me being First Mate then," Ron claimed swiftly.

"Applies to everyone. Including the Officers," Tim riposted.

"I don't think cruisers are a good idea any more. Not with Captain Bligh here in Command," Ron countered.

"I think it's a great idea Mum," Kathleen supported, coming up with Terry carrying the tray of drinks.

"Wait till you hear what Captain Bligh here is thinking before you say that," Ron pointed at Tim. "Keel-hauling us all just to start with."

"That's only if you mutiny," Tim protested. "Only if you mutiny. If you don't you're okay."

"We'd need a Marina with a slipway. But somewhere not too far away. Maybe on a river near the mouth could do. Or in a harbour." Anne was wanting to bring this back to a sensible level.

"I know someone who wants to sell a house by a river. Not far from Sandwich I think," Tim volunteered.

"Who's that?" Anne asked quickly.

"I don't know his name. But I know someone who knows someone whose Uncle has died and left him this house by the river. He doesn't want it so he's wanting to sell it. Maybe that would do."

"Who is it who knows who, whose Uncle has died?" Ron tried to unravel the trail.

"I was talking to Clive in the Spares a couple of days ago who's got a mate who he said was lucky. An Uncle of his had died and left him this house by the river and because it's no use to him he was wanting to sell it to make a few bob."

"Not now he's dead it wouldn't be," Kathleen interrupted.

"It's the nephew who wants to sell it, silly," Tim replied scornfully. "Anyway, it might be okay for what you want for the Marina. I could ask Clive if he knows any more about it tomorrow if you like."

"That sounds great Tim. You deserve to be our first Captain." Anne raised her glass. "To the one who may have kick-started Carruthers Cruisers'."

The others cheered and raised their glasses too.

And Tim suddenly felt he was really accepted at last into this close-knit family. Though there had always been acceptance **by** them, he had never felt in himself that he was actually part **of** them. Part of this family.

That feeling of never really 'belonging' had been with him for so many years that now he simply felt that was 'how things were' as far as he was concerned. That he always was and always would be in any setting, an 'outsider'. Even an 'intruder'.

It had started when he was re-Evacuated from Folkestone (where Auntie Flo and the Uncles had been so welcoming to him and the two other London 'Vaccies) to Wales though he had been the only Evacuee in the Welsh house. The son there had expected his mother to bring back a girl 'Vaccie' from the Reception Centre, not a boy. Not him. And Gareth had always treated him as an 'intruder' there. Someone who wasn't wanted at all. His foster-parents hadn't been as open about it, but they hadn't made Tim feel any more welcome.

Then when he went back 'home' to London his small brother Frank had soon begun to resent him sharing his bedroom and space, suddenly finding himself no longer being treated by their parents as an only child as he had been with the others away.

When he came out of the hospital after being bombed and so badly injured, though 'Uncle' Des, (who later became 'father') had never said anything, Tim still felt that he, mother and Frank had 'put up' with him being there more than anything else. And when he was going through a bad time of pain with his arm and leg and Frank got on his nerves just too much and he lashed out, mother always took Frank's side against him.

Even when he had chosen to come here with Dad, really for the job with 'planes, he found himself coming into an already close-knit family of Dad, Aunt Anne (he still didn't call her 'Mum' as Kathleen did) and Kathleen. So again – he was an outsider, an 'intruder'.

But now, suddenly, he felt he was one of them. Part of their 'Team'.

"I'd never keel-haul you, Mum," he blurted.

And Anne gave him a beaming smile.


"It's a fairly big house, with a fair bit of land but it's not really near the mouth of the river at Sandwich," Tim told Anne over the 'phone. As soon as he'd got to the Airfield he'd button-holed Clive. "Clive's mate is on the 'phone at work but he didn't know any more about the house."

Anne scribbled down the name and 'phone number of 'Clive's mate'. A quick call, an enthusiastic response and she arranged to meet Tom Henderson that evening.


"Do you think we're right Ron?" Anne queried doubtfully as they came to a narrow track leading from the road into trees.

"You said he said it was a narrow road and it's the right distance from Sandwich so this must be it. It's wide enough to take the car anyway."

He drove carefully down the pot-holed path, came to a sharp left turn and then they could see a large, ramshackle house set some yards back from the slow-flowing river. To one side, closer to the river, was a boathouse. A battered car was parked by the front door of the house that was facing them.

A tousle-headed young man came out to meet them. "Hi. I'm Tom Henderson. Guess you must be Mr. and Mrs. Jackson."

"That's right," Ron answered, the first to shake hands. "I hadn't realised you're American."

"Canadian really. Born the right side of the Lakes you might say. In Toronto."

"Long way to come to see your inheritance. Were you disappointed to see the shape it's in?" Anne asked.

"I was here already. Came over with the first influx of the Canadian Army and stayed on. When I saw the state of the place I decided to start work on it in my spare time but if you guys want to buy it as it is, that's fine by me. I'm going to sell it sooner or later anyway. Come inside."

They followed him through the open door into the musty-smelling hall.

"Don't let the smell put you off folks. Uncle let the place go rather badly, and when he had to go in a Home I guess it was just locked up and left. He left it to me because I'd gone to see him a few times in the Home and there's no one else anyway. Not this side of The Pond anyway." Americans (and Canadians) talked of the Atlantic as 'The Pond'.

They looked around the large, four-bedroomed house, Ron carefully checking the walls inside and out, and then studied the roof through binoculars.

"Can we see that building?" he asked, nodding at the boathouse.

"Sure. Uncle kept a small cruiser in it. I was told he was one of the 'Little boats' at Dunkirk in '40. I've fixed a couple of what looked like bullet holes in the deck anyway."

Tom flung the wide door open and they entered. Birds fluttered out with a frenzied clatter of wings through the open space leading to the river. The cruiser was out of the river supported on stilts.

"You've done those repairs well," Anne touched three places in the upper hull.

"I was a carpenter in a boatyard before I joined the Army,"

While Anne checked over the cruiser Ron checked the building.

"What do you think?" Tom asked when they'd finished.

"How much land is with it?" Anne asked, thinking of their plans.

"A fair bit actually."

Tom pointed out the boundaries, that were marked by posts set at intervals, rusty wire trailing into the undergrowth.

"Are you thinking of it as a riverside home?" he asked as they went to the house for the drink he'd offered.

"Not really. We're thinking more of a Marina for boat sales," Anne replied.

"Are you?" Tom's head snapped round. "Got - erm – got your staff fixed up yet?"

"No. We're just at the beginning planning stage," Anne replied. "I run a Chandlery business with shops in several towns in this part of the South Coast, Ron runs a Transport and Air Cargo business. We thought of extending Carruthers Chandlery into Carruthers Cruisers."

"This would give you easy access to the sea down the river, the house could be your offices and a slipway could easily be put in to the river there," Tom said swiftly, pointing to locations.

"It does have possibilities," Anne said, looking at Ron.

"What price were you thinking of?" asked Ron.

"For the lot? House, all the land, with what you've got in mind?"

Tom told them, doubling the figure the Estate Agent had talked of – but that had only been for a home, not a business premises.

"Thank you." Anne stood up abruptly.

"The price is subject to negotiation," Tom said swiftly.

"Thanks Tom," Ron stood up too.

"We'd need to price up the cost of a proper road into and round the site and the slipway, if we decided to go for it," Anne said as Ron pulled onto the main road to go home. "Then renovating the house. And building a workshop because the boathouse isn't big enough or really in the right position on the edge of the river as it is. And with the steep price he's asking, it would add up."

They drove on through Sandwich.

"He did say that could be subject to negotiation though," Ron said thoughtfully. "So we could price up the things we'd need and see where we go from there."

Three days later Anne 'phoned Tom Henderson to arrange another meeting on a Saturday.

"The thing is Tom, we could be interested, but the place would need a lot of development to put it to the use we want. Let's show you," Anne was taking the lead as Carruthers Cruisers would be part of Carruthers Chandlery.

"Fine."

Tom was immensely relieved. When he'd told his Estate Agent that Carruthers Chandlery was interested, he had been enthusiastic and told Tom what he knew about the Carruthers Group of Companies. And about Anne, Ron and Kathleen. But when Tom told him the price he'd asked for as it was a Business Sale, the Estate Agent had abruptly lost his enthusiasm.

"What price should I have asked then?" Tom demanded. "As it would be a Business deal not a House sale?"

"You could have asked for a bit more, but not doubled it. From what you've said they want to make it into and what I saw of the place, they're going to have to spend a lot of money to bring it up to scratch. A road in, hard-standing, a slipway, possibly workshops, renovating the buildings. And while the Carruthers Group is doing very well they've got a reputation of being canny business people.

"What you could do is be willing to negotiate down to no more than a third above the house sale price. See how they respond to that. But you are wanting a quick sale you said, and while it's early days yet, they are the only expression of interest you've had so far."

"Okay then. I'll see if they do contact me again. Or should I 'phone them myself? Remind 'em I'd said we could negotiate?"

"If they're pricing up their costs, which I'd expect they're doing, if they haven't lost interest altogether, give them at least till the middle of next week. And have a word with me before you do that. In the meantime I'll circulate some people that I think might be interested in doing a project like that themselves."

Tom put the 'phone down slowly. Had he messed up on the deal?

There could be other possibilities around going by what that Estate Agent had said but he was still very relieved when Anne contacted him. No one else had responded.

The three of them walked round the site as Anne made her comments.

"To start with we'd need to put in a proper road from the main road down to the riverside, put a hardstanding in for boats to be located on and a car park. The house will need a lot of work done to bring it up to standard for offices, maybe the possibility of living accommodation on the upper floors and we'd like to see if it's possible to establish a restaurant with river views as well, to bring customers in for that and hopefully they'll look at the boats as well. And *vice versa*. All of which are preliminary costs. Which will be a factor in what and where we buy, and whether we buy this place in particular."

"But any or all of which will apply wherever you locate your boatyard," Tom countered. "And here you have all the basic elements you need. A good standard passing road, so your roadworks will be much smaller than on many other locations, the land here, the house, power already laid on. All positives you could well not find elsewhere."

"How fixed is the price you quoted the other day?" Anne asked.

Tom heaved a silent sigh of relief. It sounded as though she was willing to negotiate. And he was impatient for a sale. So he was ready to strike while the iron was hot.

"I'm ready enough to negotiate. Let's put a table out overlooking the river in the sun and I'll get some drinks."

The negotiations didn't take long as Tom Henderson did not take a rigid stand on anything. He had other ideas in mind.

"What are your plans now?" Ron asked when Anne had read out the notes she'd made and Tom had agreed them.

Tom liked the way these two had negotiated and there were his other ideas.

His mother had died four years ago while he was still in the Army and he'd never been particularly close to his father. His sister had married and was living in Vancouver now, not Toronto. So he had decided to stay in the UK rather than go back to Canada when he was demobbed.

"Wa-all, that rather depends. When I first saw the size and state of this place I decided pretty quick to sell up, get some capital and go back to Toronto and see about setting up a boat building company there. That was the carpentry I was doing pre-War. But now I'm not so sure.

"To start with boat-building has moved on a lot since I was doing it, both in materials and methods. And I'm not too sure I'd be much good running a firm with all that that entails anyway.

"And maybe more important, I've met someone at work, one of the secretaries, Sally Browntree, and we've been dating a few times. She's pretty close to her folks here so I don't think she'd be too keen on going to Canada. Not that that's even been mentioned," he added hastily. "We're still only dating."

He looked round the site, then back to Anne and Ron.

"I'd still like to be connected to boats. Now suppose I was offered a job over-seeing turning this place into a viable Marina and then to run it - that would be just the ticket for me."

Anne and Ron glanced at each other.

"Besides being in boat building some years ago, what did you do in the Army? And since leaving?" Ron asked.

"I was at Dieppe, then was transferred to the Stores so I know all about ordering supplies, maintaining stocks and forwarding documentation. Then I was at the battles at Caen and Carpiquet then back to the Stores again. The job I've got now is in a builder's office. A big one. I suppose you could call me the Deputy Manager really because I'm in charge when the top Manager is out of the office which is quite often. And I've had to go out on-site myself a few times."

"Which firm's that?" Ron asked and nodded at the name. He knew George Bayliss.

"We'll put our written offer for the site in Monday and be in touch about the other," Anne said, standing up.

"Look forward to hearing from you, Mrs. Jackson," Tom replied, standing up himself.

He watched them drive off up the bumpy track, a half-smile on his face. If things worked out so he did the development of this place and then became the Manager here afterwards, it would be the perfect cover for his other ideas. Being on a river, boats legitimately going up and down it to the sea, late fishing trips that came back after dark – perfect.

He'd 'phone Jules Coublon in Paris. Tell him it was now likely that what had been suggested when they met up a month ago and he'd first told him about the house on the river, could work out even better than they'd expected.

"Started work on your wedding dress and Going Away outfit yet Kitten?" Terry glanced sideways at her.

They were sitting at Kathleen's favourite spot halfway down the Zig-Zag Path with its lovely view out over the Channel.

Ron had bought the bench and had it fixed there partly because it was there they had first met Craig Earl from which came the beginning of their Air Cargo Company and partly in memory of George Naylor, their pilot who had died in that awful air crash in Berlin during the Berlin Airlift. His name and the date was on a small metal plaque on the bench.

They would walk down the slope, take a rest on the bench, then walk on down, along the sea front then catch a bus home. It was too much of a struggle for Kathleen to walk up the slope, though she could do it.

Some months ago Terry had asked her what he could call her, just when they were alone together. Because 'Kathleen could sound a bit formal' he'd said. She had flatly rejected 'Kitty', his first suggestion, but agreed 'Kitten', "As long as you only keep that between us two. In private," she'd said firmly.

He'd agreed.

"Well - not yet," she said finally.

When Terry had first asked if she would become 'Engaged' and they had gone looking for the Engagement ring, though she knew that would lead on to Marriage – obviously - that was something that lay in the future. Far in the future. He had said he had to finish University and be settled in a 'proper job' first but he did want them to become formally Engaged. If she would of course, he'd added diffidently.

Of course she had agreed, thrilling that a man, that a man like Terry, could actually love her enough to want that. And she had been so worried when she was first injured when 13 years old that she'd never get even a boy friend 'because she had no legs', let alone someone who would want to be Engaged and then married to her.

Dad had done his best to re-assure her but she hadn't really believed him. Not really. Not deep down.

And then she had met Terry. And he was so understanding. He never 'fussed' over her, but seemed to just know exactly when she 'needed a bit of a lift'.

But now he had his Degree and was doing a Ph.D in Nuclear Engineering. Doing that had meant he was still essentially a Student – but his question brought the fact of Marriage suddenly closer. Something just round the corner.

And a Wedding Day meant a Wedding Night. When for the first time he would see her undressed. Not wearing her slacks. When she would have to take off her artificial legs in front of him – and he would see her as she really was.

And what would be his reaction to that?

She felt a surge of panic.

He knew what her condition was of course – but would actually seeing it for the first time, change how he felt about her?

"I'll have to start thinking about it, won't I?" she said, stitching a smile on her face.

"Only I've had a tip that the Atomic Energy people are going to make me an offer of a job at the end of the summer." He grinned widely at her.

"That's wonderful Terry!" Kathleen kissed and hugged him. "And you deserve it!"

That evening she went into what they still called 'The Library', but it was now as much a workroom as a place with books for reading.

She pinned a big sheet of paper on her drawing board – and then stared at it. She would design a wedding dress, not slacks she always wore to hide her artificial legs. Now much more expert with them she was confident she could wear a dress long enough to come down to the tops of her shoes without tripping over, but the Going Away outfit couldn't be a dress as long as that so it would have to be slacks again.

"Can I come in, Kathleen?" a quiet voice asked from the doorway.

"Of course Mum," Kathleen, twisted round on her high chair to look at Anne.

"What are you doing?" Anne asked, standing by her, looking at the blank sheet of paper.

"Terry asked if I'd started designing the Wedding Dress and Going Away outfit yet."

"And you're worried about it? I don't mean the designing?"

"How did you know?" Kathleen stared at her.

"I am your Mum, dear." Anne pulled over a chair to sit by her. "Want to tell me?"

"How did you feel on your wedding night Mum? Well, your – your ...." Kathleen fell silent. Mum and Dad had lived together for a long time before they were actually married and she knew they had had a long running 'affair' before that.

"At the time in the war when it first happened, most of us were thinking we'd soon be killed when the Germans invaded. Or at the very least, raped." She shrugged. "Because that's what invaders often do. So we believed anyway. Your Dad had been 'phoning me regularly and writing to me through the early months of 1940 and then he was sent to an airfield down here on an urgent delivery so he was able to actually call to see me again. You and Maralyn had already been Evacuated to Wales. I bullied the hair-dresser into seeing me first thing, told Dorothy to take the day off, then when the time was coming for him to arrive – I panicked."

"You did?" To Kathleen, Mum panicking was unthinkable.

"I did," Anne grinned at her. "We'd only seen each other for maybe an hour that first time he came with your extra clothes in September 1939, so I wondered if he'd built up a picture of me in his mind that was far more glamorous than the reality so that when he actually saw me as I am there would be a crashing disappointment. So I panicked when he actually rang the bell. I had to answer it of course and there he was. Tall, handsome, dressed in his smart overalls and his first words were, 'Anne. You look gorgeous.'"

"Lovely!" Kathleen clapped her hands, smiling.

"He told me later he'd been worried what I'd think of him! And he'd carefully rehearsed his first words and then he forgot them completely when he saw me! And then - well it seemed the most natural thing in the world for us to do."

"But you were in one piece, Mum." Kathleen came back to earth again. "You've got both legs. So what will Terry think when he first sees me as I really am?"

"He's certainly not going to turn against you," Anne said with absolute conviction. "He knows the situation already, doesn't he." It wasn't a question.

"Yes Mum." Kathleen paused. "But knowing something isn't the same as seeing it for the first time, is it?"

"I do understand what you mean Kathleen, but I also think you are worrying about Terry unnecessarily." She paused. "Just a thought, if there's no one at the hospital you want to talk to about this though they must have talked to others feeling the same kind of thing, what would you think of talking to Richard Sampson? His injuries are different from yours of course, but he must have had similar doubts when thinking of courting and marrying Daphne."

"But he's so jolly and outgoing, I shouldn't think his scarred face would worry him."

"I don't think it's only his face, Kathleen. I think the scarring goes much further down his body. I only think that because he never takes off his shirt, not even when we've all been on the beach and most of us been in swimming costumes.

"I know he's a man – but he might have had the same kind of worries. Or talk to Daphne. See what she thought at the time."

"See what you mean Mum. I'll think about doing that."


Two weeks later Anne took Kathleen and Tim to the airfield, Tim to start his shift in the Control Tower, Kathleen to meet Terry. He was flying the Club Tiger Moth back from an airfield at Whitehaven in Cumberland. He'd been at a Conference at Calder Hall where they were going to build a Nuclear Power Station, the first in the UK.

That showed just how highly they think of him, Dad had said, pleased that Terry was as 'air-minded' as himself to fly up there rather than taking the better part of a couple of days over it by traveling by train.

Kathleen was sitting by a window in the restaurant when she spotted Richard Sampson arriving. With sudden determination she stood up. Terry wasn't going to be here for an hour yet but it had been convenient for Mum to bring her now with Tim.

She paused outside Richard Sampson's door, then took a deep

breath and knocked.

"Come in," he shouted. "Hello Kathleen, what can I do for you?" he asked rather surprised. Though Kathleen was quite a frequent visitor to the Airfield, she'd never come to his office like this before.

"Can I ask you something – rather personal please? It's to do with Terry Murray."

"Your fiance?"

"Yes. That's right."

Now that the moment had come Kathleen suddenly realised just how personal the question was that she was wanting to ask and blushed to the roots of her hair.

"The – my problem is – well you know Terry and – and ---" she stumbled to a halt. "When – when the wedding – afterwards - what do you think – what ---," she stumbled to a halt again.

"I had a rather similar feeling to what might be yours," Richard said. "If you're thinking what I think you might be thinking. I worried what Daphne would think and how she would react when she saw me as I really am for the first time." He paused.

"You see, my scarring goes a long way down my body. Right down my right side to near my ankle." He paused again. "So when I went into the bedroom I left off my pyjama jacket, so I was wearing just the trousers. That meant quite a lot of the scarring was still covered but she would see the scarring did go right down my side.

"She jumped up from the side of the bed where she'd been sitting in her nightie, dashed towards me, hugged me tight and said, 'You poor wonderful darling. Thank you so much for trusting me.'

Richard bit his lip. "I loved her before but after that ..." He shook his head. "Well I guess I still worship the ground she walks on."

He looked up at Kathleen. "And I think Terry is as sensible, caring and loving to you, as she is to me.

"Remember the number of times we've met up? As kind of family group really that he has joined. So I've seen the way he looks at you, treats you.

"I think you two were made for each other. So I don't think for a second you have any need to worry about him. There's one thing though. I'm a man – obviously – so why not have a word with Daphne? For a woman's angle, I mean?"

"Thanks Mr. Sampson. I think I will." She stood up. "That's been a tremendous help. I hope you didn't mind me coming and – and asking that?"

"Glad you did Kathleen. And glad it was a help." He glanced through the window as the noise of an aero-engine became louder. "That should be Terry landing now. He was able to take-off sooner than he'd expected."


Tom Henderson signed the documents with a flourish then smiled expansively as Anne handed him the cheque to complete the purchase of the Marina for 'Carruthers Cruisers'.

"Thanks a million, Anne. Great to do that business with you." He looked at her expectantly.

"And here's the Contract of Employment, Tom." Anne handed it to him.

Tom signed the two copies and gave one back to Anne.

From next week he would be working for 'Carruthers Cruisers', his first job was to oversee the development of the site and then be the Manager of the Marina. Having already given in his notice to Baylisses he had a week to set up the other business with Jules Coublon in France that the Jacksons would know nothing about.

# Chapter 2
## Connections

The next morning Tom Henderson caught the early morning train from Folkestone to Dover for the first Ferry sailing to Calais. He could have caught the Company flight direct to Paris from Wingmore which would have been cheaper than the Ferry with his Staff Discount and of course a lot quicker, but he wanted no one in the firm to have the slightest idea of what he was doing.

From Calais he caught the train to Paris arriving there mid-afternoon.

"Hotel Maximillian'", he said to the first taxi-driver in the waiting line.

"*Oui M'sieur*," came the immediate, indifferent reply.

Tom looked around keenly as they drove through the streets of Paris, marveling at the changes since he had been there soon after Paris had been Liberated. He had been a Sergeant in the Stores then. But it was during the time he'd been at Caen after it had been captured, that he'd first met up with Jules Coublon.

Jules was the kind of guy that back in Toronto they called a 'Fixer'. During the Occupation he'd somehow been able to keep on the right side of both the Occupiers and the Resistance. He 'obtained' stuff for the lower and middle ranks of the Occupiers so they shielded him from those Higher Up and he had fed bits of information to the Resistance so after the Liberation he was not seen as a Collaborator but as having been an undercover agent for the Resistance. Luckily for him. Since then he'd gone on to carve out a niche between the criminal world and 'straight society', becoming increasingly rich in the process.

Having kept up some kind of desultory contact, on one of his weekend trips to sample afresh the delights of Paris a few months ago, Tom had mentioned the legacy of the house to Jules. Half-jokingly (because both had been rather drunk at the time) Jules had suggested calling it 'Smugglers Retreat' as a name.

Tom had dismissed his other suggestion of the house being a base for some smuggling with a laugh – his intention was to sell the house as soon as he could, for as much as he could and get back to

Toronto as soon as he could with the proceeds. But then the Jacksons had come up with their suggestion, and to his mind that had opened up a lot of possibilities with the cover that that could give. So he'd contacted Jules again.

Once settled in his room Tom 'phoned him at his nightclub, which was not in the 'best' part of town. Two hours later another taxi deposited him outside and the doorman was welcoming him effusively.

Once inside Jules' office both with a cognac and cigar, he looked at Tom expectantly. "Your 'phone call was interesting, but not very informative, *mon ami.*"

"I didn't want to be too obvious because going through an operator meant she could have listened in." He hitched his chair closer to the big desk. "The point is that Anne Jackson who's buying the house has offered me a job as the site overseer till the whole place has been renovated, and then to stay on as the Marina Manager.

"As soon as the time is right I'm going to suggest that besides selling boats and cruisers, that we rent and lease them out too. That'll mean boats could be continually going in and out of the Marina piloted by different people. And that would provide us with the perfect cover for smuggling big-time. Not in big quantities but in an almost continual stream. Little and often.

"I've still got contacts in London from my Army days that will provide the market for what we get in." Tom sat back and picked up his cognac. "So what do you think?"

"I thought it was 'Carruthers' Cruisers'. So where does this Jackson woman come in?"

"She's called 'Jackson' because she married a chap with that name but they've kept using the 'Carruthers' name for business. Though Jackson runs a pretty large Transport company now, they even call that 'Carruthers Transport' and 'Carruthers Airlines'."

"How big is the Transport? Do they come to France?"

"Sure do. Both lorries and Cargo flights. They're starting to build up their Air Passenger side too."

Jules sat forward abruptly.

"Then we could get goods into the UK by all three routes! By the cruisers and the lorries and aircraft. We'll make a fortune!"

"Not a chance!. Not yet anyway. I've already run some checks on the Jacksons. They're straight, dead straight. By that I mean honest. Really, genuinely honest. Any sniff of any funny business and they'll go straight to the cops. I don't know any of the lorry drivers or aircrew at all yet and I'd have to approach them mighty carefully to suggest anything at all. The safe way, the only way, is for me to build it up through the cruisers and give me time to check out the others. But for the Jacksons themselves – it's a strict no-no."

"Pity. But don't forget – everyone has a price. While they're on the up-and-up – okay I take what you say. But if they run into money troubles it'll be a different story. Like I say, everyone has their price. So how soon will you be ready?"

"We sort out the split first Jules. And the route through a port."

Now that Jules was seeing that he was the key to getting smuggled goods into the UK from France, Tom was quite ready to play him off against Charles Beaulac, another Fixer he knew.

He'd come to know both during the War when he was a Sergeant in the Stores the Canadian Army built up after they had captured Caen in 1944, to re-supply the front-line troops as they pushed on. Later they had switched the port of re-supply further up the French coast to shorten the supply line as they continued their advance with the rest of the Allied Forces.

But he had kept the Sergeant job in the Stores right to the end – and had continued his careful diverting of supplies to Black Marketeers. He had never been caught because he was both careful and not too greedy. So he had never responded to their constant pressure to increase the flow to them on the scale they wanted, which would have been detected.

He had kept in desultory touch with just three, Jules Coublon, Charles Beaulac and Francois Morand. Until Morand had met an untimely end from a single shot to the head a year or so before.

The Police version was it was Resistance punishment for his collaborating with the Occupiers, but Jules had just been hinting it was really because he had tried double-crossing Jules when they had been putting together a deal.

Two hours later Tom was reasonably satisfied with the deal they had put together. Coublon would organise getting the 'smuggle' to ports for him to pick up.

But he went home realising he had got himself into deeper and murkier waters than he had thought and expected. But the outlet he was planning to fix up for the smuggled goods in London was more in his small-time league than Jules Coublon now seemed to be.

"Hi Stan, Tom Henderson here. You still got your nightclub going?"

"Yeah. You coming up to see the show and want to book a table?"

"You have table bookings now then do you?"

That could mean that Stan Woodward had moved up-market from his sleazy, back-street, basement place in Soho. Or that he was just talking big which was more likely.

"We do in two of my places now. I've got three and soon I'm moving into a couple more."

Tom whistled admiringly.

"It's not so much to book a table as put a business proposition to you."

"Sounds interesting. When can you come up? If you're still in Folkestone."

"I am. What about tomorrow, say 6.00 o'clock?"

"Suits me. I'll be at the Flamingo Club. It's my newest place in Dean Street. Tell the doorman I'm expecting you."

Tom rubbed his hands together. If Stan had three and getting more in the way of nightclubs, especially up-market ones, then his customers would be just the type to want pricey French wines. It was all coming together very nicely.

When Tom walked into the Flamingo Club he was impressed. The doorman was wearing a smart black suit and bow tie, the Cloakroom girl, scantily dressed, was young, pretty and polite as she took his coat and handed him a metal check, and then 'phoned through to Mr. Woodward.

The entrance hall was expensively carpeted and the deep red wallpaper and subdued wall lighting gave an atmosphere of unostentatious wealth.

Another scantily dressed, young and pretty girl came into the hall and took him through a side-door, up a flight of stairs, then knocked on a door, opened it and announced him before closing it after him.

"You've done mighty well for yourself Stan!" Tom exclaimed, looking around then back to Stan. He'd put on a lot of weight since he'd last seen him.

"Not bad is it?" Stan smiled complacently. "Drink?"

"Please."

"Try this whisky. It's not bad." Stan poured it.

It was excellent Tom thought after trying it.

"So what's your proposition, Tom?"

"I'm soon going to be in a position to get a good steady supply of top-brand French wines, ideal for outlets like these." Tom gently waved his glass to indicate the room. "And tobacco products. At - shall we say – wholesale and Tax-free prices."

"I see." Stan paused. "What makes you think I'd be interested in wines like that?"

"The type of customers you get in a place like this would like drinks like those."

"I don't have Dining Facilities here. The premises aren't big enough. This is a Night Club. People eat, then come on here."

"According to the Menu you've got by the Check-in girl you do some snack things. So add wines to your drinks range."

"Mmm. Look Tom, I've got Partners and they own some more places including restaurants. I'd need to interest them. What sort of wines and prices are we talking about?"

Tom passed over a lengthy list. Stan took a wine list from a drawer and compared them.

"These are your actual prices?"

"They are. And Tax-free," Tom confirmed, exulting. Stan was hooked. And with the restaurants he'd talked about, the number of outlets would be increased with no effort on his part.

"How soon does this 'good, steady supply' start?"

"Three months max."

"Mmm. Tell you what I'll do, Tom. I'll talk to my Partners about this and let you know what they say? Okay?"

"Fair enough." Tom took another sip of the whisky. "Any chance of catching the floor show?"

"Be my guest. Come on, I'll get you a ring-side table."

As Tom looked around from his table he became more certain than ever he had done right in picking Stan Woodward rather than Rickie Taylor.

Tom was ready and waiting when the first men arrived at the Marina the following Monday to begin clearing the site, and when builders arrived half-an-hour later to start on renovating the house. When Anne and Ron came that evening to see how things were progressing all three were pleased.

"Anne, I've been thinking ...," Tom said as they completed their tour, "... we've been planning for boat sales, so why not add to that cruiser hire or cruiser leasing? I reckon that people could want to try out a cruiser holiday before actually buying one. So they could hire one for a week say, or lease one for a longer period – say a month at a time. Day trips too."

Anne grinned at him, then at Ron.

"'Great minds think alike'," she quoted. "We have had the same idea. But that'd be more complicated. Things like Deposits so they don't vanish with the cruiser to the Continent or somewhere even further away, and Insurance. But it's worth looking into so we'll do that. Thanks for suggesting it."

Tom waved goodbye to them cheerfully. Better and better! They hadn't needed any persuading at all.

It was two weeks later when Stan Woodward 'phoned.

"My Partners want to meet you before we come to any arrangements. Can you come up to The Flamingo next weekend?"

"Saturday afternoon would be best for me. I need to be on-site really during working hours of course."

"Sure. No problem. Three o'clock then."

When Tom walked into The Flamingo he was met just inside the door and escorted to Stan's office by a tough-looking, six-foot tall black man. His appearance was as intimidating as his silence. He hadn't been there last time Tom had come.

Inside Stan's office Tom saw he was sitting over to one side of the desk. Behind it was a very well dressed, thin man with cold, seemingly lifeless eyes of the kind that Tom had seen twice before.

One of those had been a sergeant in the Canadian Army with an impressive row of medal ribbons, that Tom had got drinking with in the Mess one night as the War was in its last weeks. He had been lamenting that the war would soon be over.

"The thing is Tom ...," he'd growled morosely, "... in the last few years I've been able to kill just about as much as I wanted to. Not just gunning the bastards down either but at close quarters, hand-to-hand as they like to call it. That is when you really live. When you look down at some son-of-a-bitch you've just killed, knowing that it was you that bested him. There's nothing like it is there?"

Tom, who had managed to avoid killing anyone, especially at close-quarters, had shuddered and left him as soon as he could.

The other was a Waffen SS officer, an Oberstambannfuhrer (Lieutenant Colonel of an assault unit) that had been grabbed pretending to be a civilian, but had been recognised.

So Tom wondered what this guy here had done during the War.

Though Stan had talked of 'Partners', this guy was obviously the one in charge. Tom wondered what part the other three guys standing around the room played in all this.

"Stan tells me you can supply us with the best wines at a good price."

His voice was unnerving too, Tom felt with a chill. A high pitched falsetto voice that didn't go at all with those eyes.

"That's right. I – well you could say I will be importing them, tax free."

"How?"

Tom had intended to keep that part of the operation to himself. The fewer who knew about it the better. But those eyes – that voice -- something about him made him change his mind. Immediately. So he told him everything.

"Peanuts," the voice snapped. "That kind of operation wouldn't keep me supplied for a single night. A small cruiser-load every now and again. Algy ...," he glanced up at the guy standing closest to him, "... use the cover Tom has got and step up the operation to supply us with what we do need. Tom, if you agree to that we'll take all that you can bring in. You got any problems with that?"

Tom felt coldly sure that if he had any 'problems' then probably he wouldn't get out of here in one piece.  He stood up stitching a smile on his face and held out his hand.

"None at all.  Pleased to be working with you."

"Algy, sort out things with Tom ASAP," the Boss as Tom now mentally christened him, snapped, ignoring Tom's hand.

He stood up and went to the door.  His bodyguard whipped it open and followed him out.

The atmosphere noticeably lightened as everyone relaxed.

"Drinks everyone?" Stan asked, moving over to the small bar.  "Mr. Frobisher?" he added looking at Algy

They all chose something and Algy moved across to talk to Tom.

"Pleased to be working with you Tom," Algy drawled, in such a British aristocratic accent that Tom wondered if it was an act.  "Did you come up by car?"

"No.  Train."

"As we're to work together you might as well go back with me in the Jag.  Then we can talk in private and you can show me over your Marina tomorrow."

"I've got a date so I'm tied up tomorrow.  No problem about Monday, though there'll be workmen on the site.  Not that they'll interfere with us."

"Tom," Algy said softly.  "Mr. Barnett said 'ASAP' didn't he? Monday isn't ASAP.  Today and tomorrow is.  Clear?"

Tom swallowed.  Though Algy was still talking in that 'aristo' accent, there was a cold menace in his tone.  As menacing in its own way as Mr. Barnett's eyes, voice and quietness had been.

"I'll – I'll put Sally off."

"Excellent.  I was sure you would be happy to co-operate." The friendly tone was back in Algy's voice.  "Let's go shall we?".

Algy put his still half-full whisky glass onto Stan's desk, so Tom hurriedly followed suit.

"Just need to pick up a few things from the flat," Algy said as he waved a taxi down.  "Mount Street, W1," he added to the driver.

Tom waited in the well-appointed lounge while Algy went into the bedroom.  Then he crossed to a big picture of a large mansion set in parkland over the mantlepiece.  Was that a picture of his place?  His family's place? It would match the plushness of this flat. Then he looked at other pictures on the walls including a family portrait on a sideboard.. He saw Algy was in it wearing RAF uniform. He looked closer. He thought so. He had pilot's Wings and some medal ribbons.

Another picture was a School photograph of youngsters about 16 or 17 he supposed. He peered closer. One of them was Algy, another looked like a young Mr. Barnett. But in the picture he was smiling and looked as cheerful as the other youngsters. He wondered what had happened to change him into the type of man he was now.

He hurriedly sat down in an armchair as he heard Algy close a bedroom door.

He decided to find out all that he could about Mr. Barnett and Algy Frobisher. He'd start with checking out that book about the Brit. aristos. 'Burke's Peerage', that's what it was called. And the 'Who's Who'. If he really was a Brit. aristocrat, that should give him some leads to start with.

"Tell me more about the Marina, the river it's on and the town of Sandwich you mentioned," Algy said as soon as he pulled away from the kerb.

Once he was satisfied with that, Algy started asking him questions about his background and what he'd done in the Army. To boost his criminal credentials Tom embellished his accounts of 'diverting' goods from the Stores,"in the spirit of 'Free Enterprise.'" he grinned.

"You'd better keep quiet about that," Algy said coldly. "A lot of us were front-line combat people and we hit shortages because scum like you behind the lines and at Headquarters were 'diverting' supplies."

Tom could have kicked himself. Seeing Algy had been a pilot in the War with medal ribbons in that photo he should have thought of that. And if Mr. Barnett had been mixed up in it somewhere or other he really would keep quiet.

"I wasn't in the Stores all the time," he lied. "I saw plenty of action too. In the attacks on Dieppe, Carpiquet and Caen f'r'instance. And other places later."

"I see. That's a decent looking pub for a bite."

Algy decided he didn't believe Tom about his war record, but so what? They weren't going into another war.

They, or rather Algy, had decided that on the Sunday they would take Sally down the river in the cruiser lodged in the boathouse, to check out the river, the access to the sea and then access for vehicles taking away the smuggled goods. Naturally Sally wouldn't be told the real reason for the trip. Algy's cover story was that he was interested in being their first customer to buy a cruiser.

At first Sally wasn't too happy about someone else coming along but Algy's charm soon won her over. To Tom's jealous disgust.

So they cruised slowly down the river in the warm sunshine, Algy, Tom and Sally chatting in a relaxed friendly way, but unrealised by Sally, Algy was making a careful check of river levels, the bends and access roads to the river's edge right along its length.

Afterwards Algy insisted on treating them all to a slap-up dinner at the best hotel in Sandwich, then went back to the house while Tom took Sally home before going to his hotel.

As soon as they'd gone Algy pulled on a pair of thin glaves and swiftly went through the desk in the office and filing cabinets. Though they were locked it took him bare seconds to open them. But all were business, all legitimate.

He went back upstairs, into the bedroom, and just as swiftly went through the two chests of drawers and under the bed. The wardrobe was locked which delayed him just forty seconds. Inside, partly hidden behind suits and coats was a large and heavy wooden box. That took him two minutes to open.

"Well, well," he murmured once he'd moved aside a newspaper. "So friend Tom has a Luger P08. Now is that only a Liberated souvenir or something more serious?"

He eased aside a false bottom. To reveal three rows of magazines for the Luger. Quick checks confirmed all the magazines were loaded as was the Luger itself. "More than just a souvenir perhaps."

A notebook was tucked down the side of the magazines. A quick flick through the two dozen names with addresses and even 'phone numbers, and he took out a tiny spy-camera. He took the notebook to the the bedside lamp and focused the light to take quick shots of all the names and details.

He had recognised the name of a fence for stolen goods in South

London, and a former French Resistance fighter now a small-time gun-runner. That meant it would be sensible to check out the rest. He carefully replaced everything as it had been.

When Tom came back an hour later Algy was sitting at ease in Tom's lounge, drink in hand, reading a Sunday paper.

"What do you think?" Tom asked, getting a drink for himself after re-filling Algy's glass.

"What do you?" Algy countered.

Tom sat down, then, "On the scale Mr. Barnett wants stuff in, it won't work. The only major road out of here is that one through Sandwich. Mr. Barnett would need lorryloads every week that our cover story won't be good enough for. A small vanload or two spread over a couple of weeks would be. So it's a non-starter as far as scale is concerned. Even if we took the cruiser into say Ramsgate, taking that amount of stuff from a cruiser would still arouse suspicion especially if we did it often. And deserted bays round here are no good for the same reasons – too much taken inland too often along narrow roads from the point of landing."

"I concur," Algy said.

Tom felt a mixture of relief, but also regret. Smuggled would have added a nice percentage to his Manager's salary but on the plus side it also meant he'd have no more contact with that intimidating Mr. Barnett. Other, smaller, nearby outlets would be possible to find though. Local pubs for sure. More in his league.

"So what we need is a commodity that is high-value, low-bulk. Then it would work excellently." Algy half-smiled. "And the commodity that is both those things is drugs. Heroin and cocaine. Which is what we're really interested in. And your cut would be treble or quadruple that from drinks."

"Drugs," Tom repeated thoughtfully. "Now that's an idea. And you're right! And Jules is into that too, I'm pretty sure. But do you have the right contacts for disposing of them? I don't."

"Indeed. But you will be going into Calais with your cruisers, not Paris, won't you? We already have a contact in Calais itself which will be better." He paused. "You do understand you do not mention me or especially Mr. Barnett to anyone else at all, don't you?" That undertone of cold menace was back in Algy's quiet voice.

"Of course not. You can't beat the 'cell-system'."

"Precisely." Algy sipped his drink. That Luger and amount of ammunition still bothered him.

"As we're pretty much partners now, have you known Mr. Barnett long?" Tom asked. Which gave Algy a lead in.

"Several years. We were in the SOE – the Special Operations Executive – during the war. You know of that?"

"Heard a bit about it. You were spies weren't you? Operating behind the German Lines?"

"We did a lot more than just gather information. Mr. Barnett was one of those who went into Occupied France, I was a ferry pilot that took Agents in and sometimes brought them out. Mr. Barnett and several of his colleagues were betrayed. Not by someone under torture, which could have been excusable to some degree, but for money. They were arrested by the Gestapo and tortured. Badly. They were then taken out into a courtyard to be shot but Mr. Barnett grabbed his Luger from the Officer in charge of the firing squad, dealt with them and in spite of his condition and that of the others, most of them managed to escape.

"I was sent to bring him home." Algy was silent for a space. "He was so changed," he murmured, staring at the floor, almost as though he was talking to himself. "Not just physically from what they'd done to him but mentally too. Emotionally. Before he'd been fun-loving, even treating going into France with the SOE almost as a game – though in training and once there he was a complete professional." Another long pause.

"He wanted to go back as soon as they'd more or less patched him up but they refused and invalided him out. But as soon as we broke out of the Normandy beach-head after D-Day, I flew him back into France. Unofficially." Another pause.

"I've pieced together what happened next. He linked up with his old SOE group in Paris and in the last days of the German Occupation there they kidnapped the Betrayer and the Gestapo torturers, took them deep into the forest region, held a drumhead Court Martial, and Mr. Barnett sentenced them to experience what they had inflicted on them and on others. It took four days and then when they were more than half-dead already they were killed and what was left of them was buried there in the forest."

Algy raised his head and looked very steadily at Tom.

"Don't ever, ever, even think of Betraying Mr. Barnett, Tom," he said very quietly. "While British police are not the Gestapo of course, as far as Mr. Barnett is concerned Betrayal is Betrayal and the Unforgivable Sin. And he would regard anyone talking to the police about any of us at all as Betrayal."

The silence dragged on, then abruptly Algy swallowed the last of his drink and stood up.

"I'm going to my hotel. If a real situation should arise you can 'phone me on this number." While he scrawled a number on a blank scrap of paper, "That is only if necessity should arise, not just because you want to chat. You will memorise that number and then burn that piece of paper. Never leave anything anywhere that can provide any kind of clue to anyone. You will simply say you have a cruiser coming in and you think I'd like to see it. We'll make a date."

Tom sat staring at the wall unseeingly for a long time after Algy had gone, then shivered. He wasn't too sure he believed everything that Algy had just told him but whatever the real story was he knew he was totally out of his depth with Mr. Barnett's gang. Even more so than with Jules. The only way out would be to do a runner back to Canada at once. Or inside a week. Without a word to anyone. Not even Mrs. Jackson or Sally. Then no one would be able to trace him. Not that Mr. Barnett would bother to, if he was careful not to say anything about them to anyone.

But the money he'd get from smuggling drugs was tempting. Too tempting. So – he compromised – he'd do it for a year or two, make enough to be set up for life, and then decamp to Canada, well away from the terrifying Mr. Barnett.-

# Chapter 3
## Expansion

"Dad, is Paris nice?" Tim asked getting into the car one evening. He had just finished his shift in the Control Tower at Wingmore Aifield.

"Never been," Ron replied. "Why?"

"Only Craig was saying how great it is now that a lot of the war damage has been cleaned up. So I checked it out in the books Mum has got at home in the Library. Okay, I know they were about what it was like before the war, but it must still be a lot like it was back then. You know, with the Palace of Versailles and places. So maybe it'd be worth going some time."

"That's an idea. We could get something from the Travel Agents and see what they say about it now. We could go on one of our flights there easily enough."

"T'r'fic!"


"Can I cadge a lift into Folkestone today, Mum?" Tim asked at breakfast two days later. "I thought I'd go into that Travel Agent's there as it's my day off and see if they've got any stuff about Paris."

"That's fine. You know, I haven't been to Paris since before the war. I wonder if it's changed much."

"Craig said they'd cleared up just about all the war damage now and I looked up things about it in the Guidebooks you've got in the Library."

Anne was pleased he'd started using the Library, the big room downstairs that used to be the Dining Room. It had made such a difference to Kathleen's outlook on life when she and Maralyn had first come to stay with her as Evacuees in 1939, twelve years ago now. Given them ambitions far beyond ideas they had had before. And which they were achieving.

"I'll be going in fifteen minutes. Alright?"

"Fine."

In the Travel Agents' Tim looked at the brochures on the shelves while he waited for one of the people at the counter to become free.

And was surprised at the places you could go to for holidays now.

Holiday Camps around the country, hotels and Boarding houses of course – including some in Folkestone and Dover he saw. But the 'Foreign Section' was really interesting.

France, Belgium, Holland – the brochures all seemed bright, attractive, with smiling people in brilliant sunshine according to the covers. Canada, America, even Australia. You'd have to be really rich to go to those places, he thought.

Spain, even Italy and places in North Africa where there had been all those battles just a few years ago. He wondered how they'd treat the English now, even if they were going as visitors not soldiers.

Spain looked different from around Folkestone too. Or any other place he had seen. Very different. The countryside, even the kind of buildings were different. Some of them looked a bit like some of those North Africa ones, he saw as he looked from one brochure to another. There'd been no battles there in the war so maybe they'd be more welcoming to British visitors.

"You looking for places to go to? Or just looking?"

Tim looked round at the girl, maybe around his own age of seventeen years, maybe a year or two older he thought, who had come to him from behind the counter.

He blushed to the roots of his hair. She was pretty, had nice scent and – and … He was still shy with girls. Very conscious of how injured, of how deformed he was.

"Looking for places to go to," he said, determined to sound adult.

"Australia? Canada? America?" she asked, not really intending to put him down, but to show this nice looking lad that she was sophisticated herself. Shame he was so crippled. She wondered briefly how that had happened.

"No. More about Paris. And Spain," he added.

"Now Spain's really good," she said taking down a brochure and turning several pages in succession to show him pictures. "It's really coming on now too. New hotels, beautiful sea and beaches, and if you go inland a bit, some of the villages are terrific. Really quaint. Different from anything in this country."

"Have you been to Spain?"

"Not yet. But I will go as soon as I can."

"How do you get there?"

"You can get a boat, so you have a sea voyage as well but 'planes are flying quite a lot into Malaga Airport which serves the Costa del Sol where a lot of this development is going on. You can buy what is called a 'Package Tour' where you get the Flight and a Hotel in same package. That's why it's called that. That way you get both together which is cheaper, easier and better. Or drive there."

"I reckon we'd only need to get the hotel places," Tim said thoughtfully.

"We can do that for you easily enough," she said quickly. "But how would you get there?"

"Maybe my Dad would start a route there," Tim said off-handedly taking the brochure from her.

As he tried to turn back to the hotel pages she saw how awkwardly he was holding it with his left hand.

"Let's go to the counter," she suggested. "Then you can look at them easier." As they moved over, "What did you mean your Dad might start a route there?"

"My father's Mr. Jackson of 'Carruthers Airlines'. We already run regular routes into Paris and some other cities and if Spain's developing like you say maybe we could start going there too."

"Then you must be the Tim Jackson who was crippled in that school bombing in the war. And your sister!" she said staring at him.

"Well – yes." Tim was embarrassed.

"Sorry. I shouldn't have said that. Sorry." She was suddenly equally embarrassed

"Doesn't matter," Tim dismissed it. "Okay if I take this brochure on Spain?"

"Of course. And this one. And this one gives the details of the flights already going to Malaga. If you want anything more, just ask for me. I'm Angela Manders."

"Thanks. I will." He stood up. "Angela."

"Did you get anything interesting Tim?" Anne asked him that evening. Tim had caught the bus home as Anne had been staying in town all day.

"Yes. Got talking to someone about Spain. Sounds really interesting."

"More than Paris?" Kathleen asked.

"Much more.  She said, this girl in the Agents, that it's really opening up for tourists now.  New hotels, great sea and sand, a lot warmer than England for much longer in the year.  So better for holidays." He looked at Ron.  "I wondered if it'd be worth us flying there.  She said Malaga's the airport for the Costa del Sol.  That's where most of the development's going on."

"Mmm.  I'll get the atlas and we can have a look.  You're a real dynamo for ideas you are Tim.  First you locate our Marina, now a new expansion for our airline," Ron declared, standing up to get it from the Library.  Making Tim grin with delight.

Ron opened the big atlas on the coffee table and found the place for 'Europe' that spread across two pages.  He traced the route with a finger then measured the distance with a ruler from Wingmore to Malaga.

"Just over a thousand miles as the 'plane flies.  Bypassing the Pyrenees and flying over the Bay of Biscay, cutting down over Madrid to Malaga – no problems that I can see.  On first look anyway," he added thoughtfully.

"But can we spare the 'planes Dad, if we were thinking of regular flights?" Tim asked.  "Aren't our schedules pretty full for doing that?"

Ron shot a look at him, inwardly delighted.  So Tim was taking an interest in the whole aircraft operation – not just the Control Tower.

"You're right Tim.  So what should be our next steps?"

"Decide how much demand there'd be?" he suggested, a query in his voice feeling Dad was putting him on the spot.

"Bang on.  So how would we do that?"

"Well I could go and see Angela, Angela Manders.  She was the girl I spoke to at the Travel Agents." That would give him an excuse to see her again.

"Yes.  But wouldn't the Manager of the shop know better than just one Assistant?"

"Suppose so." Tim was disappointed.

"So I could contact the Manager, say you had sparked our interest in possibly setting up flights to Malaga because of your conversation with Angela – and ask if we two could meet up with the Manager and her to check out some facts with them.  How does that sound?"

"T'r'ific!" That would really impress Angela!

"Right I'll phone the Manager tomorrow morning and let me have your Duty roster for the next week so we can fit the time of the meeting round our schedules."


Excited but nervous, Tim pushed open the door to go into the Travel Agents followed by Ron carrying a briefcase. As soon as Angela saw Tim she gave him a beaming smile and jumped to her feet.

"Mr. Jackson? Mr. Warner's ready for you." She went to a door at the end of the room, tapped and opened it. "The Mr. Jacksons are here, Mr. Warner," she announced and ushered them in, following them to close the door.

"Please sit down." Mr. Warner indicated seats for Ron and Tim while Angela went to sit at the side of his desk.

Mr. Warner was thin and sallow-looking, not looking particularly fit.

"I understand you are wanting to know about the demand for Flights to Malaga," he said.

"That's right, Mr. Warner," Ron answered. "As I mentioned on the 'phone I run Carruthers Airlines which includes passenger flights to Paris and a few other Continental destinations. As a result of a conversation between my son Tim and Miss Manders they drew my attention to the growth in Spain, the Costa del Sol in particular, as a holiday destination. So I'm looking into possible future demand to add Malaga to our destinations."

"I've got some figures here, Mr. Jackson. Not just from here but the three other offices we have." He passed some sheets of paper across the table. Ron positioned them so that Tim could see them as well. "As you see, Bookings are increasing steadily, especially for the Package Holidays. People seem to like the idea of getting everything done on one visit to a Travel Agent. Do you advertise through Travel Agents?"

Mr. Warner knew Ron didn't with his firm.

"No. We advertise direct to the local public. That way we can cut costs, so making our prices cheaper. As we fly from Wingmore it is the more local people who use us. But if we started thinking of Package Tours, that'll be a lot more more complicated."

"What you could do Mr. Jackson is to link up with a hotel on the Costa del Sol that Malaga airport serves, just here." Mr. Warner put a map on the desk, turned so that it was the right way up for Ron and Tim, and indicated a spot on the coast with a pencil. "The hotel is on the outskirts of a growing town so there is increasing nightlife there, it's close to the beach and it's of good though not luxurious quality. That means its not too pricey but still of a quality that visitors would enjoy."

"Have you been there yourself?" Ron asked.

"Not yet. Though part of it is ready, the hotel will be opening properly next March. But I do know the hotelier personally."

"Oh?" Ron looked at him.

"Ben Brooks had a good quality hotel in Singapore at the time it fell to the Japanese in February 1942. In the final battle before the surrender he locked up the hotel, got a British Army uniform and rifle and joined my Unit. He was a good shot and so was useful though strictly speaking he was still a civilian. After the Surrender we, and plenty of others of course, were sent to work on the Burma Death Railway as they call it now, but we both survived. After the war I came back to the UK but Ben decided he wanted somewhere warmer but not with steamy heat as in the Far East. In the end he chose Spain and because he knows hotels he persuaded some people there to back him in building a hotel.

"If you decided to run your air service to Malaga, tying it in with Ben's hotel, you could run that combination as a Package Tour. Whether you'd get enough customers from just around here though, might be questionable. That's if you decided to fly from Wingmore and just by using local advertising."

"Mmm" Ron rubbed his chin as he looked again at the figures. "How many does the hotel sleep?"

"Thirty. But Ben is already talking of increasing that. He's got enough land to add what he calls 'Self-catering units'. Where people basically look after themselves. Or buy their meals in the hotel restaurant."

"A reasonable 'plane-load then."

"Could we do a trial run Dad?" Tim asked hesitantly. "You know, book the hotel for a week and we run a flight out to take people, then another flight the next week to bring them back."

"Can't fly a 'plane empty each way Tim. Nor keep a 'plane and crew out there for a week doing nothing. The only way to make it pay is to basically run a shuttle service. Flying a 'planeload out and bring another planeload back."

"What about a weekend trial then Mr. Jackson? We do those don't we Mr. Warner?" suggested Angela. "Fly out Friday afternoon, fly back Sunday afternoon."

"Now that's an idea, Miss Manders!" Ron said at once. 'We could manage that. Would your pal go along with that Mr. Warner? My family would do it for starters. It would give us a chance to check out the hotel and see how it would work from the flying angle. If it works we'd then have to see about using Travel Agents around a fairish area from here to increase our potential. Emphasising the savings people would make flying from Wingmore rather than have the expense and trouble of going up to London."

"I'll 'phone Ben and let you know Mr. Jackson. I'll ask him how soon the hotel will be ready for a weekend visit and the cost. If he couldn't accommodate all who you might get to go I'm sure he could find places in other hotels for any over-flow."

"Excellent. In the meantime I'll sort out the Flights angle."

Once they were outside, "You did a great job there Tim," Ron said warmly.

"But my idea of a trial flight was no good was it?" Tim mumbled, thinking Ron was just 'soft-soaping' him.

"Sure it was. It was your suggestion that sparked Angela's idea. Your basic idea was absolutely right - a trial run. Then Angela took it up and ran with it as they say. That meeting was just like our Board Meetings, you know. Someone comes up with an idea, we kick it around a bit, often make some changes and come out with the best thing to do."

"Oh. That's okay then." Tim was considerably cheered.

"I'm going to go up to Wingmore to check out flight schedules with Richard Sampson anyway. Now, I can either drop you off at home for you to come up later for your Shift – or if you want to earn some overtime you can come with me to the Airfield now and start checking out some information about Flight details to Malaga."

"I'll go up with you," Tim said promptly. "What do you want me to do?"

"'Phone calls to get prices of Landing Fees at Malaga, Flight paths, exact distances involved, fuel consumption on our aircraft for those distances and so the cost of our flights and then how much we'd need to charge customers to break even and then to get a 10% profit. Okay? Or as much of all that before you have a lunch break and be ready for your Shift in the Control Tower."

"Great! If you can tell me where I get the 'phone numbers." And mother had told him that office work at the Airfield would be deadly dull!

He was working out distances in the small office that he'd been given when his 'phone rang.

He looked at it suspiciously. Who could be ringing this office? He'd only been 'phoning out and hadn't arranged for anyone to ring him back.

It rang again so he picked it up.

"Hallo?" he said guardedly.

"Is that Tim Jackson?"

"Yes. Who's that?"

"Angela Manders from the Travel Agents, Tim. Mr. Warner said he'd got the information your Dad wanted about the hotel. Can I give you the Details? Your switchboard said I should when I rang to tell your Dad."

"Sure. Fine." Tim snatched up a pencil and grabbed a fresh piece of paper. "Shoot."

He quickly scribbled down the details then repeated them back to her – something he'd learned to do in the Control Tower.

"That's it," she responded warmly. "Mr. Warner's said I'm to be the one to liaise with Carruthers Airlines. So if you're to be that for your Dad then – then we'll be chatting quite a bit, won't we?"

Tim flushed – and grinned. That sounded as though Angela wanted that too!

"That'll be t'r'ific," he said. "I'll get back to you then and let you know what Dad says."

He carefully wrote out what Angela had told him adding that Angela had said she was to be the person at the Travel Agents liaising with them. He hesitated because he hadn't finished the other jobs Ron had given to him, but then decided to take the hotel details to his office anyway. Ron was busy on the 'phone so Tim laid it on his desk and tip-toed out.

Sam Proctor took him home after they finished their shift at the Control Tower which had now closed down for the night. They rarely had late flights taking off or landing.

As he walked in the front door he encountered Kathleen just about to go upstairs to bed.

"'Night Tim," she said as he closed the door after him.

"Kathleen ...," he blurted, "... can I ask you something? Something private?"

Though she was tired, Kathleen caught the note of almost pleading in his tone.

"Sure. In the kitchen? Your supper's in the oven."

"Right." As he followed her there he shouted to Mum and Dad that he was home.

"What's it about Tim?" Kathleen asked as she sat down in one of the chairs at the big kitchen table while Tim got out his late supper.

Now the moment had come Tim felt very awkward. He was raising a subject that neither of them had ever talked about. Their injuries. Apart from that one time in hospital a few weeks after the school had been bombed, when Kathleen had wheeled herself through to his Ward. Both had been shocked then how badly injured the other was. Their mother had been told to conceal from them how bad the other was at first because they were so ill. And that other time when he had first seen Kathleen with her 'tin legs'. But that had only been about how they worked.

"You know when you first met up with Terry?"

"I should do. I was there, wasn't I?"

"Yeah. 'Course. What I was meaning was - well did he know straight off about your legs? And did it make any difference when he found out?"

"We met when Dad took me up to the Airfield one Saturday and Terry was doing 'Circuits and Bumps' with Mr. Sampson. Dad was needing to talk to Mr. Sampson so when they landed Dad went off to talk to him and Terry came across to the table where I was sittinglooking at some leaflets about the Flying School, bringing a couple of mugs of tea. As far as he knew I was just some girl that he thought he'd chat up after completing his Log.  We only used our first names so he didn't know who I was at first.

"After a bit more chat he realised who I was when he asked about Miss Dangerfield's and I told him about my legs then.  But it was only fifteen minutes later he asked me if I'd go with him to the Hippodrome in Folkestone to see a Show, so it obviously didn't matter to him then.  And as it's gone on from there, it obviously still doesn't matter.  Why?"

"Well." Tim hesitated again.  Should he wait a bit before telling Kathleen about Angela?  Only Kathleen never seemed to bother that she had artificial legs.  He was all too conscious of how deformed he looked.  His upper body anyway.  His clothes couldn't hide it.  And that girl on the beach who had stared at him that time he'd been stripped to his swimming trunks who'd said something to her parents and they had taken a quick look at him then very obviously started looking everywhere else but in his direction.  He had never taken off his shirt on the beach again.  "There's this girl at the Travel Agents and ...,"

"Angela Manders?  Dad told me about her."

"Yep.  That's her.  Only - how do you feel about your legs and and Terry?"

Kathleen looked at him soberly.

"Terry's always treated me as though there's nothing wrong with me.  Well, he does do things off his own bat without me or anyone else asking him to, that takes my legs into account – like carrying that tray of drinks for me that time, but he never fusses over me.

"There is one thing that does bother me though Tim," she said quietly after a moment.  "We're Engaged and that means some time we'll get married, we're thinking in six months to a year.  That means that on our wedding night he'll see me as I really am.  My legs I mean," she added hastily.  "What I've got left of them.  And what does worry me sometimes is how he'll react when he sees how I am So far of course my legs have always been covered with my slacks. We've never really talked about it.  Maybe we should.  Sometime."

"So maybe I could just ask Angela if she'll come out with me sometime and just see how it goes," Tim suggested thoughtfully.

"Dad said something to me once that really helped me a lot.  It was when we were still in hospital in London.  I was just getting used to the idea of having no legs and I asked him, as he was a man, did he think I'd ever get a boy friend. I was thirteen and getting interested in boys." She grinned at Tim.

"He said that what was more important than my legs was what I had in my heart and in my head. The kind of person I was, he was meaning. And I guess that was right. With Terry anyway. And if Angela's any kind of girl it'll be the same with her.

"One thing is – being injured like we are isn't our fault, is it? They're not things that happened to us because we'd done something stupid ourselves. Something that no sensible person would have done I mean."

"Yeah, " Tim said thoughtfully. "Yeah. See what you mean. Thanks."


Ron, as always, checked the big table in the Boardroom. As always his secretary, Mary Rainer, had already put everything where it should be. They smiled at each other.

Mary, widowed during the War, had no rancour about Ron doing this. She regarded it as another indication of his qualities as the Chairman of the Board. Immensely grateful to Ron and Sonia who had given her the job she had so desperately needed over younger applicants as the Carruthers Group of Companies had been expanding some years ago now, she gave the firm total loyalty.

"The latest Project sounds really exciting Mr. Jackson," she said.

"Have you ever been to Spain, Mary?" he asked.

"No. Jimmy and I motored through France to the Pyrenees but that was in 1936 and the Spanish Civil War had just broken out so that was the closest we got to it."

"Like to go?"

"Perhaps."

Ron tapped the gavel once all the Board Members were there, exactly on the set time.

"Item 3," he said once the Minutes had been read and duly signed. "An additional air route to Malaga, Spain to capitalise on the beginning tourist industry."

He explained the background in a few sentences then referred to the Costings that Tim had produced and then the details of the 'Hotel

Excelsior' from Angela.  Both had been circulated already

"Ben Brooks the hotelier is known personally to Sam Warner. They were captured by the Japs at Singapore and survived the Burma railway.  What I suggest is that we lay on a Flight to Malaga using one of our Dakotas one weekend to check the airport there, the hotel and the facilities of the area to see if it's something we want to do."

Members studied the map of the route, the details of the hotel and the way the area was being developed.

"Do we have to wait until the hotel's completely finished?  That won't be till next year and that could mesh with our projected start up date, so the trial run would be better before then.  As it's only partly completed we could make it a Company jolly with subsidised prices in one of the Daks, and sell any seats over at a higher price," suggested Richard Sampson.

"We could see how many rooms the Excelsior will have ready for when we decide to go and book rooms in other hotels for the others," Anne came in.

"What about aircraft if we take on this expansion?" Sonia as the Company Accountant asked.

"I'd suggest we get one of the new Vickers Viscounts.  They've got a production run going rather than making them to order so the Delivery Date is fairly short." Ron passed round details and Specifications.

The suggestion for a weekend 'proving run' as Richard called it was agreed and the date 'penciled in'.  Once that was agreed by the hotel they would circulate all employees on a 'First come, First booked basis'.  But it was restricted to employees and immediate families only.  To start with anyway.

Everyone round the table immediately took Bookings.

"There is another thought ...," Peter Conway said, " ... why not look at what's happening in the Balearic Islands, just off Spain, too? Check any developing tourism there.  Majorca and the other islands, making it a wider operation.  Land passengers at Malaga then island hop to one of the Balearics."

"Make a note for us to look into that.  It sounds a good idea."

As soon as this was passed on to Sam Warner he immediately

booked a place for himself and then Angela asked if she could come too, as this had originated in her ideas and she was the Liaison with Carruthers Airlines.

Ron looked down at the pages of calls for booking places that had come flooding in within hours of the details being circulated. There were enough to fill two Daks. Or a Halifax. But Malaga airport might not be able to take a big 4-engined plane of that size. He'd have to check.

To his surprise news quickly spread and they had to begin fielding enquiries from other people about commercial flights to Spain. It was beginning to look as though they could have sufficient custom to start up a regular route.

# Chapter 4
## Spain

On a cool September Friday morning two lines of people moved out of the Terminal at Wingmore to go to the two Dakotas waiting on the tarmac.

Both Frank and Tim were excited as they walked out, though Tim tried to look as though it was all part of a normal day for him. Which impressed Frank mightily.

To make sure Frank would be given time off school for the trip Ron had written to his Headmaster himself rather than leave it to May. He was not 100% sure that she would be as strong as he was in pressing for the Head's permission. She had been furious when she found what he had done, but Ron was indifferent to that.

Then to make sure that she would do what was necessary for Frank to get his Passport in good time Ron had quietly 'phoned Des Ackroyd at his office. Thankfully he had promised to make sure that she would do that – and he made sure she did by suggesting they went on a Continental car tour themselves during the school summer holiday, to be before the flight to Spain.

But to Frank a Flight was far better than a car and ferry trip. And this was a long flight too!

They strapped themselves in their seats and Tim explained what they would be doing in the Control Tower calling it the 'Pre-flight routine'. Shortly afterwards the two Dakotas took off, Craig as their Senior Pilot, leading.

Tim had let Frank have the window seat so they were able to see the countryside passing below them, then very soon they were over the sea. Tim had brought a Flight Map and an ordinary atlas to show Frank the route they would be flying. Really he would have preferred to be sitting by Angela but as Dad had suggested Frank should come, he'd accepted that that wasn't going to happen. And she was sitting with her Boss, Mr. Warner.

"Okay Kathleen?" Terry asked her. She had had a struggle climbing the steps into the 'plane.

"Sure. I'm fine." She said nothing about her legs hurting because she had badly jarred the above-knee stump when she had stumbled on the top step. There would be no way she could check it till they got to the Terminal in Malaga. The on-board toilet was really too small for her to use that comfortably.

Further forward Anne was thinking. She had seen how Kathleen had struggled. So what arrangements could they make for people like her that wanted to fly?

In Malaga Ben Brooks looked worriedly at his watch. He was more anxious about this 'proving' flight' than he had ever been about anything to do with the Hotel Excelsior in Singapore. But since the Railway he worried about things more than he ever had before. And this was a doddle compared with that, he told himself again. Which did nothing to calm his stress.

"Must be getting old," he muttered morosely. Then checked the lists on his clipboard yet again.

The Board members of Carruthers Airlines and their relatives would be staying in the Spanish Excelsior, the others he had farmed out around other hotels, holding out the promise that if this worked out well he would make sure they would get more from the same source. And then he'd gone round to check the rooms in those hotels himself.

"Time to go," he said to the driver of the lead coach he'd got as he swung aboard to go to the airport. This really was the 'Off'.

"Si Senor', the driver grinned, crashing his gears as they started.

They pulled into the Arrivals Bay in good time.

Ben picked up the binoculars he'd brought and scanned the sky finally locating two dots. They closed rapidly and he identified them as Dakotas. They touched down safely and he hurried into the Arrivals Hall. As the first passengers came through he held up a big sign marked, 'Carruthers Airlines'.

He spotted Sam Warner coming through, a tall man on one side, a younger woman on his other. Other passengers following closely.

Sam grinned widely as he spotted Ben, said something to the tall man and waved.

"Hello Ben," Sam called.

Then the passengers were crowding out behind him. Ron was impressed with the way Ben had organised everything as people were directed to one of the two coaches waiting outside without fuss.

"Nice," Anne said, looking round the room she and Ron were sharing. "I'll go and check the others."

Frank and Tim were sharing a room but Kathleen had been given a single. She had asked if that would be possible as she'd been worrying about sharing with even someone she knew. Ron had assured her that he'd booked singles for her and Terry.

"Their rooms are as good as ours," she reported back.

Ben had arranged for Spanish-style entertainment for the Friday and Saturday evenings and coach trips for the Saturday and Sunday mornings before flying back to the UK late Sunday afternoon. The rest of the time they could explore the area or use the beach and sea, soaking up the still hot September sunshine.

To Tim's frustration Angela and Mr. Warner always seemed to be together, not even giving him a chance to talk to her alone. But he didn't have much chance to do that anyway because Frank always stuck with him – and an 11 year old brother can be an unwelcome handicap at times.

On the Sunday morning Ron and Peter Conway had a business meeting with Ben. Sam Warner was not included because any tie-up would be between the Airline and the Hotel. The Travel Agent would only come in if that was agreed.

"Everything about the Hotel and your arrangements have been very impressive Ben," Ron said as soon as they were sitting in his office having waved off the Trippers.

Ben heaved a silent sigh of relief. Even if nothing came of this tie-up, he'd use that in his publicity. And the cheque for this weekend that Peter had just passed him was very welcome.

"What we're planning to do is draw our customers from the Home and Southern Counties of the UK and maybe South London because we'll be flying from our own Wingmore Airfield in Kent. That means we can undercut the costs of Landing Fees at Heathrow and whatever the Fees will be at Gatwick when that re-opens. Keeping things comparatively local for the time being anyway, will cut other costs too.

"So if we can agree a suitable price for the Hotel use we should be able to undercut the prices other companies charge for their Package Tours. Alternatively, we can simply lay on regular Flights to Malaga, leaving the passengers to make their own arrangements for accommodation. With you – or other Hotels."

"Or use Excelsior primarily for Package Tours but also sell seats just on the Flights alone and Ben provide rooms primarily for Package Tour use to be able to let rooms apart from that," suggested Peter

"Or you book rooms of different types, singles and doubles, for next season and sell those with your Flights to make up your Package Tours," countered Ben, anxious to secure firm sales.

Ron glanced at Peter, his inbred caution holding him back. That would involve the Company in a massive outlay if they booked rooms like that for a complete season, with no real indication of the possible demand.

"I think for the next season we'd better stick just with the Flights, Peter. But if you will let us have the Excelsior's details Ben – you know brochures with your facilities and prices, we could pass those on."

"And other Hotels on the Costa perhaps Ron?" Peter added.

"Yes. Spread the range of customers' choices. In Malaga – and north of there as well as down south round here which would give a greater range for our Flight customers." Ron nodded agreement.

Ben knew that that would mean he'd lost almost all the advantages he'd hoped to gain from this weekend visit.

"Or we could run it that you do give us priority as Package Tours say for the first six months to see how the demand goes, then firm up other arrangements after that try-out period." he said after a moment.

"We could prioritise your facilities to our customers for them to contact you direct. Or what we could do if that we both give them a discount and we'll pass onto you 50% of the Deposit we'd ask for each booking if they do the pairing up in our office when booking the flight with us," Ron suggested.

Ben thought for a minute. That deal was not what he really wanted but as that sounded pretty final it looked as though it was the best he was going to get. And it would mean he'd get an inflow of cash from the Deposits and his hotel would be prioritised.

"Deal," he said.

"That was a great idea of yours about Spain, Tim," Ron murmured to him, as they waited to board the coach to go to Malaga Airport. 'We've got a deal with the Hotel, so now to the next stage of getting a new 'plane for the route. I've been thinking of a Vickers Viscount, but think about what we'll need will you?"

Tim beamed with delight. And passed on the news to Frank.

"That's a pile of post!" Anne exclaimed as they went indoors after a smooth flight home. "Only from deliveries on Friday and Saturday too."

Frank scooped them up and began handing them round. They were all for Ron and Anne except for one official looking letter for Tim. Frank looked at him with curiosity as Tim ripped open the envelope, both wondering who could be sending him that kind of letter.

"It's my Call-up papers," Tim said, an odd note in his voice.

Ron, Anne and Kathleen looked at him sharply.

"Well – it's to say I'm to go to Dover for a Medical anyway."

"May I see Tim?" Ron asked quietly.

"I'll make a cup of tea while you see what it's about," Anne said as Tim handed the letter and papers to his father.

Leaving their bags in the hall they went into the Lounge, Ron reading through the documents as he went.

"Looks like just a standard, routine thing Tim. The kind of letter everyone gets at your age for National Service."

"You won't be able to be a soldier though will you Tim?" Frank asked. "With your arm?"

"I wouldn't be able to chuck a rifle around like we saw those soldiers do that time at the Tower of London Frank but I could be in an office. They must have those in the Army. Say Dad! Could I volunteer for the RAF?" he burst out, suddenly excited. "I could be in the Control Tower couldn't I? Even with my arm, 'cos I do that now. Maybe I could with those new Meteor jets! That'd be t'r'ific!"

"I'd give you a Reference for that Tim," Ron grinned at him. "You do a first-rate job there." As Anne came in with a big tray of drinks, "Tim's had his papers for his Call-up Medical the week after next."

"I'm going to see if I can volunteer for a Control Tower job in the RAF," Tim announced. "Dad said he'd give me a Reference."

"Excellent. Good for you Tim." Anne tried to sound enthusiastic.

The next morning Ron took Frank back home and Tim along for the chance to see his mother.

May kissed Tim and Frank quickly and glowered at Ron while still in the hall.

"You've made it just in time for Frank to get to afternoon school if you go straight away. You may not be bothered about his education but I am. He's taking the 11-Plus next year so the whole of this year is vital. I don't know how you worked it for him to lose three whole days just for a flight in one of your 'planes but I was totally against it and I told the school so. Frank, I've got your school bag packed and there's some sandwiches and a drink in it." She pointed to the satchel

Frank's happy look had vanished.

"Righto Mum." He swung it onto his shoulder. "Let's go Dad."

"Do you want to spend some time with your Mum while I'm taking Frank to school, Tim?" Ron asked quietly.

"Make sure you're back by two o'clock for him then. I've got to go out."

"I'll go with you and Frank, Dad in case you get held up," Tim said quickly. "'Bye Mum."

He kissed her and went to the door.

"May ...," Ron began quietly.

"I don't want Frank to be late," May interrupted.

Ron shrugged and turned to the front door that Frank had already opened.

"I thought missing school for three days for that trip to Spain was worth it Dad," Frank said as soon as Ron drove off. "In any case the last two lessons on Friday were football and that doesn't figure in the 11-Plus does it?"

"No. But what other lessons did you miss?"

"Geography, History and a couple of periods of English this morning, but I'm going to be there in time for Maths and French now and I can make up for those I missed dead easy."

"Mmm." Most of those were important for the 11-Plus exams, but they had only just started this final year so Ron didn't see missing them at this stage was of major importance, nor had the Headmaster. But it would be more important later in the year so he would take care not to take him off school again.

That evening the 'phone extension in the hall rang just as Kathleen was passing it so she picked up the receiver.

"Oh. Hallo mother," she said, startled. This was the first time her mother had 'phoned here. "Nothing bad has happened has it?" with a sudden stab of worry. A moment later, "Okay, I'll get him." She laid the receiver down on the table. "Tim, mother for you."

"Kitty ...," May began, but she had already gone.

"Hallo," Tim said guardedly as he picked up the 'phone.

"Tim. Frank's just told me you've had your Call-up papers for National Service."

"It's only for the Medical mother – Mum."

"But that's ridiculous! You can't be a soldier in your state!"

"Not a soldier swinging a rifle around but ...."

"Don't be silly Tim. You can't be anything in the Services! You've got to be fit, and you – well you're not are you? You're crippled. Both with your arm and your ankle."

Tim was irritated. Here everyone treated him as 'normal' not as a 'cripple'.

"What's your father done about it?"

"Nothing. There's nothing to do."

"That's just the sort of thing I'd expect from him. Well I'm going to do something about it. There's bound to be a 'phone number in the papers somewhere. I want to know what it is. Now. So find it."

Tim hesitated. He'd never gone against a direct order from his mother before. Even when he had decided to take the job in the Spares Department here she hadn't actually said he couldn't though she'd made it obvious enough she hadn't liked it. And he was resenting the way she was talking to him now, just as if he was a small kid instead of nearly eighteen.

And he and Frank had been talking excitedly about him joining the RAF. Even if he couldn't pilot a 'plane he certainly would be able to work in a Control Tower. He already was, wasn't he?

"No thanks Mum. I want to go. I'm going to volunteer for the RAF and work in the Control Tower of a Fighter Station. I know I can do that because I'm doing it right now, aren't I?"

"Tim," May's voice became gentle. "Why do you think they let you help out a bit in there? Your father is the Boss of the Company and he'd have given them orders to let you help out, that's why."

Tim stared at the 'phone. Was that really right? That he'd only got the job because Dad had told them to? And just to 'help out a bit'? That would mean that he really was no good. No good at anything. As he'd always thought before. Before he'd got the job in the Stores here. But then Mr. Mason had said how good he was at that and then said he'd given him a good Reference when he applied for the Control Tower job.

And Mr. Finsbury the Controller, had been letting him talk down planes for three weeks now. That wasn't 'just helping out a bit' was it? That was the job of a proper Air Controller. And Mr. Finsbury had said he'd done great.

"Tim," May said, still gently. "You do understand what I'm saying don't you?"

"Yes," Tim snapped back bitterly. "You think I'm no good at anything. But people down here know different."

He rammed the 'phone down but waited a few minutes in case she rang back. She didn't, so he went back into the Lounge and picked up the book on the RAF that he'd found in the Library.

"Okay Tim?" Ron asked. Seeing it wasn't.

"Yeah."

Ron said nothing, wishing he knew what to say, how to ask. And wishing Anne was in here. She would have known how to deal with it.

"Dad. Will you answer a question really honestly? No fudging or – or white lies or anything? Just the exact truth?"

"Sure." Ron couldn't help remembering Kathleen asking the same kind of thing before she asked him a question that had been vitally important to her. That had been soon after she had been so injured, was still in hospital, about boy friends.

"Did you have anything to do with me getting the job in the Control

Tower?"

"No.  You saw the Internal Notice about it, though I'd have told you about it if you hadn't, because you'd said before you wanted to be there.  With the Stores job you had before that, I only told you about it coming up.  Everything else was up to you and the Managers. Why?"

"But Mr.Finsbury would have known you were my father.  The Boss."

"Of course.  But that made no difference Tim.  The jobs you do at the Airfield are far too important for someone to be taken on who wasn't the best around.  In the Stores and especially in the Control Tower.  Because if you make a mess of something in that place, there could be crashes or collisions and people would be killed or injured.  That's why we always have two people in there at present and if and when we get busier there we'll need to take on someone else and you will move up to be Deputy Control Officer.  Deputy to Mr. Finsbury."

"Lumme!"

"You got the job in the Control Tower on merit Tim and don't let anyone tell you different.

"It was the same with your job in the Spares Department.  In its own way that was just as important.  You had to keep absolutely accurate records for what spares went out and when to order more. If that wasn't done we could have run out of spares, so a 'plane would have to be grounded which would mean customers would be badly let down which would affect their businesses, disappoint their customers and so on down the line.  We've got a very high reputation for reliability – and that was at least partly in your hands while you were there.

"And you had to always give out the right spares too.  If you gave out the wrong ones, at the best, time would have been lost while it was swapped for the right one.  At the worst a wrong part can cause a crash.  And you had to make sure the right re-placements were ordered at once to make sure we always had the right ones on hand in our Stores.

"Mr. Mason reckoned you were better than Tommy Turner so you got the job.  Not that he was bad – just that you were better.  I've always believed the man on the job knows best about what he needs so I never interfere. When you applied for the Control Tower job Mr. Mason did a Reference which is standard procedure with Internal Movements. So you won both jobs on your own capabilities."

He looked steadily at Tim. And Tim had to believe him.

Though both Ron and Anne offered to give Tim a lift to the Dover Assessment Centre, he refused saying they had their jobs to do and he'd get the bus.

He checked in at the desk at Reception, the papers were handed back and he was directed through swing doors into a large waiting room and told to report to the person sitting at a table he'd find in the room.

There were a couple of dozen young men in there already, sitting on the hard-backed chairs. They looked at him but no one said anything to him, then a few carried on talking quietly among themselves as he approached the long trestle table.

"I was told ...," he began.

"Papers," the official interrupted holding out a hand.

Tim handed them over.

"You Timothy Jackson?"

"Yes sir."

"Go to the table over there and fill up this form."

The man scrawled Tim's name at its top, handed it to him and pointed at another trestle table to one side where a young man was already sitting, staring down at his form.

Tim took out his fountain pen and started filling in the form with his Date of Birth, address and next of kin. The next space was 'Education History with dates'. He thought for a minute wondering where to begin then decided to start with his first Primary school in London.

"I 'ates forms," muttered the young man beside him.

Tim glanced at him, down at the form and saw he hadn't started filling in any of it.

"What's that say mate?" he touched the 'Address' space.

"Address," Tim muttered quietly.

Herbert Jones scrawled big letters across the line and then above the next line.

"An' that?"

"Next of kin."

"What's that supposed ter mean?"

"Your Mum or Dad."

"Me Dad's dead, Mum's buggered off somewhere. I live wiv me sister."

"Put her name down then."

"An' that?"

"'Education history. With dates'."

"Blimme! Ain't 'ardly been to no schools. Never went with the bombing on when I was little in London. Then I started on the Barrows wiv me brother while I was still a nipper selling anything we could pick up from the bomb damage. Then me mother buggered off with this bloke an' me sister moved down 'ere wiv 'er bloke an' I came wiv 'em. That was in the last year of the war. Since then ..." Herbert shrugged.

"You could put 'Limited' then and let them ask you if they want to know more."

"Ow do I spell 'limited'?"

Tim helped him fill in the rest while doing his own, then they took them to the man at the table who glanced through them.

"Take a seat over there." He pointed to the rows of chairs.

"You doing anything? Jobwise?" Herbert ('call me 'Erb', he said) asked.

"I'm in the Control Tower at Wingmore Airfield."

"You mean guiding the 'planes in like they did in the War? Like we seen at the pictures sometimes?"

"That's right. But the only 'planes we're using are Dakotas and Wimpeys."

"Blimme! They don't do nothink like that in the Army though do they?"

"Shouldn't think so. I'm going to ask for the RAFand for a Control Tower job. I put that down in the space for 'Preferred Regiment', especially as I already do it. I'd like to go to a Fighter Station. Especially one where they've got the new Meteor jet fighters."

"Mackeson'.

A burly young man stood up.

"Door one," he was told, the man at the desk pointing at a door, clearly marked.

More people went in and came out re-joining those still waiting.

"I made out I was deaf in one ear. Said I couldn't hear a thing," Mackeson muttered to another when he came out.

"Did they look down it? Your ear I mean. With their torch thing?"

"Yeah. The Doc said he couldn't see nothing wrong with it, but I stuck to it."

"D'you reckon it'll work?"

"Dunno but it was worth trying."

"Roger Mackeson," called the official.

"Was that me you called out?" he asked, cupping a hand round his ear.

"Yes. Go up the stairs to see the Colonel. You've passed medically fit."

"Bugger!" It was heartfelt.

Eventually, "Timothy Jackson."

"See yer mate. Best o' luck wiv the RAF," 'Erb slapped Tim on the shoulder as he stood up.

Tim went through Door One and found an elderly, white-coated Doctor sitting behind a desk checking through his form.

"Strip to the waist."

Tim did so.

The Doctor looked at him from behind the desk, glanced at the form again, then came over.

"Hold your arms out in front of you."

Tim did so, his left arm positioned awkwardly.

The Doctor checked his left arm and spent some time on the elbow joint, lifting the forearm up and down, checked the wrist movement, then spent time examining the top of his spine.

"Lift both arms above your head."

"My left arm won't go. Or stay." Tim lifted up his left arm with his right hand, let go and his left forearm immediately dropped, his hand hitting him on the head.

More checks.

"You said in your form you'd got a brachial plexus injury. What do you mean by that?"

Tim explained what it was.

"How did that happen? Your form simply says it's the result of a bombing incident."

Tim explained.

"Take your shoes and socks off."

The Doctor examined his left shoe, blocked up at the heel.

"You said the injury was a fractured Tibia and Fibula. What do you mean by that?"

Tim explained that injury while the Doctor examined both his feet.

"You put in your form you want to join the RAF."

"Yes sir. I shouldn't think I could do much in the Army except maybe office work, I suppose. But because of my experience in the Control Tower at Wingmore Airfield I could easily do Control Tower duties in the RAF. The injuries don't stop me doing any of that."

"I see." The doctor scribbled something on the bottom of the form. "Go back into the main room."

As Tim went back, 'Erb passed him going in to see the Doctor.

After some minutes while 'Erb was still in there the official at the table called, 'Timothy Jackson."

Tim stood up and went towards the stairs to go to see the Colonel. It looked as though his bid to join the RAF had failed.

"Jackson," the official called.

In surprise Tim turned back to the table. Maybe he was being passed on to the RAF after all.

"Jackson ...," the official said softly once Tim was sitting in front of his desk, "... there's no need for you to see the Colonel. You haven't passed the Medical. We can't take you into the Army. If you want to know why you should see your Doctor, he can contact us and we will tell him, then he can tell you."

"I didn't think I'd be much good in the Commandos or Paras but I did volunteer for RAF Control Tower. I already do that."

"No," the official interrupted. "We can't take you at all. In any capacity. In any of the Services. Now about your expenses for coming here."

On his way home Tim didn't know if he was glad or sorry about failing the Medical so missing his National Service. Then he decided he was probably lucky. Though he'd miss the chance of going abroad with the Services he wasn't going to be shot at either. It was a pity they wouldn't take him into the RAF though. That would have been fun.

"Dad, do you have mother's 'phone number?" Tim asked that evening.

He now used Kathleen's distinction. 'Mum' was Anne, May was 'mother'. Except when he actually talked or wrote to May. Then she became 'Mum'. Anne was never mentioned.

"Yes." Ron took out his wallet and handed a card to him.

"Thanks."

Tim went out into the hall to the 'phone extension, really to be more private, and asked the Operator to get the number . Anne was working in the Library, Kathleen was out with Terry.

A male voice answered giving the number.

"Hallo father. It's Tim here. Is Mum in?"

"Yes, I'll get her. How are you Tim?"

"Fine thank you. And you?"

"I'm well. I'll get your mother."

The stilted kind of conversations they'd always had.

"Tim. What's happened?" Panic was in May's voice. This was the first time Tim had ever 'phoned.

"I thought you might like to know how I got on with the Medical this morning. They turned me down because of me being a cripple I suppose. I tried to persuade them to put me in the RAF to go into a Control Tower but they still said no."

"Thank God!" Relief rang in May's voice. "I did tell they wouldn't pass you, didn't I? And I could have stopped you even being worried over having to go to that ridiculous Medical."

"But I wasn't worried. I wanted to go Mum. And I would have been able to do that job in the Control Tower. After all, that's what I'm doing right now!"

"Well I'm glad they were sensible about it," May declared emphatically.

"And I asked Dad about me getting the job here. He said he'd kept right out of it. It had been up to Mr. Finsbury. And he said because the job in the Control Tower is so important because of having to make sure 'planes don't crash or collide, they have to pick the best."

"And you really believe your father hadn't anything to do with it? Listen Tim, even if he didn't actually tell that Finsbury man to take you on, and he certainly should have done as you wanted to do it, he would have known your father was the Boss of the show wouldn't he? So of course he gave you the job if for no other reason than to keep in with him. Look Tim, you've got to take every advantage you can of your father's position. That's the only way you're going to get anywhere."

"No mother. I'm going to stand on my own two feet! Just as Kathleen does."

He slammed the 'phone down and glared at it. Then he grinned at what he'd just said. Kathleen didn't 'stand on her own two feet' did she? She stood on artificial legs.

Funny the way you say things. But if Kathleen could do it with her job, then he was going to do the same.

Cheerful now he went back into the Lounge. Ron glanced at him, but though he'd heard faintly Tim's end of the conversation he wasn't going to ask. If Tim raised it with him, then that would be different.


Tim waited till he and Mr. Finsbury were on shift together with no one else in the Control Tower and there was a lull between arrivals and departures. He glanced across to where Mr. Finsbury had just finished writing up the Log of the latest departure.

"Mr. Finsbury, can I ask you something please?"

"Of course," sitting back in his chair, expecting a routine question about work.

"When you interviewed me for the job here, did my father have anything to do with it?"

"Nope. He didn't say a word."

"But even if he didn't do that, was it because you knew he's the Boss of the place?"

"Tim. You got this job purely on your own merits. Your father had nothing to do with it. First of all if your father had said I'd got to give you the job and I decided you weren't up to it, you still wouldn't have got it. The job we do here in the Control Tower is far too important to pick any second-raters. Like I told you when you started, those pilots out there rely on you. If you mess up you can cause 'planes to crash or collide and then people get injured or killed. So if your Dad had tried it on, I'd've told him to push off. But less politely than that. And one of the good things about your Dad is that he gives you a job to do, and once he's satisfied you're okay, he trusts you to get on with it without constantly checking up on you. Do you know what Mr. Mason in the Spares said in his Reference for you?"

"No. He didn't show it to me."

"He said in it that one of the best things about you was your record-keeping. You'd note down in the book immediately every Spare that went out and always up-dated the running Log."

"I can forget things real easy so I had to," Tim muttered.

"Maybe you do, maybe you don't. But as far as he was concerned that was vitally important. And it's even more important here for all kinds of reasons, not least the Air Registration Board. And you're much better at doing that than Greg Marriott, the other Applicant.

"Another thing was that you had spent a lot of your own time up here learning about everything you could so you were up and running from Day One. Marriott hadn't even bothered to learn all that a Control Tower does.

"Take it from me Tim. You've earned your place on that stool. On your own merits."

Tim was re-assured. Mother knew nothing about the way things worked in this world. Mr. Finsbury – and Dad – did.


"Item 4. The viability of the Package Tours and resultant action," Ron said looking round the other Board Members. "Richard. What kind of demand does your research show?"

"I've drawn on the experience of Sam Warner as well as research in Dover, Folkestone , Brighton and Tunbridge Wells. The last to get an inland view. Here's a breakdown of the figures." He passed round sheets of paper. "To summarise: A lot of interest, particularly questions about cost in comparison with the holiday camps here that are very popular. If its much dearer then interest collapses among many. But we put the 'Levels of Interest' in relation to the 'Occupation' and 'War Service' questions. Interest was highest among the better off and then among War Service Overseas.

"So obviously our market would be among the better off (which isn't surprising) and those who've already done some traveling overseas before.

"But another angle is that very few know anything much about Spain apart from the fact Franco is seen as a Dictator and it's a poor country. Quite a few knew of Guernico, the city the German Condor Legion bombed in '37 and almost nothing is known about the Costa del Sol in particular."

There was silence as people studied the papers.

"So we could target people through Travel Agents Brochures with pictures," suggested Peter Conway. "But that would need fixing dates and prices a long time ahead."

"On top of that, or instead of, we could run Newspaper reports on our trip there – with illustrations" suggested Sonia.

"We could plan a complete Advertising strategy," came in Anne. "Immediate newspaper reports on our trip, follow-up articles on Spain generally and the Costa del Sol in particular in the Travel Section, if they've got one, of local newspapers in all the major towns across our target region. If they haven't got one suggest they start one. Then a Discounted trip for their Editors, similar to the one we did."

"Would Travel Agents join us in sharing the cost?" Sonia asked. "Or other people who are already running Tours there? Because increased interest would benefit us all."

"Travel Agents might possibly. But while I take your point about 'mutually benefiting', we're going to be in direct competition with the other providers. Perhaps Richard and Anne could draw up an advertising campaign along the lines we've covered, with costings and see where we go from there. Agreed?"

There were nods around the table.

"Item 5. Aircraft. The Dakotas are getting dated and are a lot noisier than the newer passenger aircraft.

"I'd like us to look at the Vickers Viscount. These are the details of the variant now becoming available. And because they aren't building to order the Delivery dates are much shorter than they would be otherwise."

"How many would you think of getting?" asked Sonia.

"Ideally two or three. Then we could start replacing our older Dakotas and Wellingtons. They are still viable as cargo aircraft – which is our mainstay – but increasingly less so for passengers. Now that we're moving into that market."

"I see the Viscounts cost £58,000 each," Sonia said.

"That's right," Ron agreed. The figure was printed beside the photo of the 'plane.

"Then there's the expenses of getting new aircrew, retraining ground crew, retraining aircrew at present piloting the Dakotas that you're saying we need to replace. Plus the costs of setting up the new air routes to Malaga, costs of Air Regulation compliance and the costs of setting up the Package Tours, publicity and advertising. We've no real idea of demand yet, so we've got to budget for running the first year at least at a loss.

"Looking wider, we've got to take into consideration the costs of Carruthers Cruisers we're setting up at the same time. We met the cost of the Marina itself from our Reserves, but to stock it with cruisers to sell and to hire we will be running our Reserves right down and maybe even have to borrow more.

"I didn't intend bringing up our overall financial situation at this meeting but as we're talking of expanding our Airline business at the same time as the Cruiser side, it makes me wonder if we're trying to do too much on too many fronts too quickly with not enough Market Research."

"We have done Market Research Sonia, I reported on it earlier," Richard reminded her.

"Four towns along the coast and one inland town! Which registered interest among only a limited part of the population!" Sonia turned to Ron "In the light of the financial commitments we're talking of taking on, I think we really must have an in-depth examination of our total financial situation."

Ron glanced round the table. He was wanting to go ahead with both projects. While he was 90% certain Anne would back whatever decision he made and Richard would, Richard was inclined to let enthusiasm run away with him. And Peter would certainly side with Sonia in voting for caution.

So the Board would be split – with his being the casting vote. Then suddenly his old, deep-rooted fear of indebtedness hit.

"We could put in a Provisional Order for one Viscount with a Cancellation Clause, start the ball rolling for starting Flights into Malaga because if we decide to go ahead we'll want to start early next Spring, and Richard you extend the focus of more Market Research among the likely groups you've already identified and we hold a special Financial Meeting in two weeks time if you can manage that Sonia. To clarify the situation and then make some decisions. Is that agreeable?"

It was.

# Chapter 5
## Calais

Tom Henderson looked up from the Brochures from various cruiser companies he was examining to decide on the range of cruisers he was going to recommend to Mrs. Jackson to buy for re-sale and to hire out. The outer door to the office had been wedged open and it sounded as though someone had come in. He hadn't taken on a Secretary yet because there was nothing for her to do till the place was actually operating so he stood up to check who it was. His door was pushed wide open without a knock.

"Oh. Hi Algy,"

"Good morning Tom. We want you to do a rather urgent trip to Calais tomorrow morning returning in the afternoon."

"No problem. The cruiser in the boat shed will do it fine."

"On arrival at Calais you will stroll around the town, an ex-soldier looking around a place he had known during the war. You will be carrying this camera case and take one or two shots with this camera."

Algy put a large case on the desk and took out a camera..

"Not a very big camera for that size of case," murmured Tom.

"There's room for a packet to go in a false bottom."

"Right."

"At about noon, a few minutes either way doesn't matter, you will go into the Cafe Belgard on the Rue de Concorde. It is a combined Cafe and Patisserie. You will order a glass of the Cafe red wine and a cheese roll that they specialise in, put this case on the table and start reading a copy of today's Times. This one." Algy put a copy on the desk. "The owner, Pierre, will bring across your wine and roll and then recognise you as 'his *bon ami*' from the war days when you had fought the Jerries together in liberating Calais. He will introduce you to his family which will include his 20 year old pretty daughter Silvie."

"Sounds nice."

"Indeed. When you leave after half-an-hour's pleasant chat he will present you with a big bag of the specialised breads they make and give you a packet of cheese that you will secrete in the false compartment of the camera case. Do not try any of those breads you are given. On future trips you will always go to Cafe Belgard and be very pleasant to Silvie. That will be the cover for what will be frequent trips to Calais. Do you have any questions?"

"Nope."

"I shall call down Thursday morning ostensibly to discuss cruisers when I'll collect the breads and cheese. And by the way, I shall know exactly what the bread and cheese consists of, so don't try any of your 'Free Enterprise' tricks with me. Mr. Barnett will be most displeased if you do, as well as me personally. Clear?"

Tom swallowed convulsively.

"Of course. I wouldn't try anything like that across you."

"Excellent." The friendly note was back. "I'll see you the day after tomorrow then."

Once he'd gone Tom took a swift drink from a small whisky bottle in his desk. He felt he needed it.


The next day Tom made sure he had plenty of fuel and supplies aboard, and cast off. It was early but he had a fair distance to go and his pre-war cruiser was not the speediest. Still, the weather was clear and the forecast good.

He docked at the Calais Marina, reported to the Master whose English was good and explained he had come back to 'look round the place again, the first time he'd been back since the war.' A fictitious account of what he'd done in and around Calais and he was almost feted. A query where the Rue de Concorde was, a discussion of the girl he'd met in Calais before (another fictitious account) and he was sent on his way with a grin and a slap on the shoulder.

With the directions he found his way easily to the Cafe Belgard just before noon. There were a couple of vacant small tables outside but the small cafe/shop seemed fairly crowded with customers at most of the tables or coming in for supplies from the counter where a stout man, a lady and a youngish lady were busy serving.

"Silvie," decided Tom. "Not bad - either face or figure."

He sat down at the last empty table and put his camera case on the top, then took out The Times he'd stuffed inside it, and flapped it open.

The man quickly came across, small notebook poised to take a customer's order. A swift glance as the camera case, the paper and Tom. A small frown creased his forehead.

*"Oui M'sieur?"*

"A glass of your Cafe red wine and one of your cheese rolls please. Someone told me how good they are."

*"Oui M'sieur. Merci."*

Another look at him, and Pierre went back to behind the counter from where he shot another glance at Tom who was reading the paper.

Suddenly Pierre's puzzled expression disappeared. Quickly he brought over the glass of wine and the big cheese roll.

*"M'sieur.* Do you happen to be named 'Tom Henderson? Sergeant Tom Henderson that was here in 1944?"

"Yes." Puzzled. 'Don't I know you from somewhere?" Then Tom jumped to his feet, face alight with sudden recognition. "Pierre – you're Pierre! Pierre .... What on earth's your last name?"

"Belgard! Pierre Belgard!" he half shouted.

"Of course! How could have I forgotten! Though it's been a long time."

They gave each other a bear-hug, laughing and slapping each other on the back.

"How have you been doing since then, Pierre?" Tom demanded, releasing him. The planned cover story had not covered any of that so Pierre could. And he'd go along with it.

"But what we did then, *mon ami!* That Boche stronghold, that machine-gun nest we took out between us! You with your grenades, me with those petrol bombs! *Mon amis,* Tom was a hero that day!" Pierre looked round the other customers.

"Did you get a medal for your actions that day, Pierre?"

"No. But how many actions did not get Awards!"

"True. Very true,. But you should have got *La Croix de Guerre* for all that you did that day."

Pierre shrugged modestly. They swapped more (fictitious) war stories which Pierre translated for the benefit of the other customers then a couple of them told their war stories that Pierre translated for Tom's benefit. Cynically, Tom wondered if they were as fictitious as his own. Finally Pierre introduced Marie his wife and Silvie his daughter and suggested that as Tom had come to look round the places he's known seven years before, that Silvie take him round the new buildings that made the place now virtually unrecognisable. And Tom impressed her with stories of the magnificent Marina and West End nightclubs he owned.

Their cover solidly established, Tom finally said in front of other customers that he had to go to get back to the UK, turning down Pierre's offer for him to stay overnight but promised to return again shortly. Pierre pressed on him a big bag of the range of breads Marie and Silvie made, and some cheeses and Silvie accompanied him back to his cruiser, kissed him goodbye, and waved till he was out of the Marina.

Once back home, Tom fixed himself a meal and then carefully examined the sealed waterproof packet of cheese and the breads.

"Neat," he thought.

Though the 'cheese' felt like no cheese he'd ever touched before, the packaging made it look genuine enough and you had to check really carefully to detect the place where the breads had been sliced through and rejoined. He wondered if inside the hollowed out crust, more drugs had been stashed.

With his cover firmly established in France at the Cafe Belgard, Silvie would be the perfect excuse for frequent visits out there and testing cruisers for the Jacksons would be the perfect cover this end too.

Which brought another thought. What if the cops started sniffing around and his cover got broken? They would want information about his contacts from which he could do a trade – information for charges against him being dropped. Believing forward planning for every eventuality was the key to survival that he'd found when fiddling the Army Stores before, he'd better plan for that as well.

He had little compunction about dropping Pierre in it – but he would most certainly not do the same to Algy or Mr. Barnett. Loyalty had nothing to do with it – his skin and the menace of those two had everything. Till he remembered Algy's threats covered 'anyone'.

He smiled as the perfect solution occurred to him. He'd tell the cops it was the Jacksons who were his Bosses in this smuggle racket as well as the cruiser business. That it had started when they asked him to go to Cafe Belgard to test the cruiser and pick up some of Pierre's breads. He had had no idea what they had really contained. He had become puzzled about why they wanted him to go so often, however often it was that Algy wanted him to go, but as the Jacksons were his Bosses, what else could he do? And he'd not 'reported' them to the Authorities because why should he? If rich people like them wanted to spend loads of money on fuel just for getting some French bread – that was up to them wasn't it? He was only the hired hand. He was shocked to find that completely unwittingly he'd been caught up in a smuggle racket. And Drugs of all things!

Algy walked into his office mid-morning the next day, without knocking again and twisted round the catalogue Tom was checking.

"That would be a good buy," he said touching one.

"I'm not so sure the Jacksons will want to go that high value. That a deep sea cruiser not a coastal or summer cross-Channel," Tom temporised.

"Convince them. You're supposed to be a salesman aren't you? So sell the idea to them. Say you'll need a boat like that for winter trips to Calais. Or going to Antwerp or Norway."

"Winter trips?" Tom echoed taken aback. "Testing cruisers or pleasure trips won't give cover during the winter. Okay, maybe in calm weather and with a good forecast but basically this cover won't work in winter. You'll have to work out something else."

"Tom, you don't seem to understand your part in this," Algy said softly, leaning across the desk. "You are the courier and so you do what Mr. Barnett orders through me. If we want some goodies brought in, you bring them. By whatever means is necessary. So if the weather is too bad for your cruisers you go by ordinary Ferry. Or recruit one of the Jackson's pilots. That doesn't concern me because that is what you do. What you're paid for. So do it. Clear?"

Tom nodded dumbly.

"Good. I knew you'd see it my way once things were explained to you. Now – the goodies?"

Tom went up to his flat and picked up the bag of breads and the packet of 'cheese'.

Algy checked everything carefully, then nodded.

"Excellent Tom. Your cut." He slid an envelope across the desk. "Don't spend it all at once on riotous living. Bad for your health," he added smiling. "Now that you've passed that little test Mr. Barnett wants you to go to Calais next weekend to bring back some more."

"What?" Tom had placated Sally this weekend because he'd been able to take out just one day on the excuse he was 'very busy at work'. To make the same excuse for this coming weekend would be difficult. And he could hardly take her! Especially with Silvie at the other end and the cover she was providing.

"You heard me I'm sure Tom. And it'll be twice the quantity of this little pack." Algy patted the bag and stood up. "See you next Monday."

Tom stared down at the catalogue. If he was going to do winter trips he would need something like that cruiser Algy had picked out. Not just the other, smaller ones, he'd marked to recommend the Jacksons get for the Marina. And it was so expensive that he was sure it would be a no-no for them. Unless ....

He looked up at the sound of tyres on the tarmac. A glance out of the window and he saw it was the Jacksons.

"Hello Tom," Anne greeted him as she came in through the door Ron had opened for her.

"Hello Anne, Ron. You've come at just the right time. I've picked out a range of cruisers to get."

"Good. That's just the ticket. We need to know those costings." Anne said, as she and Ron sat down in the chairs across the desk.

"There's the two catalogues I've marked and with the pages turned down for the four cruisers we should get as an absolute minimum, and I'd like you to look at that one in this other catalogue while I get us some tea."

He went off to the kitchen leaving them to look through the catalogues.

"What do you think?" he asked five minutes later coming in with a tray with drinks on.

"Would you see those four as being earmarked for hire or for sale?" Ron asked.

"Whichever comes first," Tom replied promptly. "The way I see it we need to start getting money in as quickly as possible. I know every business has to cater for losses for a time but we do need to have that time as short as possible."

"Can't disagree with that," Ron said feelingly. "What about Delivery Dates? Once the boats are here we can have our 'Grand Opening'. While we've already got plans for that, obviously we want to make that as soon as possible as this season is slipping by. It's nearly April already."

"Once you agree the type and number of boats to get I'll do a check. It wasn't worth doing that till I knew what kind of order we'd be putting in."

"I can see that. Why this big cruiser though? Surely that's far above the range we're looking at? Because that one is ocean-going," Anne asked.

"What I thought was that it would be ideal for doing trips to the Norwegian Fjords. With the seas you can get up there, the distance and so the length of time for the trip, that kind of boat would be necessary. Extend our versatility."

"Wow! That's something we hadn't thought of!" Anne exclaimed looking from Tom to Ron and back again.

Ron rubbed his chin, looking at the catalogue pictures and specification. While he was something of a visionary and had found that looking ahead and being ambitious had paid off hugely, Sonia's warning about their financial position was playing on his mind. That cruiser was expensive, double the cost of the other smaller ones they had provisionally budgeted for, and he was very uncertain of demand for trips to the Norwegian Fjords. Even for trips to see the Northern Lights. It was possible there could be but ....

"We had been thinking more in terms of people wanting short-time hires and inshore boats, not that kind of thing," Ron said slowly, tapping the pictures. "We'd really have to check out the demand before we took on buying that thing I think."

But Ron glanced at Anne. This was her project and she knew about boats – Chandlery anyway – and he didn't.

"Can see your point Ron, but to show my faith in the idea, I'll put up 50% of the cost of the cruiser myself. For 50% of the profit," Tom suggested.

"The profit from the earnings of that boat alone?" Ron asked.

Tom had been hoping neither of them would have noticed that ambiguity, then later he'd make out he thought they'd agreed he'd have 50% of the total Marina profits if he could avoid a written Agreement being drawn up. And he had the cash from the purchase price they had paid for the Marina site for his contribution to the big cruiser.

"Oh, just the big boat of course," he said as though surprised.

"Check the delivery date for that cruiser as well then will you Tom? Then we can make a final decision," instructed Anne.

"Will do."

The next weekend was a difficult one for Tom, starting with Sally. As previously he'd said about them spending the whole weekend together, a sudden switch to Saturday only made her ask a lot of questions. She thought it was 'disgraceful of the Jacksons to insist he work on the Sunday when they didn't even have any boats on site for him to sell. Then she said she would come to the Marina to help him do whatever it was he had to do, then go with him to check over the cruisers he was thinking of buying (he'd suddenly thought of that excuse) and finally she said he could come to pick her up after he'd finished so at least they would have that evening together. She made it obvious she wasn't happy at his excuse that he didn't know what time he'd be back.

As he docked in Calais, the Marina Master was sitting on a bench outside the office enjoying a pipe and the sunshine.

*"Bonjour M'sieur"*, he called. "You must like Calais to be back so soon."

Tom sat down beside him. "A pleasant town with many memories for me," he said, smiling as he presented the Marina Master with the mooring fee.

"Of course. And of course Silvie is here," he grinned slyly at Tom. "She gave you very affectionate farewell, did she not?"

"She's a very nice girl."

"She is that."

Tom grinned at him and set off for the Cafe Belgard, camera case over one shoulder, a rucksack stuffed with paper on his back.

A pleasant time with Pierre and Marie, a pleasanter time with Silvie strolling along the sea front and he went back to the Cafe to fill his rucksack with 'breads'. No 'cheese' this time but big 'sausages' instead. He set off back to the UK at six o'clock expecting to see no sign of the Marina Master at this time of a Sunday evening. So it was a shock to see him waiting there.

*"Bon soir, M'sieur,"* he called to Tom jovially.

*"Bon soir,"* Tom replied, equally jovially though it took an effort, making as though to pass him with a wave.

"Your rucksack, *M'sieur,"* the Master pointed at it on Tom's back.

"My rucksack?" Tom asked with an air of great puzzlement.

*"Oui M'sieur.* Routine Customs inspection."

"Oh. Sure." Tom swung it off his back. "It's only breads from Pierre at Cafe Belgard. Marie and Silvie make breads like nothing in England. And my grandmother so likes it."

"Of course *M'sieur."*

He checked the breads and two packets of sausage without unwrapping or feeling them.

*"Merci M'sieur."*

He watched Tom repack his rucksack and waved him on to his cruiser.

Once outside the Harbour Tom drew a deep breath of relief. He'd not expected a Customs check when leaving France, only in the UK, not that he expected anyone to bother at a place as remote from a main port as the Marina. Still, he'd established another useful layer of cover. His grandmother who liked Pierre's breads.


Early on Monday he got an irate 'phone call.

Sally announced furiously that she had gone down to the Marina and found the cruiser kept in the Marina had gone and his car was still parked by the house. So who had he taken off for a cruise because she didn't believe his story about inspecting the cruisers and in any case if he was going to see them by boat why hadn't he taken her so they would still have had a cruise together?

When she finished he waited for a few moments.

"Do you want us to finish then?" he enquired coldly. "Because if you're not going to trust me then I don't see it being worth us continuing. It's in the nature of my job I have to be away unexpectedly sometimes."

Sally hesitated. She didn't really want to finish with him, not over this. He was a good catch her mother had said and she did like him a lot. Even so .... She decided to give him a fright and keep him on tenterhooks for a while.

"I'll think about it," she snapped, expecting more profuse apologies for the past weekend and promises of different behaviour for the future.

"Don't bother," he snapped straight back and slammed the 'phone down.

Algy walked in through the half-open office door.

"Problems?" he asked, grinning.

"Nothing important," Tom grunted. "I'll get the goodies."

He went up to his flat while Algy flicked through the Desk Diary for the past week. So Tom had seen the Jacksons last Thursday about buying the cruisers had he?

He was looking out of the window over the Marina and river when Tom returned with the breads now in a carrier bag.

Algy checked the breads and sausages as carefully as before.

"The Calais Marina Master checked them this time. Said he was the Customs Officer. I spun him a yarn that my grandmother liked the breads I'd brought last time and was wanting more.

"Good thinking," Algy said approvingly.

"Yeah. But it shows he's already suspicious doesn't it? And if you – Mr. Barnett – are wanting the same amount next week, he'll get still more suspicious, won't he?"

"Mr. Barnett does. So to vary things you could always work a scheme with one of Jackson's pilots. Or use the ordinary Ferry."

"Jackson's pilots fly to Paris, not Calais. And there'll be Customs at Wingmore now with the way Continental Flights have built up and they're on the Ferry ports as well, aren't they? That's the beauty of running things just through here."

"That's your problem to sort out," Algy said indifferently. "Right. Everything checks." He laid an envelope on the desk. "A bigger cut because you've brought more goodies. And we want the same amount next week." He stood up.

"What I could do is tell the Marina Master that Pierre's breads are getting so popular that more people are asking me to get more supplies. Then I can mix in the goods with ordinary stuff. I'm picking it up while I really go to date Silvie. That'll reinforce our cover even more! If demands for the goodies pick up, so I can bring back still more with that yarn! I'd expect a bigger cut then of course."

"That's really excellent thinking Tom. The scheme's proving a dilly. You are being a real asset to our enterprise. I'll be in touch during the week to tell you how we'll want to play it."

# Chapter 6
## Too many debts?

Ron glanced round the table. Everyone had copies of Sonia's Accounts and Balance Sheet in front of them.

"I declare the Meeting Open. Sonia, will you take us through our situation."

"I'm sure you've all read the copies I've sent round, so just to summarise: All Companies in the Group are showing a profit, some larger than others, apart from Carruthers Cruisers which of course is showing no income at all, just expenditure on buying and setting up the Marina which was paid for on a technical loan from the Group Reserves. Carruthers Airlines is showing a profit, but that is the present state of affairs and not taking into account any expenditure on the projected Package Tour Section because that hasn't yet been set up. You see our Reserves for each Company are reasonable but the Group Reserves are low. Too low in my opinion.

"On the question of borrowing the amount I expect we'd need for the Marina plus the amount for buying one or two Viscounts, setting up the Flight schedules and all the other expenditures for the Package Tours, I'm not at all sure we'd get it with no solid backing on our business projections. We're having no trouble about meeting the payments on our present borrowings and there's no reason to expect a downturn in that. But as you've said Ron, you can never tell, so we've always had the policy of making sure our Reserves are sufficient.

"Floating another share issue is possible but I'm not sure it would be as successful as the couple of times we've done it before. I strongly believe, if we do go down either of those roads, that it should be on the security of the Marina and the Package Tours only, not for the Group as a whole. Then if those did flop, only those would be affected, not the Group as a whole. If we did it as a Group thing – well, I don't think we should. That concludes my Report."

"Thanks Sonia," Ron said quietly. "Comments please?"

A problem was he and Anne had a lot of personal commitment in these projects – the Marina was Anne's Project, the Package Tours his. So would those factors influence the comments? And their own attitudes of course.

He was sure the Package Tours would pay in the end but they would be in competition, fierce competition, with the Big Boys who were already operating there. And they could be ruthless. They could undercut the Big Boys with the reduced costs they had, but then the Big Boys would have the huge Reserves and borrowing capability to undercut them even more and for longer. To the extent that could ruin them.

Peter Conway finally broke the silence.

"Could the Package Tour idea be amended just to Flights? Wouldn't that be cheaper and more within our existing capacity?"

"Buying the 'planes is the major initial cost," Sonia answered. "Page eight."

Pages were turned.

"Could we lease the 'planes? Cheaper initial outlay though more expensive in the long run," suggested Richard

"Vickers won't go down that route. Not at this stage anyway. They want outright sales and there's enough demand for them to sell all they make," Ron answered. He'd already checked that.

"There are two projects under consideration," he went on, carefully not looking at Anne. "There's the Marina. And the major outlay has already been made. I mean the purchase and upgrading of the site. The stocking of the place with cruisers for sale or hire is very much less than the setting up of the Package Tour business. Do you see any problems if we just funded the Marina, Sonia?"

"No," she answered promptly. "I presume the Chandlery store at the Marina could be met from the existing stocks in the Warehouse, Anne?"

"Yes. No problem. That would mean we'd have to re-stock the store fairly soon though," she answered but distractedly.

"Then perhaps the best thing would be to do that and put the Package Tour development off for further consideration in say six months time?" Ron suggested.

"To start only considering it then could quite possibly kick the actual opening of that project right down till the year after next taking into account the Holiday Seasons and start-up times." Richard was keen to get it going as soon as possible..

"Yes," agreed Ron. He paused. "Any further contributions before we put the Proposal to go ahead with the full development of the Marina and re-consider the Package Tour Project in six months time?" He looked round the table.

"I suggest we look at it next month, not in six months," Anne said suddenly.

Ron looked at her in surprise. Nothing could alter in one month, but something might in six months.

"I'd second that," Sonia agreed immediately.

"Any other ideas?" Ron asked. After a general shaking of heads, "Then a Motion is that we go ahead with the plans to stock the Marina with cruisers for sale or hire as indicated in the documents and put the development of the Package Tour Project on the Agenda for next month's meeting."

"Seconded," said Sonia.

"Any Amendment?" Silence and shaking of heads. "Those in favour?" All hands were raised. "Carried."

"Any other business?"

There were 'No's'

"Meeting adjourned."

On their way to the Marina to finalise the details with Tom of the cruisers to buy, Ron glanced at Anne, then back to the road ahead.

"Why put the Package Tour on the Agenda for next month rather than six months Anne? It's going to take at least six months for us to see any change in the finances, isn't it? Then I reckon we'll still have to keep it under review for quite a time."

"It just seemed a good way not to lose sight of it."

Ron said no more. But that seemed a strange reason given the way they ran the business. He then had to concentrate on steering through the narrow streets of Sandwich.

"Hello Tom," Anne and Ron greeted him, almost in chorus, as they went into the office.

"We've had the Go-head for buying all the cruisers you'd earmarked Tom," Anne told him.

"Even the bigger boat for Norwegian trips?"

"Yes. On the basis of your suggestion of paying half that cruiser's purchase price for 50% of the profits from its hire or sale. In fact Tom, one of our Directors had mentioned that to some friends already and four of them said they'd be interested in a trip like that with their families. And to go on trips to Holland etc."

Tom blinked. He'd never really thought that could be a go-er with the firm. If he had he wouldn't have offered to pay half of it.

"Oh. Good. I'll get on ordering them straight away then."

"Excellent," Anne beamed. "Tell them you want cast-iron Delivery Dates. Then we can get our Advertising underway for the Grand Opening."


Two weeks later Anne looked up from the book she was reading. She and Ron were in the garden enjoying the June evening sunshine. Tim had gone indoors to the Library. He had decided to take some exams in Air Safety seeing his career in Air Control, not just at Wingmore but there was talk of setting up a National Air Traffic Control Organisation as air travel was increasing by leaps and bounds. Kathleen was out with Terry.

"We can go ahead with the Package Tours idea, Ron. With one Viscount anyway," she said quietly.

Ron shook his head.

"Not this year, next year - maybe," he said decisively.

"No. This year, Ron. Now."

"Not enough in the Reserves," he said turning the page of his own book. "Not to keep a sensible balance."

"I've got £55,000 I want to invest. And what better place than in our own Company?"

"What!!!" Ron's tone added shocked exclamation points. "Have you come into an inheritance or something?"

"Something like that. This house." Anne waved a hand to encompass it and the big garden. "It's entirely mine – ours – in the sense that any mortgage on it was paid off in my grandfather's time. So it's just sitting there – a pile of money made out of bricks."

"You've never sold it!! Where ...?"

"No. Nothing like that Ron," she smiled at Ron's horror. "I had a chat with Jeremy Hardwick, who took over from Arthur at the Bank and suggested I take out a mortgage on it. The Surveyor said it will soon be worth much more than that amount given the way house prices are shooting up but that will give enough for what we need and I can easily afford the mortgage out of my salary. So we've got the cash."

"Now wait a minute Anne – how long does that mortgage last for?"

"Twenty five years. The usual period."

"Twenty five years!!! But that means you'd still be paying it when you're ...!"

"Ron, you weren't dreaming of referring to my age, were you?" Anne interrupted, putting a dangerous note into her voice, though with a twitch of her lips. "A gentleman never, ever does that!"

"Okay. But that'll be a huge millstone hanging round your – our necks for that long!"

"Ron. You paid rent on your house in London didn't you?"

"Of course."

"So wasn't that a 'millstone round your neck' - to quote you? The only difference between paying rent and paying a mortgage is that at the end of the mortgage you've got something to show for all the money you've spent. If I – we – were renting this place, at the end of twenty five years we'll still have nothing. Would we? With a mortgage we will. And an expanded airline too."

"I know, but ...." Though Ron knew she was right, that what she was saying was only logical, he still had qualms. His way of life had once been 'never go into debt', but that had gone long ago. As soon as he had come here in fact because the Bank had immediately made a loan to him, secured on his job with Anne. "I've an idea. Why don't we pay the mortgage out of the joint Account so that I chip in half the amount for the mortgage, then it can be paid off in half the time if we choose? After all, I am living here and so are Kathleen and Tim, so I should."

Anne hesitated. This house had always been hers. Just hers. And that had always given her a sense of security. But if Ron 'chipped in' as he'd suggested, then it would be half his.

Then she chided herself. It was half his anyway as they were married. And it would certainly help because the amount of the mortgage repayments would be stretching her finances a bit.

"Done," she said standing up and kissing him. "Let's have a drink to celebrate?"

At the next monthly meeting Ron had put 'Package Tours Project' at the end of the Agenda as though it was just the 'Ticketing Reminder' Anne had suggested.

"Item 5. Package Tours," he announced. "There has been an unexpected development. Anne, would you introduce the discussion please."

"A situation arose whereby I have £55,000 to invest. I would like to invest it in 'Carruthers Airlines' which would mean we can decide which part of that company needs expansion most. Though some of our older aircraft could do with replacing as was mentioned before, none of them need that urgently. If we bought the Vickers Viscount we can augment our Passenger side rather than the Air Cargo side of the business with an aircraft that has reduced noise for passengers, less vibration, is pressurised so we can fly higher and so more economically on longer distances, with larger windows and is faster."

"Have you got a new job selling Viscounts, Anne?" asked Richard smiling. "That pitch was better than when Ron tried it."

"No I haven't. It's just that I think it's true. And I should think we could afford the extra financing we need on top of that £55,000, from our Reserves, couldn't we, Sonia? "

"No problem with that amount. But when you say 'Invest' Anne, did you mean as a loan at a certain rate of interest or a Share purchase?" asked Sonia. "Because no decision had been made about either."

Anne had already discussed this with Ron.

"I think the best way would be a long-term interest-free loan, repayment of the sum invested at the normal Dividend rate per annum per share held by me, until the capital is repaid."

Anne's offer meant the Package Tour Project could go ahead immediately and unlike a bank loan it would cost the Company nothing by way of immediate and high interest payments, and only receive a Dividend rate from Profits on their standard £10 Shares to repay the capital. Which would take a very long time. It would mean that Anne was virtually giving them the money for years. Many years. And Anne, being a businesswoman herself must know that.

Sonia was scribbling figures on a pad.

"That's a very generous offer, Anne," Richard said finally.

"Ron was as flabbergasted as you seem to be when I told him what I was planning to do," Anne said smiling round the group. Making it clear that this was completely her decision, nothing to do with Ron.

"I Propose that we accept Anne's offer of £55,000 on the terms she suggested and use it to set up the Package Tours Project as proposed by Carruthers Airlines," Sonia said.

"I Second that," Peter said quickly.

Ron got nods from the others, giving no indication himself.

"Proposal carried," he said formally. "Any other business?"

# Chapter 7
## Wedding plans

Kathleen got out of Terry's car unaided feeling a tremulous excitement as he got out from behind the driver's wheel.

"Are you really sure about this Terry?" she whispered as she took his arm.

"I am," he said emphatically. "Any doubts yourself?"

"Not the slightest."

As they went into the house she knew this was the Rubicon for her, for them both. Though they had been Engaged for eight months with Marriage of course implied, they were now going to tell Mum and Dad their actual Wedding plans. Terry had already formally asked Dad for permission to get married when he'd asked about them becoming Engaged. He'd wanted to do it that way he had said.

They went into the house and Kathleen peeped into the lounge.

Good. Mum and Dad were in there listening to the wireless and Tim was out. He had said he was going out with Janice tonight which was why they'd picked tonight. He was 'Going Steady' with Sonia's twin daughter now.

Kathleen and Terry went into the lounge and went to stand together by the empty fireplace because the June evening was still warm

"May we have a word, Mr. and Mrs. Jackson," he asked formally.

"Of course," both answered, making guesses of what this was about, while Ron reached out to switch off the wireless.

"Kathleen and I have been Engaged for eight months now and when I asked permission for that Mr. Jackson, it meant also we'd be wanting to get married. We'd like that to be on the 20th September, if that's alright with you."

"Of course it is!"

Ron stood up quickly to shake his hand and kiss Kathleen, Anne following seconds later to kiss them both.

"Any ideas where – and other things?" Anne asked.

They were instantly in deep discussion.

"Mum, do you think we really ought to ask mother to the wedding?" Kathleen asked Anne abruptly next morning. Anne was taking Kathleen into work at Miss Dangerfield's dressmaking workshop.

"What does Terry think?" Anne asked, not deliberately prevaricating but his ideas would be important.

"He thinks we should. But – well - we haven't had any contact with her at all since that Court case. Even long before that really. She hasn't sent me a letter, a Christmas Card or a Birthday Card. Even though Frank does."

Anne knew how strongly Kathleen blamed her mother for the loss of both her legs in the bombing of Thompson Road School by keeping her in London when she had so wanted to return to Wales after her father had got over that double pneumonia bout in March 1942. Tim had never blamed their mother in the same way. Though his injuries were severe enough, they not as bad as Kathleen's.

"Are you asking Frank?"

"Of course." Kathleen hesitated. "He should be able to travel down here on the train by himself shouldn't he? He is thirteen and Tim was about that age when he brought Frank that time."

"Wouldn't that make him feel his loyalties were split between coming to your wedding but without his mother, and yours, being invited too?"

Kathleen was silent till Anne pulled up outside Miss Dangerfield's workshop.

"I suppose you're right Mum," she sighed. "We ought to send her an invitation with Frank's. And I suppose we ought to invite Des Ackroyd as well. Go the whole hog."


Ron picked up the 'phone on its second ring

"Mrs. Ackroyd for you Mr. Jackson," Joan the Receptionist told him.

Ron hesitated. After that verbal confrontation on the 'phone when George Naylor had been killed flying into Berlin on the Berlin Airlift the day after Arthur died, he had insisted on any contact from May would be by letter not 'phone except for any emergency about the boys. So it had to be an emergency.

"Put her through please Joan."

"What's happened?" he demanded.

"I've had the invitation for Kitty's Wedding," May said abruptly. She never called her 'Kathleen'. "Included in it is Frank of course – and Des. You including him surprised me I must say."

So it wasn't any emergency about Frank.

"Kitty told me that she wanted one to be sent to all three of you," Ron said neutrally. "Her view as I understand it is that he is a natural part of your family as you are married to him and so is Frank's step-father."

There was a moment's silence.

"Have invitations gone to the Davies's?" The real point of the call.

Kathleen's Welsh foster-parents. All three had been devoted to each other and they had been heart-broken when May had kept Kathleen in London in 1942, and even more so when she was so injured.

"Yes, they have," Ron said quietly.

"Even though it's their fault Kitty's injured like she is? Because if they hadn't sent me that letter all this would never have happened."

Ron set his lips. This was a new distortion of May's on reality. The letter had been sent to them both by the Davies's when May had visited them and Kitty (because May always referred to her as 'Kitty' Ron did the same when talking to her) and had told them about their 'unsuitable' relatives for looking after Kitty. As a result the Davies's had feared might they would take Kitty away as she was a girl and approaching working age, and so had suggested in November 1940 that 'if anything should happen' to Ron and May in the bombing of London that was at its height to prevent those 'unsuitable' relatives taking Kitty away, would they sign Consent Forms for them to Adopt Kitty to be activated only in those circumstances'?

Ron, having seen that kind of situation before as he was a Warden, had been totally in favour, May adamantly against. So she had taken Kitty back to London in March 1942 when he had been so ill with double pneumonia – and then refused to let her go back. Tim had been brought back in the September because the bombing had slackened and other children were being brought home. But it was barely four months later the school had been bombed at the onset of the mini-blitz.

So even though it was May who had insisted Kitty stay in London and had threatened to Divorce Ron, get custody of the children and get the Court to Bar him from ever seeing them again if he tried to force her to let them go back to Wales, she was now using that letter to divert her guilt feeling away from herself. Ron was sure the psychiatrists May had seen on the occasion of her complete break-down after the school, would have some kind of term for it. They had for everything else.

"The whole point is, it's what Kitty wants, May. So I hope, and expect, that you will say and do nothing to the Davies's to cause trouble at the Wedding. Or before or afterwards. I want that day to be the happiest in Kitty's life with no upsets whatsoever."

"If they go, then I won't," May declared. "Because I'll have plenty to say to them as soon as I set eyes on them I can tell you here and now. So you'd better tell me what they decide to do. Or better, instead of you giving them preference over me, just stop them coming altogether. D'you hear?"

"I hear you May," Ron said quietly. "And what about Frank if you do decide to stay away? Because Kitty wants him here."

May hesitated.

"If he's set on going whatever I do or think, I won't stop him," she said finally.

"I'll let you know what the Davies's decide to do as soon as I know," Ron promised. "How is ...?" The 'phone was slammed down on him.

Ron shrugged, then frowned. If May decided not to come that could save a lot of tension and possible trouble. Because though she didn't hate Anne in the same way she hated the Davies's, she still had plenty of resentment and antagonism towards her.

That evening when the 'phone rang at home Anne and Kathleen were in the Library at her big design table working on the designs for the bridesmaid's dresses. Kathleen had already done the basic design for hers. Janice and Sandra, the twins, were there, thrilled with being invited to 'the design party' as Kathleen had called it. Tim was there as well just to be near Janice not because he was interested in dress design. He wasn't.

"Hello?" Ron said into the 'phone by him in the lounge.

"Hello Ron. Hywell Davies here."

"Hello Hywell. Were you wanting to speak to Kathleen? She's ...."

"It's really you I want to speak to Ron. First of all anyway. Are you alone?"

"Yes. Everyone else is in the Library working on dress designs. I'm banished. Luckily for me."

"I can imagine! Dressmaking would not be my cup of tea either. The thing is Ron, is May going to be at the wedding? We want to come of course, we dearly want to, but if May is there – well I'm not certain that – well what her response to seeing us there would be. So we're thinking that perhaps ...." He floundered to a stop. "I don't want anything to happen to upset Kathleen's big day you see and if that meant we should stay away then ...."

"May 'phoned me this morning about things."

"Did she accept?" Hywell asked quickly.

"Yes and no. She wanted to impose conditions."

"That she'd come if we didn't, I presume," Hywell said flatly. "In that case we'd better ...."

"Hywell," Ron interrupted. "Kathleen wants you and Edith to come very much. She doesn't want her mother there but felt she was duty-bound to include her with the invitation to Frank. Well, it was Terry who felt they were duty-bound. So if you accepted and I really hope you do because Kathleen wants it so much, then I'll 'phone May tomorrow and tell her. Personally, I'll be delighted if she does stay away because that'll make things a lot easier in other directions besides you and Edith."

"If you are sure that will be the best, Ron." Hywell sounded a lot happier.

"I really am sure. What I suggest you do, ring back in about ten minutes and ask to speak to Kathleen. Don't mention May or our conversation and simply tell her that you and Edith are thrilled at the news of her wedding, thank her for the invitation and of course you will come."

"Thank you Ron, thank you. We're – well – thank you. I'll do as you suggest. Goodbye. And bless you."

Tim wandered into the room, hands in his pockets, looking fed up as Ron put the 'phone down.

"Dressmaking lost its appeal Tim?" Ron grinned at his expression.

"Janice is more interested in that than in me," he muttered disconsolately.

"All it means is that you have some different interests as well. You're not interested in dressmaking, is she interested in the technicalities of Air Control?"

"Not really."

"And you are?"

"Sure. It's interesting. And it's my job."

"That's it son. Just as Mum here and I have differences in our interests as well as plenty of shared."

"S'pose so." But Tim was not consoled. After all, Mum here and Dad were **old** weren't they? Not young like him and Janice.

The 'phone rang that Ron answered.

"Hello Ron. Hywell here. Is Kathleen available by any chance?" As though they had not spoken just a few moments before.

."Sure Hywell. Nothing's wrong is there?"

"We're fine. We've had the invitation to Kathleen and Terry's wedding. We'll reply in writing of course but we hoped we could have a chat with her as well."

"I'll get her. She, Anne and her bridesmaids are designing the bridesmaids' dresses but I'm sure she'll tear herself away to speak to you and Edith."

"I'll get her Dad," Tim said hurrying out. With Kathleen out of the way, maybe Janice wouldn't be so distracted.

Kathleen came quickly, hoping that Uncle Hywell was going to say that he and Aunt Edith would be coming. Ten minutes later she hung up beaming. They were coming. And bringing Maralyn too!

It was 3.00 am that she jerked awake, suddenly panicking. If mother came, how would she react to Aunt Edith? And Aunt Edith to her? Surely they would become friends on this very special day? Maybe it would mean a big reconciliation. For her sake.

The next day Ron waited until 10 o'clock before 'phoning May.

"May? Ron here."

"Well?" May's tone was very abrupt.

"Kitty was 'phoned by the Davies's last night. They are coming and bringing Maralyn."

"Didn't you do something to put them off?"

"No."

"Then did you tell Kitty that if they're going, I'm not?"

"No. Look May ...," he put a conciliatory note into his voice, "... for Kitty's sake won't you please come to the wedding and if you won't be fully reconciled to the Davies's at least be pleasant to them?"

"You heard what I said. If you want me there, and Kitty wants me there, then put the Davies's off. That's all you have to do." The 'phone went down.

Sighing, Ron put his down and stared at the pictures of the aircraft they used on the wall while he thought.

Should he tell Kathleen about this 'phone call or not? She was delighted at the Davies's coming. If he told her about May's ultimatum would she think that she ought to put them off in favour of her mother – simply because she was her mother? Or would it be Terry who'd press her to make the decision that way? Anne had told him about Kathleen's own reluctance to invite her at all and there hadn't been any hesitation at all over the Davies's.

Another factor was that they had always kept in touch with Kathleen (they'd even taken to calling her 'Kathleen' now, though when she had been with them they had called her 'Kitty'), and her mother hadn't at all. Not since Kathleen had left the London hospital to come to the one in Folkestone.

Kathleen had never stopped blaming her mother for her injuries, and then that Court case May had organised against him had antagonised her even more.

But he had to acknowledge in fairness to May, Kathleen's attitude towards her had been so antagonistic from the moment she had been told she was having to stay in London after he had recovered which became even more intense when she realised she had lost both legs in the bombing of the school, that he had to feel some sympathy towards towards May, riven with guilt as she had been. Must have been surely. Perhaps still was.

Kathleen had been just as antagonistic to him at first, blaming him in equal measure. But that had changed when he had broken down and actually cried in front of her in hospital. And then later it had changed towards him even more. That was after Anne had told her of the way he had rescued her from the wreckage of the school, risking his own life to do so, Anne had told him. And she had discovered what had happened, not from him but from Ralph Smith the Chief Warden at Ron's Post who had had it from one of the team of rescuers who had been with him..

No, he decided, he would say nothing to Kathleen, and see if and how May responded to the invitation.


Terry looked sideways at Kathleen. They were checking through the list of the invitations they had sent out and the replies they had received. From everyone except her mother.

"So now we know how many are coming, we can give the numbers to the Caterers," she said.

Terry hesitated. He knew how reluctant she had been to even inviting her mother.

"What if our invitation hadn't got to your mother? Lost in the post I mean," he said carefully.

"Funny that only hers had been lost, don't you think?" Kathleen said coldly. "She obviously just can't be bothered."

"And Frank?"

"If mother even told him. I wouldn't it past her keeping quiet about it altogether."

"If you'd still like him at least to come, as you wanted before, we could ask your father to send another one. Addressed to Frank this time but still inviting the three of them as before."

Kathleen hesitated. She'd been so relieved at receiving no reply at all seeing that as maybe the way her mother had decided to play it. Just not answer. A snub – but so what?

"I'd rather just leave it Terry," she said finally. "She may simply have not got round to answering. But we must go on the figures we've got for the Caterers," she added hastily. "And it'll only be three more if she does decide to come."

"If that's what you want, Kitten," Terry said promptly.

And Kathleen relaxed.

The next day Terry 'phoned the Operator to get Mr. Desmond Ackroyd's number. He gave the address. In a few seconds he had the number and was dialling for it. He was certain that the Invitation must have gone astray because surely Kathleen's own mother would want to come to the wedding of her only daughter?

"Is that Mrs. May Ackroyd please?" he asked when the 'phone was picked up.

"Yes," May was cautious, wondering who was ringing her.

"I'm Terry Murray. I'm marrying Kathleen on the 20th September and we did send you a Wedding Invitation. As we haven't had a reply I was wondering if you'd had it."

"Does Kitty know you're 'phoning me?" May snapped.

"Well – no." Terry guessed that when she used the name 'Kitty' she must be referring to Kathleen.

"Her father said you had invited the Davies's. I told him in no uncertain terms that if they were going, then I wasn't. He's quite happy to invite that horrible pair even though they were planning to kidnap Kitty when she was a young girl during the war and even wrote to tell me that. I rescued Kitty from them and then I get rewarded by being blamed for everything. Even Kitty's injuries as well, when it was all that letter's fault. And theirs." May slammed the 'phone down and burst into tears.

In Folkestone Terry slowly replaced the receiver.

What on earth was all that about? What on earth could have happened over the Davies's? Kathleen had only ever spoken of them as being loving and caring for her. That they'd looked after her wonderfully the whole time she'd been in Wales. So what was this about their planning to kidnap her? What letter had May been talking about? How had she rescued Kathleen? What was this tangle of mysteries he was marrying into?

Kathleen had simply told him that her mother had taken her home from Wales when her father had been extremely ill and she and the Davies's had expected her back within a month. But then her mother had 'forced' her to stay in London and it was directly because of that she had been in Thompson Road school at the time it had been bombed resulting in her injuries. Nothing about any letter.

He could hardly ask Kathleen – she'd probably explode at him for 'phoning her mother at all!

Mr. Jackson would know the truth of course – but how would he take his 'phoning his ex-wife?

After worrying about it for two days Terry decided he would have to talk to Kathleen's father. And simply take his anger at 'phoning Kathleen's mother without Kathleen's knowledge. He 'phoned him at work to ask if he could go to see him at the office, not at home. And would he please not mention this visit to Kathleen.

Ron cancelled a meeting with Sonia to see Terry immediately, worrying what the problem was. Was Terry having second thoughts about marrying a girl as disabled as Kathleen?

"Take a seat Terry. What's the problem that you needed to see me about so urgently?"

"It's about Kathleen. Well not her as her, but .... Well I'd better start from the beginning."

"That's usually the best place," Ron tried to smile.

Terry explained his 'phone call to May and why he'd made it, including Kathleen's wish to accept the non-reply on its face value.

"There's obviously an awful lot of things in the background to this and the relationship between Kathleen, the Davies's and Mrs. Ackroyd, and I think I need to know about them. If I'm to be a good husband to Kathleen now and in the future."

"But you don't want to ask Kathleen herself?"

"Well, to start with I don't think she'd be best pleased about my having 'phoned her mother about this at all."

"I think you're right about that," Ron agreed.

"And there may be things about this that you know about as Kathleen's father, married to the ex-Mrs. Jackson and perhaps knowing things about the Davies's that Kathleen herself may not know about, so I thought it better to ask you. I hope you don't mind me asking," he added, suddenly diffident about prying into past family secrets.

"I'm glad you did. Marrying into our family as you are I guess you have a right to know. Know the real truth as against May's beliefs. Delusions in some ways really.

"To understand things I need to give you some background and tell you things you may already know. Kathleen and Tim were Evacuated here to Folkestone when the war began in 1939,

Kathleen coming here with Maralyn to live, Tim with the Abbots. I met Anne and we fell in love. My marriage with May was pretty much dead anyway but I make no excuses for myself. Then the children were re-Evacuated to Wales in 1940 and Kathleen went to live with Mr. and Mrs. Davies. They took wonderful care of her and they and Kathleen became devoted to each other. May went to see the children and in talking to the Davies's spoke of relatives we had that she regarded as 'unsuitable to look after the children' which was why she'd agreed to Evacuate them at the beginning. She also told them that if anything happened to us (May and me) in the bombing that was still going on, then those relatives could take the children away. Foster parents had no rights you see.

"So they wrote to us saying that if we signed Consent to Adopt papers then, should anything happened to us then they would be legally covered against those 'unsuitable' relatives taking Kathleen away, and for it to be written into the Consent documents that those Consents would only apply in the special circumstance of May and I being killed.

"I was a Warden at the time and had seen these kinds of situations happen so I thought it an excellent way of safeguarding Kathleen. May saw it as a plot to 'kidnap' her.

"I became very ill with double pneumonia in March 1942 and in delirium kept asking for Kathleen. May had her back home ostensibly till I was better, but then refused to let her go back to the Davies's. She told me that if I tried to insist on her going back she'd Divorce me, claim Custody of the children and get me Barred from ever seeing them again.

"The only offer I'd have been able to make to the Court was sending Kathleen back to foster-parents in Wales, so a Solicitor Anne checked with on my behalf took the view that May would be bound to win Custody, less likely to succeed in getting me Barred but it still could happen. May would have stayed in the house with the children before and after the Divorce so they would have been no safer from the bombing that was still going on intermittently and I wouldn't be there to look after them. So I had to give way."

He was silent for a few minutes staring into space, grim-faced at his memories. "When May told Kathleen she was not going back to Wales...," he went on, " ... she felt betrayed. In spite of our argument over it May told Kathleen that I agreed with her keeping Kathleen in

London. Kathleen told me that later. Then of course, the school was bombed, Kathleen was so injured and she blamed us both for keeping her in London.

"May and I were both devastated and blaming ourselves. Both for her injuries and for keeping Kathleen in London. May was blaming herself for doing it, I was blaming myself for not standing up to her in spite of what Anne's solicitor had said."

"But Kathleen doesn't blame you now," Terry said softly after Ron had been silent for a space. "Not least because you risked your own life to rescue her."

Ron looked at him sharply.

"Kathleen told me. She knows it because Mrs. Jackson told her, she said, and she had got it from your Chief Warden who'd had it from one of the rescuers who was with you."

"Any number of people were doing things like that at that time," Ron said abruptly.

"Possibly. But Kathleen feels she owes her life to you. She is still totally antagonistic to her mother though."

"Yes." Ron hesitated but decided to say no more. It would be up to Kathleen whether she told him about that Court case.

"I was wondering about sending another invitation to them but addressed to Frank. To make sure they had got the Invitation but it's obvious that they have had it. But would Mrs. Ackroyd have necessarily even have told Frank about it? Given the circumstances?"

"Yes," Ron said positively. "Whatever our personal feelings and opinions about each other, May has always been perfectly fair about the boys' contacts and relationships with us. But Frank must feel he's in a difficult situation. He may well want to come, but could also feel problems about it knowing his mother's feelings. I write to him every week, and get occasional replies, usually when something has happened about school. Kathleen and Tim sometimes write.

"So I suggest you take no further action yourself and see how the situation develops with Kathleen and Frank."


"You've got two letters this morning, Kathleen," Ron said two weeks later passing them across the breakfast table. It was a

Saturday so they were all eating together. Tim was not on shift.

"Getting popular," grinned Tim.

"Wonder who they're from. Oh, one's from Frank." She ripped his open first, and quickly scanned the two page letter.

"Says thanks for the Wedding invitation, but they won't be coming. They're going to be in Belgium at that time. He'll be sending a Wedding present nearer the time. School's okay, taking more exams."

Ron frowned but said nothing. Surely Frank would be back at school then after the summer holidays and in any case the wedding was on a Saturday at 2.15 pm. But if that was the excuse they were using it could be thought of as plausible.

Kathleen opened the second letter. "Oh. This one's from ...." A slip of paper dropped from the folded letter. "... it's from Des Ackroyd," she added, an odd note in her voice. "He says they won't be coming as well but wish Terry and me a very happy day. And he's sent a cheque as our wedding present 'from all of them so we can get what we feel would be most useful to us'." She glanced at the cheque. "Goodness! It's for £100."

"Lucky you!" Tim said enviously. "You'll be able to get loads of stuff with that."

Kathleen was reading and re-reading Des's letter trying to see something, some indication of the way her her mother might be feeling in it.

Was she just indifferent? Not bothered enough to even write? Because it was Des who had written the letter.

Was she resentful? Kathleen knew she had behaved badly towards her after being kept in London when Dad was better. And her losing both legs just because mother had done that. And all the other things mother had done. Like lying over saying Dad had agreed to her being kept in London. And then even pretending it was she who had arranged for Aunt Anne and Uncle Hywell and Aunt Edith to come to see her in hospital so quickly when it was Dad who had the idea and done all the arranging of it even sorting out the hotel for them to stay in. And mother had gone away for the week they had been in London.

After all, it was she, Kathleen, who had held out this olive branch to her. Really because Terry had wanted it. But sending the

Invitation as they had, or Dad had, which if mother had accepted, come and been happy for her and Terry then perhaps things could have changed between them.

But she hadn't even been bothered enough to reply.

Kathleen abruptly left the room.

Anne and Ron glanced at each other and Anne gave five minutes then followed her. She checked downstairs then went to Kathleen's room, finding the door ajar. She tapped on it.

"Come in,"

Anne went in to find Kathleen sitting at the dressing table, a letter pad in front of her.

"Mum, you know so much about people – why wouldn't mother have at least been the one to send me a letter, even if she wouldn't come? And why wouldn't she come do you think?"

Anne hesitated. Ron had told her about May's ultimatum. If she told Kathleen what would her reaction be? Perhaps it would antagonise her even more. On the other hand she felt, Kathleen was a grown woman now, not a child, it was her wedding and her mother. So she should be the one to make the choice between the Davies's and her mother with full knowledge, she decided.

"You know about the letter that Aunt Edith and Uncle Hywell sent to your mother and father after your mother visited them when you were still in Wales?" It was not really a question.

"The one where they said they'd be willing to Adopt me if anything happened to mother and Dad and asking for them to sign Consent to Adopt papers?"

"That's the one Because if anything – bad had happened to your mother and Dad, your 'unsuitable relatives' as your mother called them, could have taken you away and Hywell and Edith wouldn't have been able to stop them."

"That's right. We had a special lesson about it at school once. So it was a great idea!"

"I agree. So did your Dad. But your mother saw it differently. She saw it as a plot 'to kidnap you' which was how she put it to your Dad. So when he was so ill she saw her chance to take you back to London and then keep you there."

"I remember. And that mother threatened to Divorce him, claim

Custody of all of us children and persuade the Judge to Bar him from ever seeing any of us again so he had to give way. I remember you telling me all that a few years ago Mum."

"That's right. But your mother is now blaming Hywell and Edith's letter for everything. A psychiatrist I talked to once said that was so she could 'exteriorise the guilt' he said – to feel it wasn't her fault."

Anne waited.

"I see. So for mother to come, I'd have to un-invite Uncle Hywell and Aunt Edith I suppose," Kathleen finally said grimly. "Well, I'm certainly not going to do that. If mother won't bury the hatchet after all these years, after what happened to me which proved that Dad and I were right about me going back to Wales, not even for my wedding, then – then I don't want her there. I'll simply write to Des thanking him for the cheque. And Frank."

# Chapter 8
## Suspicions

Tom Henderson was whistling cheerfully as he brought the new big cruiser, the 'Sea Swallow', into the Marina in Sandwich. Another biggish load of drugs equaled more cash money equaled a quicker route to the top of the big rackets in London. Unless he decided to move into the Gang scene that seemed to be building up in Brighton. Being a smaller scene he could become a Big Player there more quickly and there were fewer big toes to tread on.

Once again the trip had gone smoothly. The Master at the Calais Marina had been as friendly as always and now didn't even bother checking the boxload of breads that he was now always bringing back from Pierre. He had swallowed the story they were proving very popular with Tom's relatives and friends and that he now was even thinking of starting up a regular business importing the breads into England on a commercial basis.

His cheerful mood vanished as soon as he put his key in the outer door to the office and his flat above. The door was unlocked and he was 100% certain he'd locked it when he'd left this morning.

He carefully reached inside for the baseball bat resting against the wall behind the door curtain. It was no longer there. Which meant someone had known about it and moved it.

He eased back. He wanted some other kind of weapon then. And there were lengths of wood around near the slipway that would do. He eased away from the door.

"Come in old boy, don't stand on ceremony," came from inside.

"Algy! What the hell are you doing here? And in my office too," Tom exploded angrily, pushing the door open wide.

"Just bring in the goodies you've brought Tom. Then we'll talk." The bantering note had gone from Algy's voice.

Now worried Tom reached back, picked up the box he'd put down to unlock the door, and went in. Algy was leaning against the door to the upstairs flat. That door was ajar and Tom knew that too had been locked this morning.

"How ...?" Tom began.

"Shut and lock the front door. And come up to the flat."

Now even more worried, Tom did as he was told. Algy was in the lounge when he got there, sitting at ease in one fireside chair, a drink in a glass on the coffee table near him, a second empty glass on the coffee table opposite, a bottle of Tom's whisky in the centre of the table.

"Sit down." Algy indicated the chair opposite. "Why did you talk about your trips to Calais in The Dog and Doublet?"

"I was only talking to my new girl friend." Tom was surly, resentment surging.

"So Sally's no more?" Algy raised his eyebrows.

"She started asking questions."

"Then you were wise to get rid of her. Unless she knew something."

"She didn't."

"Let us hope you are telling me the truth about her. It would be a shame for such a pretty girl to meet with an accident. A permanent accident. What do you know about Penelope?"

"Pen ---? How do you know her name's Penelope?"

"What do you know about her?" Algy's voice was like a whip-crack.

"I went into The Dog and Doublet, for a drink, she was there, we got talking, I bought her a drink and dinner and we made another dinner date. That's it."

"Who is she? Who are her relatives? Where does she live? What does she do for a living?"

"I don't know! Good God man, it was our first date. You don't give a gorgeous girl like her the Third Degree on your first date!"

"So though you knew nothing whatsoever about her – you started telling her all about your weekly trips to Calais. What if I told you she's a female cop!"

"Wha-at! Is she?"

"And blabbing about your doing a weekly trip to Calais would sound alarm bells loud and clear in any copper's mind."

"Oh my God!"

"Luckily for you she isn't a cop. She's one of ours. I wanted to check how much of a fool you are. And you're a double-dyed fool to talk to a complete stranger like that. The next thing you'd have said to impress her with would be that you've got a Luger and 200 odd rounds of ammunition in your wardrobe. And that would really have landed you in trouble if she had been a cop. So remember – in any future contact with anyone, male or female, you keep your lip buttoned about everything."

Tom stared at him. That gun had been hidden! Locked away securely.

"You've bloody burgled my place!" he snarled.

"Listen Tom, you are a complete novice in this game," Algy snapped. "You think you're big-time because of the racket you played at for a few years in the Army Stores, but you haven't got even half-decent locks on your doors. It took me about thirty seconds to get into your front door, less than that to unlock the door to your flat, fifteen seconds to find the key into your wardrobe just to check how long it would take me to find it and just over a minute to get into that box in the wardrobe.

"If you do want to stay in this game you've got to wise-up a hell of a lot. Do you want to? Stay in this game?"

It took Tom less than two seconds to decide. Not just for the money, but for his neck. If Algy could talk so easily about Sally 'meeting a ;permanent accident', what would Algy do to him? Because he (Tom) really did know plenty.

"'Course I do," he croaked.

"In that case get some proper locks on your doors. And find somewhere better to hide your weapon. Somewhere that an 'teenage burglar on his first pop won't find it."

"Right."

"You're going to have a different cargo next weekend."

"Right." Tom was not going to ask what it was. In the war sometimes Missions were on a 'Need to know' basis. If he 'needed to know', Algy would tell him. So he'd keep his lip buttoned, as he'd just been advised.

"You'll be bringing some guns. Handguns. Lugers."

"Wh-at!" As far as Tom was concerned drugs was one thing – guns something else entirely.

"There will only be a few. Well, two dozen. No ammunition. I've had a look at the ammo you've got in your wardrobe. You don't need 200 plus rounds, around 20 is more than enough for you, so Mr. Barnett will buy the spare 200 you've got. That of course will be in addition to the fee you'll be getting for bringing the Lugers – which will be half as much again as for the drugs consignment which you will also bring.

"The cover story, if one's needed, is that Pierre had put you onto the chance of getting some spares for the cruisers you've got here. That there was no sale for them in France. There will be some spares on the top just in case there is any check and the Lugers will be hidden in genuine spares boxes underneath. You will do the trip Sunday morning, I will arrive late Sunday afternoon to repair your car. That'll account for the Spares if any cover is needed."

"Yes." But Tom knew he was going to be worried sick till this time next week. Not just about the Lugers – though that was bad enough – but what the hell had he got himself into with this mob? Talking of 'meeting permanent accidents' like that.

.

Tom dashed to his office to grab the 'phone as it kept ringing leaving a potential buyer looking over the day-boat he said he was thinking of buying.

"Hello Mr. Henderson, Terry Murray here. I was wondering if you had a boat free on Sunday afternoon for me to hire to take Kathleen Jackson out in. I've never driven one before so would you need to come to pilot us? We'd only want to stay in-shore - not go right out into the Channel I mean."

"No problem. But I'm in the middle of a sale right now so could you come down before Sunday and we can talk about it then?"

"Fine! What about at six this evening? I want it to be a surprise for Kathleen."

"See you then." Tom put the 'phone down quickly and dashed back to the customer. Ten minutes later he had made his first sale. Only a day-boat – but it was a start, he felt.

Terry arrived soon after six and Tom took him along the line of four cruisers. As the day-boat was sold, he couldn't have that.

"That's a nice-looking boat!" Terry said, pointing.

"It is, but that one would be a bit much for your first trip," Tom said quickly. That was the cruiser he took to Calais. "This one would be more suitable. Both because it'll be your first trip and for in-shore."

"Right. So would you have to come?"

"I could. But I'm sure Kathleen would prefer it to be just you two," Tom grinned at him.

"I'd prefer that too really," Terry grinned back. "I was thinking about the safety factors but if you reckon showing me how the controls work and telling me about any problems with currents and things round here will be enough – that's fine by me."

"Come tomorrow evening and I'll have the cruiser ready and we can do a chug up and down the river which will give you a feel for it. What time will you want the boat from on Sunday?"

"Two o'clock?"

"No problem. It'll be ready and waiting. Do you want a hamper on board or will you bring your own refreshments?"

"What do you do in hampers?

"Come into the office and see the range."

When Terry left, Tom was well pleased. A sale and a genuine hiring. It would mean leaving for Calais Saturday evening to make sure he would be back in plenty of time to get Terry on his way before Algy came.


Tom listened to the forecast Friday evening with growing dismay. Strong blustery winds increasing from mid-day Saturday, but easing early Sunday morning to give a bright and sunny afternoon. Though it would be fine for Terry and Kathleen, it would be anything but for his trip across the Channel Saturday evening. The Jacksons would expect him to be there Saturdays of all days of the week now as most customers would come then. Still, he had ridden out enough rough weather on Lake Superior back home so he reckoned he'd be able to cope with anything the English Channel could throw at him.

On Saturday though the weather began to close in earlier than forecast. The wind picked up steadily from early morning then squalls began lashing the Marina quickly increasing in frequency and strength.

He wondered about 'phoning Algy to tell him this weekend's trip would have to be postponed because of the storm and then the hire on Sunday afternoon, but he could go across Monday. He could always tell the Jackson's if they found out he was away, that he'd taken a buyer out on a 'sample trip'. Algy himself could come.

Relieved at the idea he reached for the 'phone. Then stopped.

As an ex-flyer Algy would know all about the dangers of rough weather of course – but in wartime usually that's of little consequence unless it's really abnormally bad. This weekend's weather wasn't. Not really. .In wartime it would have been ignored. And though this wasn't wartime Tom was suddenly reluctant to use this excuse remembering Algy's and even more, Mr. Barnett's attitudes.

He dropped his hand. He'd go after closing the Marina early today on the basis that no one would be coming to look at boats on a day like this. Putting on oilskins he went out to check over the cruiser.

At three o'clock he put up the 'Closed' sign, and went to the cruiser. Which was a pity because he missed the call from Algy five minutes later telling him to cancel the trip because of the weather.

Once he was beyond the quieter river and in the open sea the wind hit him with a new ferocity, smashing rain against the windscreen and bodywork. He already had the wipers going full pelt and thanked God that the cabin was weatherproof so he was dry and reasonably warm. Though he was normally a good sailor he began to feel distinctly queasy as the boat pitched and gyrated in the increasing seas.

Though he was running pretty much parallel with the Cross-Channel ferry routes he was crossing the through-Channel routes at virtually 90 degrees. Though he was keeping a watch for shipping he knew only too well he was a speck in the ocean to one of them and his chance of seeing one depended very much on his being at the top of a wave.

He was five miles off Calais when it happened.

Without realising it he had drifted Westwards from his planned course that gradually coincided with the Ferry route as they closed Calais Harbour. Though the Marina was separate, they were close.

As he breasted the top of a 15 feet high wave and stared around, with a sickening jolt of fear he found himself only sixty feet from the towering side of a Ferry steering for a collision within a hundred yards.

With a yell, he twisted the wheel to get away. But this dropped him broadside on into the trough between the waves.

Two seconds later the cruiser was swamped as it slammed sideways into the base of the next wave. Daylight was cut off under tons of water crashing onto it. The cruiser shuddered, the engine hesitated, then picked up again as Tom slammed the throttle wide.

The cruiser bobbed to the surface, still broadside on to the next wave. Another frantic twist of the wheel turned the cruiser another ninety degrees so it was now facing back towards England. The wave crashed over it, shooting it forward to burrow into the wave that had almost drowned the cruiser just seconds before but somehow it struggled to the surface again.

On the top of the wave Tom glimpsed the Ferry, now past him and the patch of calmer water on its leeward side, where the Ferry was shielding it from the wind and squalls.

But to get to it, and to comparative safety, Tom had to go broadside on to the wave pattern coming at an angle from the coast of France.

Tom shrugged. He had to do it. Try it anyway.

He waited till the crest of the wave was just past him, then twisted the wheel as fast as he could and rammed the throttle wide.

The cruiser responded immediately, cutting across the wake of the Ferry at an angle. Another twist of the wheel at full throttle and he shot past the stern of the Ferry and into the patch of calmer water.

Tom eased the throttle just to keep pace with the Ferry and tried to calm his pounding heart and the fear that was still coursing through him at his very narrow squeak. He decided he'd write a strong letter of commendation to the boat-builders as he patted the wheel in relief. Till he remembered Algy's warning not to talk at all.

Nearly an hour later he gently motored into the calmer waters of the Marina, drew up to a vacant mooring spot and stiffly climbed onto the jetty to secure mooring ropes before staggering back into the cabin to mix himself a stiff drink – a very stiff drink.

Slowly his still jangling nerves quietened as he decided what to do. He'd stowed blankets in the cabin's under-bench storage boxes and some supplies so he could easily bed down here for the night. But he needed to get away very early tomorrow to make sure he was back for Terry and Kathleen with this weather. So he'd better go to

Pierre's Cafe right now to make sure he'd get the gear loaded on his boat early to make his early getaway. And a proper hot meal there would be much better than the soup and sandwiches that was all he had on board.

The Marina Master's office was closed so if he did get the gear on board tonight he would be well on his way back to the UK before the office opened in the morning. That would avoid any chance of a Customs check.

He shrugged on oilskins because the wind and squalls were still blowing hard on shore, and made his way through the now familiar streets to Pierre's.

It was less crowded than usual, not surprising the weather being what it was, and Pierre stared at him in consternation.

"Tom! I wasn't expecting you till tomorrow!" Pierre hissed as soon as he joined him at his table.

"Complications my end," Tom muttered back equally quietly. "They mean I've got to get back to England by mid-day and with the weather the way it is I've got to leave a lot earlier than usual. Which means I need all the gear to be aboard either tonight, which would be best or by five tomorrow morning at the latest."

"That'll break the normal routine that everyone is used to."

"So what?"

"Tom. It's one thing for you to come for breads each weekend – though I'm getting comments about that now despite your cover of visiting Silvie. But who's going to believe you've just come for breads when you dash in and out like this in weather like this?"

"Then you'd better get all the gear here to be loaded on board very early then so I'm away before anyone's about."

"Even more suspicious if anyone does happen to be about!"

"Who'll be about at the time I need to get away? If I'm not back by mid-day questions are going to be asked my end. Dangerous questions by dangerous people."

"The breads are no problem. You can have them now if you want them." He rubbed his jaw. "The other? I make 'phone call."

Ten minutes later he was back with a steaming plate of food that he put onto the table in front of Tom.

"They'll be here by three," he muttered. "Morning not afternoon."

"Great! I knew you could sort it!"

"You tell Algy that," Pierre grunted.

"Will do."

He was too keyed up to sleep as he kept a watch along the quayside, waiting for the hours to drag by to three o'clock. But it was nearer half-past four before a van quietly drew to a halt by his boat.

Four men dropped down from the back, two more from the front. The two kept an obvious watch from the front and rear of the van while the four hauled wooden cases out of the back and brought them over to The Sea Swallow, two to a box.

Tom stepped onto the quay and pointed into the cabin. Without a word two men dropped into the cabin and took an end of the boxes one at a time and hauled them in to stow in the inner cabin out of sight. Just as silently they climbed out.

"That's it Tom," Pierre, one of the four men, muttered.

"See you, presumably next weekend."

"Tell Algy about the questions and suggest a break for a few weeks or even months," Pierre said and walked off rapidly after the other three.

The van eased away as Tom cast off the ropes, and stepped into the cruiser. The wind was still blowing quite hard but it was easing and there were fewer and lighter squalls. So it should get quieter on the way back.

He started the engine and eased away from the quay. Slowly and as quietly as possible he set off for the Marina entrance without lights on even though it was still quite dark.

There was only one scare. As he left the Marina he was almost run down by a fishing boat passing the entrance to go into the Harbour. The Captain yelled at him something about lights, Tom yelled back 'Sorry', but still delayed switching them on till he was past the Harbour entrance as well as the Marina's. That meant that if anyone saw them suddenly go on they couldn't tell whether he'd come from the Harbour or the Marina.

He arrived back at Sandwich just before mid-day, exhausted but in good time to finish getting the other cruiser ready for Terry and Kathleen.

They were on easing their way back into the Marina having had a lovely short cruise at just gone 6 o'clock that evening as Algy arrived driving a garage van, not his Jag. He was wearing mechanic's overalls.

"Did you do the trip, Tom?" he asked quietly as they watched Terry approaching the moorings slowly and cautiously.

"Of course."

"Only I 'phoned to cancel it in view of the weather forecast. You weren't around. So what did you do?"

"When did you 'phone?" Tom demanded, staring at him.

"Soon after three."

"Damn. You must have missed me by a matter of minutes then. I left at bang on three after closing early."

"Any problems?"

"Nothing I couldn't handle." With Algy Tom wanted to sound capable and resourceful.

"Get the goodies?"

"Yep. I'd better see these two in first before we check them over. Go in for a drink if you want. You know where it is."

"I'm a visiting mechanic to do a job Tom, not a friend of the family this time. Keep in role for God's sake."

Irritated at his contemptuous tone Tom went to grab the line Kathleen threw at him and took a turn round the bollard while Algy went over to Tom's car, raised the bonnet and pretended to tinker with the engine. Then Tom grabbed the other line from Kathleen, hauled on it and Terry cut the engine as the cruiser was close-hauled.

"Can we have a look in that cruiser? The Sea Swallow?" Kathleen asked once they were on dry land. "Because we'd need one that size to go cross-Channel wouldn't we?"

"Can we make that another time please Miss Jackson?" Tom said quickly nodding at Algy. "Only I'm rather tied up with him and I've got to get that problem sorted urgently. In any case you'll need to take a course in Navigation before venturing cross-Channel"

"Can we talk about that, because I fly a light 'plane and had to do navigation to get my Pilot's Licence," Terry asked.

"That's okay. Call me tomorrow?"

"Will do."

Five minutes later Kathleen and Terry were on their way, both delighted with the way their afternoon had gone.

"A drink Algy?" Tom asked, once they were out of sight.

"Not a bad idea now that they've gone. We need to talk."

Wondering what that meant Tom led the way inside?

"So you went yesterday for the goodies. Why? You go on a Sunday morning."

"Two reasons." Tom handed him a whisky. "The weather forecast was bad as you know and I had a Sunday afternoon booking. That girl is the Jackson's daughter. If I'd turned that down there'd have been questions from them as we're in the cruiser Hire business."

"Fair enough. So what time did you get back from Calais?"

"Just before mid-day. And they weren't supposed to pick up the boat till two so I had enough time to get it set up for them."

"So what time did you leave Calais?",

"05.30 hours. The sea were still high so I wasn't able to travel at full speed and I had to make sure I was back here before those two arrived."

"What time were the spares loaded?"

"Finished about five. No one was around to see. And I sailed with no lights till I was right out of the Harbour area."

"Right."

"But Pierre said people had been making comments about my going every weekend, in spite of the cover story of me being devoted to Silvie. Said we ought to stop operations for a couple of weeks or months.

"Another thing is that now we're in August and I've sold one boat and had a hiring – that could build up. It had better because if it doesn't the Jackson's might decide to cancel the project altogether. On the other hand you could hire a boat a few times yourself or use someone else to pilot it. That'll keep the Jacksons happy and keep the cover of the Marina going."

"Mr. Barnett has been thinking along those lines."

"Great minds think alike," Tom grinned.

"Yes." But Algy didn't seem to think that 'great minds' applied here. He stood up abruptly. "Let's see the goodies."

"I've kept the boxes in the cruiser," Tom told him. "They were heavy, filled as they are, for one person to shift."

On the boat Algy unlocked the strong wooden boxes, moved side the top layer of engine spares, then undid a large flat pack of brake pads. Except that he took out a Luger still in oil wrapping. A check on two more, then he re-packed them.

"Help me to the van with them."

Together they lifted the two boxes into the back of the van already crammed with varied mechanics spares and tools. Algy hauled out a similar box.

"Let's go and get your ammo."

"Look Algy ...."

"And why the hell did you want over 200 rounds? Were you planning to start a war all on your ownsome?"

"They were offered so I took 'em."

"So you must be glad to sell a few on at a profit."

Algy taking 200 rounds of the ammo leaving him with only 20, to Tom was not him 'taking a few', but he wasn't going to argue, not with Algy. Who had Mr. Barnett behind him. And he was still going to make a profit anyway. A very good profit, as that Jerry soldier had been only too glad to just give him the gun and ammo in exchange for Tom's silence about him.

They were just putting that last box into the van when a car pulled into the car park. The driver got out, shot a quick glance at them, hesitated then went towards the office.

"Won't be a moment sir," Tom called out and got a wave back. The new arrival changed track to come towards the cruisers. Algy quickly slammed the door of the van closed, and went to the driver's seat.

"Thanks for fixing that Sam," Tom called out as Algy started the engine and quickly drove off.

"I'm thinking of hiring one of your smaller boats," the visitor said.

"Of course sir. What do you have in mind?" Tom was instantly the salesman.

In Calais the Marina Master was chatting to Charles Jaquet as they sat in the sunshine on the bench outside the office.

Disabled in the war Claude Frassot considered he had been very lucky to be given this easy job of collecting the Mooring Fees and making the occasional Customs check. The Marina could be busy at times but not often and his hours could be lax at least to some extent.

"That chap – Silvie Belgard's English boy friend – I nearly ran him down early last Sunday morning," Charles said casually.

"He didn't come last Sunday," Claude frowned.

"I'm sure it was him. He was running without lights too but it was just light enough to see him when he was that close." He held his hands six inches apart. "I yelled at him and he shouted something back but he still didn't put his lights on till he was well outside the Harbour area."

"Outside? He wasn't coming in then?"

"Nope. I thought it a bit strange him leaving so early, it must have been about 05.00 hours. Usually he's here for the day isn't he? Still maybe he came Saturday this weekend."

"He hadn't arrived by the time I closed shop at four. The weather was so bad I wasn't expecting anyone would be coming or going."

"I know! I was out in it remember!" grunted the fisherman. "But some of us have no option but to go out. Unless the weather's downright dangerous and even then sometimes. Seamen like that fellow are only fair-weather people."

"But he still came across, late at night in bad weather and then went back very early Sunday morning," muttered Claude thoughtfully. "Odd."

"So he got a message that made him go back to England urgently. Or he suggested something to Silvie that she didn't like and she threw him out," grinned Charles.

"But if that was all it was why did he leave in such bad weather and run without lights till he was right out at sea? Which is not only illegal, it's downright stupid. Especially in a harbour area. Unless what he was wanting to slip away unnoticed. In which case – why? I'm going to check Silvie is still alright." He heaved himself to his feet and picked up the walking stick he needed. "I'll do it discreetly and don't you say a word to anyone Charles. It could be that whatever it is that the Englishman is up to, Pierre and Silvie are involved in it somewhere too."

When Claude arrived at Pierre's Cafe he found that Silvie was inside humming happily as she served customers. So either she was a very good actress or she was genuinely happy and nothing untoward had happened to her. Having known her from childhood he was pretty sure she was no actress.

Thoughtfully he went back to his office. And decided he would have a quiet word with the Gendarmes and put these oddities to them. See what they made of it all. More likely than not he was making something out of nothing - but it was odd, to say the least.

It wasn't until late afternoon that a young Gendarme strolled up to the Marina Master's office. Twenty minutes later after taking Claude's Statement of all the events surrounding Tom Henderson, and Pierre and Silvie Belgard, he was hurrying back to Headquarters at speed. There were a lot of far-reaching enquiries to get started because the Belgards were already suspected of being small-time fences. This sounded much, much bigger so they would need to be started by someone far above his rank. But he'd still get some credit for having reported it.

# Chapter 9
## The Paris connection

Ron stared up at the huge sheet of paper pinned to the wall. For this exercise of planning for the Package Tour Project he had decided that different sheets of paper spread across his desk just wasn't good enough. He needed something the size of a wallchart to get a complete view of all the details that needed to be dovetailed from so many different organisations and different people within those organisations.

At the same time he needed to include costings for each element and the profits from each element or at whichever stages.

The purchase of the aircraft was relatively simple and easily costed.

Then came the aircrew needed for it, whether their existing groundcrew had the capacity to deal with it with retraining – or whether it needed more mechanics.

Then came the links into Ben Brooks' hotel in Spain. Or should they go for more than just his? And how far should they stretch from the hotel they'd already tied up (provisionally) with Ben.

That could be the Package Tour element. But if the seats weren't full could they sell the empty ones just as Flights? How do you balance the two? And time the cut-off points for those with the timing of the holiday seasons?

Then the question of how to use the Viscount apart from the Saturday Flights to and from the Costa del Sol? Keep daily Flights to and from Malaga? Or go to other Tourist destinations? Or use it to replace one of the aging passenger Dakotas?

Or, on the other hand, he could approach Tour Operators for them to Charter the Viscount to take their customers to wherever? Then they would have the problems of filling the Flights! Less profit perhaps but halving the worries, which might be worth paying for.

He'd have to work out the costings for various destinations to put to Tour Companies. But they might not be willing for Flights starting from Wingmore. But using the arguments the Costs would be less because of cutting out the Landing Fees from London airports might win them over. That was an alternative to put to the Board.

One blessing was he didn't have to worry about the arrangements for Kathleen's Wedding. Anne had made it very clear that she wanted to do it with Doreen, Terry's mother. As Anne and Kathleen did treat each other as mother and daughter he had been delighted. That would bring them even closer together.

That brought another thought. Terry. Not about Terry himself, he was only too happy about him marrying Kathleen. It was what he had said about Tom Henderson after last weekend.

He'd had to go to Sandwich on business Saturday afternoon so called in at the Marina to check if the hire for Sunday afternoon was still possible in view of the weather. Not only was Tom not there, The Sea Swallow wasn't there either. He thought he must have just taken it down the river a bit for some reason, never thinking he'd have gone any further with the bad weather. He 'phoned again Sunday morning as though the weather was moderating and the forecast was better, he still wasn't sure about going. He'd got no reply. Worried, but because he was picking up Kathleen mid-morning, having lunch together in Sandwich then going on to the Marina he'd said nothing to her.

Very relieved at seeing Tom and The Sea Swallow had come back by then he had simply said to him that he'd 'tried to catch him latish Saturday afternoon to ask about the weather'. Tom had said quickly that 'he must have been down at the boathouse so out of the office and missed the 'phone call'.

Puzzled because of course he'd visited not 'phoned but wanting to get off, Terry had said nothing more to him. That evening when they got back home he'd mentioned it to him and Anne.

That had puzzled them too. Not so much that Tom had been away from the Marina with a cruiser because a potential buyer would naturally want to try one out though with the weather as it was, surely he wouldn't have taken a potential buyer out in those conditions? But why had he lied saying he had been in the boathouse when really he was not at the Marina at all? So where had he been that needed a trip in that kind of weather – and how long had he been away? Had he been away overnight, because he hadn't answered the 'phone early Sunday morning either? So why had he lied about it?

Ron turned back to the wallchart and his costings. These were the immediate problems he had to deal with. Tom and his mysterious comings and goings could safely be left till later.

"Tom, we want you to do some checking," Algy said to him three days later. This time they were in the restaurant of a Five Star Hotel in Ramsgate. Algy had insisted that if they were going to eat somewhere, 'it had to be somewhere half-way decent'.

"Oh?" Tom was wary.

"We need more supplies of goodies. Not the specials. More in quantity and frequency."

Tom heaved a silent sigh of relief. 'Specials' were guns and ammo. He was a lot happier with drugs.

"The thing is, with people making comments about your trips to Calais we've got to pick some other routes. We can organise Dunkerque and Boulogne as well as Calais reasonably easily so we want you to suggest to the Jacksons you advertise to do some trips to those places using The Sea Swallow."

The Sea Swallow could carry up ten passengers comfortably enough even though it was the one he used to go to Calais by himself.

"We'll book six of the places on some of the trips, fill the rest with whoever you like. The less connected with you or the firm the better in fact. Camouflage."

Tom nodded. That made sense.

"But we also want another route in. Not seaborne. Air."

"Air?!"

"So sound out the pilots that fly to Paris, establish contact with your Jules Coublon and see if he can supply our type of goodies. If not we'll have to organise someone else. Fix whatever price you can with Coublon, see what the pilots or other aircrew want, and come to me with a price. If we can agree that then you'll be in business. And if you do that right your cut should work out a hell of a lot bigger than the Fee we give you just as our carrier."

Tom stared at him. This was sure upping the ante! It would put him among the Organisers, the Bosses. And by cutting him out of the direct smuggling he would be that much in the clear as well.

"Already been doing it and I've made some contacts now," Tom said smugly. "So I"ll check things out and let you know."

"Excellent Tom. Ah. Here's the steaks and wine. I was glad this place had that wine in stock. It's a first class vintage. You'll like it."

Tom did. And revelled in the thought this would soon be his normal lifestyle. Just as it was with Algy.


Two days later Tom went to the Airfield early. He was looking to meet up with Toby Watson and Phillip Grover. They were pilots that were now making regular late afternoon cargo flights to Paris. They stayed overnight near the airport to return, fully loaded again early the next morning. Careful enquiries during several visits he'd made to the Airfield 'out of interest' he'd said had found that for those Early Morning Arrivals there were no Customs checks. 'Too early for those clock-watchers', Toby had laughed.

"Hi Phil, Hi Toby," he waved a hand as they came into the Cafe for the Full English breakfast that was now their routine.

They joined him at his table carrying their plates.

"Good flight?"

"Routine. Gets almost boring," Phil responded.

"Staying in Paris boring?" Tom echoed unbelievingly.

"You been there?" Toby asked.

"Sure. Stationed there during the War, after the :Lberation of course and been back many times since. I know a smashing nightclub there, The Montpelier," he winked. "Still going strong too."

"Where's that then?" Toby was interested.

"Rue de Montpelier." Tom hesitated just a moment. "Look, when are you going again? To Paris I mean."

"This evening and back tomorrow morning. Then we've got two days off," Toby answered. "Why?"

"If I could sneak aboard your flight I could take you there, introduce you to the owner, Jules Coublon, and you'll have a night to remember! That I promise you."

The pilots looked at each other.

"Cargo flights don't take passengers," Phil said slowly. "Regulations."

"But Tom could sit in the Flight Engineers place in the cockpit as we don't take one on the Paris trips, couldn't he?" Toby suggested.

"In any case I won't be an ordinary passenger, will I? I am an employee of the company even if I'm not aircrew. Anyway, who's going to know?"

"Done," Toby said happily.

"See you later then. Hang on though – what about Customs? The Custom's guy will know I'm not aircrew won't he?"

"Customs? What Customs?" Toby grinned. "Customs Inspectors don't bother with short-haul regular cargo flights like ours - especially at the times we go and come."

They separated, all well pleased, Tom to make a carefully worded 'phone call to Jules.


In The Montpelier Toby and Phil found that Tom was treated as a favoured customer, they were shown to the best table for the floor show, with friendly Hostesses to attend to them. Tom disappeared just as the floor show began.

"So what is your proposal this time, Tom? The last one died the death didn't it? I was - disappointed."

"So was I, Jules, so was I. But I got a sudden offer that paid a hell of a lot more that just smuggling in the bit of 'booze and baccy' I could carry from a cruiser without raising curiosity my end. But that meant I had to use sources already in Calais.

"But things have moved on and now I can put Paris in the conduit. For 'goodies' shall we call them of the high-value, low-bulk kind. Which means I could bring you in as we talked of before. But this time bigger and better."

"Which involves those two?" Jules jerked a thumb at the door.

"Right. They are pilots of cargo flights from Kent to Paris and back for Carruthers Airlines. As I'm still the Marine Manager of the Carruthers Group, if we can reach a deal then I can bring them in as the air carriers. On regular flights too."

Jules studied him for a moment. If Tom was for real this time, he could expand his operations overseas rather than just around the Parisian drugs scene. And because he would be selling in bulk not the more usual small or even tiny packets it would be a lot more profitable. He was sure that was what Tom was now talking about.

"You're talking about heroin and cocaine, I presume?" He wanted it in clear words before he said anything about possible supplies coming from him. Because had Tom's suggestions before been just a come-on, before putting the real question?  This one.  What if Henderson was really a 'grass' as the British seemed to call betrayers?"

"Of course.  What else could be so profitable with low bulk?"

"Supplies would be no problem for me to provide," Jules said after a moment.  "At the right price and with fool-proof arrangements."

"Excellent.  Quantities and prices then," said Tom leaning forward. Now for the bargaining.

Fifteen minutes later he shook hands with Jules, deal concluded. Once Tom had convinced Toby and Phil.  And both had shown they were willing enough to bend Regulations.  But this was a totally different order of magnitude of course.

He joined them in time for the last ten minutes of the floor show.

"Like this kind of life, lads?" he asked when that was over, waving his hand around the plush nightclub and pointing at the expensive drinks on the table.

"Sure do," Toby replied at once, patting the thigh of Stephanie the Hostess sitting close beside him.  Phil was with Yvette.

"Well, play your cards right and you can enjoy this – and more any time you want to with no one else knowing anything about it.  Tax-man, Bosses - or wives.  No-one except us."

The girls stood up.

"As you talking business, we leave you.  Just for now, I hope." They blew them kisses and left.

"Nice girls," Tom observed.

"Sure are." Phil glanced at Toby and back to Tom.  "So what's this about Tom?  Smuggling booze and cigs?"

"Drugs," said Toby flatly.  "It must be.  Bigger money, small bulk, easily smuggled on our flights.  Right?" He looked steadily at Tom.

Tom knew this was the crunch moment.

"Any problems about that?" he asked softly, looking from Toby to Phil.

They looked  again round the club.  Stephanie and Yvette chatting with other customers.  The expensively dressed men and young women finishing off expensive drinks, and he had seen the expensive cars some of them had arrived in.

All in marked contrast to his ordinary rented terraced house in England, Toby thought. Okay, it was in a nice enough house in a nice enough area and the wages as a pilot were pretty good – until you compared it with these people with their kind of money and lifestyle.

Phil's ideas were going along the same lines. He'd be able to move out of his present bed-sit. into a really nice flat.

Just for doing a dead easy smuggle, all this could be theirs too. And as Tom obviously had an in with the Boss here – maybe they could get in for the Show for free every time! And Stephanie and Yvette.

"No problem to me," Toby declared.

Tom looked at Phil.

"Are you in with us Phil?" Tom asked.

Phil hesitated, then nodded, brushing aside his worries of the consequences if they were caught.

"Right. So let's talk about your take in this," Tom said authoritatively.

Ten minutes later that was settled with no real argument from Toby and Phil. Both felt out of their depth and it was free money wasn't it?

"Right. I'll go and sort out the goodies for the morning, then we can go back to the hotel for the night. Unless you make your own arrangements of course." He winked at them.

Just as Toby had forecast, there were no Customs to be seen at Wingmore so Tom gathered up the two small bags of drugs from each pilot they'd hidden in their overnight bags, and set off for the Marina to 'phone Algy.

By 4.00 p.m they'd done a deal which pleased Tom but left Algy thinking Tom was a sucker. He should have stuck out for a much higher price than the one he settled for.


As August passed into September, pressures over the myriad negotiations on the Package Tour/Flights Schedules, and Kathleen's wedding preparations pushed the puzzle about Tom to the back of Ron's mind.

Tom was reporting to Anne a good take-up on Hire and Charter use of the cruisers of different sizes for visiting Calais, Boulogne and Dunkerque or fishing trips with the occasional boat sale, so it was proving profitable which was excellent for its first season.

Unknown to any of them, in France investigations were spreading out from Pierre Belgard's Cafe and Patisserie after the tip-off by Claude Frassot, the Marina Master. Unknown to him Pierre had been suspected for a while of being a small-time fence selling stolen items from petty criminals to his customers. This though seemed to indicate something rather different and bigger. When Tom (Frassot did not know his last name) went off every time with a big bag of 'breads' from Pierre's Patisserie the Gendarmes wondered what those 'breads' had really been. But they were not yet ready to move.

It was also noticed that the Belgard's lifestyle had abruptly improved. Pierre bought himself a new expensive car and Silvie had now got a car too, smaller, but also brand new. Decorators came into their flat and a lot of new furniture. And he had begun looking at houses over-looking the beaches in the newer, rather expensive estates

As far as could be seen his clientele had not increased enough to fund all those things. What was different though was a regular visit of an unmarked van to the Cafe. When that was followed it led them to a dancehall suspected of supplying drug users.

It was then seen that Tom and The Sea Swallow was not coming to Calais quite so frequently, but that Silvie began going off in her new car and meeting it and him in Dunkerque or Boulogne. Of course she could have just been going off to see her English boy friend, but it was noticed the bag of breads had now become a large box. Containing what?

Because of the English connection the British Police were contacted who very quickly found that 'Tom' was Tom Henderson, the Manager of Carruthers Cruisers where The Sea Swallow was based. He had recently taken to running daylong cruises to Calais, Dunkerque and Boulogne.

British police began going in the other direction - Henderson's contacts. There was some evidence to show he'd met Algy Frobisher at the Marina. So did that mean that Lancelot Barnett's gang was also involved?  They were certain he had to be.

Frobisher was known to have had a distinguished war record and Barnett had done 'something hush' in the War, but now they were suspected by the Metropolitan Police of running a gang with widespread rackets.   An unsubstantiated rumour talked of the running of drugs and guns.

While investigations went on into Tom's background including his war service and contacts on the Continent at that time and since, other officers began probing the Carruthers Group of Companies to see how far up that chain the involvement went.

The Carruthers Group also ran lorries and aircraft to the Continent. To Calais and Paris among other cities, with very regular flights to Paris, both cargo and passenger flights.   Alerted, the French investigators followed the regular pilots and found most of them visited the Paris nightspots when staying overnight, among them the Montpelier nightclub owned by Jules Coublon which was regarded as one of the shadier nightclubs.

But the Carruthers personal and business reputations were high and rock solid.

"And what better cover can you have than that?" Detective Superintendent Wilson asked Detective Sergeant Revell cynically. "Look at all they've taken on just recently business-wise?  Opening the Marina place, then a Package Tour business with a new 'plane - a Viscount no less!  And then this Wedding that must be costing a fortune too!  They've got to be strapped for cash in all kinds of directions.  Getting a link-up with crooks like Barnett and Co. would give the Carruthers a desperately needed cash injection as well as big steady profits."

"There was that big cash injection of £55,000 odd that was bunged in sir.  No indication where that came from," supplied Revell.

"Exactly.  Proves my point.  The Jacksons go regularly to the Marina so I'm willing to bet a packet they're the brains behind the set up.   No point in trying to follow everyone that goes there.  We haven't got the manpower to do that anyway."

"Sir, I've been thinking," Revell said a while later looking up from the file.

"Goo-ood," Wilson said, sarcastic approval echoing in his voice.

"Our main action is against people in this country because this is where our villains are. While the French will have their own cases against their gangs of course we've got the other part of the operation this side of the Channel with the guys going over there for goodies that they bring back here to dispose of."

"Can't fault your scintillating analysis so far." Revell was used to Wilson's sarcasm and was always careful to hide his irritation.

"So shouldn't we go across to Paris to check out the score there to get the full picture first hand? To inform our assessments here?"

Wilson looked at him.

"Are you proposing, Detective Sergeant, that we visit Paris to investigate a nightclub or two and their activities over there, stay the night and fly back to the UK the next day? All on Expenses?"

"Plus discussing all the ramifications of the case with our counterparts in Calais – yes sir."

"So – a Flight to Paris, hotel, nightclub, rail to Calais and a Ferry back to the UK. That would probably take two nights. When we can exchange Reports at a fraction of the cost?"

Revell reckoned he'd lost the chance of a French nightclub visit on Expenses, but persisted.

"Reports don't give us the 'feel' of the case sir. Only a personal visit could do that."

"You know Revell, I can see you going a long way in the police. It's a great idea. The other thing is whether we ought to fly both ways to Paris to fit in with normal flight patterns as part of our cover. So we don't get the Ferry from Calais back to the UK."

"So see about fixing us a hotel in Paris for three nights with an option on a fourth. We could well get back from the round train trip to Calais too late to come back till the fourth day. But don't make it one of the very best hotels – we don't want to hammer the Taxpayer too hard."


Three days later they took the 10.30 Flight to Paris from Wingmore Airfield and were impressed by the efficiency of the operation.

Delivered to their hotel by taxi, Wilson congratulated Revell on his choice. The hotel was good but not overly expensive. Not really.

Deciding to focus on the shadiest nightclub they took their seats in good time at The Montpelier but the nearest tables to the Floor were either already taken or marked 'Reserved'. Their seats were close enough to give a good view of the floor show though, the pretty Hostess escorting them assured them in delightfully accented English.

They accepted proffered Menus and were glad that they were on Official Expenses. Everything was pricey. In keeping with their image of prosperous English businessmen they ordered lavishly.

"Can you tell me who owns The Montpelier?" Wilson asked the waitress bringing them another cocktail after the excellent floor show was finished.

"*M'sieur* Coublon, *M'sieur,*" she replied busily.

"Is there any chance we could meet him? I have a business suggestion he might be interested in."

"I would have no idea, *M'sieur.* But I could mention it to our Manager, if you wish?"

"Yes please."

It was fifteen minutes later that a gentleman in evening dress came to their table. Revell noticed a couple of burly men, also in evening dress had come into the room from another door and were drifting slowly and casually over to them.

"Good evening, *M'sieurs.* I am the Manager. I understand you have expressed a wish to see *M'sieur* Coublon?"

"Yes please."

There was a pause.

"May I enquire what it is about? If you have a complaint of some nature I am sure we shall be able to resolve the problem without troubling him."

"We have no complaint at all, *M'sieur.* Everything was superb. The food, the service, the floor show – everything. It's a business proposition that I feel sure he would be interested in."

"I deeply regret he is not available *M'sieur.* Perhaps he could reach you? A hotel address perhaps? A telephone number?"

Wilson hesitated.

"I shall be at this number tonight until tomorrow morning about midday. Then I am not sure of my movements. I have a series of business meetings in various places for the next two days." Wilson scribbled his name, the Room Number and telephone of the Hotel on a card on the table advertising facilities of The Montpelier and some other establishments as he spoke.

"If I am able to speak to *M'sieur* Coublon before then, I shall pass on your information. And your permanent contact points?"

"Only those, thank you."

"Of course, *M'sieur* Wilson."

Once safely outside, walking looking for a taxi, "What's your proposition going to be sir?" Revell asked.

"Talk of wanting to buy into The Montpelier. Then move on to hinting at smuggled – wine, cigarettes and then even more careful hints about drugs."

Revell was impressed.

In his beautifully furnished and decorated office, Coublon listened to his Manager's assessment of Wilson.

"He has the smell of the *flic* about him," his Manager said positively.

"Mmm." Coublon looked at the card the Manager had given to him. "But he has a 'proposition'," he murmured thoughtfully. "Emile, check out with the hotel about those two." It was one of the many who carried cards advertising The Montpelier.

When Revell had booked the rooms he had used Wilson's rank to get 'good rooms', so Emile established in minutes who they were and reported back to Coublon

"Now are they 'bent coppers' as the English term it – or are they operating 'under-cover' but very badly." He paused. "Emile. Tell them now that I will meet them here at 10.00. In the morning."

Wilson was not happy about Emile's message that the hotel passed on to him immediately. It was 2.00 am. So having been woken up himself he proceeded to wake up Revell with the same message.

Promptly at 10.00 the taxi deposited them outside The Montpelier. With only a short delay they were shown through to Jules Coublon. Revell looked round the office, impressed.

"Please sit down gentlemen," Coublon said in excellent English. "I understand you want to see me about some kind of business proposition." He put on a puzzled air.

"That's right," Wilson replied. "The point is my colleague and I are very impressed with your operation here. (Coublon inclined his head modestly) and we would welcome a chance to invest in it. And perhaps transfer its type to London."

"I see. That is very kind of you I'm sure but I have no need for any investment from outsiders here. And if you wish to start a similar operation to mine in London – well I don't hold any kind of patent on my style."

"No. Quite." Wilson paused. "Connections I have in London are keen to import certain items. At discounted rates. Fine wines of the type you have here, cigars and cigarettes. As examples of their many and wide interests."

"There are excellent wine importers in London are there not? Though it's many years since I last went there I am sure I remember seeing some. In your Bond Street if I remember correctly. But I'm sure any London taxi driver would be able to take you."

"Quite. Really I was thinking more of goods that are more profitable. And much less bulky."

"I confess I do not follow you." Coublon put on an air of puzzlement

Wilson decided he had to be more open. "Drugs."

"Aspirin? Laxatives?" Now with a smile.

Wilson knew he was being given the runaround. He stood up abruptly.

"Thank you for your time, Coublon," he snapped.

"Not at all. Detective Superintendent Wilson." Coublon waited till they were by the now opened door. "By the way, I wonder if your superiors at your Scotland Yard know that you are wanting to move into drug smuggling yourself. Perhaps it is my duty as an honest French Citizen to inform them of your activities.".

Revell was worried. Wilson wasn't.

"We were under cover. Even the Chief Constable knows you have to work in character. And we're Kent police anyway, not the Met.."

Their visit to Calais was more fruitful. They established good links with the French investigators, visited Belgard's Cafe and the Marina and talked to Claude Frassot who positively identified Henderson's photograph.

The time was approaching when the decision to rope them all in for questioning would have to be made.  Or start following the Jacksons whenever they visited the Marina, then arrest him, or her or both, on the way back at some stage to catch them with drugs in their possession.  Assuming they were the brains behind the racket.

But that timing would need to be co-ordinated with the French police for arrests their side of the Channel, to stop one side alerting the other.

# Chapter 10
## Wedding

Ron was sitting in the lounge with the photographer, waiting for Kathleen to come down the stairs in her Wedding Gown. Anne was with her and she would be whisked off to the church ahead of Kathleen and him following in the Bridal car.

Like most fathers at this time, he supposed, his mind went back over the years.

Kathleen's birth, babyhood, in her case Evacuation, the bombing, her terrible injuries, her battle back and her now being made Miss Dangerfield's Partner in her very highly regarded Fashion house. Her wedding present to Kathleen who was determined to be a 'working wife'.

And Anne. The lady who had given Kathleen a real ambition those many years ago. Ambitions greater than anything he or May would ever have thought of.

Anne. The vast changes in himself that Anne had wrought as well as Kathleen.

Noises came down the stairs. Anne and Kathleen.

Ron glanced at the photographer.

"Let battle commence," he grinned.

They went out to meet them.

Kathleen was followed down the wide carpeted stairs by Anne carrying the train of the gown Kathleen had designed herself.

"Hold it," the photographer snapped as they neared the bottom of the stairs and took one quick shot with both in, then another of just Kathleen.

He scurried outside to take more as Kathleen paused by the front door, by herself, with Ron, then with Anne as well.

They helped Kathleen and her train into the car, another photograph, then Anne and the photographer were off to the church while Ron waited with Kathleen for a few minutes to give them time to get there.

"Dad, do you remember that time when I thought this day could never come?" Kathleen asked quietly.

"After the school you mean?"

"More about the next day – unless it was the day after that – when I asked you if you thought a boy could ever be interested in me as a girl friend being as I was. Do you remember?"

"I'll never forget," Ron said quietly.

"It was what you said to me then that – well inspired me I suppose. That having no legs didn't mean the end. That a boy could like me for what I had in my heart and my head. So I decided that I would make a go of my dressmaking ideas. And when Terry began to show an interest in me I could really believe that he really did love me. That it wasn't just pity for a cripple."

Ron squeezed her hand as the Driver started the engine.

"You had shown him what you had in your head and your heart that made him fall in love with you I should think."

Ron felt uncomfortable talking about those kinds of feelings, especially knowing the Driver would be hearing every word. But he really did believe what he was saying.

"And Mum. She believed in me too. Not only when I first wrote to her about my ambitions for dress-making and a fashion shop, that was soon after we were sent to Wales but after the school too. I really do owe everything to you two."

"Anne's a wonderful lady, Kathleen."

"You both are. Well, not you as a lady of course, but you know what I mean. As a man. As my Dad."


The Bridesmaids, Sonia's twins, Sarah and Janice, were eagerly waiting outside the church. There was a flurry of excitement among by-standers as the Bridal car swept into view then drew up.

With care the Bridesmaids, Ron and the Driver helped Kathleen and her dress out of the car, up the churchyard and as the organ peeled out Ron and Kathleen, followed by the twins walked slowly down the aisle.

Ron had to keep his eyes firmly ahead, jaw clenched to keep his composure as Kathleen went forward on his arm. Then they were standing by Terry. He glanced at her beaming. She beamed back, revelling in this moment.

Afterwards they went back through the church crowded with well-wishers, Kathleen's eyes flickering from side to side recognising and smiling at friends she'd known for years like Maralyn, some more recently, people from work, Aunt Edith and Uncle Hywell and Marayn, Tim of course – but no mother, Frank or Des, finding she had mixed feelings about that, then out into brilliant sunshine and more people, then people were crowding out from the church, photographs, official and crowds of others – and then suddenly a Fly-past to 'Ooohs' and 'Aaahs' from the crowd, of all the aircraft of Carruthers Airline.

The Reception in a big Marquee in the field next to the Church, speeches. And Kathleen waited for Dad as Ron stood.

With Anne's help he had drafted a shortish speech, funny as well as elements of seriousness that he'd learned by heart but had kept the safeguard of notes.

He looked around the large, happy crowd, glanced down at Kathleen and Terry – and suddenly his eyes glistened with tears at the memory of Kathleen in the hospital bed the morning after the school had been bombed.

"It's okay Dad," Kathleen whispered to him. "You've made everything just fine."

"Kathleen, Terry, everyone. Thank you for coming," he began.


Late that evening he and Anne were sitting relaxing in the lounge both feeling utterly exhausted.

"A really marvellous day Ron," Anne said quietly.

"Yes, it was. But I must say – I'm glad it's over now that it all seemed to go so well." He paused. "Anne. Would you really have liked a wedding like that? When we were married?" Theirs had been a very quiet wedding.

"No," Anne said promptly. "That one was right for Kathleen, our wedding was right for us."

"I think that too," Ron said, pleased. And relieved.

# Chapter 11
## Arrests

It was a cold and wet early November morning when Ron and Tim set off for the Airfield. He dropped Tim off at the Control Tower and sped back to his office in Folkestone to finish off some of the details of the Contract with Malaga Airport. Landing Fees had been agreed after some negotiation but that hadn't been too bad. Anne would be coming in later, now that all the Companies in the Carruthers Group were housed in the same suite of offices.

"Good morning Mr. Jackson," Mary poked her head round Ron's door when she arrived. "Tea?"

"Yes please."

Their usual routine. Five minutes later that all changed.

Ron's door was pushed open abruptly and a man walked straight up to his desk holding out a Warrant Card in one hand, sheets of paper in the other, two uniformed Constables close behind.

"I'm Detective Superintendent Wilson. You Ronald Jackson?"

"Yes."

"You're under arrest on Charges of Smuggling illicit goods into the United Kingdom." He slapped the sheets of paper on the desk. "Arrest warrant, Search Warrants."

Ron stared at him, looked at the Identification Card then picked up the Warrants to study them briefly.

"Would you tell me what all this is about, Detective Superintendent?"

"We'll be doing that alright. At the Station. So come along."

"Just a moment. Mary?" Ron shouted.

Mary appeared in the doorway looking thoroughly frightened.

"I'm so sorry Mr. Jackson! They wouldn't let me tell you they were here."

"Don't worry. I'll need you to tell Anne and ...."

"She's already been arrested," snapped Wilson.

"What?" Ron glared at him ferociously. "Then Mary, get hold of Mr. Howard and tell him what's happened."

"She can't. No communication to anyone."

"James Howard is our Solicitor," Ron snapped back. "We are entitled to legal representation in this country. You are civilian police not the Nazi Gestapo. Mary, after contacting James, contact Sonia."

"I said she can't contact anyone! Okay, I'll allow your solicitor but no one else."

"Sonia is my sister-in-law. I have a severely crippled son working at the Airport Control Tower who will require a degree of care this evening," Ron glared at Wilson.

"Well – okay then. But just her."

"You'll need to sort out my Diary for the rest of today at least Mary," Ron said standing up. He didn't want Wilson to start asking questions about how crippled Tim really was. He needed no one to care for him really, but it was a way of making sure the news got to Sonia quickly in view of the bans Wilson was putting up. Between them Mary and Sonia would be able to handle things. "Shall we go then Detective Superintendent?"

"Make sure you bring all the papers here," rapped Wilson to the Constables.

"I shall want receipts for every single file and every single document you take," Mary snapped immediately.

Ron stifled a smile as he grabbed his coat as he went through the door, closely followed by Wilson. Those Constables were not going to have an easy time of it.

Ron was put in a cell at the Police Station and left. He used the time to think things through. Especially about the smuggling accusations.

The only times he and Anne had been abroad were a couple of recent trips to France and the weekend flight to Malaga, and they hadn't smuggled anything then. So were the accusations related to the firm? Which had to mean the cruisers and the airline. Pilots and aircrew. Most of their flights were cargo that only had pilots aboard but the passenger flights did have a Steward or Stewardess aboard as well. But Henderson with the cruisers! What Terry had said about him weeks ago.

The door view panel was whipped aside and the rattle of keys in the lock announced his confinement in here was ended. For now.

"Sit down Jackson," Wilson said, pointing to the chair on the other side of the wooden table he and another policeman were sitting at. The constable had a wad of paper in front of him. .

Wilson rattled through the Caution and required Ron to sign that on the top sheet of paper in front of the Constable who went on to write out the questions and Ron's answers.

"When did you begin your smuggling operation, Jackson?" Wilson asked abruptly.

"I'm not involved in any smuggling operation," Ron answered promptly.

"I've a witness that says you set up an organisation to smuggle in drugs to the UK from your contact in France."

"He or she is lying," Ron snapped flatly.

"How long have you known Pierre Belgard?"

"Never heard of him."

"Why did you set up a cruiser sales and hire Marina on a deserted stretch of river miles from anywhere?"

"The Marina is not miles from anywhere. It's located just two miles from Sandwich on a well used road and the river has a lot of cruiser traffic from further upstream passing the Marina as well.

"We had the idea of extending my wife's Chandlery business that included dinghy sales at that time, to selling cruisers – a logical extension. We heard that Tom Henderson was wanting to sell a house and land by the river that had been left to him in an Uncle's Will, inspected it, decided that with some development it would make a suitable Marina and bought it. All the documents relating to that are in our office so available for your inspection.

"We decided to take on Henderson as the Manager as he wanted the job, had been in boats on Lake Ontario in Canada before joining the Canadian Army. He was in the Dieppe Raid, lucky to survive that apparently, and was then in the D-Day landings in Normandy and was in the front line pretty much right through except for the short periods he was in the Stores. That kind of war service is a big Plus as far as I'm concerned. And then he had excellent references from Bayliss's, the big building firm here in Folkestone.

"He's developed the cruiser hire side of the business very well, beyond our expectations I must admit and sold some cruisers too."

"Really? If you believe all that, then Henderson has had you for a real sucker. He was not in the Dieppe Raid, he was never in the front line with the Canadian Army, but he was in their Stores throughout the entire war. He was in France and there were some suspicions he was diverting supplies to the Black Market but he was a canny operator and nothing was ever proved against him."

"Do you have proof of that?" Ron challenged him.

"I've been in touch with the Canadian Army Records."

"Then I have been had," Ron said slowly.

"How long have you known Algy Frobisher and Lancelot Barnett?" Wilson switched tack.

"Never heard of them. Who are they?"

"Barnett was in SOE during the war, Frobisher was a pilot in a 'Hush' Squadron that flew them and supplies in and out of France."

"I wasn't in either."

"I know. But those two now run one of the most vicious Gangs in London, if not **the** most vicious. You must know that because they dispose of the drugs your organisation brings in."

"I don't run any organisation bringing drugs or anything illegal into the UK."

"Going on to something else. You've got crimes of violence in your record."

"That was Assault and Criminal Damage. For which I was fined just a shilling on the Assaults and sixpence for the camera."

"You knew the Magistrates or something?" sneered Wilson.

"No. I was fined that amount because of what the Magistrate called 'The totality of the situation'."

"What's that supposed to mean?"

"The reason for me thumping Tam Jerningham, a Reporter."

"And what was that?"

"My daughter was sixteen at the time. Three years before that she lost both legs through injuries in a bombing incident in January 1943. Jerningham was a Reporter on one of the local papers and for some reason wanted to manufacture some dirt on Mrs. Jackson, my wife. Miss Carruthers as she was then. My daughter was working for Miss Dangerfield, the costumier. On this particular evening she was waiting outside the workshop for me to pick her up. I'd been delayed and when I got there I found Jerningham was attacking my daughter, one of her artificial legs had broken and she was on the ground and he had a hand inside her coat, molesting her. Another man, the photographer, was standing by doing nothing to help my daughter. I pulled Jernigham off and thumped him. Found out exactly what he'd done and said, and thumped him again to reinforce my order for him to stay well clear of my daughter and Miss Carruthers in future."

"And the Damage?"

"The photographer had taken some shots of my daughter. I – remonstrated with him, totally accidentally of course, knocked the camera from his hands and, just as accidentally trod on the camera, broke it and ruined the pictures he'd taken. The Magistrates said they had to convict me of the offences because I'd thumped Jerningham after I'd got him away from my daughter so they rejected my Plea that I'd only hit him to rescue my daughter, to make sure they didn't both turn on me there and then, and to make sure he didn't molest my daughter again. They said that there had been no real need to smash the camera. So they fined me the small amounts they did and then warned Jerningham and the photographer to keep well away from my daughter and Miss Carruthers in future or they'd go to prison. The level of those fines showed what the Court thought about the whole thing. The Court was on 12th February 1949 so you'll be able to check the Court Record."

The Constable taking the notes scribbled something on a separate piece of paper and slid it across to Wilson. He shot a quick glance at it, then re-read it.

"Get someone else in, I'll need to talk to you," Wilson said to him.

Another Constable came in and the other two went out, leaving Ron with the Constable silently watching him.

Ron thought rapidly over the interview. Five minutes later Wilson and the note-taking Constable came back in.

"Look Jackson." Wilson leaned across the table. "Make it easy on yourself . We know you set up the organisation for Henderson to bring in the stuff but we really want to nail Barnett and his Gang and you can help us a lot in that. Finger Barnett and Frobisher for us as the people you passed the drugs on to and we'll make sure you and your wife get the lightest possible sentence."

"Did you offer Henderson the same deal?" Ron asked.

"That's nothing to do with you."

"It has everything. If Henderson had set up the organisation he'd have had a good idea of the reputation you said Frobisher and Barnett have if he was passing stuff onto them. So if you did offer that kind of deal, by naming me as the organiser he could keep their names out of it and get himself the easier sentence." He paused. "Unless he has already fingered Frobisher and Barnett as you put it," he added slowly, knowing that may have got him nowhere after all.

Wilson looked at Ron thoughtfully.

The fact he had connected those two with this was not because Henderson had named them. He had said he knew nothing about them even when he was shown Frobisher's photo.

But Frobisher had been stopped by a Motorbike Patrolman for Speeding in his Jaguar in Sandwich. Routine checking with the Vehicle Licensing Office had confirmed the name and address Frobisher had given. Later he had seen Frobisher chatting to Henderson at the Marina when he had gone there, out of uniform, to book a small cruiser for a trip, and Frobisher had been driving a battered garage van and been dressed like a mechanic not in smart gear as when he'd been driving the Jag. Curious because the two characters didn't match he had contacted a pal in the Met. who had told him about Frobisher and Barnett. The Patrolman had been brought into the Enquiry as a 'Local Bobby', and had mentioned it.

Taken with that, Jackson's ideas made a lot of sense.

"I'm going to Release you on Police Bail, Jackson. Pending further enquiries. Do you have a Passport?"

"Yes."

"You'll have to hand it in to this Police Station immediately. And you are not to go to the Marina. Those Conditions will be in your Bail. If you break them you will be imprisoned for Breach of Bail. Do you agree?"

"Yes. Can I go to my office here in Folkestone?"

"No problems about that."

"What about my wife?"

"She's already been released on Bail. Same Conditions."

"Then I can go now?"

"Go through the Statement the Constable has been writing out and sign each page. Anything you don't agree with, we'll go through again. In the meantime I"ll get the Bail Forms."

Wilson left the room, and the Constable passed the pages of writing to Ron. Once he'd read each page, Ron signed it at the bottom. When he'd finished Ron passed them all back.

"No queries. Can I go now?"

"When the Detective Superintendent comes back with the Bail Forms." The PC paused. "I don't suppose you'll remember me Mr. Jackson, but I was in Court when you were there that time. I confirmed everything you said about it to the Super."

Ron nodded but said nothing. They sat in silence for five minutes till Wilson returned.

As Ron went out into the General Area, Anne jumped to her feet, face suddenly aglow at seeing him. James Howard got to his feet more slowly.

"I understand we're both free to go, Anne," Ron said quietly.

"Thank God!" she exclaimed, grabbing his arm.

Once outside, Howard stopped them.

"I'm sorry I could not be with you Mr. Jackson but I thought I should give priority to your wife."

"I'm glad you did. Have you time for us to have a Conference in my office?"

"I have an hour free so by all means."

They left the Police Station to walk to the office where Ron's car was still parked and to make some 'phone calls, Ron first to Richard at the Airfield to pass a message to Tim in the Control Tower, Anne to Sonia.

"Ron, we'll need to meet to see how we're going to handle this, publicity-wise," Richard said urgently as soon as Ron had explained what had happened at the Police Station.

"What do you mean, Richard?" Ron was puzzled.

"News like this is bound to hit the headlines, locally at the very least."

"Why? What for? It's not newsworthy at all. And I'd rather not anyway."

"Of course it's newsworthy Ron! 'Carruthers Cruisers suspected of being used in a Drug Smuggling Racket.' 'Managing Directors questioned by Police for hours'. Those could be the headlines. Ron, it's not just you and Anne in this. It's the children. And the Company. What do you think our customers will think when they read that the Carriers they use are a cover for a smuggling racket? Because they'll think it's the Airlines too. And the lorries."

"I get what you mean, Richard." Ron was now consumed with a fresh anxiety. It was not just a personal matter as the last time he was in Court. The consequences of this could be much wider. And immediate if the Airline customers started pulling their Contracts. "Could you come to our place in about an hour Richard? We're at the office in Conference with Mr. Howard but we should be home by then."

"I'll meet you there."

"What happened in your interview with Detective Superintendent Wilson, Mr. Jackson?" Howard asked.

Ron went through it while Howard took more notes.

"Excellent. Both of you told exactly the same story in response to the same type of questions," the solicitor said at the end. "By reinforcing each other in that way, independently I mean, it has given strength to your accounts. I could quite see that the police will now eliminate you from their enquiries and follow up your suggestion regarding Henderson's version. Please contact me if you should be contacted again by the police." He left to hurry to his next appointment.

"Hope he's right about that," Ron grunted. "But there's still the publicity angle Richard talked about."

"Let's get hold of Anthony Reilly, the Editor of the Journal. Get in with our side of the story early." Anne suggested.

Ron nodded.

"Great idea Anne. He's given backing before in a lot of ways. I'll suggest we meet him tomorrow morning. We want him, not one of his Reporters. That would have given us a chance to talk things over with Richard tonight."

"I'll ring him and set it up." She picked up the 'phone while Ron went through to settle some matters with Mary. When he went back Anne was just putting the 'phone down. "He'd already heard we'd been arrested. Said he was glad we'd been released without Charge."

"We're still on Police Bail though Anne, so we're not out of the woods yet."

"No. But because we've not been Charged he reckoned that means they must now realise their case against us is shaky. And Mr. Howard was even more definite wasn't he?"

"So what's the score with Reilly?"

"He'll meet us here tomorrow morning at nine. But if we want to after a talk with Richard we can ring him either at the office or his home tonight. He gave me his home 'phone number."

"Good. Let's get home then."

Ten minutes after they walked in Tim arrived brought by Richard and then Sonia knocked on the door having brought Kathleen from work.

Sonia bustled around getting them something to eat while they sat around the big kitchen table and Anne and Ron told them what had been said during their interviews at the Police Station.

"It sounds to me that Henderson set the thing up, and then he implicated you to avoid mentioning those two gangsters, just as you thought, Ron," summarised Richard at the end.

"Dad ...," began Tim hesitantly, " ...I don't know if it means anything but I've seen that Henderson getting into the cargo flights piloted by by Watson and Phillip Grover a couple of times. Going out late and at other times coming in on their early moring returns. My shifts don't cover both ends of those flights.

"Nothing was said about our flights to me by Wilson, just the cruisers," Ron said slowly,

"Nor to me," Anne was just as definite.

"But if Henderson was the organiser he could have involved those two. Because why else would he fly out in a cargo flight when we've got more comfortable passenger flights going almost every day? It's against Regulations to start with."

Ron went into the hall for the 'phone.

"Jimmy ...," Ron said when he was through to the Flight Office. " ... have Toby Watson or Phillip Grover cleared with you about taking Tom Henderson on cargo flights to Paris with them?" A brief pause. "Right. Are they on a trip to Paris tonight?" Pause. "Right. Thanks." He pressed the receiver rest to clear the call, then got through to the Police Station. "Is Detective Superintendent Wilson there? It's Ron Jackson here. I need to speak to him urgently." Pause. "Okay, I'll speak to Detective Sergeant Revell then." Moments later, "Detective Sergeant Revell? Ron Jackson here. I was at the Station earlier being questioned by Detective Superintendent Wilson. I've got some information that needs to be acted on tonight or very early tomorrow."

He finished the call then rang Anthony Reilly to put him off. They were going to be tied up in the morning.


Ron arrived at the Airfield in his car followed by two police cars at 6.30 am. Followed by Wilson and Revell Ron went straight to the Control Tower.

"Is Watson's Flight from Paris on schedule, Sam?" he asked the Duty Controller.

Sam glanced at the Status Board.

"Yes Mr. Jackson. He's reported that he took off on time with a two-thirds cargo aboard. Weather fine and clear. Expects to arrive on schedule at 07.30 hours."

"Good. Keep to the usual routine. Don't mention anything about the police cars or me being here."

"Right Mr. Jackson."

The police cars were hidden in a hanger as out in the open they'd have been seen from the air and Toby and Phillip needed to be caught unawares.

They landed on time and as usual parked the 'plane near a hanger for unloading, switched off the engines and walked to the Flight Office carrying their Pilot's bags and overnight luggage.

They were laughing at something Toby had said as they walked in but abruptly lost their smiles as they saw the police and Ron waiting for them.

Toby swung round as the door was shut behind them and saw a

policeman standing by it, arms folded, staring at them grimly.

"Put your bags on the counter and empty them," Ron, standing at the counter, said quietly.

Toby and Phillip glanced at each other, put their overnight bags on the counter and released the catches.

Nothing but overnight kit.

"Flight bags as well."

Slowly Toby and Phil complied.

Ron glanced at Wilson and up-ended Toby's bag. Two large packets about 4 lbs. each fell onto the counter among the papers and maps. He repeated that with Phillip's bag with the same result.

Wilson picked up the packets one at a time and felt them carefully before going on to the next. He cut a small nick at one end of each, put the tip of his finger in and checked the powder now on his finger.

"Toby Watson and Phillip Grover, you are under arrest for attempting to smuggle suspected drugs into the United Kingdom," Wilson intoned, adding the customary Caution.

"As you are likely to be held for some time Toby, do you want me to let Betty know?" Betty was Toby's wife. "I presume you've no objection to that?" Ron glanced at Wilson.

"No."

"Anyone you want me to inform Phillip?" Ron asked next.

Wordlessly he shook his head.

Ron watched them being handcuffed and led out to the police cars. He'd go and tell Betty after the children had gone to school. Toby often didn't get home till then so that would be time enough. And he'd have to see about getting replacement pilots. Permanent ones. Because even if Toby and Phillip were released, having done this he could never employ them as pilots again.

And this was another angle they'd got to sort out publicity-wise.

On the way to the Police Station, Wilson decided he would question Grover first leaving the older, and he judged tougher, Toby Watson to stew for a while.

He had Grover whisked into the Interview Room as soon as they arrived and then he looked at the pale Phillip almost paternally.

"You know Phillip, I'm inclined at this moment to think you got almost trapped into this by Watson and Henderson."

Grover nodded vigorously, relieved at this friendly approach.

"That's right. Tom Henderson had come with us to Paris, pretty irregular that was too, against Regulations in fact, but Toby okayed it and he's the Senior Pilot to me, and then he sprang the thing on us in Jules Coublon's nightclub."

"And then when Watson agreed, you felt trapped again. That you couldn't get out of it." More as statements than questions.

"That's right," Grover said, again nodding vigorously. "And then it just kept on growing till we were bringing in stuff almost every flight. Henderson wasn't usually with us though."

"So how did Henderson get it from you? Or did you pass the stuff straight to Ron Jackson?"

"Mr. Jackson?" Grover stared at him. "He wasn't involved in this at all. In no way. It's Henderson who has the contacts. Henderson would arrange to meet us somewhere, and we'd hand the stuff over to him. He knew Jules Coublon from the war he said. Used to do deals flogging him stuff from the Canadian Army Stores where he was a Sergeant. He knew someone at Calais too, someone called Pierre. Don't know his other name."

"What about the UK end? He say anything about that?"

"Not much. But he and Toby had one over the eight one night and started swapping War stories. There's some bloke called 'Algy' involved somewhere but Henderson suddenly clammed up and wouldn't say anything more about him."

"Anything about someone called 'Barnett'?"

Grover tried to remember, then shook his head.

"No. Pretty sure he didn't. Not that he said anything much about that 'Algy' either.

"So who did Henderson say he passed the drugs on to?"

"He didn't say. Said we had to operate on a 'cell system'. As though we were an SOE group in the war, he said."

"Right. Look Phillip. We'll need you to put what you've just told me into a written Statement and then because you've been so helpful I'll release you on Bail straightaway. Oh, just one more thing, when did Henderson tell you Jackson had planned the whole thing? Organised it?"

"Mr. Jackson? Like I said, he didn't have anything to do with it. Tom Henderson said that we mustn't talk to anyone about what we were doing of course, and said 'Take bloody great care that that straight-arsed idiot Ron Jackson doesn't get a sniff of it. Because if he did we'll all be in dead lumber.'"

Sitting in the cell in the Ramsgate Police Station, Henderson went over every angle of the interviews he'd had with various police since being arrested carrying a caseful of drugs from The Sea Swallow. He did this before and after every session to make sure he kept his stories straight.

Yep, he was sure he'd given away nothing about Algy and Mr. Barnett. That he'd diverted all the blame and all the UK contacts onto the Jacksons. He'd consistently denied knowing or having even heard of either of those other two. By admitting everything about Calais and not mentioning the airline route, even his admissions were limited. It had been a bad moment when they'd brought in that copper saying he'd seen Algy at the Marina and knew who he was, but he'd still stuck to saying that the copper was mistaken. And he'll keep on saying that.

# Chapter 12
## Trials

Tam Jerningham stumped into the Bar of The Speckled Bear in Ramsgate and spotted Sam Rawlings sitting alone in a corner, a pint in front of him. Tam collected his pint and joined him.

"Hi Sam."

"Hi Tam."

Both grinned as always at their similar sounding names.

"Any news?" they both asked at the same instant. Both being Reporters, Sam on one of the local papers, Tam now eking out a precarious living as a Freelance, they were perfectly happy to swap leads. Sometimes.

"Got something that might develop into something sometime," Sam said. "There's a bloke in the lock-up here that works for Carruthers Cruisers of Sandwich. He's accused of smuggling stuff. Officially they're saying it's just 'booze and baccy' but there's a rumour that drugs are involved in it somewhere. They're playing it tight because they want to go right up the chain before they shout loudly about it I suppose."

Tam went very still. Carruthers Cruisers surely had to be one of the Carruthers Group of Companies. And so Ron Jackson.

An angle sprang immediately to mind. Not just a small bit in a Local, but a real biggie! One that could even start him on his way upwards, to being an employed Reporter on one of the big London papers again.

"Is that one of the Carruthers Group of Companies then?" he asked as casually as he could. "That lot based over in Folkestone?"

"Could be." Sam looked at him narrowly. "You got something on them then? If so you ought to share it as I started the lead."

"Maybe. But probably not. If anything does come of it, I'll tip you the wink, don't you worry."

He finished his pint slowly as they talked about other things, hiding his impatience, then went out to the small battered van that was all he could now afford and set off for Sandwich. In the town he picked up a sign for 'Carruthers Cruisers', soon arrived at the entrance and drove in. As he went round the sharp bend, the house and Marina became visible. A police constable was sitting on a bench under the shelter of a verandah who quickly got to his feet as Tam's van approached.

Tam pulled up and went towards the young PC.

"Hi. I'm Jim Hogan, a friend of Ron Jackson. I'd arranged to meet him here about buying one of his cruisers. That one." Tam pointed to the The Sea Swallow, the biggest there. "Is there some kind of trouble seeing you're here?"

"This is a Crime Scene I'm guarding," the PC said importantly.

"Good Lord! Nothing's happened to Ron has it?"

"He's been arrested for organising a smuggling racket. Using those cruisers as a cover."

"Arrested!" Tam spluttered. "How come? I'd never have thought he'd do anything like that! He's always been so – so respectable."

"Best cover there is. Respectable outside, villain inside."

"When was he arrested? And what about Mrs. Jackson?"

"She's been arrested too. She's up to the neck in it an' all."

"What were they smuggling? Wines? Tobacco products?"

"Drugs. And we've found a gun and ammo hidden in there." He jerked his thumb over his shoulder at the house.

"Oh dear." Tam appeared completely at a loss. "Well – I might as well go. Jackson's not going to be in a position to sell any cruisers now, is he? And in the circumstances I wouldn't want to get involved with him in any way at all about anything. Thank you for telling me, Constable."

Shaking his head sorrowfully, Tam went back to his van.

The PC sat down again. That Hogan seemed a nice bloke, he thought. Different from Jackson. Then he had a sudden qualm. Had he said a bit too much? He shrugged. If anyone ever said anything about it, he'd simply deny saying anything to anyone. There were no witnesses here so it would be Hogan's word against his. And it was nothing to do with him if Hogan did say something to his mates in the pub, was it?

On his way back to Sandwich, Tam pulled over to the side of the road and reached for his address book. He soon found the address he was looking for, and went hunting for a telephone kiosk.

"Nice to see you again Mrs. Ackroyd. It has been a long time," he said affably to May.

"It has been indeed," May said, smiling . They had been on the same side against Ron before, though that hadn't worked out as expected. "Please come in." As soon as she'd shut the door, "Come through to the lounge. Would you like tea?

"That would be great thanks."

Tam looked round the well furnished room while May got it. She's done alright for herself, he thought. A lot better than that Council house she'd lived in once.

"I was intrigued by your 'phone call about my ex-husband," she said, coming in with the tray. He had deliberately made it sound mysterious.

"He's got himself in really serious trouble this time," Tam said, taking the cup and saucer May was holding out to him.

"Does it involve Kitty? Or Tim?" That had been May's only worry.

"No. She and Tim are completely in the clear. It's nothing to do with them though it is with his new wife. She is equally involved according to my information. Did you know they have set up Carruthers Cruisers?"

"No. What's that?"

"It's a firm they set up to sell and and hire out sea-going cruisers. That's their story officially. But they were using it as cover for smuggling all kinds of things into the UK."

"Good heavens! What about his airline? They go all over the Continent I believe. Was he using them too? And his lorries."

That was a new idea to Tam. Sam had only talked about the Cruisers. But if Jackson was using cruisers to smuggle stuff in he'd be bound to have used the aircraft too. And lorries.

"You are exactly right, Mrs. Ackroyd."

"Well I can't say it surprises me," May said, sitting back in her chair with her tea. "I could quite see that woman and him setting up those things just to hide that kind of criminal activity."

"He was a lorry driver for NAAFI before and during the War wasn't he? So he had plenty of chances then for 'helping things fall off the back of the lorry', if you get my meaning?" Tam grinned at May. The wartime words for stealing goods from lorries for the Black Market.

"He had. Not that I ever saw any benefit from it," May smiled back. "But why exactly have you come here to tell me this Mr. Jerningham?

Tam hesitated just briefly. Did May still hate her ex-husband to the degree of wanting to really hit him? As when she'd used him (Tam) to get at Ron and Anne before? Or they had used each other because he'd had his own reasons for going along with her. As now.

"The thing is Mrs. Ackroyd, I can use this information I have, to get at your ex-husband in a harder way than we were able to before. Then the Editor of the local paper I was on killed the story and then your ex-husband must have got at the Magistrates to deal with the case in the way they did that made that story a non-starter with the Sundays too.

"But with this kind of story – involving drugs and guns as it does, it will be of national interest not just local. So a local Editor simply couldn't kill it. I'd go to a London Evening to start with, then get on to a Daily to pick it up and then others will start running with it too. Quite likely the Sundays – and they'll be bound to make an even bigger splash. The London connection will be reinforced by his links with here because the drugs and guns must have come up to London."

"Do you know that as a fact? Bringing drugs and guns into London?" May was shocked at this Especially the guns.

"It's the most likely destination for them. So I'll put it in the story as 'a likelihood'. If you're careful with the way you write, all kinds of angles can be implied so people will believe that way, without you actually stating something as a fact.

"So what I'd like you to say to me, either as flat statements or by mplication, various things I can use. Without me saying they actually came from you," he added hastily.

May closed her mouth on her objection to being directly quoted by name.

"For example, what you said about his lorry-driving days with NAAFI. I can word it in such a way as to imply that he was stealing stuff without saying as much, and that you 'never saw any benefit from it'. That focuses it all on him, and that you were the poor, and innocent, wife."

May nodded. That sounded good.

"What do you want to ask me?"

When Jerningham left an hour later he had a series of articles laid out in his mind. And he knew which Editors to approach.


Ron cheerfully took the top file from the second box of files that Detective Superintendent Wilson had said he could have back three days after he had first been arrested.

He was thinking that the action he had taken over Tim's information about Henderson going on the cargo flights to Paris had convinced him that he and Anne were in the clear. He didn't know that Phillip's responses had reinforced that idea, which was now beginning to make Wilson think that perhaps Henderson's accusations against them had been lies to divert police attention away from Frobisher and, presumably, Barnett.

"Let's check these against your list Mary, so we can see what might still be missing," he said cheerfully. "We'll have time to do at least some before we knock off for the night."

His 'phone rang.

"Mrs. Ackroyd on the line for you Mr. Jackson. She says it's very urgent that she speaks to you."

"Something must have happened to Frank. Put her through, Joan," Ron said at once, putting the 'phone on 'Speaker' so that Anne who was going through the files with them would hear too

"Yes May, what's happened to Frank?" he snapped urgently.

"It's not about Frank."

"If it's not about Frank whats so urgent that you had to 'phone me?" Ron snapped impatiently.

"It's an article in tonight's evening paper. I didn't say half those things that Jerningham says I did. You must believe me. Des was furious with me when he saw an early edition and said I had to 'phone you straight away to explain." May's voice was a mixture of worry and defiance.

"What are you talking about?"

"It's a thing in the evening paper, it's a London one so maybe you don't get it in Folkestone. It says about you and Anne being arrested on Charges of drug smuggling and gun-running using your cruisers and airlines and lorries to do it. And it says, 'He (meaning you Ron) claims to have rescued his daughter from the wreckage of the school but his former wife very much doubts the truth of that'.

"And then it says, 'He worked for NAAFI during the early years of the war when rationing was at its worst but he was never actually prosecuted for helping 'goods fall from the back of his lorries'. His former wife says she never saw any benefit from those activities.'

"And then he says that I said that I wasn't at all surprised by you being arrested on Charges as serious as those. The drugs and gun-running things I mean.

"Then it says 'The police have confirmed that guns and ammunition were found on the firm's premises', and it says again that I said I wasn't surprised about that either as you'd always liked guns and firing them.'

"And then ...."

"Send a copy to me in case I can't get a copy here," Ron interrupted harshly. "I'll read it for myself and see about suing them. And you as well, especially about NAAFI and guns. And next time keep your bloody trap shut to that bastard."

He slammed the 'phone down, breathing heavily.

His 'phone rang again.

"I'm sorry Mr. Jackson but it's Mrs. Ackroyd again. She's – well she's begging to speak to you again."

"Put her through Joan." Furious though he was, that was at May and her lies – and Jerningham - not Joan so it wouldn't be fair to bite her head off.

"Well?" he demanded once through.

"I thought you ought to know Ron ...," this time May was almost timid "...only Jerningham talked of going to the Dailies and Sundays with the story as well."

Ron cut her off.

"Joan, get me Mr. Sampson at the airfield please. Let's carry on with the files Mary."

Five minutes later his 'phone rang.

"We've another publicity problem, Richard." Ron explained.

"Sounds as though you really have got grounds for suing this time

Ron. Look, I know you've always used the Howards as your Legal Eagles but I know a guy that does quite a lot of handling this kind of thing – suing for defamation of character and so on, so he'd have more specialist knowledge of that area. I could have a word with him, then when we see what's actually in the papers we can decide what action to take. But as your ex-wife has denied immediately making those statements you might have a difficult job to prove she did even if Jerningham insists that she did. You'd have to use her against him and then him against her."

"I'm not so much out to get her, Richard. Not really. Not if she didn't say those things that  Jerningham says she did."

"Sure. But that's only what she's saying to you now. But it may not go as far as going to Court anyway because my pal will most likely recommend trying to settle it out of Court, part of which would need to include a public retraction of those allegations."

"That's what we need really," Anne interrupted. "And as soon as possible. So we'll do what you suggest. And maybe we could get the police to make a public statement something like the allegations were made against us, have been thoroughly investigated and have been found to have no truth in them whatsoever."

"We'll have a go at getting that too."

The postman delivered a packet from May with the next morning's mail. Ron opened that first and spread the newspaper out on the kitchen table. Anne and Tim came over to read it with him.

"The Headline flared 'Flawed 'Hero' arrested on drug and gun-running Charges'.

"That's a double lie to start with," Anne said touching the sentences about Kathleen's rescue. "Your Dad has never 'Claimed' he rescued Kathleen, Tim. But I know he did because I've talked to Ralph Smith, your Dad's Chief Warden who had it direct from one of the team of rescuers he had with him at the time."

"Dad ..." Tim put his finger on the paragraph about guns,"...did you have any guns at home?"

Ron was silent for a few moments.

"I suppose it'll be alright to tell you now that the war's over, but don't you tell anyone else Tim. In the War I was a Warden as you know. But early on, before the bombing really started some of us Wardens were asked if we'd be willing to volunteer for some training to be a Resistance if the the Jerries invaded and occupied us. I did and so did some others but we weren't allowed to tell anyone, not even our wives and kids. So I had some training in handling guns and explosives on some of the days and nights when as far as your mother knew I was on my 'overnight' runs lorrydriving for NAAFI. We weren't given guns to have at home because we had to be a secret army. In the end of course with the Jerries not invading I just kept on being a Warden. I never told your mother any of that but going by what she says there, maybe she did know all along."

"Or maybe she just wanted to blacken your character still more, linking you with guns," Anne said quietly. "If she even did say it, given what Jerningham is doing and what she said to you on the 'phone."

"It's time we were going to work. We'll pick up the Dailies on the way."

Richard was already waiting for them at the office when Anne and Ron arrived. They went through the newspapers but only found a half-column on an inside page in two of the Dailies and they were purely factual with none of the comments attributed to May in the previous evening's newspaper.

"We must still go after the evening newspaper and Jerningham Ron," Richard declared. "And May. I know that she 'phoned you, and maybe she did sound contrite on the line, but she is very directly involved and she is quoted. Then if she denies saying those things in her defence, we can say we'll use that in hitting Jerningham and the paper.

"The other thing is that paper could well run more stories. By slapping a lawsuit on them immediately we may be able to stop them in their tracks."

"Richard's right Ron," Anne agreed.

"Okay. Let's contact your pal, Richard. See what he says."

"I've already provisionally fixed a meeting at his office for 11 o'clock. I'll just confirm it." He reached for the 'phone.

Francis Newcome was a middle-aged, keen-eyed, athletic looking man in a well-appointed office in a quiet street behind Dover's seafront.

"Suppose you summarise your situation, Mr. Jackson," Newcome said briskly once introductions had been made by Richard.

Briefly Ron told him how they'd been arrested, the alleged offences and what had happened. The fact they knew Tam Jerningham from a previous encounter some years before, what he was saying Ron's former wife had told him and about May's 'phone call. They put the newspapers on the desk, open at the correct pages. Throughout Newcome had been making notes.

"Richard told me that he thought we should sue the newspaper, Jerningham and Mrs. Ackroyd, Mr. Jackson."

"I'm not too happy about suing my ex-wife but I can follow his reasoning for it."

"I see. While I can perhaps understand your feelings about that Mr. Jackson, I do agree with Richard. So we could use a backdoor tactic. At the same time as writing to the newspaper I send her a letter about suing her with a demand that she make a public apology and withdrawal of her published comments as well as demanding a substantial sum in compensation, both to you personally and to each one of your Companies for damage to your and their reputations.

"But then the day after she would have received the letter you 'phone her to say you are not too happy about the 'substantial damages' that I'd demanded from her in the letter, that the real culprits are Jerningham and the newspaper and you personally felt that damages should only be paid by those two. If she would be willing to support your claim against the other two, repeating her telephoned comments to you that she had not made those published comments to Jerningham, then you might be able to persuade me and the Carruthers Group not to pursue the damages claims against her personally."

Ron stirred uneasily and shot a sideways look at Anne. He didn't like these kinds of dealings. How was it right to frighten May – and Des – in this underhand way?

"I understand what you're thinking Ron," Anne said quietly. "But May must have made some kind of comments to Jerningham for him to use what he did in the way he did. And she will be let off a major part of the hook she's put herself on if she agrees to do what is the right thing after all."

"I'll think about it," Ron muttered finally. "What line will you be taking with Jerningham and the newspaper? And what about the Dailies?"

"The Dailies have only accurately reported the facts, all of which are true from what you've told me, so there are no grounds to sue. The evening paper is very different. So we hit them hard, demand massive damages for both of you, Mr. and Mrs. Jackson, personally and on behalf of all and each of your Companies, the Damages to be doubled for the publication of each of any further articles. As that will mount up massively very quickly that should bring them to an immediate halt. I'll start that by sending the Editor a telegram as soon as we've finished to prevent anything further being published tonight.

"I shall also contact the other major evening papers to inform them of our action, your entire innocence and something of your background. Richard has already given me some ideas."

"Well – if you think that would help the case."

"It most certainly would. Now this comment by Mrs. Ackroyd about guns. Have you had or used guns in the past? In wartime? Or since?"

"I was a Warden and a lorry driver for NAAFI, not in the Services and never had any guns at home," Ron said flatly.

"So Richard told me." Newcome paused. ""Were you in one of the 'Stay-behind' groups?"

Ron shot a quick look at him. How the hell did he know about that Top-Secret matter?

"I was in the War Office at the time, Ron. Home Defence," Newcome said.

"I can't say anything about that," Ron said finally.

"Of course not," Newcome nodded. "You wife has no basis for what she said then? Of her own knowledge?"

"None whatsoever," Ron said emphatically.

"Thank you. About the tactics in relation to Mrs. Ackroyd?"

"If you really think that would be the best way." Ron nodded reluctantly.


Ron passed a very unpleasant two days worrying about May's reaction to the solicitor's letter. And Des's too. If he had been 'furious' with May for the article, what would be his reaction to the letter demanding 'substantial damages'?

At 10 o'clock on Thursday, he 'phoned May. To his surprise Des answered.

"Des? Ron Jackson here. Do you know if May received a letter from my solicitor yesterday?

"Yes. But she only told me this morning." Des's tone seemed to hover between anger and worry. "How much do you have in mind for the 'substantial damages' you are demanding?"

"That's what I wanted to talk to May about."

After a pause, "Why not talk to me? After all, I shall be the one paying them."

"That's true enough I suppose, but it was May who talked to Jerningham."

"It was. But I will be the one paying for her mistakes."

Ron really did want to talk to May, but Des was obviously blocking that. Maybe he was worried about her talking them into more trouble rather than out of it.

"I was going to tell her that personally, I'm not at all keen of hitting her with any kind of financial damages at all. That's the solicitor's idea. To hit everyone. For me, May is different from Jerningham and that newspaper though. They need to be hit and will be. She doesn't. Not with a massive damages claim. So she won't be."

"Thank you Ron," Des said after a pause. "Thank you. My solicitor whom I contacted immediately May told me, said the sum could well be several thousands of pounds altogether."

"So my solicitor said. There is one thing though."

"Yes?"

"I'm sure that Jerningham has deliberately misquoted May or even reported things as quotes that she never said to sensationalise the story. So I'd want her to be willing to be a witness against him to that if necessary. If it should come to that. But, between ourselves, as far as we are concerned we are hoping to settle out of Court."

"I see." A long pause. "Suppose – just suppose - May is unable to say precisely that on oath in Court? That she couldn't deny making those kind of statements to Jerningham?"

"What I said earlier about the damages was not intended as a bargaining counter, Des. It stands whatever May is or is not able to say in Court on Oath."

"I very much appreciate that Ron." Des paused. "I'm sure that May will want to write to that Editor immediately to correct what was alleged she said to Jerningham in the article. About how she was misquoted and that she demands that he print her letter as prominently in the newspaper as the article. Though I can – shall we say – draft the letter, I can't guarantee the Editor will print exactly what is in it."

"I realise that Des. And thanks."

"Of course."

Ron felt pretty sure that Des would keep his part of the pact. The plan had worked. He hadn't particularly want to hit May. Not really. In spite of everything. But he had wanted a public retraction.


Detective Superintendent Wilson looked again through the papers scattered across his desk. They didn't really answer the question of who to believe. Henderson or the Jacksons.

Henderson was unshakable in his statements that it was the Jacksons who were the organisers of the smuggling ring. That they would come to the Marina to collect the drugs from him and he had no idea of where they disposed of them next. He insisted that he knew nothing of anyone called Frobisher or Barnett and that the policeman who said he saw the chap Frobisher at the Marina was simply wrong.

And then there was that newspaper article that had talked of them gun-running and that Jackson had handled and 'liked' guns, confirmed by his ex-wife. Then they had found that Luger and ammunition in Henderson's flat at the Marina. At first he'd assumed they were Henderson's but he had told them they weren't, that the weapon and ammunition had given to him by Jackson 'to look after'. So, Wilson wondered, had there been gun-running to someone as well, though Henderson denied that flatly. Jackson had said he knew nothing about the weapon and fingerprint testing showed only Henderson's prints on the gun and ammunition.

If gun-running was part of the racket and they were being passed on to Frobisher and Barnett then that spelled big trouble for the Met.

But against that were the statements from the Jacksons, backed by Grover that the Jacksons knew nothing about the smuggling at all. And it was Jackson himself who had alerted him to the Airline smuggling that had caught those two pilots red-handed..

Or had that been a deliberate sacrifice of some underlings to maintain his cover of respectability?

He could pull in Frobisher on the strength of the PC's statement that he'd stopped Frobisher for Speeding in Sandwich and had clearly recognised him at the Marina talking to Henderson though Henderson had denied that Frobisher had ever been there. Which was then suspicious in itself.


"Sit down Frobisher," Wilson ordered.

They were in an Interview Room at a London Police Station so a Met. Detective Inspector and a Constable were in with them. He had filled in a lot of Frobisher's background before they'd arrested him.

Algy Frobisher shrugged, sat down opposite Wilson and the Detective Inspector, smiling at them benignly.

"You were stopped in Sandwich, Kent for Speeding 27$^{th}$ June," snapped Wilson.

"Was I?" Frobisher frowned as though puzzled.

"Here's a copy of the Speeding Ticket and Receipt that you'd paid the fine." Wilson pushed them across the table.

Frobisher studied them.

"Ah yes. So my sins committed in Kent have caught me up even in London. It was most unfortunate, you know. Touched the accelerator just a miniscule too heavily by mistake. But a Jag has pretty powerful acceleration you know. Or perhaps you don't. In any case, I have paid my debt to society as you see from the receipt for the fine that I paid immediately as an honest citizen. So why does a Detective Superintendent of the Kent Constabulary come all the way to London to pursue me on this very minor matter that has already been settled?"

"You were also seen at the Carruthers Cruisers Marina that is currently being investigated for smuggling offences."

"Not possible. I've never been there. Where is this Marina anyway?"

"Just a couple of miles down the road from Sandwich."

"Is it really? Well I'm not interested in boats so I wouldn't go to look at any, anyway. Too slow for my liking."

"You were clearly identified as talking to Henderson there. By a Police Constable."

"And exactly when was that supposed to have been?"

The DI knew that Frobisher would produce an alibi for whatever date they selected in about five seconds flat with half a dozen witnesses swearing he was somewhere else at the time. And the PC hadn't been able to give an exact time.

"We know that Henderson passed on smuggled drugs to you, smuggled in on Carruthers Cruisers from Calais," dodging the question.

For a split second Frobisher's lips tightened, spotted by both policemen, thinking Henderson must have betrayed him.

"Who's Henderson?" Frobisher asked.

"Manager of the Marina. Hires out cruisers and uses that as a cover to smuggle in drugs."

"And so – simply because I happened to be driving through that pleasant little town called 'Sandwich' because I was curious to see what a town with that odd name looked like, at one time, an offence was committed at some other place miles away from the town, at some other time, by someone else and lo and behold, I'm suddenly a suspect of being involved in it!

"Tell me Wilson, just how many hundreds of other people have you arrested solely because of those two factors? Or did this Henderson chappie suddenly announce that he'd had an inspiration and produced my name out of his conjurer's hat?"

"We know you were there because of the PC's evidence."

"So presumably it was not this Henderson that produced my name out of his hat after all! It was just a PC – who apparently can't even give you a date when he says he saw me."

He looked from one to the other enquiringly with raised eyebrows.

"Dear me gentlemen – I use the term very loosely – I shall have to consult my solicitor with a view to seeing how much in the way of Damages I can claim from you both individually and the Chief Constables of your respective Police Forces as well, for Wrongful Arrest, Harassment, and the Besmirching of my good name.

Accusing me of smuggling."

"How's Barnett doing nowadays?" the DI cut in unexpectedly.

"Barnett? Barnett?" Frobisher frowned. "I don't think I know any Barnett."

"Come on Frobisher, you know damn well who I mean," the DI snapped impatiently. "Your mate, that lousy villain Lancelot Barnett."

Frobisher's lips tightened and he glared at the DI.

"If you are meaning MISTER Barnett, Craven, my friend is not well. Which is to be expected in the circumstances. That you know damn well about. Injuries that he got while fighting for his country while you were skulking here like the bloody coward you are." His slightly mocking tone had vanished as he growled the words in his fury. He slammed to his feet. "I want to go. Now. You bloody pair with your accusations make this room reek," he snarled.

"You can go," the DI said quietly and Frobisher stormed out, immediately followed by the Constable.

"My God!" whispered Wilson. "That really got to him, didn't it?"

The DI nodded soberly. "Yeah. One thing I'll say for Frobisher – and it is only this one thing – his loyalty to Barnett is total. Stems from what happened to them, especially Barnett, in the war years.

"It's an odd thing about Barnett, he runs that gang of his as though it was his old SOE Group – complete loyalty to each other. So he looks after his villains and expects total loyalty in return."

"From villains?" Wilson sneered. "They're not loyal to anyone but themselves."

"Normally yes but not in Barnett's case. He gets it partly by personality, partly because his real Gang members know he is totally loyal to them too. Other people by fear or rewards.

"One guy did try to double-cross him. As it happens I was the copper that found the body. Not a pretty sight. Nothing could be proved against Barnett but the story went around."

As Wilson went back to Folkestone he knew that interview had taken him no further forward except to emphasis that Frobisher and Barnett were certainly not people to cross. Which would give Henderson the strongest possible reason not to 'betray' them, and so the maximum incentive to divert attention on to the Jacksons.

The trouble was, he had no one else in the frame beyond

suspicions of those two and they were only suspicions, with no hard evidence at all to back them, that really it was Frobisher who had collected those drugs, and maybe guns too, from Henderson. Or thev Jacksons. He had no real evidence against anyone beyond Henderson and the pilots.

Beyond them was only Henderson's Statement and that was all against the Jacksons.

Grover had said he knew nothing about the Jacksons' involvement. But that could be simply explained by Henderson having covered for the Jacksons until he was in the frame himself.


"What do you want now?" Ron demanded, looking at Wilson and Revell with a mixture of worry and irritation as they came into his office.

"Just a little chat," Wilson said as he and Revell sat down without being invited to. "You know, Henderson is completely unshakable in his evidence that he handed the drugs over to you and Mrs. Jackson."

"And we are just as unshakable in our denials," Ron riposted immediately.

"Which makes what lawyers call 'a conflict of evidence'," Revell commented.

"So you have to decide who to believe. Henderson, a crook you caught in the act of bringing in the drugs on one of my cruisers – or me against whom you've got no evidence at all, someone who's never committed any offence of dishonesty and has an impeccable record. I know who'd I believe in a choice between those two."

"Of course you would," agreed Wilson. "But then you've not been in my position of hearing the same kinds of things from equally 'respectable' people when they've been in the same position as you are now. So I'm not nearly so ready to take statements on their face value from anyone any more.

"In this kind of situation the police usually take the line it should be left to a jury to make the decision based on evidence given to them in Court by both sides at the time."

Ron stared at him, worry surging. That sounded as though they were actually going to put him and Anne on trial! God knew what that would do to their reputations - personally and the Companies.

And could you trust a jury to acquit innocent people? There had been plenty of miscarriages of justice before.

"So we'd have to put both you and Mrs. Jackson on Trial," Wilson was saying. "With those kinds of very serious Charges against you, you're bound to both be Remanded in Custody. Held in prison for weeks on end while the Court processes are gone through.

"On the other hand, if you admitted it was you who collected the drugs from Henderson, then Mrs. Jackson could be dropped out of it altogether," he added softly,

Ron looked bleakly at the two policemen, thinking furiously.

That would get Anne out from under, but if he took the line they were suggesting, everything they had built up together over the past 15 years would still be ruined.

His admitting he'd organised the racket for smuggling in the drugs and guns would destroy everything. His reputation with the children, his friends, the Companies. And he'd get years in prison. On the other hand if he and Anne fought this together then in spite of the worst these police would do, their reputations and their Companies could be cleared.

If the Jury decided the right way. And if they didn't – would it be any worse? Yes. Anne would be in prison too.

"You know damn well neither of us had anything to do with it and that Henderson is lying to make out his part was smaller than it really was," he snapped.

"You'll have your chance to prove it. If you are determined to stick to that story," Wilson responded.

"It's not for me to prove I haven't smuggled drugs and guns in. It's for you to prove I have."

"We've got Henderson's Statement."

"Which is a pack of lies."

Wilson and Revell stood up.

"Ronald Jackson, I am Arresting you on the Charge of importing illegal drugs into this country. Anything you say will be taken down and may be used in evidence against you," Wilson snapped.

"I need to notify my Solicitor."

Wilson smiled slightly. "I'm sure your secretary will do that for you. And notify anyone else."

Ron buzzed for Mary.

"Mary ...," Ron said as soon as she came in, notebook in hand, " ... I've been arrested again on the same Charge as before. Notify James Howard will you please?" He glanced at Wilson. "Will I be Remanded in Custody, as you put it and for how long if I am?"

"You'll appear in front of the Magistrates tomorrow morning and they'll decide."

"And what about Mrs. Jackson?"

Wilson hesitated. "We won't be arresting her. At this stage."

"So notify Mrs. Jackson as soon as she gets here from Deal, Mary. And anyone else you consider necessary. And cancel my appointments for the next couple of days." Ron indicated his diary. "Well?" he glared at Wilson as he stood up. "Are we going?"

In Court the next morning the Magistrates listened to the police evidence of Ron's arrest, fixed a date for Committal for Trial to the Quarter Sessions at Lewes and immediately granted Ron Bail till then. The Prosecution raised no objection.

As expected there was more publicity, including in the London newspapers. Especially the evening paper they were suing who had made only a partial retraction centred around the statements Jerningham had attributed to May.


Barnett and Frobisher had a regular morning routine. Together they skimmed through all the London newspapers, the previous evenings, the dailies and nearby locals, which Barnett described as 'Intelligence gathering' which had proved immensely useful to them many more times than once.

"Some interesting bits in a couple of locals on that Jackson that Henderson used as cover for us, Lance," observed Frobisher.

"Oh?" Barnett looked up from his pile of newspapers.

"On his background. Putting bits together, he was in Lewisham during the War, driving for NAAFI, so was Reserved, but became a Warden, was involved in a fair number of rescues during the Blitz, rescued his daughter in a school that was bombed in '43 when she'd had both legs smashed in the wreckage at the risk of his own life, started up firms in '44 using the name of his girl friend in Folkestone that he later married who was Carruthers. And interestingly, from the beginning they have had the policy of giving priority to employing ex-Service people especially wounded ex-Service people still suffering from their effects. And all their Companies have maintained that policy since. He's now remanded on Bail pending Trial on Drug smuggling. Ours."

"Let me see." Barnett took his time reading the articles. "Did he have any connection with us?"

"None. It was Henderson's idea to start with and we developed them. Jackson was not involved at all at any stage. Henderson said there was no need to cut him in and later he said if Jackson got a whiff of anything he'd put the slammers on it. I suppose he gave the cops Jackson's name to make out he was only a cog and to keep us out of it. I'd made it clear to him early on we'd see that as 'Betrayal'."

"Mmm." There was a silence. "Maybe I'm getting sentimental in my old age Algy – but I like the sound of Jackson. We'll keep track of what goes on about him."


A month later the Committal Proceeding rattled through and Ron was Remanded, again on Bail, to Quarter Sessions.

Two weeks later Henderson, Watson and Grover appeared there. They all pleaded 'Guilty' to the Charges of Drug Smuggling and again Henderson named Ron as the person collecting the drugs from him that had been smuggled in on the cruisers and the aircraft. Grover felt he couldn't contradict that in Court (after Henderson had 'explained' certain things to him while waiting in the cells below the Court before Trial) though he still couldn't forget Henderson's earlier insistence that Jackson must never know. His Barrister didn't mention it in Court when he tried to show that Grover's part was minimal, though he'd told him about it earlier

Henderson was sentenced to four years prison, Watson and Grover to one year each.


Ron and Anne stared miserably at the newspapers reports. If Henderson had got four years, how much more would Ron get? As Henderson had made it clear again that Ron was the main organiser?

The police would be bound to make a lot out of the fact that Ron was giving them no more names of people he'd passed the drugs on to. He hadn't because he couldn't. But they would say he was 'shielding the rest of his gang'.

On the day of the Sitting, Ron and Anne made their way to Lewes, and he Surrendered to his Bail as required and was put in a cell even though he was pleading 'Not Guilty'.

It was early afternoon when his case was called and he was whisked up the stairs to stand in the Dock.

The Prosecuting Barrister outlined the Case against him. That Ron had set up Carruthers Cruisers and Carruthers Airlines either with the intention of using them as cover for his planned Drugs Smuggling operation or developing that use afterwards perhaps to fund the further expansion of both Companies into the Tourist field. The main evidence against him was from Tom Henderson, the Manager whom Mr. Jackson had appointed to the Marina and then chosen to organise the actual smuggling operation. He had already been sentenced to four years imprisonment for his part in the offences having pleaded Guilty. He would call Mr. Henderson first.

Henderson came into Court from the cells, looking around boldly. He caught Ron's eye, then looked away quickly.

He took the Oath and looked at the Prosecuting Barrister.

"Mr. Henderson, would you please tell the Court how Mr. Jackson approached you to set up the Drug Smuggling operation."

"He didn't," Henderson said immediately.

"I beg your pardon?" the Barrister said blankly.

"Mr. Jackson didn't approach me to set up any drug smuggling operation. It was all my idea," Henderson repeated, looking steadily at him but with the faintest of smiles.

"Then how was it raised?"

"Like I just said, it was my idea, my smuggling operation. Ron Jackson had nothing to do with it at all."

Ron was staring at him as bewildered as everyone else in Court, wondering what the hell was going on!

"In your Statement to the Police at the outset you said that he did and you've repeated it many times since. I'll read the Statement to you." The Barrister scrabbled through his papers.

"No need to. I admit I said it then. But I was lying."

The Barrister stared at him, then rallied.

"In a Court Hearing earlier when your case was dealt with, you said, on Oath I remind you, that he approached you with the suggestion."

"Sure. I said that then. What I'm telling you now, is that then I was lying."

"Or were you telling the truth then, but you're lying now, perhaps because you have been threatened." The Barrister looked very openly at Ron. "But I can promise you total protection from any threat that may have been made against you to change your story. And that any reward promised for changing your story now is meaningless."

"I'll tell you again," Henderson said with an air of weary patience. "I'm telling you, the Judge, the Jury and everyone else, the truth now. Ron Jackson had nothing whatsoever to do with my smuggle. I was mighty careful not to let him know because I knew that he would go straight to the cops if he heard the slightest whisper of what we were doing."

"What about the gun found in your flat? You said earlier Jackson had given you that 'to look after'" The Barrister was getting desperate.

Henderson grinned at him, at the Judge, at the Jury.

"It was mine. I 'liberated' it from a Jerry soldier towards the end of the last war. No one else knew about it. Including Ron Jackson."

"So tell us why you named Mr. Jackson as the Organiser earlier then?"

Henderson grinned triumphantly again at him, the Judge and the Jury.

"Simple. It took most of the heat off me, didn't it? If I wasn't the Head Honcho, but just one of the guys, I'd get sentenced according. Lighter than if it was known I was the Boss. And Jackson was the obvious fall-guy for that."

"So why have you changed your story now?"

"I got the lighter sentence didn't I? You can't increase it now.and Jackson wasn't bad as a legit Boss. Certainly better than some I've had. So telling the truth about him now, puts us square."

"If you expect us to believe that you lied on Oath before ...," began the Judge.

"I did lie before!" Henderson shouted abruptly losing his self-satisfied smirk.

" ... and you are telling us the truth now ...,"

"Which I am!"

" ... then you are liable to a Charge of Perjury which carries a sentence of imprisonment which could very well be added to your present sentence," the Judge finished but looking at the Prosecuting Barrister.

"So what?" Henderson shrugged.

"Your Honour, to uphold the dignity of the Court I cannot see there can be any alternative but to prosecute this Witness for Perjury. If he persists in his present story."

"Well?" The Judge looked at Henderson.

"I lied before. Not now. Ron Jackson had nothing at all to do with it. I was bloody careful that he didn't get to know, because I knew that as soon as he did he'd run off to the cops," Henderson said emphatically.

"Do you wish to make a Submission, Mr. Jenkins?" The Judge looked at the Defence Barrister who so far hadn't said a single word.

"Yes indeed Your Honour. As the chief or indeed the only Witness the Prosecution has against my client the Defendant, has changed his story totally and has told this Court his previous Statement implicating Ron Jackson was lies and emphatically declared that Mr. Jackson 'had nothing at all to do with it' – to quote him, I ask the Court to Discharge Mr. Jackson without any stain on his character whatsoever."

"Do you want to make any observations, Mr. Simmonds?"

"No." The Prosecuting Barrister knew he had a dead case.

"Gentlemen of the Jury ...," began the Judge turning to them.

Outside the Court, smiling delightedly, Anne and Ron were photographed, had questions shouted at them and, on the quick whispered advice from Richard, told the Reporters they would be holding a Press Conference in the Bar of the nearby hotel in fifteen minutes.

In the cells, Henderson buried his head in his hands trembling, but with relief.

Jackson was free. Henderson knew he would get a bad grilling from the cops about who he'd passed the drugs on to, but that didn't worry him in the slightest. He'd simply stay shtumm. Not say a single word at all to them no matter what pressure they brought on him. If they prosecuted him for Perjury and he got more time – what the hell?

The vital thing, the only thing of any importance, was that Jackson had been freed. So Barnett and his goons wouldn't be coming for him in the nick. Or afterwards.


The day after Frobisher and Barnett had read about Ron being sent to Quarter Sessions in the newspapers, as soon as Algy had joined him, Barnett had said abruptly, "Algy, get a message to Henderson. He's got to get Jackson off the hook. If he does, the bonus for his silence stays. If he doesn't, I shall be displeased with him. I shall feel Betrayed."

"Sure Lance. Right away."

Frobisher hurried out. He had to give some instructions to a solicitor.

The next morning a smartly dressed lawyer arrived at Canterbury Prison to see Henderson 'about the forthcoming Appeal'. As he hadn't put in an Appeal or asked to see a solicitor Henderson was rather puzzled but decided he had better see him. Mr. Barnett had sent a message to him via a solicitor twice before.

"Mr.Barnett is concerned about your comments about Mr. Jackson," the Solicitor explained in a quiet 'Oxford' voice.

Henderson relaxed, sat back in his chair and pushed his hands into his pockets.

"There's no need for him to worry tell him. Jackson knows nothing about either Mr. Frobisher or Mr. Barnett. In fact he knows nothing about nothing. What I've said would have hit him like a bombshell," he grinned.

"Quite so. So why did you name him as the Organiser?"

"It's the Top Guy in the organisation that cops the big sentence isn't it?  So by pitching him as that I became only one of the smaller guys so I got a smaller sentence."

"Though Mr. Jackson was, and is, completely innocent?"

"Why should that matter to me?"

"Because it matters to Mr. Barnett.  For reasons that I do not know, Mr. Barnett is displeased that you have involved Jackson in the way you have.  You are to extricate Mr. Jackson from the position you have put him in."

Henderson stared at him.

"Why?  What's Mr. Barnett want that for?"

"As I have already told you, I don't know his reasons and nor would I tell you if I did.  But understand this Henderson, if you do not do what Mr. Barnett wants, indeed if you do not actually succeed in doing what Mr. Barnett wants, then the consequences upon you will be dire.  Severe.

"Do I need to point out to you that you will be in prison for the next four years, incarcerated with many extremely unpleasant and violent people?  People who for many reasons would take a great deal of pleasure in making your life extremely unpleasant, not to say extremely hurtful physically, if Mr. Barnett's wishes are not carried out.  And I was to add that should you somehow manage to survive all that will happen to you during the sentence, you will still never make it back to Canada alive afterwards.

"However, carry out his wishes and the bonus on release for your silence stands."

The solicitor stood up and drew on his gloves, then leaned across the table to stare Henderson in the eyes.

"Be sensible for once in your miserable life and do exactly what Mr. Barnett wants," he almost whispered, but with menace throbbing.  "Exactly what he wants.  Which means that Mr. Jackson must go free from the Court.  A suggestion.  At Jackson's Trial, assuming he pleads Not Guilty, you will be the main if not the only Witness against him.  Change your story and say that before when you were implicating him, you were lying.  As you have just told me you were."

"But don't they have laws about Perjury in this country?"

"They do.  But an additional period in prison here, if that happens, would be infinitely preferable to the dire consequences to you of incurring Mr. Barnett's displeasure.    He will feel he has been 'Betrayed' by you."

Henderson went pallid as he remembered, sickeningly, what Algy had said happened to people who 'Betrayed' Mr. Barnett.  So his relief was as great as theirs when Ron walked free.


For the next three days much of Ron's time was taken up with 'phone calls and personal contacts making sure that every single past and current customer of the Carruthers' Group of Companies knew that he had been completely cleared and why Henderson had made the accusation in the first place.  He also made sure that the news was widely publicised in newspapers, radio and TV.

At his insistence Customs set up a highly visible system of frequent spot checks at Wingmore and the Marina to emphasise there was no possibility of smuggling in anything at any time.

Another Manager was appointed at the Marina and two more pilots were recruited to replace Watson and Grover.  He asked Detective Superintendent Wilson to do Police checks on them, and followed up all the applicants references extra carefully.

# Chapter 13
## Confrontations

"It'll be your 21$^{st}$ Birthday in three months Tim. We're thinking of celebrating with some kind of shindig. Any ideas?" They were driving to Wingmore.

Tim shot a look at Ron. He'd been thinking the same.

"Well I suppose we could make it formal – a dinner and dance to follow. Or just a quiet family do." He knew which he'd prefer.

"It's a big day, Tim! We can't let it go with just something like a quiet family do! So you draw up a guest list – but maybe not to include the whole town of Dover in with the whole town of Folkestone for it."

"Thanks Dad."

"And any ideas about a birthday present? Something suitably special of course."

Tim hesitated. He knew what he'd really like but that would be just too special.

"I was wondering about trying some driving lessons Dad. So maybe a course of them?"

"You mean on a left hand drive?"

Ron was conscious of Tim's semi-paralysed left arm for gear changes and his left ankle that was still giving him a lot of trouble at times, for operating the clutch.

"No Dad. I want to get a normal car sometime." He paused. "I think I could do the gear changes okay." He paused again, then confessed. "Terry has been letting me try his a few times on the perimeter track at the Airfield."

Ron had always believed in encouraging Tim to push himself to the limits of his capabilities so when Terry had 'phoned him about Tim hinting at it, Ron had quietly encouraged it, neither of them telling Tim that Ron knew.

"Could you manage it okay?"

"I'll need a lot more practice to drive properly. On proper roads at proper speeds."

"Did it cause much pain? In your arm and ankle?"

"A bit. But that should get better as I get used to it I should think."

"I'll contact a Driving Instructor and book some lessons straightaway then. I'll book ten of them round your shifts and we can see how we go. We'll need to see about a Provisional Driving Licence for you but you could have some lessons at the Airfield as that's private land while that's coming through."

"Cor! Thanks Dad." Tim had been expecting to wait till his 21$^{st}$ to start!

"Dad, would it be okay for this number to come to the shindig? As a Dinner-dance?" Tim handed Ron a list that evening.

Ron glanced down the list and passed it to Anne.

"I'd like to invite Mum – mother as well as Frank," Tim added, almost defiantly.

"Of course Tim," Ron said at once. "But you didn't invite father. Des."

"Well, I didn't think you'd like that. As things are."

"He did look after you while you were in hospital and afterwards till you decided you wanted to come here," Ron said quietly. "And he is married to your mother. So unless you definitely don't want him to come I think it would be nice to invite him as well."

"Right. I will then," Tim declared happily.

As he'd expected, when he told Kathleen she made it obvious she was not happy about it but he wasn't put off. He had never been as 'anti-mum' (as he put it) as Kathleen had been. He had never blamed her for bringing him back from Evacuation even though it was only four months later he'd been so injured when the school was bombed that midday.


The night before Tim's 'shindig', as he called it, May barely slept. At times she almost regretted accepting the invitation, but as Frank was wanting to go and Des felt they should, she felt she couldn't refuse. It wasn't that she didn't want to go to Tim's 21$^{st}$, it was how Kitty would treat her when they met as they were bound to, that worried her. It was different from Kitty's wedding though. The Davies's from Wales would not be there.

They were driving down to Folkestone in the morning intending to arrive at the Hotel where it was being held just before the time of the dinner and decide on the time of leaving on how they were treated. They wouldn't stay to the end though as it was finishing quite late and she had insisted they came home that evening though Des had suggested they could book rooms to stay at the hotel and come back the next day. She was expecting an uncomfortable time.

Ron had arranged that the top table would curve down into the two side tables rather than set square across the top. On the top table was Tim (as the Guest of Honour) with Janice by him at Tim's special request, Ron and Anne on one side, Sonia, Sarah, Kathleen and Terry on his other Curving down but on the side table from Anne, were Frank, May and Des, then other guests mostly from the Airfield but a couple of people Tim knew because of Janice, and on the other side were Richard and other Board members and a few other guests.

They had made good time to Folkestone so May, Des and Frank strolled along the sea front and up the Zig-zag Path. They got to the hotel five minutes before they were called in to Dinner. They still had time to check the Seating Plan at the door so were able to make their way straight to their places without milling around looking for place-names.

Inside the door Tim and Ron were greeting the guests as they came in.

"I'm very glad you were able to make it," Ron said quietly shaking hands with Des (who'd come in before May and Frank) then May and Frank.

"So am I," Tim said, shaking hands with Des, then he hugged May and gently punched the 15 year old Frank on the arm.

As soon as they sat down May covertly glanced around, immediately seeing Kitty (as she still thought of her) with a tall young man who must be Terry, her husband. May had never seen him before apart from that photo in the newspaper years ago now. But Kitty did look well, May was glad to see.

Then Kitty caught her eye – and immediately looked away without smiling before turning to say something to Terry. May's tentative smile vanished.

Des said something to her that she barely heard. "What did you say?" she asked hurriedly.

After the excellent dinner, Ron tinged a bell as he stood up.

"Before I propose the toast to our Guest of Honour, Tim, I'd just like to say a few words.

"He told me I must not say anything to embarrass him." (Some laughter). Ron glanced down at him. "Tough." (More laughter) "Some years ago – on the morning of the 21$^{st}$ January 1943 to be exact – I looked down at a 9 year old lad lying unconscious in a hospital bed, badly injured by a Jerry bomb. I had been told by a doctor the night before that if he lived, which was doubtful, he would be permanently crippled, probably in a wheelchair and never be able to work or lead a normal life." Ron paused. "He did live didn't he? After all he's right there before our very eyes! (More laughter). He's not in a wheelchair. And from the day he left school – he's worked! (Cheers) At least Mr. Finsbury at the Control Tower tells me he works! (Laughter) And two days ago Tim was awarded his Air Controllers Certificate so now he's a fully qualified Air Traffic Controller. (Cheers and applause)

"It's not just that either," Ron went on quietly. "Tim has always pushed himself to the maximum of his capacity and has done things, achieved things, that that awful morning I never thought he ever would or could. As soon as he arrived at Folkestone he announced he wanted to buy a bike. He'd already saved up the money for it. I must admit I was doubtful, but I believed he should tackle life head-on and uninjured kids want to have a bike. So we got it, he learned to ride it – skinning his knees several times and necessitating repairs to his clothes (Laughter) but he did it. (Cheers and applause)

"But not so long ago he decided he wanted to put the rest of us in still more peril – he wanted to learn to drive a car! I suggested a left-hand drive with the gear on the best side to change with his right hand but he threw that idea out of the window straightaway. He insisted he wanted to drive a 'normal' car. I'm very pleased to tell you, yesterday morning he Passed his Driving Test." (Cheers and Applause) "I shall of course be putting a national alert out for the whole population to be aware of the peril we are now in. (Laughter)

Ron looked down at Tim. "I'm more proud of you that I can possibly say, Tim," he said quietly. He looked up speaking more loudly. "You know, I nearly forgot that vital matter on a birthday, especially a 21$^{st}$ Birthday. The present." Anne handed him a smallish packet. "A model car to add to the collection you've built up over the years. (Some cheers and 'Aaahs'). There's another one a bit bigger outside the hotel. But I think you have to fit these into it somewhere." He held up a bunch of car keys. "With our love and Best Wishes".

There was a burst of laughter and applause. Anne began slapping the table and calling, 'Speech! Speech! Speech!' Others joined in and Ron propelled Tim to his feet, scarlet-faced.

"Well – all I can say is thank you all very much for coming, and Mum and Dad for laying all this on. And that car is the greatest present! Say – it's not a Rolls Royce like the model is it?" he added in pretended panic.

"No son, it's not a Rolls Royce," Ron assured him.

"Thank God for that!" Tim mopped his brow. "That would be a bit powerful for me. Until next week anyway. But in fact, today is even better than my 21$^{st}$. Janice Richards has agreed to get Engaged. To me, not someone else," he added to laughter. "Her ring is open to inspection," he added holding up her left hand. "Thank you."

Tim sat down to more cheers and a kiss from a blushing Janice.

"The Bar is open, and a band will be playing in five minutes if you would like to go through the door there to the Ballroom," Ron announced. "Great speech Tim," he added quietly. "And congratulations. You kept that quiet!"

"I couldn't be sure she'd say 'Yes' until I actually asked her. You never really can be sure, can you?"

"I haven't proposed to all that number of women Tim!"

"I did ask Aunt Sonia last week to make sure it was okay to ask Janice."

"You didn't tell me you were going to do that, Tim!" Janice said.

"It was a case of doing things in the right order, Jan. But if she'd said 'No' I'd've asked you to elope with me to Gretna Green instead."

"That's alright then," Janice smiled.

Then people were clustering round to look at the ring.

May looked across the table at Kitty, but she had joined the group round Janice. May hesitated wondering whether to join them. It was the natural thing to do – all the other women were.

"I'm going to look at Janice's ring and – and have a word with Tim," she said with sudden determination standing up.

"Sure. Let's go and have a word with your father, Frank." Des wanted May to have a clear field to talk to Kitty. If she could.

Ron saw him approaching and went towards him.

"Thanks for coming Des, Frank," he said.

"Dad, there's that pilot over there, can I go and talk to him about the RAF? There's something I want to ask him," Frank asked eagerly.

"Sure. He's Craig Earl."

"Right." Frank hurried off.

"Tim's looking ahead to National Service. It's a couple of years off of course but he's quite keen on doing it in the RAF," Des said quietly.

"As a pilot?"

"No. Tim's got him interested in Control Tower work. So Frank's wondering if he volunteered for that ahead of time whether that would give him a better chance of doing that."

"His architects work in your firm wouldn't keep him clear?"

"No," Des looked across at May. "May thinks if Frank went into the RAF in Air Traffic Control that would be safer than in the Army."

"Can't disagree." Ron looked down at the floor then back at Des. "I wouldn't want you or May to think I'm trying to poach Frank and from what I gather from his letters he's really focused on being an architect like you. But if during a holiday you'd like him to have a 'taster' in Air Traffic Control, I could lay on a stint in ours for him to try. It would be what we call an 'Observational Placement' that we do lay on for young people on quite a regular basis."

"Thanks. But I'm not sure how May would feel about that."

"I understand. Erm – how is she?"

"Well enough." It was clear Des wasn't going to say more.

"Right. Thanks for what you did with the newspapers."

"It was necessary to put right what she'd said about you. Especially what you did at the school. Rescuing Kitty, Kathleen, I mean."

Ron looked at him sharply.

"I happened to be talking to Ralph, our Chief Warden, some time ago. You remember him I'm sure. That was after our – conversation when you collected Tim's gear to come down here. He told me what you'd done. I told May. Unfortunately not until after she'd done the article with Jerningham. I wish I'd told her before but – well I hadn't."

Ron nodded and looked across at her. She was talking to Terry. Kathleen was now nowhere to be seen.

"How is Kitty?" May asked Terry quickly. She had gone up to him having seen Kitty had gone somewhere.

"Well enough thank you, Mrs. Ackroyd." His tone was carefully formal. Not the kind of tone she'd hoped from someone who after all was now her son-in-law.

"Does she – does she have any trouble with her legs?"

"She has what is called 'Phantom pain' with them from time to time, but she never complains. And of course she has to take care about jarring them."

May nodded.

"Does she ever talk about me? Did she say anything when she knew I was coming here to Tim's party?"

"Not really."

That means she did, May thought immediately.

"I didn't intend her to be injured the way she was, Terry," she said almost angrily. "Though anyone would think I had, the way she acts towards me."

"I'm sure you didn't Mrs. Ackroyd. Intend her to be injured, I mean." A brief pause. As May was about to move away, "Mrs. Ackroyd, may I ask you a question please? Perhaps it's impertinent but it seems pivotal to Kathleen's attitude towards you."

"Well?"

"Why did you feel as you did about the letter you had from the Davies's, Kathleen's Welsh foster parents, in late 1940?"

May went white as she swung back to face him.

"What do you mean?" she hissed.

"They wrote to you and Mr. Jackson suggesting that you name them as prospective Adopters for Kathleen in the event of you and Mr. Jackson being killed in the bombing that was still going on. As that was to safeguard her future against what you had described to them as 'unsuitable relatives' taking her away in those circumstances, I wonder why."

"The Davies's were planning to kidnap Kitty!" May growled.

"How? As that Adoption was only to come into effect if you and Mr. Jackson were killed? That was to be written into the document."

"Ron agreed with me."

"No Mrs. Ackroyd, he didn't. And you threatened to Divorce him and get him Barred from ever seeing Kathleen or the boys again. So he had to stay silent, even to Kathleen when you insisted on keeping her in London after he recovered, because a solicitor had advised him that in all the circumstances it was a virtual certainty you would have got Custody if it did go to Court. You later had Tim home and then the school happened."

"And don't you think I haven't tortured myself with that knowledge day and night since? And with the way Kitty hates me?" she hissed.

"I'm sure you have Mrs. Ackroyd." Terry paused. "You won't know this of course but since before our wedding when I suggested to Kathleen that we should invite you, I have been trying to put that precise point to her. And have asked her to consider what she would feel in those circumstances about our child or children if and when we have them."

May studied him intently.

"Then you think I was right to do what I did? Even though things turned out the way they did?"

"No Mrs. Ackroyd, I think you were totally wrong. In my view those Provisional Consent to Adopt papers should have been signed and Kathleen should have been allowed to go back to Wales as soon as Mr. Jackson recovered. Then my wife would not have been injured." He paused. "But we are in the situation we are. If you would like me to I'll continue to press Kathleen to change towards you. But I can't promise I'll succeed."

"If only you would do that I'll be eternally grateful Terry."

She glanced around. There was still no sign of Kitty.

"I must go and find Kathleen, Mrs. Ackroyd," Terry said, nodding to her and went off into the Ballroom.

May looked over to Des. Ron was just turning away from him and heading towards the Ballroom.

Des came over to her.

"Shall we go into the Ballroom? Frank's already there."

May nodded, not trusting herself to speak. At last she had someone she could count as a friend, or at least someone on her side, in what she felt was the 'enemy' camp.

As she and Des walked into the Ballroom Anne immediately came up to her from talking to Sonia.

"Hello May, would you like a sherry? Or something else? Des?"

"Just a very small sherry please. As I shall be driving back tonight," he answered quickly.

"Of course. May?"

"Yes please. A dry sherry would be nice."

Sonia chatted with them about their trip down, traffic and the weather while Anne went to the Bar for the drinks and May looked around. She finally saw Kitty sitting at a small table on the edge of the dance floor talking to Terry seriously, their heads close together.

"Kathleen, what better chance than now to go up to your mother and talk to her?" Terry was saying gently. "I'm sure she does want a reconciliation and that's really why she came."

"Does she?" Kathleen's tone was bitter and cynical. "If she really does then she could come over to me couldn't she? She's got two normal legs so that's no problem for her is it? I can't even dance with you.

"And it's not only that Terry. Look what she's tried to do to Dad. Tying up with that louse Jerningham. Twice, if you count the time she backed him taking Dad to Court that time because he hit him while Jerningham was attacking me. And then that awful article about Dad smuggling in drugs and guns. That Dad had nothing whatsoever to do with."

"She did get the paper to retract that article a couple of days later didn't she?" countered Terry.

"Only after an awful lot of damage had been done to Dad's reputation. And she's not even apologised to Dad for it as far as I know." She looked across to where Mum and Aunt Sonia were talking to Des and – mother.

Des was looking at his watch. He said something to May, she hesitated, shook her head, then went off. Des immediately came towards Kathleen and Terry.

"We're going to be leaving soon Kathleen, Terry. So we're going round saying our 'Good-byes'. Thank you for inviting us."

Kathleen struggled to her feet.

"It was Dad and Tim who invited you all to Tim's party, not me," she said coldly. "But thank you for coming Mr. Ackroyd. And Frank."

Des looked at her soberly.

"Over the years your mother has paid a very heavy price for her past mistakes Kathleen and ...."

"Has she?" Any more than me for her stupidity and bloodymindedness?" she snapped.

"No, she hasn't. But she has been racked by guilt and ...."

"Has she? Has she really?" Kathleen demanded. "When she first came to see me in hospital after it had happened she said she was sorry. Just the once. But if she really was as sorry as all that, she certainly didn't show it.

"Not like Dad. He actually cried and Dad had never, ever done that before. Dad really meant it. And since then I've found out what she did to stop him letting me go back to Wales after he got better from that illness. Threatened to Divorce him, get Custody from him and get him Barred from ever seeing any of us again, didn't she? If she had listened to Dad, Tim and I would be fit and strong, not crippled as we are. And then what she's done to Dad since! Her sorry? Don't make me laugh!" She stuck out her hand. "Goodbye Mr. Ackroyd."

"Kathleen," Des said as he took her hand. "Please ...."

Kathleen wrenched her hand away.

"I said 'Goodbye Mr. Ackroyd'."

Des inclined his head. "Goodbye Kathleen."

He turned away and walked out after May to collect Frank from the group clustered round Tim and his car.


"Dad. How old do you reckon someone should be before they get married?" Tim asked unexpectedly.

They were tinkering with Tim's car some months later. Not that it was having any particular problems Ron was thinking but maybe Tim was using that as excuse to be able to have a quiet word.

"Now you're over 21 Tim, really it depends on when you think you can afford it. A house, either rented or bought, your income to keep you both if Janice is going to give up work. Or how you will work the finances if she keeps on working for however long."

"Janice does want to keep on working. Mr. Sampson has said he really needs an Administrator, or Personal Assistant he called it, in his office at the Airfield now which would suit her fine. And we've found a house at Wingmore which would be handy for work for both of us. It needs quite a bit doing to it so it's cheap enough for us to be able to afford. We should be able to manage that work between us. It's more decorating than anything else I think."

"I see." Ron glanced at him sideways. "Have you and Janice got a date in mind?"

"I've yet to ask Aunt Sonia really but we've been thinking of May or June next year. That'd mean we'd have time to get the house bought and fixed up and I should have had another pay rise by then too."


"Wonder who that is?" Anne looked up at the scrunch of car tyres on the gravel. "It's too early for Tim to be back."

Ron went to the window to peer through the curtains into the October evening, a month after Tim's party.

"It's Terry and Kathleen. Hope nothing's wrong."

When they followed Ron into the warm room Kathleen's face was glowing not from coming in the cold to the warm room but with suppressed excitement too.

Terry fussed around her to sitting down comfortably, then looked at Ron and Anne.

"We've something to tell you," he said, then glanced at Kathleen.

"I'm expecting a baby!" she burst out. "I am but Terry is as well of course! Except he isn't because he can't as he's a man. Oh you know what I mean."

"Lovely Kathleen! Oh I'm so glad for you!" Anne bounced out of her chair to hug and kiss Kathleen, then Terry.

Ron, more controlled, shook Terry's hand then kissed Kathleen. While he'd hoped that her leg injuries hadn't affected anything else he had still worried they had. But obviously not. As long as the baby wouldn't be affected.

"When?" was Anne's next question.

"The doctor says April. But we only want the family to know for now." Kathleen looked from Anne to Ron. "My Folkestone family. And Terry's of course."

Anne and Ron nodded, Kathleen's message very clear. And then Anne and Kathleen were into the depth of feminine talk.

"Let's leave the women to talk about their angle while we put the kettle on to celebrate, Terry," Ron suggested with a grin.

"Did the doctor think Kathleen's injuries would cause any difficulties Terry?" Ron asked gruffly as he busied himself putting on the kettle.

"He was certain the injuries wouldn't." Terry paused. "When Kathleen and I were getting serious but before we were Engaged, apparently Kathleen went off to see the doctor 'for a check-up' as she put it to me after we were Engaged. She wanted not just a few re-assuring words about it but a proper and thorough physical examination. He gave her the 'all clear'. When she did tell me she said it was to 'let me know the facts'. That she was 'alright'.

"I told her I was glad but it wouldn't have made any difference if it had gone the other way. I loved her as her, not her as a brood mare. That made her laugh," Terry added, smiling himself.

Ron smiled back then sobered.

"You know Terry, soon after the school, before she'd been fitted with her legs, she asked me if I thought she'd ever get a boy friend in her condition. I said what counted in a real relationship was what was in her heart and in her head, not just physical things." He paused. "I couldn't have asked for a better husband for my daughter than you Terry." He swung away quickly, pretending to be busy with putting cups on the tray. "Sorry to go mushy and sentimental on you."

"Thank you for saying it Mr. Jackson."

Terry knocked, then pushed open the lounge door.

"Is your conversation now of a level a couple of respectable gentlemen can overhear?" he asked.

"Just about," Kathleen grinned impishly at them.

It was on a Thursday afternoon in April when Joan hurried into a Board Meeting after a perfunctory knock on the door and put a note in front of Ron. Listening to Richard's figures on the Cost-Benefit of running another Advertising Campaign for Autumn Flights to Malaga, Ron glanced down at the note.

"Sorry to interrupt Richard ...," he said quickly, " ... a message from Anne. She's just taken Kathleen to the hospital. Terry's on his way down from Calder Hall. I'm off to the hospital. Sonia, take over the Chair will you? Speak to you later."

"Give her our love Ron," Richard called after him as he hurried out, abandoning his papers.

Ron strode quickly into the hospital's Maternity Wing. It was, he felt, the second worst worrying time in his life. The first was when he was on his way to the school after the bombing.

But then, when May was having Kathleen, that was as worrying as this, he supposed.

"How is she?" he hissed, seeing Anne sitting on one of a row of chairs some distance down the corridor from the Delivery Room reading a magazine.

"Fine. Nothing to worry about."

"No?"

"No. Giving birth is a purely natural function for women, Ron. As I've told you before. And so has Kathleen. Many times."

"Maybe." Ron sat down by her. "But when it's the first time."

"And what about the three children you've had already, Ron Jackson?" Anne asked, raising her eyebrows. "But as it is the first time for her – you're forgiven."

"It's all very well for you to talk. You've been as much on tenterhooks as I've been."

"Can't deny that," Anne admitted. She glanced at her watch. "Terry didn't give me an ETA for arriving at Wingmore."

"I'll give the Control Tower a ring. See if they've got anything yet."

Ron went out to the 'phone box in Reception and in a few minutes was speaking to Tim, the Air Controller for the day. Roger Moreton was the new lad they'd taken on now that Tim was fully qualified.

"Terry's ETA was twenty minutes as of ten minutes ago on our last contact."

"If you can tell him, the baby hasn't arrived yet so there's no need to break his neck getting here."

"I'll tell him Dad. Give Kathleen our best from everyone here,"

"Mere males are excluded from the Delivery Room at this time, but thanks all the same. I'll tell her as soon as I can."

Ron re-joined Anne.

Twenty minutes later a passing nurse asked if they'd like a cup of tea. They did.

Terry arrived just as the tea did. Obligingly the nurse went into the Delivery Room to check progress, and was out two minutes later.

"Shouldn't be long now," she said cheerfully but not really helpfully. "I'll bring another cup, Mr. Murray."

"What was that?" Terry started up fifteen minutes later, staring up the corridor from where the cry had come.

"Something's happened," Ron said unnecessarily,

"Sit down both of you," Anne said calmly, not having moved from her chair. "They'll tell us when there's any news."

"How the hell can women stay so calm about these things?" muttered Terry, slowly sitting down.

"Beats me," Ron agreed.

It was ten minutes before the door opened.

"Mr. Murray?" asked the nurse.

"Yes." Terry started to his feet.

"Congratulations. You have a beautiful baby girl. Would you like to come in?"

Terry hurried forward and the door closed behind him. Five minutes later a nurse came towards them.

"Mr. and Mrs. Jackson?"

"Yes," they answered together, standing up.

"You may come in to see your granddaughter."

They looked down at Kathleen, nursing the baby, her face just visible between the swaddling bands, Terry sitting by the bed, beaming.

"She's as beautiful as her mother," whispered Ron.

"Men have no imagination do they, Mum?" Kathleen smiled at

Anne. "Terry ,said exactly the same."

"Neither have I then," Anne said, a catch in her voice. "I was just about to say that myself."

"Have you decided on a name for her yet?" Ron asked.

"Yes. Anne Edith."

Anne's eyes filled with tears. She loved Kathleen as though she was her own daughter, so this was the nicest compliment Kathleen could have paid her. Edith, Kathleen's Welsh foster-mother, would be just as delighted she was sure.

That evening after her visitors had gone and 'Little' Anne was tucked up in her crib beside the bed, Kathleen turned on her side to be able to look at her.

Aunt Edith would be glad they had included her name in 'Little' Anne's she was sure. Mum had said she would 'phone her with the news as soon as she and Dad got home. It would be nice if she and Uncle Hywell were able to come to see them both.

Which turned her thoughts to Evacuation. How on earth could mother have sent Tim and her off to the care of total strangers when she could have gone with them? Okay, that would have left Dad alone in London but when she and Terry had talked about it once he said he would have wanted her to go with the children in those circumstances. But mother had actually refused to go when she could have gone and Dad had wanted her to.

But then, if she hadn't been Evacuated as she had been she'd have never met Mum – Aunt Anne as she was then. And she had made such a mammoth difference to the whole of her life. In every respect.

But mother had thought that Aunt Edith had been trying to steal her from her (mother). Maybe she had even thought the same of Aunt Anne. She hadn't, but without meaning to – Mum – Aunt Anne had done just that!

What if someone really did try to steal 'Little' Anne's love from her!

And Kathleen suddenly realised what mother had meant when years ago she had said that Kathleen would understand why she wouldn't let her go back to Wales, 'when she had children of her own'.

Though she had been totally wrong about Aunt Edith setting out to do that, that was just what had happened.


A week later May was studying an envelope addressed to her in vaguely familiar handwriting that the Postman had just delivered. What made it stranger was that it was postmarked 'Folkestone'. The only people who wrote to them from there were Ron writing to Frank or, very occasionally, Tim writing to them all. This wasn't from either of them.

She shrugged. There was only one way to find out – open it. Using a kitchen knife she slit the envelope and took out the single sheet of notepaper and a photograph.


'Dear mother,

Yesterday I gave birth to a baby daughter  Her weight was 7lb. 2 ozs. She is perfect – having both legs.

We have named her 'Anne Edith Murray'.

We are enclosing a photograph that Terry took not long after she was born.

Yours,

Kathleen Murray


May re-read it several times with mixed feelings but with anger quickly becoming the dominant one.

So Kitty had had a baby girl! Which was her first grandchild!

But she hadn't even let her know she was pregnant! So that she, her mother, could have been there with her through that time. Supporting and advising her. Leading up to and then through the birth.

Instead she would have had that Carruthers woman doing all that! When she had had no children of her own to even know what it was really like.

And then Kitty had named her after her two foster-mothers without giving her real mother even a mention! Could there be a greater insult? Or clearer indication where Kitty really put her priorities? To the two women that May had been sure had wanted to steal Kitty's affections. To kidnap her really. This, if nothing else, had proved just how right she had been all those years ago.

And then Kitty's way of signing off the letter. As though it was a formal letter to a business acquaintance rather than one to her own mother.

She grabbed a pen and paper to write a scathing letter back. To tell her just how right she had been when Kitty was a young girl about those two women that she liked so much – that they were both treacherous busybodies determined to persuade or bribe her to get her away from her own mother. And that it was now high time for her (Kitty) to grow up and realise just what sort of people they were, to have behaved like that towards a young girl who had been committed to their care.

Her letter covered five pages, spattered with capital letters and underlinings. She pushed it in an envelope ready to post when she went to the shops. She was about to drop it in the Post box when she paused, then stuffed it back into her bag. She would show it to Des first. He had a way of expressing himself and might think of more things to add. It would mean it wouldn't go until tomorrow, but that wouldn't matter.

She managed to contain herself until Frank had gone to bed before showing Kathleen's letter to Des."What do you think of that?" she said.

And remembered a previous time she'd said those same words. The time when the Davies's had sent that letter suggesting she and Ron sign Adoption Agreements for them to Adopt Kitty. They had made the excuse that would only be 'if something happened to her and Ron in the bombing' but she (May) had seen through that straight away. Ron had been too stupid to see it though.

Des read the brief letter carefully, then looked at the photograph.

"Looks a bonnie baby, doesn't she?" he said neutrally.

"And that's what I've written in reply. Only you can sometimes word things better than I can, so I can always re-write it if you do. Or if you think of other things I can add." May passed him her reply.

Des read that even more carefully.

"What are you really wanting to do, May?"

"Tell her exactly what I think of her, of course! Not even telling me she was pregnant. And naming the baby after the Carruthers and

Davies women with never a mention of me. And that tone of her letter! And don't forget the way she ignored me at Tim's 21$^{st}$."

"May. Would you really like a reconciliation with Kitty?"

"Of course I would," she snapped immediately. "That goes without saying."

"Does it? And do you?" Des asked quietly. "And how far does your letter take you along that path?"

May stared at him. Not believing that he wasn't backing her and her letter 100% instantly.

"Are you're saying it's all been my fault then?" she demanded.

"No." He paused. "Not entirely. Kitty's responses to you after you kept her here in London after Ron had recovered were bad. Wrong. But we are dealing with the present situation. What it is now. After that period when she was kept here in London against her will, after the school, after what happened to her in the school, after what happened in the hospital. And the care that Ron and Anne Carruthers have given to her ever since. And the care the Davies's gave to her when she was in Wales."

"So what you're saying is ....," belligerently.

"Listen to me May," snapped Des.

May glowered at him but stayed silent.

"At work we've been doing a project for a Clinical Psychologist who during the War was a Student doing some research among Evacuees. So apart from pure business we talked about her studies. Particularly because of our own experiences with the children. At the time of her research some of the children were still away, some had come home. Among the children were those who had had good experiences, others bad, others that she called 'neutral'.

"Among those who had 'good experiences' there was quite often what she called 'Transference', especially when children were young and with the foster-parents for many months or even years. That was when the children 'Transferred' their feelings for their natural mothers to their substitute mothers – their foster-mothers. That sometimes caused problems between them and the natural mothers, but other times both families became firm friends.

"After the war she did what she called 'Follow-up Studies'. Where the two families had become friends, the feelings of the children for their natural mother had returned to her. However, when it had resulted in antagonism between the natural and foster-mothers the children had split loyalties, which often resulted in resentment against the natural mother on return home. Especially in the early months. And all kinds of problems resulted." Des looked at May steadily. "So Kitty's reaction to her situation here, complicated by the circumstances under which she stayed in London was not so uncommon."

"So you and that Psychologist woman think that the children should have stayed with the foster-mothers do you? I bet she didn't have any children of her own to talk that rubbish."

"No, she didn't have children at that time, but has had two since. Nor did she think the children should have stayed with their foster-mothers," Des replied. "But her advice would have been to make friends with the foster-parents, which would avoid the split loyalties for the child. Kitty in this case."

"Tim was glad to be home. And he has never blamed me for being in the school," snapped May.

"Agreed. But as I understand it Tim's experiences were not as caring and loving as Kitty's in Wales. So naturally their reactions to coming home were different.

"Now May, it will be up to you to decide what kind of letter to send in response to Kitty's. Either the letter you've already written – which I would expect would deepen the rift between you. Or send a very positive letter saying how delighted you are that she and Terry have had a baby girl, she looks lovely and could you possibly see her and them, either at their home or they would be very welcome here. And make no mention of the baby being named after Kitty's foster-mothers. That could then produce a warmer response from her – and things could lead on from there. Not guaranteed of course, but certainly more possible.

"Another possibility would be to send a letter as neutral as Kitty's is, thanking her for the news and photograph, glad everything is alright with her and that you would like to be regularly up-dated on her progress."

"Or I could ignore it. Just as she's ignored me for years and at Tim's 21st," May snapped.

"I wonder if she felt you ignored her in not going over to her then yourself," Des said, looking very directly at her.

"I'm going to bed," she snapped angrily, standing up.

May did not reply to Kathleen's letter for a week then sent the 'neutral' letter.

Kathleen read it, then shrugged. The reply was more or less what she'd expected.

# Chapter 14
## Family reconciliation?

Two days after sending her reply May got two letters by the same post, both postmarked 'Folkestone'. One was in Ron's handwriting, the other was Tim's.

She opened the letter from Ron. Inside was a card inviting 'Mr, and Mrs. Ackroyd and Master Frank Jackson to the Marriage of Mr. Timothy Jackson to Miss Janice Richards, daughter of the late Mr. Arthur Richards and Mrs. Sonia Richards at St. Saviours Church, Folkestone at 2.15 PM on 15th May 1956, and Reception afterwards at the Grand Hotel, Folkestone."

Though Tim in his occasional letters to them had mentioned this Janice, he'd not given any idea that their relationship was as serious as this!

She ripped open Tim's letter.

Dear Mum, father and Frank,

I don't know if you've had the official invitation to my wedding to Janice from Dad yet. It's at St. Saviours Church in Folkestone at 2.15 on the 15th May and there'll be a Reception afterwards.

We've got a house in Wingmore near the Airfield which will be handy for both of us for work as Janice has now got a job there too. She wants to keep on working after we're married, for a while anyway.

I hope you'll all be able to come because it would be lovely to see you there.

Love,

Tim

May read it several times with mixed feelings. It seemed a genuinely warm invitation from him. But why hadn't he told her about the way things were going with Janice and him? Surely he should have been over the moon about things?

But come to think of it – he had. Not directly and personally to her but at his 21$^{st}$ he had announced their Engagement.  So a wedding was usually pretty automatic after that wasn't it?

She got out a letter pad and pen and wrote a warm and loving letter straight back.

Of course they would go.  And stay overnight in Folkestone and would like to go to look at the house at that place Wingmore, wherever that was.

And, she decided, if Kitty chose to ignore her again, she would do just the same straight back.


They went down to Folkestone the day before the wedding early, having arranged to meet Tim at the Airfield, the first time they had been there, at the time he'd be coming off-duty.  He would take them to the house so they could see all over it.  They had already booked two rooms at The Grand Hotel which would be convenient as the Reception was to be there.

They were stopped at the Gate but the Gatekeeper had their names on his clipboard and directed them to the Restaurant.

Even May was impressed as Des drove them and Frank pointed out the different places.  He had taken up Ron's invitation to spend three days in the Control Tower with Tim and had become determined to volunteer for the RAF to work in a Control Tower for his National Service.  Carefully not telling his mother he was also determined to volunteer to go abroad as well.  He could be posted abroad anyway of course but he wanted to make sure of it.

As Des parked by the Restaurant a light 'plane came in to land and taxied over to where others were parked.  Its engine was switched off but the pilot spent a few minutes more in the cockpit before jumping down to the ground and walking over towards the offices and Restaurant.

"That's Terry!" exclaimed Frank. "I'm sure of it."

"He's rich enough to have a 'plane of his very own?" exclaimed May incredulously.

"No.  At least he didn't have one before.  But when he has to go up to Calder Hall, that nuclear place up in the Lake District, he hires a Flying Club 'plane to fly himself up there.  He did that during that time I was in the Control Tower with Tim.  He saves days of time, he says. Hi Terry!" he yelled waving.

Terry looked over to them, waved and disappeared into the office.

"That's rude of him! Not even bothering to come over to us," May snapped.

"He's got paperwork to do as soon as he lands. Everyone has to," Frank explained quickly.

"Let's get a cup of tea," Des said hurriedly. He hoped May was not intending to find fault wherever she could.

The Canteen had been radically upgraded over the years and now had both a Snack Bar and a Restaurant. As they only wanted a cup of tea they went into the Snack Bar. Des collected teas and cakes while May and Frank secured a window seat with a view across the Airfield. As a passenger 'plane took off Des arrived at their table with a laden tray and Terry walked in through the door. He collected a mug of coffee and came over to them carrying a large briefcase.

"May I join you?" he asked, smiling round all three.

"Please do," Des answered, pulling out the fourth chair.

"Have you just flown down from Calder Hall?" Frank asked eagerly.

"That's right," Terry answered. "As when you were down here before in the Control Tower and talked me down that time."

"Frank talked you down?" Des asked quickly.

"Not talked me down as giving precise instructions in a blind-flying situation but gave me wind strengths, directions and course to steer for landing."

"I was only passing on what Tim told me to," Frank confessed. "He was the Duty Air Controller at the time."

"Well you did a good job of it. I'd say you're both naturals for the job."

Frank beamed, pleased at such an accolade from a 'real' pilot.

"So what were you doing at Calder Hall? Making more atom bombs to kill millions at a time?" May demanded.

"We don't make any atomic weapons at Calder Hall at all," Terry said promptly. "We're developing the site for generating electricity for the country and that alone."

"Really." Cynicism rang. "I know that's what they say!"

"That is exactly what is happening, Mrs. Ackroyd. I'm there and I know," Terry said emphatically, staring at her very directly. "How's the architecture going Frank?" he added, switching his look to change the subject.

"Fine. It's really interesting." Frank was uncomfortable with the obvious tension between his admired older brother-in-law and his mother. "It's taking a lot of studying, but it's really interesting."

"Good. Glad you're liking it." Terry drained his coffee cup. "Must dash. Still got a stream of work to do."

"Aren't you going to tell us how the baby is? My grandchild," May enquired icily.

"Anne is fine, Mrs. Ackroyd. Progressing well, gaining weight as she should, pays attention to everything going on around her. We reckon that she's going to be really bright as she grows up."

"And when do I get to see her? For real I mean, not just in a small photograph?"

"We've already got an appointment for tonight. So at the Reception after the wedding would be more convenient all round. Everyone will be busy in the morning getting ready for the wedding, of course. As it's at 2.15 and we have to be at the Church well ahead of that time. So see you at the church tomorrow. Weather forecast isn't too bad, thank goodness."

He hurried off before any objection could be raised.

"Well what do you think of that?" snapped May. "I was expecting to see her this afternoon or tonight,"

"As it's nearly six o'clock it would be getting too late today anyway. They'll be getting her to bed shortly," Des observed mildly. "Ah, here's Tim." He waved and Tim waved back as he came over, kissed May, shook hands with Des and gave Frank a grin.

"Do you want more tea? Or something else? Or shall we get over to the house? Janice is at her house still sorting things out for tomorrow with her mum."

"We've got dinner booked at the hotel for eight so perhaps we'd better get to the house as we might spend some time there," Des suggested. "Are you in your own car or will you travel in ours?"

"I'm still living at home so ...,"

"You're not!" snapped May. "You're living down here, not at

home."

"I've driven here," Tim dodged the issue. "If I lead the way we'll be there in ten minutes as it's this side of the village."

"Let's go then," Des said, standing up.

"Okay if I go in Tim's car?" Frank asked,looking from May to Tim.

"Fine by me," Tim said quickly as they moved towards the door.

"How's Kitty? Kathleen?" Frank asked as soon as they'd set off. "Still as anti-Mum?"

"Yeah. Only hope they don't fall out publicly at my Wedding. But obviously I wanted to ask everyone."

"Yeah." A pause. "But why is Kitty so anti-Mum? You're not. I'm not."

"Goes back a long way Frank. As far as I know, 'cos I don't suppose I know the full story from both sides, Mum kept Kathleen in London once Dad was better from some illness he had when Kathleen wanted to go back to Wales. She'd got very close to her foster-parents there. But not as close as to Mum here – I mean Aunt Anne. I was just glad to be back from being Evacuated. Then of course the school happened and we were both crippled. So Kathleen blames mother – Mum - the London one - for that."

"Yeah, I remember now. Dad said something about it years ago didn't he? But you don't blame Mum for it."

"Why should I? Mother – Mum – wasn't to know that the Jerries would bomb a school, was she? That's the way I look at it anyway. And I was really glad to be home."

They drove the rest of the way through quiet country lanes in silence, past some farm buildings, then on the outskirts of a small village, he pulled into the drive of a cottage, Des close behind them.

"This was a couple of fairly derelict farm cottages," Tim told them as they approached the front door. "The farmer had no need of them so put them up for sale and we were lucky enough to get them fairly cheap. This way."

He led them in.

"We've done up this side, which was one small cottage but we've knocked a way through to the other one and we're in the process of doing that one up."

"You've done all this?" May asked incredulously, as she looked at the freshly painted kitchen, lounge and then up the stairs to the bedrooms.

"Not just me!" Tim grinned. "People have been really great. A whole lot of people from work came on two weekends, having a blitz on the house while others did a blitz on the garden which was like a jungle. Dad organised them like an Army Drill Sergeant and it was amazing what they did in such a short time. This is the part we're still doing."

He led them through a door to the other half of the semi-detached cottages.

"A pal of Mr. Sampson's is a builder and he's re-plastered all the rooms in this side because water had got in and ruined what was there. So that's got to dry out before we can do any painting."

"And he charged a pretty penny for it I'll be bound!" said May.

"He did it as a wedding present he said. Even the materials," Tim said quietly. "And we were lucky in other ways too. The Airfield had a big pre-fab. store hut that we were going to scrap because we were going to build a modern workshop on the site. I mentioned it when the farmer and I were negotiating the price for this and he offered to knock something off the price for the store hut. The Board agreed he could have it just for taking it away, so we got that bit knocked off the price too!"

"Why didn't you ask father's help in designing this interior for you?" May demanded.

Tim flushed. He had thought of that but had then decided not to, partly because of the distance Des would need to come several times to do that kind of job, partly because he kept the 'London part' and the 'Folkestone part' of his life separate and partly because he and Janice had known from the outset exactly how they wanted it. So why use an architect who would have had to come all the way from London?

"They've done exactly what I'd have suggested down here," Des said quietly. "Are you keeping the two small bedrooms this side or knocking them into one bigger one? That way you'd still have a three-bedroomed house."

"That's exactly what we're already doing, father," Tim said. "It's a bit cluttered upstairs with building materials but come up to have a look if you want to."

They did.

"What are you doing tonight Tim? Having a Stag Night Pub Crawl?" Des asked with a smile once in the kitchen again.

"Not really. I've got to keep a clear head for tomorrow," Tim smiled back. "Wouldn't do to fluff my lines in the Church."

"Then have dinner with us tonight," May said, almost as though it was an order.

"Sorry. But - I've already got something already booked," Tim said uncomfortably, going red-faced.

"What?"

"It's not exactly a Stag night Mum, not a Pub Crawl type anyway, but it is with a group of close friends. To celebrate my last night of freedom, as one of them said." Tim stood up, taking keys out of his pocket.

May set her lips but said nothing more.

As they drove in their separate cars to Folkestone, Tim heaved a sigh of relief. It was a good job mother hadn't asked who the 'Stag night' was with or who the 'friends' were. They were having a quiet dinner at home with Kathleen, Terry and 'Little' Anne.

When Dad had said it was 'to celebrate his last night of freedom' – Mum had immediately asked him if he wanted his 'Freedom' back then. Dad had promptly said she had made 'the bonds of matrimony so pleasant it wouldn't be worth it'.

They had all laughed and Mum had called him, 'the world's worst flatterer'.

Just the sort of 'joshing' they all liked.

Tim hoped he and Janice would have the same type of marriage Mum and Dad had.


The Wedding Day was overcast but not heavily so and it stayed dry and the ceremony went like clockwork.

When they gathered outside for the Official Photographs the photographer arranged them in different groups, then called out, 'Parents of the happy couple with them please'.

"There'll be two group photographs for that," Ron said to him quickly. He crossed to May, "Would you come with me to stand as

Tim's parents, May?"

May looked at him surprised. She had been building up resentment all morning anticipating this routine photograph – and expecting to be excluded from it.

"You are Tim's mother May, and both he and I want you to be in this."

Almost numbly May went to stand with him by Tim and Janice with Sonia by Janice on the other side.

"Smiles please!" called the photographer. "Excellent."

He looked at Ron. Two groups?

"Thanks May," Ron said quietly, clearly a dismissal as he beckoned to Anne.

Angrily May stepped out of shot, but was unwilling to make any kind of scene in front of so many people, so many strangers.

As more photographs were taken, May was watching from a distance, feeling isolated and resentful.

"We're glad you came, mother," a quiet voice said behind her.

May spun round.

Kathleen and Terry were standing there, Kathleen holding 'Little' Anne, now nine months old in her arms.

"Would you like to hold her?" Kathleen held her out.

May stared at them, then slowly reached out and took her.

'Little' Anne looked at May, smiled at her, then looked around at all the other people and the activity.

"She's beautiful," May whispered. She glared at Kathleen. "So why did you keep her away from me? And why on earth did you name her after those two awful women!" she demanded. Aggressively, not as a genuine question. Not as a hurt question either.

Abruptly grim-faced, Terry reached out for 'Little' Anne. For a moment May resisted, clinging to her, then let her go.

"Let's go and be photographed with Tim and Janice, Terry," Kathleen said icily.

# Chapter 15
## Pub brawl

"It's come, father," Frank looked up from the letter he'd just opened. They were on the train going up to the office.

"May I see?"

Des quickly glanced through the short letter ordering Frank to 'Report for Basic Training to RAF Padgate, Warrington, Cheshire.' There was a separate sheet of 'Travel Arrangements' and a Rail warrant.

"Do you want to go abroad?" Des asked, handing it back.

"Yes." Frank was emphatic.

"Well there's enough trouble-spots in the world where we're involved. Germany, Cyprus, Malaya, Kenya. Korea's an armed stand-off though the shooting war seems to be over. For the present anyway. And the politicians call this peace!" Des added cynically.

But to Frank going to a war zone didn't worry him. It was exciting, exhilarating. Not alarming.

Once at Padgate, he threw himself into the training with enthusiasm, from Parade Ground drills to firing weapons and bayonet practice as well as Classroom work. He even got used to the non-privacy of the barrack-room within a week. So he wrote enthusiastic letters home to May and Ron, expecting Ron to pass on news to Tim and Kitty. Kathleen.


"What about coming with me to Liverpool, me old stamping ground, Frankie?" Harry Climber asked cheerfully. They'd got their first '24'. A Pass to go out of Camp.

For some reason that Frank couldn't really understand but still welcomed, Harry from the back streets of Liverpool had palled up with him. As far as Harry was concerned Frank was 'posh', but because he was as enthusiastic as Harry himself was at tackling everything from Route Marches and Obstacle Courses to firing weapons and bayonet practice, he thought he was 'Okay'. Both were a lot different from many National Servicemen who disliked and resented being 'pulled away' from their homes and jobs. Then when

Frank was put in charge of a Sub-Section Team of ten competing with other Teams on a 3-day, 2-night Long-range Exercise in the Lake District he'd not only got all the map-reading right but he got them first back to their temporary camp and their hot meal on both nights.

As far as Frank was concerned Harry knew his way around, was always cheerful and as keen as himself on everything.

Then talking quietly in the NAAFI one night Frank found that Harry had had relatives injured and killed during the war, and that he had been 'bombed out' twice. So they found the experiences Frank's brother and sister had had, made another bond. So they became inseparable.

"Why not? It's too far for me to go home with trains the way they are," Frank responded at once. "And I've never been to Liverpool."

Frank looked round the back streets of Toxteth where Harry was taking him to his sister's. His mother had been killed during the bombing when he was two and his father had disappeared. So he had been more or less brought up by an Aunt but for the past two years had lived with his older sister. More or less.

"What you doing here?" she demanded as soon as she opened the door and saw Harry. "Gone AWOL?"

"Nah. It's great there. No, we got a '24' and I've brought Frank over to see the place. This is Sheila, me sister, Frank."

"Oh. You'd better come in then."

They followed her down the dank smelling corridor to a kitchen.

"Cuppa tea then?" Ungraciously.

"Yes please. Thanks." Frank was feeling uncomfortable at this cold 'welcome'.

She looked at him, surprised at his accent.

"You're not from round here then?"

"No. London."

"Whereabouts?" as she put a battered kettle on.

"South East. Lewisham."

"Never heard of that bit. Did you get bombed much?"

"Some. Harry said you'd got bombed out twice. And your Mum was killed."

"Yup. Anything like that happen to you?" But not really interested.

"My sister and brother were badly injured when their school got hit. I wasn't there though. I was only four at the time."

"Oh. Tough."

"It was worse for you though, wasn't it? What happened to you. With your Mum and everything."

Sheila looked up at him from making the tea, surprised at his sympathy.

"Guess so." She handed them mugs of weak tea. "There's no sugar."

There was desultory conversation as Frank drank the hot tea quickly. Then they could go from this unwelcoming place.

The front door banged open and moments later an unshaven burly man dressed in rough, dirty clothing walked into the kitchen.

"What you doing here then?" he growled as soon as he saw Harry. "Deserted already? Couldn't hack it?"

"Brought Frank to see a bit o' Liverpool. We got a '24'. Came ter see Sheila. An' you o' course."

"Right. Liverpool's out there, not in 'ere." He jerked his thumb over his shoulder. "Me dinner ready yet, Sheila?"

"Coming right up, Sid," she said hurriedly, turning to the oven.

Frank was already on his feet, tea only half-gone..

"We'll be on our way. Thanks for the tea Sheila. 'Bye Sid."

"What's the rush, Frankie?" demanded Harry, following him into the street. "I was just going ter ask Sheila for somethin' to eat! I'm starved."

"Let's find a cafe then. There must be one around somewhere. It's not as though we were exactly welcome there were we?"

"Oh, they're always like that. Nothing to bother about," Harry said carelessly. "Still, if it's a cafe you're wanting there's some down at the docks. They're not posh restaurant places but the grub's not bad. Better than the Camp's anyway."

"Sounds just the ticket. Lead on McDuff."

"Who's 'e when 'e's at 'ome?"

An hour later they sat back in their chairs feeling comfortably full. After seeing the place from the outside Frank had been pleasantly surprised at the food.

"So what do we do now?" Frank asked. "You know the sights about the place."

They wandered round the city which was still showing plenty of signs of the bombing it had endured during the war, till they stopped outside a pub,

"This is where you begin your real education Frankie," Harry announced. "The start of your first pub crawl."

Some hours later Frank was feeling distinctly 'odd'. A very full feeling, a certain wooziness of the head, unsteadiness when he was walking – but Harry seemed able to drink pint after pint with none of those effects. And as the numerous pubs they had visited all had a similarity of smells and beers, why they had to go from one to the other he wasn't quite sure. Harry seemed to know not only where all these pubs were, but all the barmen and barmaids as well.

They were in another that to Frank seemed louder, and more crowded than the others when Harry put yet another pint on the table in front of him. Frank knew he was expected to drink it though all he really wanted to do at this minute was to find a quiet spot and go to sleep.

Then voices even louder than the background chatter penetrated. He looked up blearily. A man, a couple of years older than Harry, was glaring at him.

"I told you to keep out of this pub, 'Arry Climber. Said if I ever saw you in 'ere again I'd sling you out on your ear, didn't I?"

"I got just as much right to be in this place as you 'ave, Dinko," Harry was roaring back just as aggressively.

"Not if I say you ain't. This is my pub and what I says goes. An' I says clear off."

"Since when 'ave you owned this place? 'Cos you don't. It ain't your name over the door is it?"

"But I still says who can come in and who can't. And you an' your mate can't. So 'op it."

"Well we ain't."

Dinko grabbed Harry by the shirtfront and someone hauled Frank to his feet by his collar and pushed him towards the door.

Frank yanked himself free and swung round. The man shoved him hard in the chest making him stagger backwards into Dinko who pushed him back.

"You duff up that one, Irish," Dinko shouted

Grinning, Irish swung at Frank. Instinctively Frank ducked feeling a massive surge of fury and shot his right fist up in a sizzling upper-cut.

Not expecting it, Irish staggered backwards, collided with a table and fell over it with a resounding crash.

Frank whipped round to see Dinko hit Harry in the face while still holding his shirtfront, which he tried to parry but couldn't stop altogether.

"Hey Dinko," yelled Frank.

Dinko glared round at him, and Frank hit him with a straight left in the eye as Harry kneed Dinko in the groin.

He bent over with a grunt and Frank was hauling him away from Harry when a bottle hit him on the shoulder. It had been aimed at his head but Frank was moving fast. He whirled round, snatched the bottle from Irish's hand and smashed it across the side of his head.

Arms grabbed him from behind, pinning his arms to his side. He stamped backwards, thankful for the Unarmed Combat drills at the Camp, and the grip relaxed with a yell.

Another kick and he broke free. Yet another kick backwards, another yell and he whipped round to see Dinko with his hands now round Harry's neck. A double punch, one to the kidneys another to the side of Dinko's head and he staggered. Harry broke free and shoved Dinko hard into another table which collapsed under him.

"Let's go Frankie!" Harry yelled.

But Frank had only one thing on his mind. To hit Dinko and Irish and keep on hitting them till they were senseless. At least.

Harry grabbed him by the arm and hauled him towards the door.

"Leggo! I want to get at 'em," Frank shouted, resisting but then Harry had him outside the door.

"Come on," Harry snapped, still pulling him with one hand, whipping the remains of the bottle away from Frank's hand with the other and dropping it into the gutter. "Dinko an' all his mates'll be after us in a sec."

His anger waning, Frank started running with him, up a side road, through an alley (nearly tripping over a dustbin) along a side road, another alley and then Harry slowed down, panting.

"I think we're okay for now, but we'll keep going."

"Where to? Oh My God, I do feel bad." Frank stopped and suddenly vomited Into the gutter.

Harry waited patiently.

"I know a place where they'd got just the medicine for you," he said as Frank straightened up, wiping his mouth with a handkerchief.

"Where's that? A hospital? Or a mortuary?" Frank groaned.

It proved to be another pub. Frank went into the toilet to wash out his mouth – to find Harry had another pint waiting for him when he came out.

"No thanks Harry. I just couldn't manage another drop," he said pushing it away.

Harry's face clouded.

"You leave a drink from another bloke it's an insult round 'ere Frankie. Means you don't think nothink of the bloke what's buying it for you."

"You know it's not like that, Harry," Frank said quietly.

"It is where I come from. Round 'ere. And we're round 'ere, ain't we?" he snapped aggressively.

"Okay then, okay." Frank took a sip. "But then when we finish these, I buy you one."

"'Course."

"Then you'll feel you have to buy me another one – so we keep going all night long. Until we both flake out I suppose."

"'S'right. That's the fun of it," Harry grinned, anger forgotten.

"They're in 'ere, Dinko!", came a sudden shout from the door.

"Move it," Harry dived for a back door.

He looked round to see Frank was already moving – but towards the main door, grabbing up a bottle from a table, his face furious. Harry groaned and dashed back to him.

"You can't fight Dinko's lot on your tod. Come on!" Harry grabbed his arm.

Not wanting trouble in his pub, the Landlord whipped open the back door, pushed them out and slammed and locked the door after them.

"Let's get 'em, Harry!" Frank shouted. "Round to the front. That's where they are! Gettem from the rear! Tactics!"

"Don't be a bloody fool, Frankie! There's too many of 'em. Come on," Harry yelled, pulling him along forcibly.

They dashed off again.

"Where we going to now then?" panted Frank as Harry finally slowed down.

"Might as well go to the railway station. No point 'anging round 'ere now, not with Dinko's lot on the 'unt for us. So we might as well go back to Camp sooner rather than later."

Once on the train Frank was asleep in seconds. Harry nodded off too but roused as they pulled into Padgate Station. Waking Frank was not easy. At Harry's insistence they stopped at a pub they passed on the way back to Camp, 'For the drink we missed in Liverpool'.


Next morning at Reveille Frank and others were still sleeping heavily, but made it to Parade – just – bleary-eyed and feeling decidedly unwell.

"What a sorry looking lot you lot are," roared Sergeant Keys, making Frank and most of the others wince. "'Itting the bevvies last night was you? Well don't worry because 'aving done it meself before, I know just 'ow you're feeling right now. So I'm going ter be nice and considerate this morning, ain't I?"

"Yes Serg," they chorused hopefully and obediently, heads aching, agreeing as always. As they'd learned it best to do.

"What am I going ter be?"

"Nice and considerate, Serg."

"Right. So as a lot of you are feeling what we might call 'a bit delicate' we'll just take a gentle stroll round the Parade Ground this morning instead of the usual run. So what do you say ter me?"

"Thank you Serg." they chorused gratefully.

The Sergeant switched his look to a glare at them.

"But you lot are a disgrace to the Queen's uniform fer gettin' so disgustingly drunk last night. Don't matter if you was in civvies then, you're in uniform now. So you'll do the gentle stroll at the double! Got it?"

"Yes Serg." Mournfully.

"Right turn. By the right – at the Double - march!"

While they made an effort, the Sergeant kept his smile hidden. Sweating it out of them was the best or at least the quickest cure he firmly believed.

At lunch time Frank and some others couldn't manage their usual amount. He just picked at it. To his amazement, Harry seemed unfazed by the amount he'd drunk last night either this morning or now, stacking his plate as high as he usually did.

"Harry, last night," Frank began.

Dim, confused memories, unless they were his imagination, were bothering him.

"Yup? Great sausages these, ain't they?" holding one up.

Frank shuddered, his stomach not yet recovered.

"Did I drink much?" he asked.

Harry sorted through his own memories.

"'Bout fifteen pints I should reckon," he exaggerated, but not by much.

Frank stared at him. That many?

"And – was there a bit of a fight?"

"A bit of a fight? Frankie, you piled into Dinko and 'is mates like you get into a pub fight every night of every week!"

"Oh – My – God!" Frank stared at him, jaw dropping. "I remember us drinking a fair bit in a few pubs and then – did I really hit someone with a beer bottle?"

"You did. Dinko's sidekick – a bloke they call 'Irish' 'cos that's what 'e is. I was a bit occupied meself but I think 'e'd 'it you with it first, but then you busted it on 'is 'ead. Luckily you didn't 'glass' anyone with the bit still in your 'and. If you 'ad the cops would have been called for sure."

"Won't the cops be after us anyway? Because of the fight?"

"Nah!" Harry was definite. "No one down our way would want the cops sticking their noses in over a little thing like that!"

"When 'Irish' hit me I was so mad I could have killed him Harry! I'd never felt like that before. At any time."

"That was only the beer talking," Harry said carelessly. "Nothin' ter worry about. It can take some people that way. You ever been drunk before?"

Frank shook his head.

"That's it then. So you ought ter get a medal fer last night, Frankie. First pub crawl - first drunk – first pub fight - first bottle-smash. And then you grabbed up another bottle to 'ave another go at them in that other pub when they caught up with us again. A real tiger you are when you want ter be!" He laughed loudly.

"You sure we won't be reported to the police by anyone?"

"Nah. Not for a little thing like that," Harry said again. "Not down our way in Liverpool. Not when there was no real damage done. And no real injuries. Mind you, we won't go back there for a bit. Dinko and his crew will be on the lookout for us. So we'll do our drinking round 'ere instead."

Frank pushed his dinner plate aside. In no way was he going to get drunk like that again. Not if it could make him get as angry as last night over things. Not when he could have killed someone. Or 'glassed' someone. And if Harry got offended – well too bad.


"At ease Jackson."

Frank stood at ease in front of the Group Captain's desk. Basic Training was over.

"So you want to be in Aircraft Control, Jackson?"

"Yes sir. I have had some experience in the Control Tower at Wingmore Airfield, Kent, sir."

"So I see from your Application Form. I'm pleased to tell you you've Passed the Proficiency Test, so you're being Posted to that Section for further training."

"Thank you sir."

"Collect your Orders on your way out, Travel Warrant home for three days Leave now you've finished Basic Training." He paused. "Have you thought of making a career in the RAF?"

"Not really sir. I'm planning to be an architect."

"Mmm. Think about it. You seem to have the right qualities."

"Thank you sir." Frank saluted, about-turned and marched out to pick up an envelope with his name on.

He glanced through the papers on the way to the NAAFI. He'd arranged to meet Harry there to swap notes after he'd 'phoned mum and dad.

"What you got, Frankie?" Harry asked when he walked in ten minutes after Frank sat down at a table with a mug of tea.

"Air Traffic Control? What about you?"

"RAF Regiment. Otherwise known as 'Rock Apes'. Guarding you guys and your airfields and 'planes. So we might meet up again some time."

"Could be. You packed up and ready to go?"

"Packed up. I'm meeting Daisy in Warrington at five, after she's finished work. Her Mum's letting me stay with them till I 'ave to go off so I'll 'ang around 'ere for a bit.

Frank stood up and held out his hand.

"All the best Harry."

"Same to you Frankie. And don't you keep getting drunk and inter fights."

"Sure thing. And the same to you."


Three weeks later Frank was standing in front of another officer, a Squadron Leader.

"Rush job, Jackson. You're flying out from Northolt to Cyprus tomorrow to join manning the Control Tower at RAF Akrotiri."

"Yes sir."

"Been casualties, so no time for the usual Leave period before going, I'm afraid."

"No sir. Permission to inform my parents of my going sir? And where I'll be?"

"Permission granted. But give no reason for the rush."

"No sir. I'll tell them it's just a routine Posting."

"Exactly."

"But you always get Leave before you go abroad Frank!" May

protested on the 'phone. "It's called 'Embarkation Leave.'"

"Not with this Posting, Mum."

"Well I'm going to do something about it! It's not as though we're at war or anything so there can't be anything really urgent about it. I'm going to 'phone your Base."

"No Mum," Frank snapped. "You're not going to 'phone anyone at all about it. I'm in the RAF, I've had my Orders and that's it. Finish. I'll write to you as soon as I get to Akrotiri. Got to go as I've got a heap of things to do. 'Bye."

He rang off quickly, wishing Mum would realise he was not a little boy who needed her or anyone else to fight his battles. Not that there was any battle to fight. He'd already spoken to Ron, who had listened, told him to 'keep his head down out there' and to contact him giving his BFPO (British Forces Post Office) address when he could.

After they'd rung off, Ron stared at the papers on his desk. EOKA was being very active in Cyprus just now, demanding 'union with Greece', assassinating people who disagreed with them and especially British Service people, so he wondered if Frank was being rushed out because one of the Air Traffic Control people had become a casualty. In fact three of them had been travelling in a Landrover when it was blown up. All had been killed.

Ten minutes later when May 'phoned him demanding he 'do something about it', he told her that Frank was now a serving airman so 'subject to Orders'. If anyone 'made a fuss' it would be noted in his Service Record. Surely she didn't want that to be a blot on Frank's right at the beginning, did she?

# Chapter 16
## Postings

Frank looked down through the window as the 'plane banked to come into land at Akrotiri glad that, as far as he knew anyway, EOKA had no anti-aircraft weapons.

It touched down and he joined the rest of the passengers standing up to get his hand luggage. The heat hit him as he stepped out of the 'plane to go down the steps to the Terminal.

"Bit warmer than London, Serg," he muttered to the Flight Sergeant in front of him.

"Sure is. In every sense," he replied looking over to the Terminal where non-Service Cypriots were working. A wagon towing trailers were coming towards the 'plane to off-load cargo. "Any one of those could be an EOKA terrorist planning to plant a bomb on board."

Frank looked at him. "Yeah. Suppose you're right."

He looked uneasily at the many working around them. Then he shrugged. They could be as loyal to the British as any Serviceman, he supposed. The trouble was – how can you tell whether they were or not? What is in another person's mind?

Once through the Terminal with his kitbag over his shoulder he joined the others going into their Barracks down the road from the Airfield. Orders were awaiting them.

Frank ripped open his envelope. He was to Report to the Control Tower at 18.00 hours – four hours time. They weren't giving him much time to get bored, he thought. First priority – where was the Mess to get something to eat? If they were still serving.

They were.

He was able to get transport to the Airfield where he showed his orders to the RAF Policeman at the Gate and was waved through.

"LAC Jackson reporting for duty, sir." He held out his orders to the Flight Lieutenant in the Control Tower.

"Good. We were told you were coming. We're short-staffed at present. Casualties. What's your experience?"

Frank told him.

"Okay. We've got two transports coming in, in the next twenty minutes. Let's see how you do."

Frank took his seat and put on the headset while he scanned the panels of information while the Flt.. Lt. stood behind him, watching his every move.

The radio squawked and he was busy.

Once the transports were safely down, he clapped Frank on the shoulder.

"Good. You did just fine. Control the next transits in and out, while I'm doing other things. Like me you'll be on duty till 06.00 hours."

"Yes sir."

Frank settled down. Once those were in and out, there was nothing scheduled for another half hour. He began to wish he'd brought some of his architecture study books from the barracks. While he'd expected this work pattern because this was the way it had worked at Wingmore at its less busy times, he hadn't thought it sensible to bring them to his first spell on duty. To start with he hadn't known how busy it was going to be here.

Using the powerful binoculars he looked round the Airfield from the excellent viewpoint of the Control Tower. In the northern direction was the big Limassol Salt Lake, more towards the east were woods, fields and then the beach and sea. On the other side were the buildings of the Airfield.

As darkness began to fall a Canberra photo-reconnaissance aircraft came in. Presumably it had been over-flying the Troodos Mountains where EOKA were believed to have their main bases. Venom ground-attack 'planes were on their hardpoints – none were listed for action tonight though one was always at 'Readiness'. The Meteor night-fighters were on their hardpoints as well. They weren't scheduled for action tonight either.

Then it was full darkness though there was a half-moon occasionally covered by clouds. The lights on top of the perimeter fence had come on illuminating the ground underneath them but there were limits to each area so there were small patches of deep shadow between the lights.

One of the lights blanked out.

"Flight! One of the perimeter lights has gone out," Frank snapped, staring at it through the binoculars.

"It happens." The Flight Lieutenant got up from his desk and came across. "We gave the job to a local Contractor, good for PR and local relationships you see, and bulbs sometimes blow either because they were faulty, or wiring gone wrong somewhere. We'll do a report and they'll fix it tomorrow."

He went back to his desk but Frank was still staring at the now wide stretch of blackness.

"There's a big black blob there by the fence now, Flight. It wasn't there before."

Sighing, Flight came back, took the binoculars and looked.

"Nothing I can see."

He put them down by Frank who immediately picked them up to look again

"Can't see it now, but I'm certain it was there before." Frank paused. "Flight, what if that blank out was sabotage, that blob was some terrorists grouped where they were cutting the wire to get in and the blob's gone because they're now inside? A bunch that must be aiming to hit the 'planes we've got parked?"

"Fanciful." He paused. "But all too possible." He picked up a 'phone. "I'll get the Rock Apes onto it."

Seconds later three Landrovers roared out from a hanger, headlights blazing, one driving towards the fence, the other two towards the 'planes to get between them and the fence.

Gunfire erupted towards them from by the fence, one headlight of the 'rover driving to the fence plunged into darkness. Immediately a Brengun mounted on that 'rover fired back, lashing where the gunfire had come from. It stopped abruptly.

The other two 'rovers increased their speed.

A searchlight switched on pointing at the sky then dropped till the area between the Venom night fighters and the fence was lit up like day. Half-a-dozen figures hugging the ground were suddenly visible.

"Drop your weapons, and stand holding up your hands," came a bellowed order from the 'rover, first in English then in (bad) Greek.

Covering gunfire came from two on the ground as the others leaped to their feet and dashed towards the Venoms.

The windscreen on one of the 'rovers shattered and it abruptly twisted and went tumbling over and over as the driver died.

At the same instant the Bren on the other opened up silencing the gunfire in seconds, then hit two of the four running towards the 'planes.

The remaining two hurled home-made grenades at the Venoms, then dived headlong.

One grenade exploded, wrecking its target, the other went over but damaged another Venom, but then they raked more Venoms with stengun fire till they ran out of ammunition including some re-loads. They flung the now useless weapons aside, and stood up arms held high.

Troopers leaped from the 'rover to grab them, others went to the fallen terrorists as a fire engine hurtled towards them to put out the blazing Venoms,.

"You did a good job there Jackson," the Flight Lieutenant said "If you hadn't spotted the terrorists we wouldn't have warned the Rock Apes and God knows how much damage they'd have done. Be interesting to know what their intentions were."


In England, May fretted, Ron worried. Every mention in the newspapers or on the radio or TV of the activities of EOKA was followed and analysed to see what danger Frank was in.

The attack on the Airfield was mentioned with just the comment 'it had been repulsed with minimal damage being done'. When a letter arrived from Frank three days later it said he had arrived at Akrotiri but made no mention of the attack. Not knowing it had already been reported back home he had assumed he shouldn't mention it for 'Security reasons'.

When May wrote to him she said it had been in the newspapers, had he been near it at the time?

"What can I say about it Flight? Anything?" Frank asked.

"Better not say what you did Jackson. If they talked to the 'papers they could report it as being a full-scale battle. EOKA would love that kind of publicity. So wait till you get home to tell them what really happened. And even then tell 'em not to talk to the 'papers. For now, better to keep it to that you know what happened but weren't involved.. With the Services, Security is vital but another factor is not to give any chance for the Enemy to make propaganda out of it."

Frank nodded. He could see that. Pity. Mum might have told Pauline who lived next door what he'd done. She'd said she'd write to him, but hadn't replied to either of the letters he'd sent her so far.


"Fancy a trip to Limassol tonight? Only I know a smashing *taverna* there," Trevor suggested.

Trevor had been in Cyprus two months and this was Frank's first Saturday night off-duty. Limassol was their nearest town outside the Sovereign Air Base.

Frank hesitated. Did Trevor have in mind a pub crawl like Harry's? In no way was he going to get drunk like that again. Not just because of 'the morning after' but because of the way he had reacted to the beer.

"I ration myself to one or maybe two pints at the most," he said.

"That for the whole evening?" Trevor asked incredulously.

"Yup. The thing is, the last time I got drunk I smashed a bottle over a guy's head. We'd got into a bit of an argument in a pub."

"That must have been some argument! And I thought you was a quiet sort of bloke with you always reading them books! Okay you stick to your two pints. Or glasses of *ouzo*. They do have beer here but in the *taverna* I usually drink *ouzo*. So you'd better be careful what you drink of that if beer takes you like that."

The bus dropped them off in Limassol and Trevor guided him down to the old port area with a view over the harbour and ships. "This is the place."

The *taverna,* facing the sea had tables and chairs outside as well as inside.

"Hi Mariam," Trevor beamed up at the pretty young waitress from an outside table. "Two *ouzo* please. *Ouzo* is the traditional Greek drink," he added to Frank as Mariam moved off. "More so than beer. There's *Retsina* too but *ouzo* is better. I think so anyway."

"You know Mariam then?" Frank asked.

"Just a bit, and only here. Her old man's a bit too protective I think to let her really go out with me. I've tried."

A middle-aged man sporting a luxuriant moustache came out with two small glasses, a small jug of water and two small plates of *mezes* on a tray. He glared at them, snatched the note that Trevor held out and marched back into the *taverna* to get some change.

"What's this?" Frank pointed to the plates.

"They always serve it with *ouzo*. It's bits of fish, chips, olives and cheese. *Feta* cheese. Put a drop of water in the *ouzo.*"

Trevor poured in a little, turning the *ouzo* a cloudy white.

Frank took a cautious sip.

"Nice isn't it? Nothing like you get at home."

"You can get it in off-Licences sometimes. Try the *mezes.*"

Frank did so as the 'barman' as Frank thought of him, came back out and slapped coins on the table by Trevor.

"Sir. Can you tell me where the old buildings of Limassol are?" Frank asked him slowly and clearly.

"Why?" The word was almost a snarl.

"In England I am an architect. I design buildings. Houses. Big houses like castles sometimes," he added imaginatively. "I want to see some old buildings here. To see their ideas."

"Oh. There Limassol castle."

"Where do I go to see that?"

The man studied him, then gave directions. Then hesitated. "There are other places at Amathus, Kourion and its amphitheatre and Kolossi castle."

"How do I get to those places?" Frank made notes.

"You really interested in Cyprus? As a place? A country?" he asked, almost unbelievingly.

"Yes. I read what I could about its history as soon as I knew I was coming here. And since being here."

"But you British. At Base."

"Yes. But that doesn't mean I'm not interested in this country and its history. Because I am."

Over the next few weeks Frank visited the places, went back to the *taverna* several times and chatted with the owner of where he'd been and what the owner knew of their history. And found that he knew a lot. And he began to get a bit more friendly.

"You likely be here next Saturday?" the owner asked him quietly from behind the bar a month later. Frank had gone in to pay.

"Probably. Not sure at the moment." He didn't know the roster of duties.

The owner glanced around. No one was watching, so he leaned forward as he passed over change.

"Don't come. Just – don't come," he whispered. And turned away quickly to see to bottles.

As soon as Frank got back to Base he went to see the Intelligence Officer.

"What do you make of it Jackson?" he asked when Frank had described his contacts with the *taverna* owner and his warning.

"I think he must have been indicating there'll be trouble in Limassol next weekend, sir. Either for me personally or against any British visitors to Limassol."

"We've had no whispers from anywhere else about any trouble brewing so I shouldn't worry about it too much."

"No sir."

Frank saluted and left, fuming at the IO's patronising tone.

He found on the Monday he was scheduled for duty the next weekend so he couldn't go anyway. He watched from the Control Tower as Trevor and a bunch of others caught the bus for Limassol. Trevor had smiled at the warning too.

An hour later two ambulances raced from the Base, heading towards Limassol. When he went off-duty he looked around for Trevor to check if there had been any trouble at the *taverna*.

"Sorry Frank. Trevor's bought it. And two others that were sitting outside the *taverna*," Hugh Scanlon said, when he finally went to the NAAFI to ask if anyone there had seen him.

"What happened?" Frank was stunned.

"Trev and some others had gone to this *taverna*. They were sitting outside at two tables pushed together when a motor-bike went by, slowed as it drew alongside them and chucked a grenade. Got the lot of them. Two of them were killed, the others injured. Wasn't that the *taverna* you go to?"

"Yeah."

"Guess you were lucky to have been on duty then because it would have got you."

"It would have," Frank responded slowly.

So the owner had given him a warning. But didn't that mean he was in EOKA?

"We've pulled in that *taverna* owner you told us about Jackson," the Intelligence Officer collared him on his way back to barracks. Frank had decided to get a quick letter off home to let them know he hadn't been caught up in the 'atrocity' as it was bound to be reported "He insists he doesn't know a thing about anything and denies absolutely giving you any kind of warning. Apart from warning you off about chatting up his daughter a bit much. Which she confirmed as soon as we asked her."

"I see sir," Frank said grimly.

"You want to say something, Jackson?" snapped the IO.

"Sir, if you hadn't pulled him in I could have gone back as a friend sympathising with the terrible thing that had happened to his *taverna* and how glad I was he and Mariam were safe. Then if he does have links with EOKA I might have got some more out of him later."

"Could try that, I suppose."

"Won't work now sir. Because with the line of questioning he had he'll know I must have told you so he'll most likely chuck me out of the place on my ear as soon as he saw me."

"Or worse given all the circumstances. Better stay away from Limassol for a bit then."

"I intend to sir."

The Intelligence Officer looked at him. Jackson had been right from the beginning and his idea about handling the owner of the *taverna* was right too. But wanting to show he was on top of things the IO had immediately ordered the owner to be arrested and questioned. And then had had to release him as there was no real evidence against him and he had stuck to his story despite the hours of questioning. While he was now an Identified Suspect, Jackson's tactic would have been better. Could have been more productive in the long run. But it was too late now

"Ever thought of making RAF Intelligence a career Jackson?"

"No sir. Once I've finished my National Service I'm going back to being an architect."

"Mmm. Well think about it. You could go a long way."

As EOKA became still more active, the travels of off-duty Service personnel around Cyprus became more restricted, much to Frank's frustration. The main purpose of his wanting to be Posted Overseas was to explore the countries, but the possibility of kidnapping and/or assassination was a strong deterrent to wandering around sight-seeing.

"Jackson. You're being Posted," the Base Commander told him.

"Back home sir?" Frank asked eagerly. He was in the last eight months of his National Service and his time in Cyprus was now boring. Unable to explore in the Troodos Mountains because that was where the EOKA bands were mainly based – somewhere there anyway – they were effectively confined to the towns nearest to the Sovereign Bases.

"'Fraid not. You're going to RAF Eastleigh, just outside Nairobi. Kenya."

"Mau-Mau country, sir?"

"That's right. You're flying there next Monday, 09.00 hours. So in five days time.

Kit ready, Frank reported to the Flight Office at 08.30 hours.

The flight south was uneventful, Frank being wedged in with boxes of supplies stacked pretty much all around him. If Cyprus had been hot, Nairobi was hotter. On reporting to the Flight Office he was met by a Squadron Leader.

"You're just over-nighting here, Jackson. Tomorrow you fly up to Nanyuki Airstrip. It's here." He took Frank over to a large wall map. "We're here at Eastleigh, Nanyuki is near enough 90 miles away, just there." He grinned at Frank. "You'll not be living in the lap of luxury like you were in Cyprus, you'll be living under canvas, working under canvas and because it's over 6,000 feet up in the foothills of Mt. Kenya it can get quite chilly so I'm told. I've never been there. As a consolation you get an extra shilling a day as a 'Hard living allowance' and a tot of rum.

"I don't know whether you've been naughty to get Posted there or if it's a mark of trust because you're going to be the commanding Air

Controller there." He paused. "I guess it must be a mark of trust because you've been promoted to Flt. Sergeant too. Tomorrow morning you'll pick up a loyal Kikuyu as a Deputy Air Controller to go up with you. He's already had some experience but we want you to bring him on. Take a seat because I need to give you a Briefing about what's going on up there." He shouted to an African Orderly for some tea.

"Basically you're going to an airstrip that is on the edge of the Aberdare Forest and mountain range area with some white settler farms nearby. It's where the Mau-Mau are mainly grouped but though their activities are less than they used to be they're still going on, so we are still operating from there. A lot of it is leaflet dropping and recce, with only some ground attack when we pick up targets like Mau Mau camps."

"Any chance of exploring the Forest? What's the wildlife like up there? And scenery?" asked Frank.

"Scenery is fantastic, wildlife plentiful, but security is too dodgy to go wandering up there either alone or in small sight-seeing groups. Hopefully at some stage in the future it'll be safe because there's the Aberdare on one side and the foothills of Mount Kenya on the other. Maybe at some stage they'll start getting more tourists like they are in Europe now rather than just a few wealthy Big Game Hunters. If they do it'll do the local economy a lot of good. But not yet."

"Pity. But if that's the way it is, that's the way it is."

"But maybe, if you reckon your Deputy is up to handling Air Control on a quiet day you could do a flight over the area for an hour."

For some hours Frank sought out everything he could find of the Aberdare region. It all confirmed what the Squadron Leader had said.

The next morning he met a Kikuyu with the widest smile he'd ever seen, making him smile in return. They saluted each other and Frank held out his hand.

"Hi, I'm Flt.Sergeant Frank Jackson. Pleased to meet you."

"I am LAC Gachara David Mweri," the Kikuyu said, beaming.

"Great. I understand you'll be my Deputy up a Nanyuki."

"That is so sir. I am most pleased we will be serving together. I believe our aircraft is ready for us."

"Let's go to the Flight Office and get going then."

Frank swung his kitbag onto his shoulder, beating Gachara to grabbing it, and together they walked over to the Flight Office to check out.

"You'll fly up with other supplies in the Dakota warming up on the tarmac. Best of luck," said the Dispatcher briefly. "They've almost finished loading," he added pointedly.

Frank looked round the 'plane as they strapped themselves in. So this was the military version of the 'planes that Dad had had flying from Wingmore from the earliest days of the Air Transport arm. Interesting.

The short flight to Nanyuki airstrip took them over forest, then touched down just outside the village. They taxied up towards the collection of tents that served as Reception and several grouped in tidy lines, as the living quarters for staff.

ERKS doubled out to unload as the door in the side of the Dakota swung open and Frank and Gachara went down the short stepladder. Carrying their kit they walked together to the tent with the sign 'Flight Office'.

"Flt.Sergeant Jackson and LAC Gachara David Mweri, Air Controllers reporting for duty sir," Frank snapped, saluting.

"Good." Squadron Leader Beamish stood to shake Frank's hand, ignoring Gachara. ""We'll go to the Communications and Air Control Tent and I'll introduce you to Harrison. He's the present Air Controller but he's due to be Demobbed so he's really anxious to get away."

"How long have we got for him to bring us up to speed, sir?" asked Frank.

"Two hours. Until the Dak. is ready to go back to Nairobi. So chop-chop. No time to waste."

"Let's go Gachara," Frank said, dropping his kitbag.

"There's no need for him to come," Beamish said. "He can get your Quarters – your tent – ready. Then he can join the other Kikuyu in their encampment."

"Sir...," Frank said quietly, " ... as I understand it, LAC Mweri is my Deputy. So he needs to know everything I do."

Beamish looked at him sharply, lips tightening.

"There's no time to debate this with you now, Flt.Sergeant. So he can come. Then we'll need to have a discussion, you and I."

He strode out.

"Sorry about that," Frank muttered to Gachara, feeling he'd been treated shabbily.

"Don't be sir. That is usual in Africa," he muttered back, equally quietly. "Do you really want me to come?"

"Yes."

In the Air Control tent a Flt.Sergeant looked up and as soon as he saw Frank, leaped to his feet.

"Glad you're here, very glad I can tell you, Flt.Sergeant. Right. To update you." He broke off seeing Gachara.

"LAC Mweri is my Deputy, so he needs to be updated as much as I do," Frank said quietly.

Harrison glanced at the Squadron Leader who nodded at him so Harrison spoke directly to Frank, pointedly ignoring Gachara.

"The Mau Mau seem to be running down their activities in this area so we've reduced the number of aircraft here. We've still got Harvards and a couple of Venom ground attack to fly patrols and support the farms if they're attacked and a Canberra comes across on photo-recces ever so often.

"There's farms here ...," he touched six places on a map on an easel, " ... that we are in radio contact with 24 hours a day. Besides the 'planes we've got a small Detachment of RAF Regiment here and some Kikuyu loyalist Home Guard and armed police.

"There's ground patrols and recce flights and we go in when we've got some Intelligence of locations but we're also on constant readiness in case there's attacks on any of the farms which there are sometimes. Anything else you want to know?"

"Call signs lists?" Frank asked.

"Here." Harrison tapped a clipboard on the desk, looking at his watch. "You'll need to see off the Dak. And take care with it as I'll be aboard. Permission to leave sir?" he saluted the Squadron Leader.

"Permission granted."

Harrison doubled away as Frank sat down at the desk, checked the Movements Sheets and checked the radar screen, Gachara by him.

"Calling D-45," Frank said into the mike.

"D-45. Ready for departure in 30 minutes."

Frank acknowledged, and sat back in the chair. One Departure, the Dak, in 30 minutes, Arrivals listed as two Venom returning from Patrol in 45 minutes.

"Mweri, take over," ordered Beamish. "Jackson, a word."

In the Squadron Leader's 'office' he sat behind his desk while Frank stood at attention in front of it.

"How long have you been in Africa, Flt.Sergeant?"

"Just under 24 hours sir."

"I've been here over thirty years. I was born here. So I think I should know more about Africa and the Africans than you do, don't you?"

"Yes sir."

"Furthermore I've been in the RAF here more years than I care to remember, I have managed to reach the rank Flt. of Squadron Leader so I also think that I know the ways of the RAF here better than you. Don't you agree? Flt.Sergeant?"

"Yes sir."

"So when I give orders to you, one of the Servicemen here, I expect them to be carried out immediately without any question or hesitation. Do you understand?"

"Yes sir."

"Excellent though many Africans and Kikuyu are as individuals, you simply can't expect as much of them as you can of Europeans. To do so would be grossly unfair to them."

"I understand sir."

"Do you." Bleakly. Not liking Frank's tone.

"I may have misunderstood sir, the part that the Kings African Rifles played during the last war. But I had understood they fought alongside and as part of the British Army against the Japs in Burma. And are doing so with us against the Mau Mau right now."

"Are you trying to argue with me?"

"No sir. Trying to clear up what might be a misunderstanding on my part."

"Are you." Bleakly again. "Understand this Flt.Sergeant. You are in command over Mweri and therefore responsible for every mistake he makes. Furthermore he will have his place in the Kikuyu encampment and you do not associate with them as equals. There are Europeans in this Camp both RAF and RAF Regiment and you will find companionship among them. Standards of Discipline will be maintained while I am in Command. Do I make myself clear?"

"Yes sir."

"Go and take command back from Mweri. It's almost time for the Dak to take off. Once the last of the Venoms are down, you're both on duty till 20.00 hours when air operations close here for the night, subject to Emergencies."

"Yes sir." Frank saluted, about turned and went to the Air Control tent.

He hadn't been formally Reprimanded it seemed, but he had no doubt that a black mark was now on his record. It looked as though he simply had to accept this way of doing things here. Or he would get into serious trouble.


"Well, well. Fancy meeting you 'ere, Frankie lad!"

In the Mess tent Frank turned round at the half-familiar voice and found himself staring into Harry Climber's face.

"What are you doing here?" Frank asked, equally pleased to see someone he knew. Especially Harry.

"Remember I was Posted to the RAF Regiment? So I'm 'ere guarding this place. Nursemaiding you lot really. Not on me tod o' course. There's about twenty of us 'ere now. Plus Kikuyu. Come and 'ave a drink. It's not as good as Liverpool beer but it is beer, sort of. It's not too bad really."

They swapped stories of where they had been over the past year, others joined them, tried to ply the new Air Controller with drinks but Frank stuck to his 'no more than two pints', and finally his 'oddity' was accepted.


Three months later Frank was well settled in. He'd had a weekend Leave in Nairobi (shared with Harry), gone to Nanyuki village a couple of times, but there was nothing much to see there. It would be many years before it became a start-off point for tourists to the Aberdare Forest and Mt. Kenya.

He had wanted to trek into Aberdare Forest but was warned off because of Mau Mau gangs crossing his path, but to compensate he had been able to grab the Observer's seat in the Harvard patrol flights a couple of times. He'd not been allowed to accompany a foot patrol.

"You are not here as a tourist, Flt.Sergeant," Squadron Leader Beamish had rasped.

There had been little real action apart from the regular air and foot patrols. The pacification programmes were working by now, the Kikuyu loyalists were far outnumbering the Mau Mau fighters as the concessions to Self-rule already made by the British were becoming more widely understood and accepted. There had been a couple of alarms from a farm or two, 'planes were dispatched to deal with them followed up by foot patrols but there had been no real attacks on them.


Frank sat back in his chair in Air Traffic Control and stretched his arms above his head, yawning. They were soon to close down Air Traffic Control for the night as it was nearly dark and the last 'plane had landed, though the Radio Watch desk would still be manned.

The alarm klaxon suddenly blared from the radio on the far side of the tent. Immediately the Duty Officer (a Kikuyu Serviceman) cancelled it as he snapped, 'Nanyuki Air Base' into the mike.

"White's Farm under attack by Mau Mau. We need help urgently," came over the radio.

"Back-up coming," snapped the Duty Officer as he hit the Camp Klaxon, just as another call came in, then more. Every farm in their area was being attacked at the same time.

Beamish came running in, closely followed by the Captains of the Kikuyu Detachment and the RAF Regiment.

"Report," he snapped.

"Every farm is being attacked by Mau Mau at the same time it seems sir. At least, the messages have come in one after the other."

"Switch on the runway lights,Flt.Sergeant. Ready for all aircraft to be deployed."

"Lights already on sir. Ready to Dispatch as soon as aircraft notify they're ready," Frank snapped.

"Gentlemen. I want every man deployed to support the farms including all ground forces. You've already got your designated zones. Move it."

"Sir," the RAF Regiment Captain interrupted, "That would leave the Base completely undefended. So ...,"

"Captain. All those farms are being attacked right now. And they've all got women and children living there. The farm families as well as their Kikuyu staff. So – oh very well, leave three. That will be sufficient to safeguard a Base that's under no kind of threat at all. Flt.Sergeant," he snapped to Frank, "You take Command here. I'm leading the fighters. Hold them till I'm ready and in command."

He ran out.

Pilots reported in as they were ready but were still held until the Squadron Leader cut in to say he was ready for take-off. One after the other they roared off.

At about the same time Landrovers and lorries crammed with troops sped out of the Gate. Suddenly the Base was quiet.

"Have you informed the farms backup is on its way?" Frank asked the Duty Office.

"Yes sir. As the 'planes took off."

"Good work."

A minute later Harry hurried in.

"Frankie. I'm told you're in Command 'ere now. Sir." Harry snapped to attention and peeled off a sizzling salute, making no attempt to hide his grin.

"So I've been told - Corporal," Frank grinned back. It vanished.

"Kioni." Frank looked at the Duty Officer. "Have all the farms been attacked at the same time like this before?"

"No sir. Usually only one, sometimes two farms at a time, but never all of them attacked at the same time like this."

"Then either it's a big move by the Mau Mau – or I wonder if they're diversions to pull our people away to raid our Weapons Store. Harry..," Frank snapped now urgently, " ... post whoever you've got here around the Weapons Store.   Get them well dug in, well weaponed up and all round the place.  And we all here will need weapons double quick.  Hand guns and Stens.  Move! Take over my place, Gachara."

Frank slipped to the tent door as Harry dashed out, dropped down and peered out.  Everything seemed quiet.

He slid around the tent to check all sides.  No movements that he could see.  Then Harry and another man arrived, carrying weapons and ammunition.

"Men in position sir.  But that means the Gate's undefended."

"Can't be helped."  Frank, Gachara and Kioni snatched up the weapons, and loaded them as he spoke.  "The fence round the place could be penetrated all too easily anywhere so they could by-pass the Gate anyway.  How many men have you got?"

"Two plus me and Phil here.  And you three."

"Bloody hell!" muttered Frank.  "Gachara.  We've got to make sure this Communications tent is safe-guarded as much as the Weapons Store.  So ...,"

An outburst of gunfire crashed into the quiet from the Gate.

"You two back to the Weapons Store.   Gachara, alert the Squadron Leader.  Kioni, check the situation of the farmers and how determined those attacks are."

He rammed a handgun in his belt and snatched up a Stengun thankful for the weapons training he'd had in Basic Training, slight enough though it had been, he now thought.  At least he knew one end of a gun from the other and how to point it in the right direction.  He slipped outside.

Silhouetted against the landing strip lights were three crouching figures running towards him.

He lay down and waited till they were closer, then he opened up with the Sten.  The three fell.

Frank stayed where he was.  He might have missed.  They might have gone to ground in time.  They might be dead.  No movement from them that he could see.

He eased back into the tent.

"Report."

"Squadron Leader said we had to cope," Gachara snapped.

"All farmers say attacks determined, but not sure how many attackers," put in Kioni.

Frank slid outside again, circled the Communications tent.

No one seemed about round here but the gunfire was now almost incessant from the Weapons Store.

"You'll have to look after yourselves for a time. They need back-up at the Weapons Store," Frank whispered, poking his head through the tent doorway.

Outside he dropped to the ground and crawled as quickly as he could towards the Weapons Store. If he stood to run he'd be seen against the airfield lights just as he'd seen those others.

He aimed towards one of the muzzle flashes going towards the Store, answering muzzle flashes could be seen coming from three points round the Store, and fired a double shot. There was a shout, a hurried movement, he fired again and the figure collapsed.

He switched his aim to another muzzle flash and then return fire started coming in his direction. He quickly rolled a dozen yards and fired again.

There came a shout from the attackers, then a dozen people sprang to their feet and ran towards the Store.

Frank set his lips and fired a continuous burst towards them.

His Sten fell silent, ammunition gone. A re-load as quickly as he could, then a fresh burst. Bodies dropped, but then he saw the last two were right by the Store. Two figures rose from the ground to meet them, and Frank had to cease firing because he could hit the defenders.

A faint noise behind him. He rolled without looking up, and a machete slashed down at where his head had been a second before.

He whipped up his Sten gun pulling the trigger. One shot that missed, then just faint clicks. Ammunition gone.

More desperate rolling. The machete was stabbed downwards, rather than a slash, and it cut down into his shoulder, not his chest.

A grab for the handgun in his waistband as the machete was raised again by the now grinning Mau Mau warrior.

The gun came free. No time to aim so a double shot. The second one hit.

A look of surprise came over the African's face and then he collapsed on top of Frank. He pushed off the body and staggered to his feet.

No gunfire was coming from the Weapons Store direction now but people were running into the Communications Tent. That had to take priority now.

Frank set off too, at a stumbling run, somehow managing to ram a fresh magazine into the Sten as he went.

He got to the tent door.

Inside Kioni was lying out on the floor, the Mau Mau who had just shot him was smashing the Communications set. Another was rifling through a desk drawer, stuffing papers into a satchel and a third was grinding the muzzle of a rifle against Gachara's head.

"Tell your Commander ...," he was saying when Frank pushed in, swaying from blood loss but Sten gun pointing.

The rifle swung round to Frank but Gachara launched himself bodily into him, both going flying.

Frank's three shot salvo got the Mau Mau smashing the Communications set, another brief burst caught the one rifling the desk already bringing up his gun as he turned to face Frank, then Gachara and the Mau Mau, fighting like tigers on the ground collided with Frank, sending him sprawling.

Gachara came up on top kneeling across the Mau Mau's legs. Frank saw the Mau Mau pulling a knife from his belt aiming it to stab Gachara in the side. He scrabbled forward for the knife arm, grabbed it as a shot hit him in the thigh from the doorway. A fourth Mau Mau had come.

Frank slumped forward, the knife slashing across the side of his chest, diverted from stabbing Mweri.

Gachara hammered the Mau Mau with a ferocious upper cut.

A double shot came from outside the doorway then another, but Frank was already unconscious.

Two seconds later Harry appeared in the doorway, Stengun switching around. But the Mau Mau were all down.

"Sergeant badly wounded," snapped Gachara. "I tie this Mau Mau, you see to Sergeant then I contact Squadron."

Gachara wrenched wires from the wrecked Communications set

and turned to the unconscious Mau Mau as Harry snatched the First Aid kit from his belt and knelt beside the rapidly bleeding Frank.


Frank opened his eyes and looked around. Memories came back. Gunfire. A knife. Gachara.

But he wasn't in the Comms. tent. Odd. He was in bed. A camp bed. He cautiously swiveled his eyes.

He was in a tent. A couple more beds were beside him. With people in. Wires and tubes were leading from his arm to – was that a bag of blood on a stand?

"You awake now, Flt.Sergeant? Feeling better?"

Then Gachara came into view from where he'd been sitting at the foot of the bed, out of Frank's line of sight.

"Where am I? What happened, Gachara?"

"You in Hospital Tent. You took knife meant for me, Flt.Sergeant Then you shot by new Mau Mau at door, but Corporal Climber got him. They putting blood into you now because you lost much. I get Orderly."

He vanished while Frank frowned, trying to remember. But a lot was confused.

Good God, he suddenly realised! He had to get back to the Comms. because Gachara wasn't there! He'd just been here!

He struggled to sit up but felt as weak as a kitten! He'd better start doing those training runs that Harry kept on at him about.

"You just stay right there, Flt.Sergeant," a quiet voice ordered, as hands pushed him back on the bed.

The white-coated Orderly checked tubes, the bag of blood and fussed around.

"But I've got to get back to Air Control! There's air movements that have got to be controlled," Frank insisted.

"That's being taken care of."

"But Gachara, LAC Mweri, was in here just a minute ago!"

"Another Controller's already been flown up from Nairobi to assist him, so that's taken care of. Now are you awake and feeling okay? The Squadron Leader wants to see you ASAP."

"Right. Where's my uniform then?"

"He'll come to you. So I'll tell him you're okay."

Frank struggled to co-ordinate his thoughts.

Ten minutes later the Squadron Leader appeared by his bedside, pulling up the chair from the foot of the bed.

"How're you feeling Flt.Sergeant? Fit enough to make a Report?"

"Yes sir." He was. More or less. And it was the expected answer.

"So exactly what happened here?"

"After the Squadron had gone I thought the Mau Mau might attack here as the pattern of attacks on all the farms at once hadn't Flthappened before. That was what I was told when I checked. I thought those attacks could have been diversions with their main objective being our Weapons Store here as well as trying to wreck the place. Corporal Climber had few men so I ordered that they be deployed round the Weapons Store itself and that LAC Mweri, Corporal Kioni and I be armed.

"The Mau Mau did attack both the Weapons Store and the Comms. They must have breached the Fence in at least two places because a group came towards the Comms. from a different point to the group attacking the Weapons Store. I dealt with those coming towards the Comms. then I gave some assistance to the Weapons Store, came back to the Comms. when we came under attack again. That's it I guess sir."

"So it was your decision to leave the Gate unguarded?"

"Yes sir. I considered the two targets they would be after would be the Weapons Store and maybe the Comms. I considered that as there were no 'planes here to defend anyway it would be better to defend those two points in view of our very limited manpower."

"And you considered that you would need to be armed as well and then go to get involved with defending the Weapons Store? When your prime responsibility was to maintain Communications."

Frank set his lips wondering just how many Charges he was going to be facing at his Court Martial.

"Yes sir. Because LAC Mweri was perfectly capable of handling that. As he proved by his conduct throughout. As for weaponry, it was fortunate that we did have some as it meant we could not only defend the equipment but our lives."

"I disagree, Flt.Sergeant. It was not just fortunate." He paused, then smiled. "It was in fact excellent tactical planning and execution on your part. Every one of your decisions was right."

Frank stared at him. That sounded as though there wouldn't be a Court Martial after all.

"Now for your future. We can't give you the medical treatment you really need here. So as soon as you can be freed from those gadgets ...," he gestured at the stand, " ... you will be transferred to a hospital in Nairobi. It's possible you will then sent back to the UK but that's likely to depend on how much of your National Service you'll have left when they reckon you'll be fit to be Discharged. Unless you're minded to make the Air Force your career."

"No sir. I plan to be an architect."

"Pity. We could do with people like you." He stood up.

"Sir. How's LAC Mweri?"

"He's likely to soon be Flt.Sergeant Mweri. I'm recommending him for promotion. And Corporal Climber to Sergeant. Neither were particularly wounded though both had some scratches and bruises. But they both did very well. I'll see you again before they fly you out."


Frank was sitting up in bed reading a month old newspaper two hours later when Gachara came in beaming.

"How you doing Flt.Sergeant?"

"All the better for seeing you Gachara. Are you okay?"

"No injuries so okay fine." He sat down. "I told you go to Nairobi soon." He looked down, twisting his hat in his hands, then looked up. "Sir. I must thank you for saving my life. If you had not taken that knife strike I would be dead. So thank you sir."

Frank was embarrassed.

"Don't talk daft, Gachara," he mumbled.

"Not daft. I know it true." He smiled widely again. "Squadron Leader tell me he's recommending me for promotion to Flt. Sergeant." He hitched his chair closer. "Then soon I apply for pilot training. To really be Air Force man."

"That's great Gachara! Can't think of a better bloke to get it! And to go on still further."

Gachara looked at him then glanced round.

"My real ambition is something really big, my friend," he said quietly. "The Mau Mau are wrong in what they do. The British Government have been saying from before they started about measures of independence. Some day I sure we get full independence. Be our own country. And can get an Air Force of our own." He stopped, wondering if he had said too much.

"I can't think of a better bloke to head it up, Gachara," Frank said just as quietly, holding out his hand. "I really hope you get it. You deserve to."

Gachara pumped his hand, grinning widely again.

"If I do I'll send you a personal invitation to visit our country again. In more peaceful times. So we can tour the Aberdare Forest together."

"That sounds great!"


Frank roused an hour later to see Harry sitting beside him.

"Hi Harry. You haven't been there long, have you?"

"Not long. How are you doing?"

"Dead lucky I think. Harry, thanks for what you did."

"What's that then?"

"Gachara said you got the guy who was just going to get me."

"Just paying you back. When you came charging out earlier you got enough of them to stop us getting over-run. We were able to settle the last two so I came across to you as there was a lot of noise coming from the Comms."

"Mighty glad you did."

"Yeah. By the way, they reckon now that those attacks on the farms really were diversions to pull as many of us as possible away from here so they could raid the Weapons Store, just like you thought. The Mau Mau had got a couple of vans outside the Gate to bring their guys in and load up with all the guns and ammo they could and blow up the rest. They got most of that from the guy Gachara knocked out. Mweri got a message off to the Squadron Leader and in the end 'e sent two 'Arvards back but they wasn't what we needed. We needed more boots on the ground." He grinned. "Or maybe we didn't because by the time the 'planes landed, we'd already got it sorted for them."

"From what the Squadron Leader said my congratulations are in order. Sergeant."

"'E said 'e'd recommend it, don't mean I'll get it."

"Bet it does. You certainly should do."

After Harry had gone Frank wrote a careful letter home.

# Chapter 17
## Back home

May opened the evening newspaper to see if there was any news from Kenya. This evening Des would bring home the morning Daily they had but ever since Frank had been sent abroad to Cyprus and then Kenya she taken to getting an Evening one as well. And she was living in dread of getting that telegram beginning 'Her Majesty regrets ..."

If they sent them now. Now that Elizabeth was Queen after the death of George V1 in 1952.

It was the main headline on Page 3 that blazed, 'Deadly attack by Mau Mau on Nanyuki Air Strip" that grabbed her attention. With near panic she read of 'Many deaths among the attackers' and 'Several wounded among RAF personnel including Flt.Sergeant Jackson who led the heroic defence.' But details were tantisingly few, though it did say that Frank's injuries were not 'life-threatening'. But that could mean anything. It could still mean they could leave him permanently crippled. Just as Kitty and Tim were.

So she would just have to wait days or weeks till a letter came from Frank himself. Or someone.

That sparked a thought. Several of Ron's people were ex-RAF! Maybe they still had contacts! She snatched up the 'phone.

"Have you heard about Frank?" she burst out as soon as she was through. "He's been wounded out in Africa."

"I know. I've already got Richard Sampson chasing up his contacts in the Air Ministry to find out details of his injuries and whether he'll be coming home to the UK. If he is."

"What do you mean **if** he is?" May demanded. "Surely they must send him home now that he's been wounded!".

"As we don't know how badly wounded he is beyond the fact they're not 'life-threatening', to quote the newspaper report, and the hospitals in Nairobi are first-class, he may already be on his feet and be fully fit in a couple of weeks. In which case as he's still got nearly three months of National Service left they may decide to keep him in the sunshine of Kenya rather than send him back to the beginning of winter here."

Ron was speaking as re-assuringly as he could while he knew that the 'not life-threatening' comment was not nearly as comforting as he was deliberately making it sound. After the first few weeks Kathleen's and Tim's injuries could have been described as 'not life-threatening' – but they were still severely disabled as they called it now, not 'crippled', though in reality it was just the same. He didn't know May's thinking had been exactly the same.

"You will let me know as soon as you hear anything? Anything at all?"

"Of course I will May."

"I mean as soon as you know anything? At any time of day or night."

"Of course I will May," Ron repeated. He put the 'phone down.

"Did Richard have any idea how long it might take?" Anne asked.

"Not really. Depends on where his contacts are in the Air Ministry now and how soon they can find out what."

Though he had spoken re-assuringly to May, Ron did not sleep much that night. Nor did May.

Ron was in the Flight Office at the Airfield at 10.30 the next morning when Richard hurried in.

"Just had some top-level gen, Ron," he said, beaming. "Straight from the RAF Chief Medical Officer at the hospital in Nairobi. Turns out he remembered me from 1940 when he was a Junior Doctor in my treatment team so he was ready to be more open than usual.

"Basically Frank had a stab wound from a machete into his left shoulder, then he was shot in his right thigh and a knife slash across the chest. Luckily that wasn't a machete. The wound was more consistent with the Bowie-type knife found by the Mau Mau that did it. Also luckily it was a slash not a stab so it's more of a flesh wound that bounced over the ribs rather than penetrating between them.

"The more dangerous wounds are the machete through Frank's left shoulder and the shot in the thigh. Dangerous because of their possible disabling effects because they're not 'life-threatening'."

"Only 'possible disabling effects'? queried Ron.

"'Likely' was the word he actually used," Richard said quietly. "And they'll be sending him back to the UK for more treatment later on."

"Right. Thanks for finding all that out so quickly Richard. Look, I'm going to have to be careful with the wording I use to May. So I'll tell her a 'superficial chest wound and other damage to an arm and leg that doesn't seem too serious at this stage'. If she gets back to you through the Company 'phone numbers, will you back that?"

"Sure." Richard repeated the phrases back to him. "Will you be saying the same to Anne, Kathleen and Tim?"

"I'll tell Anne the full facts, but use the same words to the other two. But I could see them pumping you for more."

"So can I. But I'll back you okay. One more thing. Apparently they're going to recommend Frank for a gong for his leading the defence of the Airstrip. The Distinguished Conduct Medal."

"That sounds good! And thanks. I'll get on to May now." Ron rang May. "Richard Sampson was able to find out some details from the hospital in Nairobi, May. Frank has three wounds I understand. One is what they call 'a superficial chest wound'. That means a cut that doesn't penetrate deeply, or a skin-deep wound only. A second was some damage to a leg and third an arm that don't seem too serious at this stage. So summing up, Frank is wounded but long-term effects are not too likely. And they'll most likely be sending him home to a hospital in the UK for final treatment."

May let out a huge sigh of relief.

"And they're going to recommend him for a medal for leading the defence of the Airstrip. The Distinguished Conduct Medal, Richard said. Better not say anything about that though in case it doesn't work out."

"Alright. I'll tell Des though."

"Of course."

Ron 'phoned Anne and Kathleen then went across to the Control Tower to tell Tim.

As a 'plane was just coming in from Malaga he waited till it was taxiing to its Arrivals point at the Terminal and was Impressed by the calm way that Tim handled it.

"Got a moment Tim?" he asked.

Tim glanced at the Status Board of incoming and outgoing Flights.

"There's nothing for fifteen minutes, Dad."

"It's about Frank."

"Yes?"

Ron went through what he'd already told May and Kathleen.

"I see," Tim nodded. "Any indication how much he'll be disabled? His arm, his leg or both?"

"I did say **some** damage to an arm and leg that doesn't seem too serious at the moment," Ron reminded him.

"You did, Dad." Tim looked straight at him. "And probably mother will swallow it. But I don't and most likely Kathleen won't because when we were injured we weren't told the full facts at the beginning. And a wound in either or both those places coupled with him being sent back to the UK for 'final treatment', makes me think it's more serious than just superficial wounds."

"Just between ourselves Tim, you're right. But if your mother does try to pump you for more details, just repeat what I've told you, will you? Because that's exactly what I told her. There's no need for her to worry before she has to. The reality is that some longer-lasting damage could have been done."

Tim nodded grimly. "So that'll be all three of us Dad."

"Yeah. But whatever physical damage there is, I bet he'll overcome it just as you and Kathleen have done."

"Yeah." Tim glanced at the Status Board. "I've got that 'plane due in ten minutes Dad."

Ron grinned at him and slapped him on the shoulder.

"A tactful way of telling me to push off, Tim. See you."

Ron went back to his office to 'phone Anne again.

Three days later he received a letter from Frank in which he gave more details of the severity of his injuries and Ron became increasingly grim as he read it. The stab in the shoulder had severed muscles, nerves and tendons so there was going to be a degree of paralysis at present not possible to say exactly how much. 'So I know a bit how Tim must feel now', he wrote. "The shot in the thigh has chipped the bone, splintering a chunk off it so they're working out some way of strengthening it. Ideally they'd like to graft another piece of bone into the place but the favourite seems to be to screw a metal plate each side to bridge the gap. So I'll be partly on the road to being the original Tin Man.'.

He then added that he'd written a rather different kind of letter to 'Mum'. 'No sense in worrying her sooner than need be."

The next day another letter came saying he was to be transferred back to a hospital in the UK on the 15th of next month – 'so too late for Christmas'.


May and Ron were waiting side by side outside the Ward of the RAF hospital just outside Aylesbury. There was snow on the pavements and grass outside but the roads had been clear enough. Neither commented on this being the 20th January, that awful Anniversary, the date when Thompson Road school had been bombed. Des and Anne were waiting in the Visitors Tea Room as the Rule of 'Two Visitors only', was strictly enforced here.

The Ward's double doors opened and a nurse appeared.

"You may come in. Half-an-hour Visit only this time please."

May and Ron went in together, then May dashed forward to Frank, halfway up the Ward. He was looking pale and thin but was smiling broadly

"Hello Mum, hello Dad. Nice to be home I must say. Even though it's a lot cooler here than Kenya."

"How are you Frank?" May asked, almost managing to keep her voice under control.

"Not too bad really. The arm's just a bit weak at present and the leg will soon be fixed up. They tell me I'll be Discharged in a few weeks." A briefest pause, "So how's things in father's office Mum? My job's still there is it? I've been keeping up my reading. Pretty much anyway."

"I suppose so. I'm sure it must be." May was rather bewildered at the way Frank was talking. Not saying anything of what had happened, just asking about his job! "Frank, what …?" she began.

"What's the Airfield like Dad? Busier than when I was last there I suppose. And the cruisers?" Frank cut across her.

Following the lead that Frank was clearly giving, Ron and he kept the conversation on those topics.

"Can we see the doctor for Frank Jackson, please?" Ron asked a nurse once they were outside the Ward.

"Of course. Come this way please."

"Please sit down, Mr. and Mrs. Jackson," the doctor invited, indicating the two chairs on one side of the desk.

May opened her mouth to explain their situation but the doctor was talking straight on, so she closed it again rather than interrupt.

"I don't know how much your son has told you about his injuries of course, but they are mending as well as can be expected considering how serious they were."

"Serious? But I'd understood they weren't particularly serious!" May burst out.

"Ah." The doctor obviously felt he had been wrong-footed.

"I think perhaps Frank has rather minimised the exact nature of his wounds," Ron said quietly. There was no way that could be kept up now that they were talking to the doctor, but Ron felt that now they had seen Frank, now that he was home, May would be better able to face whatever the truth was. "Perhaps you could explain exactly what the position is as of now. As we shall need to be caring for him in a few weeks."

"A few weeks? I'm afraid it's going to be a matter of several months rather than just a few weeks."

May felt a clutch of fear.

"Perhaps you had better tell us exactly what the score is Doctor." Ron said quietly.

"There is the matter of patient confidentiality, you know. If he hasn't seen fit to tell you exactly what happened."

"Doctor," Ron said quietly. "While I recognise that medical principle, we are determined to know exactly what our son's situation is. Now either you can tell us, which I would prefer as then we can ask anything else we may need to know to care for him when he is discharged, or we shall need to go back and ask him directly. Right now. You must recognise we are his parents."

The Doctor capitulated

"Very well. First, he is past the initial dangerous period. That was when he had lost so much blood he had to have urgent blood transfusions. But that was done in the Field first of all, then in Nairobi. So that's been sorted. Now we're putting right, as far as we'll be able to, the more serious shoulder and thigh wounds.

"The shoulder wound was a deep stab. Apparently it was done by a machete. That chipped the right shoulder joint but also severed some nerves and tendons. That will result in a degree of paralysis, how much has yet to be determined because the exercises he will need to do will undoubtedly help lessen that over time. The thigh wound was a gun shot that damaged the upper thigh bone. That is being rectified by the metal plate that has been inserted. As a fully grown man of course that means a far simpler repair job than if he'd been a child or adolescent who would be growing all the time."

"So war has now crippled my third child," May said bitterly. "The two older ones when they were children and now my youngest through a foreign war when we had no need to even be there. A more or less paralysed arm, and a damaged leg. So he's now a cripple too. And they call this peace!"

The Doctor and Ron looked at each other. Ron gave the slightest shrug.

"Thanks for telling us the score, Doctor," he said quietly. "Is it possible to give some estimate of when he might be Discharged?"

"Most likely in about three or four months. Which would have been about the time he'd have finished his National Service."

"Right. Can we have the details of Visiting Times, and is there anything he needs that we might be able to supply? Additional to the standard hospital facilities I mean."

"He doesn't really need anything, but I'm sure he'll appreciate any of the extra goodies his Visitors bring or send in," he smiled standing up. "Reception will give you a leaflet about Visiting Times etc."

Anne and Des were talking quietly together when May and Ron walked in.

"I'll get some more teas," Des said at once standing up.

"We'll tell you the score when Des comes back, Anne," Ron said quietly.

He was soon back.

"Thanks Des. This is the score as we got it from Frank's Doctor," Ron said, and repeated it. "That's all of it isn't it May?" he asked for confirmation.

"So how soon are you going to move in on him?" May demanded harshly, glaring at Ron. "Bribing him to leave me and join you lot in Folkestone? You were quick enough to talk to him about the Airfield weren't you? And the cruisers. Going to offer him a job there, are you? To get him away from me just as you did the other two?"

Ron stared at her, bewildered.

"As far as I know Frank's interest is architecture not Air Traffic Control or cruisers. He's always said he's kept up his reading about architecture for his future exams and he said that again just now didn't he? His letters have been full of things about the local architecture wherever he's been." He looked at Des. "Has he written to you any different?"

"No." Des seemed as bewildered as Ron. "What's made you say that May?"

"His past record," May snapped, jabbing a finger at Ron. "He bribed Kitty to go to Folkestone and then did the same with Tim. Got him away from me by promises of an Airfield job and God knows what else. I wouldn't be surprised to find he'd promised Tim that he'd take over the firm at some stage in the future."

"I don't think this is the time or place for this, May," Ron said quietly. "Beyond the fact that I most certainly didn't 'bribe' either of the children. It's true enough I told Tim about a job vacancy that was coming up but that was because he'd said he wanted a job around 'planes. But he applied for the vacancy in the Control Tower off his own bat when he saw the Internal Notice that went round everywhere. And I certainly didn't make any promise about him taking over the firm at some time'. I can't do that anyway because I don't own it. It's not mine."

"Oh no? You're the Chairman, aren't you? That's what it says on all the stuff you send out anyway. Or is that a pack of lies?"

"I was elected to that position by the Board. And they can just as easily replace me. But we're talking about Frank. What he wants to do for the rest of his working life. He shows talent as an architect doesn't he Des?"

"Yes," Des answered promptly. "And he's had some useful ideas about incorporating some of the things he's seen abroad into a project I've got on the go right now that we've been corresponding about." He hesitated momentarily. "My only anxiety is whether the damage to his shoulder will hinder his control of his instruments but I've also no doubt we'll overcome those if there are any."

May was about to go out of the door for shopping the next morning when the 'phone rang. She was half-expecting a call from Sheila

Mansfield about tomorrow's meeting of the Women's Group that they both went to, so she almost ignored it. Sheila could ring back later. Then she decided to answer it – it could be someone else.

"Hello Mum," Frank's voice sounded cheerful. "Got a moment?"

"Of course Frank. How are you feeling?"

"Not too bad. Just got back from some physio. Could you ask father to bring some books the next time you come? They are architecture books so he may already have them, but if he hasn't and if he could get them I'll send him a cheque. And I'd like some kind of smallish Drawing Board I can use here in bed if he can get one too. I've got some ideas for a 4-bedroomed house that could appeal to a certain niche market and I want to start work on them. The books I could do with are ...."

"You're still going to be an architect then? You don't want to be an Air Controller at your father's airfield? Or something with the cruisers?"

"Of course not. Being an Air Controller was a great experience at the time at Dad's Airfield and it meant I got a cushier number for National Service than I might have got but I'm only interested in being an architect as a career."

"A cushier number! But you got badly wounded doing that."

"Sure. But it would have been a lot tougher tramping through the jungles of Malaya if I'd been Posted there in the Army wouldn't it? By the way, it's been confirmed I'm getting a gong for what happened in Kenya. Now the books I need ..."

"Just give me a moment to get a pencil and pad. Right."

Frank read out the titles of the books he wanted.

"Got it. I'll ring father about them now in case he's got them in the office and we'll see about bringing them this weekend. And what do you mean about getting a 'gong'?"

"They say it's for 'leading the successful defence of the airstrip'. The DCM or Distinguished Conduct Medal. I feel a bit of a fraud really because the others deserve a medal just as much as me but I don't know whether they'll be getting one. They should do."


Three months later he was collected from the hospital by Des and May and taken home. He walked with just a slight limp but used a stick and he kept his left arm in a pocket so his arm did not dangle.

He had impairment of shoulder movement and some paralysis but was able to use the arm and fingers sufficiently to handle his architect instruments.

Des and Ron had arranged a 'Welcome Home' party for two days later where they all came together at a hotel in Bromley. The two had felt that could be a 'neutral' place with no particular memories from the past for anyone to distract from the purpose of the party.

Kathleen and May exchanged a few civil words.

# Chapter 18
## Nuclear war

It was nearly three years later on the 1<sup>st</sup> September 1961 when Joan buzzed Ron in his office.

"Mr. Ackroyd for you, Mr. Jackson," she informed him.

"Oh. Right. Put him through please." This was unusual though not unprecedented.

"'Morning Ron. Is there any chance you can be in your office early this afternoon and be able to spare me an hour or two?"

"I'm going to be here all day battling paperwork so I've got no appointments at all."

"In that case can I be there at 11.00 and take you out to lunch?"

"Sure. But Anne and I lunch together when we're both in Head Office."

"Alright. I'll take you both then."

Intrigued Ron 'phoned through to Anne to let her know.

Though they had become more friendly over the past few years since Frank had come home from his National Service, Des had never before paid visits to them in Folkestone like this.

Anne was waiting in Ron's office when Des arrived exactly on time.

"Come on in Des," Ron held out his hand that Des shook. "No trouble I hope?"

"Not family trouble," Des assured him.

"Tea or coffee?"

"Coffee please."

Ron 'phoned through to Mary then sat back.

"We're all yours Des."

"What do you know of the present state of the Cold War, Ron?" Des asked abruptly.

Ron looked sharply at him. This was totally unexpected.

"Only what the general public knows. I've read the news on the international situation in the papers of course but I've no sources of private information."

"'I see." Des paused. "What I'm going to tell you is just for you two. Frank has met and started dating an American girl and they have become pretty close."

"He's told us something about her. Sophie Gartland. If it's the same girl." Anne commented.

"That's the one." Des paused again. "You must both regard this as completely confidential to you two for good."

Mary knocked and came in with a tray of tea and coffee. She closed the door after her as she left but Des still went after her and checked no one was listening outside the door. Ron frowned, wondering what was coming.

"Sophie is the daughter of a very high-ranking American Air Force officer who's asked us to do some designs for a house they're adapting in a village near the American Air Base at Upper Heyford, near Bicester where they're living. Sophie is actually sharing a flat in Lewisham as she's a Medical Student at the Hospital. Frank first met her when he was going there for treatment to his arm. Some complications had arisen – not too serious though. A Contract about their house arose from that and so it was sensible for Frank to be the one to go down with her to the house to study it and draw up some plans.

"RAF Upper Heyford is a Major Base of the American Strategic Air Command in this country though there are several others. That means their bombers carry nuclear bombs as part of the Mutual Assured Destruction Strategy between the Western Alliance and the Soviet Union. You know the idea?"

"Who doesn't? Otherwise known as MAD. It's that both knows the other side will destroy with nuclear weapons either Alliance that attacks them. The idea being that both sides will be deterred from attacking the other at all because in the end it will be too costly,"

"Exactly. However there is a flaw in the argument. And that is that if it ever does come to the crunch, if the Leader of the one side decides the Leader of the other will 'chicken out' (as the phrase is) under a threat from the first side, they could then use the threat of nuclear attack to try to get their way."

"And if the first Leader has got it wrong ...," Anne said.

"Exactly." Des paused, then hitched his chair closer to them and lowered his voice. "Apparently there is some talk among some

American high-rankers, very very unofficially, about the present President of the United States, John F. Kennedy, and the possible consequences of his recent behaviour towards the Soviet Premier Nikita Krushchev. Apparently there is some feeling that he was too indecisive over his handling of their Bay of Pigs invasion of Cuba when it was being repulsed last April and then his handling of the situation was weak when Krushchev ordered the building of the Berlin Wall last month.

"So they're concerned that Krushchev could take it into his head to push the United States even more and whether Kennedy will respond weakly again. Or over-react but out of weakness rather than decisive strength. Coupled with that there have been noises of Cuba going even more pro-Soviet and that Krushchev is responding positively to that. As he would.

"And if the Soviets should take it into their heads to base nuclear missiles there to threaten the United States to strengthen their side of MAD,..," Anne put in.

"Exactly. But from their points of view it would be the common sense thing to do," Des nodded.

"Especially Castro's," Ron said thoughtfully. "If only as a deterrent to the Americans trying another and bigger Bay of Pigs invasion. And that could then lead on to a massive confrontation between the Soviets and the Americans. And that could bring in the use of the nuclear bombers the Americans have based here. As at Upper Heyford. Hence the Americans concern. And as those nuclear bombers are here, our concern. And we have nuclear weapons ourselves and are allies of the Americans."

"Exactly," Des said again. "So the question is, what do we do about it?"

"I don't think I have a great deal of influence on either of those two," Ron commented. "Though I could try offering them a free trip to Spain if they back off I suppose," he added with a grin.

"Ignore him Des," Anne advised. "What do you have in mind? Because I'm sure you have something."

"The Government are trying to do two contradictory things at the present time – maintain the theme of 'Mutually Assured Destruction' while at the same time half-heartedly promoting the idea of self-build Shelters including putting out a booklet on how to do it."

"What's the point of building a Shelter, even if it's possible against nuclear explosions, when you'd come out to a lethally radioactive world if you did somehow survive the bombing?" demanded Ron.

"Exactly," Des said for the fourth time. "That is exactly the picture conveyed by the 'Mutually Assured Destruction' scenario, isn't it? But what if that scenario is, in fact, an unlikely one?"

"What?" Anne and Ron stared at him.

"I had a rather senior politician with the Ministry of Defence, who shall be nameless, contact me three weeks ago wanting me to design what he called a 'nuclear fallout shelter' for him. So he gave me a rather detailed Briefing. How many nuclear rockets do you think the Soviet Union have?"

"Thousands. All able to hit anywhere in the world." Ron answered promptly. Anne nodded agreement.

"That was what I thought. In fact, they are reliably estimated to have less than 30 missiles able to hit the US from Russian territory at this time, but many more shorter range able to hit Europe, including us and an unknown number of 'plane-carried bombs."

"So - thousands."

"Possibly. But 'planes are a lot more stoppable than missiles. Now if you were a Commander, what would you want to eliminate first and quickest and so use nuclear weapons on them?"

"Enemy headquarters, Command and Control and their nuclear weapons sites," Anne answered.

"And do we have a headquarters and/or nuclear weapons sites near here? Near Folkestone I mean?" Des asked quietly.

Ron and Anne thought about their area, then going further afield.

"Not that I know of," Ron said, looking at Anne who nodded agreement. "But there are all the ports along the South Coast, the fighter Bases still around and Dover Fort. Which could be targets."

"But which they're hardly likely to expend a nuclear weapon on," Des said dismissively. "Because those places aren't any kind of immediate threat to them in this kind of confrontation. So the only problems round here are far more likely to be from the radioactive fallout from any nuclear explosions further away."

"And the location of where that comes down is dependent on wind conditions at the time," Ron said thoughtfully. "So Terry said when we were talking about nuclear accidents at Calder Hall once. Or Sellafield as they're calling it now."

"Which means that a nuclear fallout shelter does make sense," Des finished. "While an all-out nuclear exchange is possible – if the stated threat of Mutual Assured Destruction fails and it operates for real. However, NATO Generals are now talking about 'a limited nuclear exchange', as being the more likely scenario. Which is why both sides now have what they call 'battlefield nuclear weapons'."

"But that would immediately escalate to an all-out exchange surely?" suggested Anne.,

"Under MAD – yes. But not in the 'limited nuclear exchange' scenario. Now where's a good place to eat where we can continue talking privately? I'm pushed for time because I don't want to be late back home and frighten May by this kind of talk."

"I'll go along with that," Ron backed him. "Never mind frightening us of course!"

Sitting at a table in an alcove in a nearly deserted Hotel restaurant, while they were still looking at menus, Ron looked up at Des, "Those Anderson Shelters in the last war were pretty strong, weren't they? If they were built a lot bigger, deeper and stronger, would they do?"

"That was to be **my** brilliant solution after you two were supposed to be floored by the question!"

"Wouldn't it have to be ever so deep though to survive a direct hit or even a near miss?" Anne asked.

"It would. But I should think we'd be very unlucky indeed to get one of those, as we were saying earlier," Ron answered. He turned to Des, "If we decided on one of those how big would it need to be?"

"And we'd have to do something to make it airtight as radioactive fallout is made up of dust and small particles," Anne put in.

They stopped talking while a waiter collected their orders.

"These are the designs I did for the politician." Des took a big sheet of paper from his briefcase and unfolded it. "That was for a family of five."

They examined it.

"So you have included filters for the air supply." Anne touched points on the drawing.

"Are you having one at your place?" Ron asked.

"We have practical problems. We have mains sewage and water pipes going across the back garden halfway down that go right along our row of houses and we've got gas and electricity coming into our house across the front garden from the main pipe and cable going down the road. There's no way to avoid them or even re-direct them to give us the needed space. That was why we had a Morrison Shelter in the last war."

"Any idea where our pipes run, Anne?" Ron asked.

"No. We'd have to check it out. Des. I think we need to think in terms of our four families if we go along with the idea of a 'limited nuclear exchange'. You, May and Frank as one, Kathleen, Terry and 'Little' Anne as the second, Tim and Janice as third, and us." She blinked. "And Sonia and Sarah. And what about Dorothy and John?" She looked at Ron.

"Let's be practical. Des, how much space is needed per person, for food storage, water supply, the other supplies that might be needed? And how long do we have to plan to stay in there? Days? Weeks?" The problems were mounting by the second it seemed to Ron.

"If you are seriously thinking about this, the first thing is to pick your site. The best place is in the garden by the house, so you'll need to check the run of the pipes through it. Then decide how much space you've got to play with because that's going to determine the number of people you can accommodate. And you may well have to think about individual places for the individual families rather than them all being together." He looked at them steadily. "You were talking of four families Anne. If it happens it will be a time of very high psychological stress for everyone. There's not only whatever is going on outside, but people will be living for 24 hours a day in close crowded conditions for some time. Even the best of families can fall out with each other under such conditions. And there have been major stresses between people that are still not resolved."

Ron and Anne nodded, well aware of what he was talking about.

Des folded the drawing quickly as waiters came, and gave it to Ron. No one said anything while the waiters were busy

"If you can spare the time I could come and look at your garden to see what suggestions I can make," Des suggested.

"We have time," Ron said promptly.

"And Dorothy's not there this afternoon so there'll only be us," Anne added.

They ate in silence, each busy with their thoughts.

"I must admit it feels kind of strange to know that it might be possible to survive some kind of nuclear war if it does happen," Anne said suddenly. "I'd more or less assumed that with everything that's been said in the newspapers and things, that if one did start – that would be the end of humanity. Most of it anyway. Including us. A fatalistic approach to something believed inevitable I suppose."

"A lot of people think the same," Des said. It's a weird kind of peace – MAD."

"But it does have a mad kind of logic to it," Ron put in. "Until they all dis-arm. Though I can't really see that happening."

"No," agreed Des.


At the house Des looked around the garden with some trees and a large flowerbed at the front and the large lawned area at the side that went round to the back with the vegetable area at the back with a greenhouse and garden shed.

"Depending where the Services pipes and cables run you've got a good area there," Des said, pleased.

"There's something in the house that could be useful," Anne said suddenly.

She led them into the house through the kitchen door that she unlocked, into the hall and opened the door into the cupboard under the stairs. She handed out brooms, mops and a vacuum cleaner to Ron who put them in the kitchen out of the way, and then she hauled up the strip of lino on the floor, revealing a large trapdoor.

"I never knew about that!" Ron exclaimed. "Secret passages!"

"A big cellar. Except it's never been used as a cellar. Not in my time anyway," Anne corrected, hooking a finger through the ring-handle set at one edge and struggling to heave it up. "Hadn't thought about it for years so it had slipped from my memory. But talking of living underground for weeks jogged it I suppose. Ron ...," she added, giving up, " ... why should I struggle when there's a man standing by doing nothing!"

She moved out of the cupboard to make room for him.

He took out a penknife and scraped away the accumulated dust and debris in the joints and round the hinges, put his finger in the ring-handle, tried it then twisted it and heaved up the trapdoor and they looked into pitch darkness.

"I'll get torches from the kitchen Ron." Anne dived off coming back moments later with three big torches.

"I'll let you go first Ron and Des. There could be rats down there," she said, handing over two torches, keeping the third for herself.

"Thanks. And I was always told  it was polite to let ladies go first."

Ron flashed his torch around showing a dust covered ladder with wide rungs leading down at an angle to a dry earthen floor five feet below. A lot further over were walls stretching up to and beyond the ceiling of joists and floorboards.

"This must be the size of the whole house!" he muttered, and clambered down the ladder to stand on the floor, half-crouching for his head to clear the joists, Des and Anne following.

"How old is this house Anne?" asked Des.

"About 150 years I think.  It was built in my grandfather's time anyway.  I could get the Deeds from the Bank Storage for the exact date if you need it."

"Just wondering.  But that would account for this type of under-house space.  But it's massive!"

Ron had been exploring.  The exterior walls showed that it was the same area as the house, and it was divided into 'rooms' too as load-bearing interior walls were set onto foundations too.  But there were no doors set in the walls.

"How about this!" Ron exulted.  "A readymade Shelter!  But any chance of us being able to drop the floor a foot or so Des?  It'll be wearing to go around on our knees if we do have to use it for real."

Des had been exploring too but he went over to an exterior wall and dug down into the dry earth at its foot, then went to another and dug down there, then at two interior walls.

"It'd be sensible to put buttresses right along the lengths of all the walls to do that but that should be no real problem.  Then we'd have to strengthen the roof of this a lot just in case the house was demolished.  Air is coming in so we'd have locate that and put a filtration system in place and bunk beds etc. But I think you're absolutely right Ron. You've cracked the problem Anne!"

Over the next three months all the work was done using some Contractors that had done other work for the Government in building underground Posts for the Royal Observer Corps and a Regional Seat of Government so news of this Shelter wouldn't be spread by gossip..

Ron and Anne debated how much to tell their staff and friends as tensions grew and the rhetoric hardened between the United States and the Soviet Union. The propaganda war that became steadily more alarmist between the 'Ban the Bomb' Unilateral Nuclear Disarmament groups and the 'Pro-nuclear Deterrent' groups, grew with demonstrations, parades and publicity material. But they decided they couldn't possibly provide Shelters for everyone and their families.

They spoke privately to their friends on the Board and found a mixture of fatalism, dismissal of it all as 'politicians posturing', with Richard Sampson being the only one to treat it seriously and deciding to take some action.

So Anne and Ron put together an anonymous booklet giving all the information Des had given them about nuclear weapons, radiation fallout dangers and Anderson shelter construction (but not about the divisions and doubts among the Americans) and leaving copies around in the Canteens where people could take them if they wanted to.

They invited Kathleen and Terry to dinner one evening and while 'Little' Anne was sleeping took them down to the 'Cellar' as they called it rather than 'Shelter', though work hadn't started on it yet. Like Ron, Kathleen was amazed that it had been there all the time without either she or Maralyn knowing anything about it.

Terry listened to their description of what they were going to do and of why they were doing it, looked round carefully without saying a word and just as silently went back with them to the kitchen while Anne made some coffee.

"Well? What do you think?" Ron asked him directly. "That we're mad?"

"No," Terry answered promptly. "I've been looking at our place, the house and garden, to see if something similar was possible there."

"I'd noticed you looking about the place but I thought you were thinking of decorating or getting a garden shed or something!" exclaimed Kathleen.

"I didn't want to worry you unnecessarily," Terry responded. He hesitated. "Just between ourselves, we've been assessing things at the Plant (he used this rather than 'Sellafield') on counter-measures we should take covering a whole range of possible attacks including nuclear missiles. That's because of the way America and the Soviets seem to be squaring up against each other. I was going to raise it with you as well Dad when I could do it discretely. When you invited us tonight I thought I'd make a chance. I might have known you'd be ahead of me," he added with a wry smile.

"That was Des's doing," Ron responded. "So it's up to you. Either do a Shelter at your place or come in here with us."

"Come here," Kathleen said promptly. "If you're sure there's enough room."

"Good," Anne said with heartfelt relief.

"As Des put you onto it Dad you said, what are they doing?" Kathleen asked next.

"Des has done a survey of his garden and because of the run of water, sewage and gas pipes across them it won't work. So we make room for them here."

"Oh."

"And Tim and Janice? And Aunt Sonia and Sarah?"

"We're putting it to Tim and Janice tomorrow night. Sonia says she believes the nuclear deterrent is enough to stop things happening at all," Anne said. "But we'll have room for them if it doesn't."

Tim looked at Anne and Ron unbelievingly.

"Dad – surely the Russkies wouldn't be so utterly daft to risk anything like that!" he protested. "Or the Yanks. Have you read the 'Ban the Bomb' leaflets?

"Yes, I have," Ron said quietly. "All of them. Made a point of it. The thing is, it's not our own Bombs that I'm worried about. They're obviously not the ones pointing at us. Nor are the American ones.

It's the Soviet ones that are. If the Soviets and the Americans start, we would certainly become involved. I don't see the point of us debating the merits or otherwise of our being allies of the United States or why we could - or might be – targets. Those factors are beyond our control."

"But they aren't! If enough of us get together we can stop this madness altogether!"

"We could debate that too Tim. But at this immediate point of time there is this confrontation between East and West in the Cold War and the build-up of tensions over Cuba. As it's a Communist State they can bank on the backing of the Soviet Union. Which could bring in the possibility of a nuclear exchange. We are preparing this Shelter in case that happens. If it doesn't – great! We can go right on living our normal lives which is exactly what we want to do. We wanted you to know that we have this facility and if the crunch does come, there is a room here for you and Janice."

"And mother, Des and Frank?"

"Yes. Partly because Des is unable to do one at their place."

"What about Mum and Sarah?" asked Janice.

"She doesn't think it's needed. She believes the politicians are sensible enough for the nuclear deterrent to hold. But there is room for them as well if they aren't."

"Good. Thanks tremendously." Janice jumped up from her chair and kissed both Ron and Anne.


The strengthening of the structure of the Shelter was completed by the end of December 1961. Now there was only the stocking it with food for it to be ready for use. Water would only be put into the storage tanks at the time it was going to be used for real.


News filtered out that facilities of different types were being attacked on Cuba. Put down to 'attacks by the Resisters to the Cuban regime' by the Americans, it only emerged decades later that these were more down to the CIA 'Operation Mongoose' after the Bay of Pigs invasion had failed.

In February 1962 to tighten pressure on a Communist regime, the Americans launched an 'embargo' against Cuba.

In May 1962 Krushchev quietly suggested to Fidel Castro, the President of Cuba, that the Soviets could place Inter-Mediate Range Nuclear Ballistic Missiles (IRBMs) on Cuba as a deterrent to another invasion attempt by the Americans as all this could be leading up to another, stronger, invasion attempt, this time openly supported by them.

From the Soviet strategic point of view it would also mean that all of continental United States would come within nuclear missile range, something that the Soviets couldn't yet do with their small number of Inter-Continental Nuclear Ballistic Missiles (ICBMs) from Soviet territory. This would be the counter to the much larger number of American ICBM Nuclear weapons based in the US and the other shorter range nuclear missiles based in NATO territories around the Soviet Union.

That was formalised in a secret Treaty signed in July 1962 and construction of the missile launch sites began the next month, materials coming in ships from the Soviet Union.

These were quickly spotted by the Americans and closer and more detailed surveillance was set up on Cuba itself and the Soviet shipping heading there.

That Surface-to-Air missile sites (SAMs) were in position and being added to and that other sites for the IRBMs were being built were identified.

There was intense debate about response measures in the White House with the President setting up the EX-COMM crisis committee. Ideas of what to do about it, ranged from bombing the sites to a full-scale and immediate invasion. Finally it was decided to totally blockade Cuba, but to call it a 'quarantine'. There were legal and propaganda reasons for this as technically the two countries were not at war with each other. And to demand their weapons removal in return for lifting the 'quarantine'.

But though trying this tactic, President Kennedy didn't really expect his offer to work and thought this was bound to end in a military confrontation. Quite probably a nuclear one.

Both sides put military and nuclear forces on alert - in the Soviet Union as well as America and Europe as increased Soviet shipping headed towards Cuba. More American warships moved into position to enforce the 'quarantine'.

The date was 15th October 1962.

On the 22nd October 1962, President Kennedy went on the radio and TV to make a public announcement of the 'quarantine' of Cuba saying that it would be enforced by a ring of American warships that had already been deployed round Cuba 'to prevent offensive weapons' being delivered to Cuba. Second, he demanded that the missile launch sites be dismantled and any and all 'offensive weapons' already in Cuba be taken back to the Soviet Union as well. Third, that any nuclear missile strike against the US launched from Cuba would be deemed as having been launched by the Soviet Union itself.

Implicit in that was the threat (made publicly before) that any attack on America or its Allies by the Soviet Union would bring an immediate and devastating nuclear response.

But enough had been leaked beforehand for Anne and Ron to have already started to stock up the Shelter with food etc.

That afternoon Joan slipped into the Boardroom where the monthly meeting was in progress. Ordinary life had to go on despite the growing confrontation in the Caribbean. She put a note in front of Ron. It read, 'Mr. Ackroyd is on the 'phone. He says he needs to speak to you urgently'.

"I'll take it in my office," he murmured. Aloud, "Would you excuse me please. Urgent personal matter."

"Hallo Des?"

"Two quick matters Ron. Sophie 'phoned Frank from the hospital. She said 'They were now on Alert'. That is NOT referring to the Hospital. Also May is very, very worried about things. Panicking in fact. So I told her about the 'Cellar'. How nearly ready is it?"

"Being activated as we speak. So by all means come whenever you want to."

"She's so frightened Ron, sure that London is going to be nuked any minute, so – tonight?"

"Fine. Who'll be coming? And any idea of time of arrival?"

"The three of us because Frank and I can work from there as easily as from the office in London. And we will be re-assurance for May. Sophie's going home to her parents' place. Apparently there are facilities there. We should arrive between eight and nine o'clock if that's alright with you."

"We'll have a meal ready."

Ron went thoughtfully back to the Boardroom. So the Strategic Air Command nuclear bombers were now on higher Alert then. Sophie's phrase meant that they were to be ready to go from their Bases at fifteen minutes notice. Which meant the American military forces State of Readiness had been moved up to 'DEFCON 3', from 'DEFCON 4 or 5', the usual State of Readiness.

Richard looked at him as he went into the room and raised his eyebrows. Ron nodded once. Richard set his lips and looked down at the blotter in front of him. Sonia looked from him to Ron.

"Major trouble brewing?" she queried.

"Could be moving that way," Ron replied abruptly. "We had reached Item 6 of the Agenda, I believe."

Des reached them soon after 8 o'clock, Ron going out to meet them as soon as he heard the crunch of tyres on the gravel.

"Come on in. Let me help you with your cases."

He was shocked when he saw May in the hall light. Her hair, now grey, was untidy, she was dressed almost as untidily and she looked wide-eyed, terrified and thin. Ron had only seen her looking like this in the days after the school was bombed. And then just before she had that complete nervous breakdown when she'd become suicidal.

"Come on in, May," he said gently as Anne came hurrying out from the kitchen, drying her hands.

"Hello May. Everyone. Come on through to the kitchen. Dinner's all set out there."

"Aren't we going to eat in the Shelter?" May burst out.

"Not unless you really want to May. But if you do, we can."

"I'm sure we'll be alright to eat in the kitchen May," Des said gently. "But do we have time just to have a look at the Shelter before we eat, Anne?"

"Of course. You do the honours Ron, while I dish up. I'll give you a call."

"This way," Ron went to the hall cupboard door.

"In there!" May said blankly.

"To start with." Ron flicked on the light and indicated the already open trapdoor. "Down here."

He went down the new ladder and across to a small table while May came down, followed by Frank and Des. They looked around.

"My word Ron! You've made a difference since I saw it last!" Des exclaimed.

"It is meant to be home from home," Ron grinned.

The floor had been dropped by two feet, and lino now covered floorboards, the walls were painted light blue, the ceiling a deeper blue and landscapes and seascapes were on the walls. Curtains covered doorways in loadbearing walls leading into smaller 'rooms' which were furnished with bunkbeds. In the main area chairs were scattered around.

"We've a small kitchen area, washing and toilet facilities, a generating motor outside in case mains electricity supplies are cut off and an air filtration system," Ron finished.

May looked around.

"When Des said you'd got a Shelter I pretty much expected an Anderson shelter kind of thing. Not this!" She shook her head. "But I don't see how even this will survive a direct hit from the thousands of bombs and rockets that'll rain down on us the second war starts." Her voice had started rising in panic.

"Who says that number, May?" Ron's voice was gentle.

"These. By people who know and aren't afraid to speak out! But I bet you haven't even looked at these." She produced a wad of leaflets from her bag and flapped them at Ron.

As Ron took them Anne called down that dinner was dished up and ready to eat.

"I'll read them while we eat," Ron said, leading the way to the ladder.

Once seated round the table and eating, Ron picked up the first leaflet from the pile beside him, glanced at the top page and put it down before going on to the next.

"You're not even reading them!" May exploded after half-a-dozen.

"Read them all a long time ago May. Ah, this is a new one." He read it carefully and then went through the rest as he had treated the earlier ones.

"Well?" May challenged, at the end.

"To give you some background – when I came here in 1943 I applied to join the Wardens. They didn't need me but I kept in touch till the war ended. A couple of the people I took on had been Wardens. Ralph Smith, our Chief Warden in London in 1939 got the job as the Emergency Planning Officer down here when they were set up. When things started getting warm in the Cold War, and then after Des alerted me to things I got in touch with him again. Since then I've attended Briefings both with them and some Military people."

"So they've brainwashed you!"

"No. I'm too old and cynical for that May. When these leaflets were produced I questioned a lot of what I was being told. And did so still more as more were produced. I was luckier than most because though Terry is on the Civil side of nuclear power obviously he knows a lot about the effects of nuclear explosions. While there's a lot of truth in the leaflets, they also exaggerate the problems."

"How?" May's voice was still aggressively demanding.

"Take this statement about 'thousands of nuclear rockets and bombs will rain down on Britain as soon as any war starts'. Remember what was being said before the last war about bombs?"

"But they did come."

"But even the worst hit cities weren't as devastated as much as was forecast, were they? Not even London.

"Furthermore nuclear weapons are far more complicated to make than ordinary ones – the nuclear explosive bit as well as the rockets themselves. And the Soviets simply don't have enough to 'rain thousands down on us' – if they'd even wanted to. If you've finished lets go into the Shelter again where I've got maps to show you what I mean."

"You go. I can bring the coffee down," Anne said quickly.

Ron led them over to a small desk. Behind it pinned to the wall were large maps of Europe and the UK. On the desk were pens, pads and a telephone. On another small table nearby were a radio and a transceiver, both with wires leading up to the ceiling and aerials outside.

"Let's look at the Soviet position," Ron said, pointing at locations as he talked. "Russia there, the US there, the European NATO countries round this side, Turkey round there. We are there. So we are probably the smallest country of all of them geographically speaking. Now as the Soviets have a limited number of nuclear weapons of all kinds it's simply not possible for them to 'rain thousands' down on us - and also everyone else at the same time. Especially America being the size it is. The reason the Soviets want to locate missiles in Cuba is to be able to hit the US hard from a closer range. So how many are they going to need over there to 'rain down' missiles all over all that country? And then all the countries of NATO? And still have enough to do the same to us?

"They'd need millions of them. And what is so different about Britain for them to decide to pick just on us to do that? To hit us harder than anyone else? To start with, other countries are much closer in distance to Russia than we are, aren't they? All with nuclear weapons based on their territories and their ground forces closer to the Russian border ready to attack the Soviets' own territories if war starts. So in fact we aren't as dangerous to the Soviets as they are from that point of view, are we?"

May studied the map. What Ron was saying did make sense. Then something else produced a clutch of fear.

"What about the radioactive fallout from even one bomb here that would blanket the whole country?"

"To start with, the amount of fallout depends on how big it is and whether it's what they call an 'airburst' or a 'groundburst'. An airburst means the area of damage is greater from the downblast but a groundburst scoops up loads of bits of dirt, buildings and what-have-you from the ground and drags it high into the air. Bigger pieces fall to the back to the ground quickly, smaller bits start drifting away borne by the wind to fall back sooner or later."

"Exactly!" May interrupted.

"Where they fall depends on how far the wind or air currents take them. Let's look at the UK map," Ron said. "Suppose there was a nuclear strike - there, for example. Near enough in the middle of the country. If the wind is West to East almost all the fallout will be carried that way more or less. But air currents can move in different directions at different heights and take the smaller dust particles with them."

"So just as I said - it DOES come down everywhere!"

"Anywhere, May, anywhere. Not everywhere. Not over the whole country. So - is that 'blanketing the whole country from even one explosion' accurate?"

May looked at the sketch, at the maps on the wall and visibly relaxed.

"See what you mean."

"They are making a very important political point, though I think they're over-stating their case and then coming to a wrong conclusion. That if we dispose of our nuclear weapons, ban all of them from this country then others will follow our example. I don't see that happening if we did.

"No one has followed our example when we scrapped our arsenal of chemical weapons in 1957, five years ago, have they? Everyone who had them then has still kept them. And some more countries have got them since.

"Would it make us less of a target if we didn't have any nuclear weapons here? I'm not so sure about that either. If they decided to invade us they could use nukes to knock out our main defences even if we didn't have any nukes – people are not usually sporting in war are they? But the whole point of deterrence is to stop any war of any level starting at all."

"If you believe all that then why the Shelter?" But May's tone was now much more an enquiry.

"Because deterrence might break down. Fail. Not work. So I considered there was enough potential danger to do this." Ron waved a hand around the Shelter. "You know I always want to play double-safe but especially in war. And this time it was me that controlled this decision. Just as important – Anne agreed with me." He looked steadily at May.

She dropped her eyes.

"When are the others coming? It's getting late." She glanced at her watch.

"When they decide it's time to come," he replied evenly.

"What d'you mean by that?" May's eyes widened. "The Russian rockets could come any minute! Any second!"

"May!" Ron snapped, cutting into her resurgent panic. "See that?" He pointed to the transceiver. "I have a direct radio link to Emergency Headquarters. Any move up to what they call 'DEFCON

2' which is when the Armed Forces are put on a Readiness to deploy and Engage at less that 6 hours notice indicating war could be about to break out, I'm notified instantly by the transceiver.  And by our telephones if that doesn't get a response.  'DEFCON 1' means 'Nuclear war imminent'.  So by us moving when 'DEFCON 2' is activated from 'DEFCON 3' that it is at present, it means that everyone will have ample time to get here."

"Oh."

May stared at him, wanting to believe.  To be re-assured.  Ron looked back just as steadily.  May relaxed again.

"Alright then, Ron." She looked around "Did you say our room is over there?"

"That's the one,"

"All the beds are made up," Anne said, coming forward.  "But if you need any more blankets, just say."

Upstairs in the kitchen Des looked at Ron.

"Is what you said to May about the transceiver 100% accurate Ron?" he asked quietly.

Ron checked the door was pushed to.  "It's 100% true that Ralph will contact me.  The rest is 90%."

"And the odd 10%?"

"That the declaration of 'DEFCON 2' may not give everyone enough time to get here.  But there's no need for May to know that.  Or that the Soviets could decide to make what they call a 'pre-emptive strike'.  Hit us with no build-up or warning.  Which will give us 4 minutes they say from launch to detection to hit.  The deterrent factor is that they know that still gives us time to launch our nukes in retaliation within that timespan – so they decide not to launch in the first place."


Throughout the 23$^{rd}$ and 24$^{th}$ October the Soviet ships sailed steadily on towards Cuba.  The number of American warships round Cuba was increased.  Their submarines tracked both the surface ships and Soviet submarines close to American shores, and surveillance aircraft patrolled – very obviously.

Newspapers, radio and TV kept up constant news programmes.  Ron, Anne and the others took to carrying portable transistor radios with them. May sat in the Shelter keeping a constant listening watch on the transceiver and telephone.

On the 25th October the first of the Soviet ships approached what the EX-COMM had privately defined as the 'boundary line', though the American ships were poised further back from that. Once they reached that, it would be the time for an 'Action' decision to be made. The strategies had already been decided, but now the time had nearly arrived to activate them.

"Pull back our ships 10 miles, shifting the Boundary Line closer to Cuba by that amount. We've still got room enough. And go to 'DEFCON 2'," ordered President Kennedy

All American forces around the world went to Readiness to attack on orders being given, for launching ground attacks on the Soviet Union including using tactical nuclear weapons. Missiles were readied. Strategic nuclear bombers were now at their Holding Points at the borders of the Soviet Union, poised to penetrate Soviet Air Space. As one group began to run low on fuel, they were replaced by others fully fuelled up.

To many people nuclear war seemed not only possible but likely if not now inevitable. Because the Soviet Ground and Air Forces were on their Maximum Alert too. At their ground borders with their Battlefield nuclear weapons poised and their Strategic Bombers with nuclear bombs ready on board were in the air too. Shorter range missile troops were ready too

Any level of attack by anyone on either side, could begin WW3.


May was at Ron's desk in the Shelter that had the transceiver, telephone and a radio on, constantly listening for any snippet of news. As she had been sitting since the early morning after they had got there. Her anxieties had been diminishing as time went by with nothing happening - until President Kennedy's broadcast. Then she had wanted everyone in the Shelter immediately but had finally reluctantly accepted that if she manned that post with everyone promising to be at the other end of the telephone for a call from her, constantly updating her on their whereabouts, then they would be able to carry on with their normal lives.

The transceiver suddenly shrilled, making May leap from her seat in shock. She snatched up the receiver.

"Shelter," she snapped as she had been told to reply to it.

"Ron there?"

"No, but I can get a message to him immediately." Again as she had been told.

"Tell him, 'Ralph called and said, 'DEFCON 2.' Got it?"

"Yes."

The transceiver cut off. May picked up the 'phone and rang Ron's Folkestone office number. She prayed he hadn't gone elsewhere without telling her.

"Mr. Jackson immediately," she said as soon as Joan answered.

Forewarned Joan put her through immediately.

"Yes May?"

"'Ralph called, 'DEFCON 2'. That was what he said to say to you, Ron."

"Des and Frank at home?"

"Yes."

"Tell them. I'll contact the others." Ron cut the call and tapped Anne's number on the internal 'phone while dialing Kathleen's number on the outside line.

"Anne. 'DEFCON 2'." and put down the Internal 'phone knowing that Anne would be relaying the message to Sonia who would then contact Sarah. He tapped his fingers impatiently while Kathleen's 'phone rang insistently. She was supposed to be working at home with 'Little' Anne today but she wasn't answering.

"Hallo?" she panted at last.

"Dad here. 'DEFCON 2'."

"Oh my God! And I had to be in the loo! I'll contact Terry."

Both rang off and Ron dialed the airfield.

"Richard? 'DEFCON 2'."

"Roger. I'll alert Tim and Janice."

"Thanks."

This had been a cause of bitter, though private, argument between Ron and May. She had tried to insist that Ron tell Tim he had to come home immediately the 'situation got worse'. Ron had said Tim's job at the airfield was essential, everyone else would be doing their jobs so when it was his shift, he, Ron, would not pull him away. His job was too important with aircraft in the air needing to be guided down and alerted to other aircraft in their vicinity. When May took Tim to one side and tried to persuade him to 'go sick' he flatly refused for exactly the same reasons – but that Janice should go to the Shelter. She had immediately said her job was just as important as Tim's to the Airfield so they would go together. Or not. And if things really did blow, they would join the others in the Airfield Shelter.

As soon as Richard had been alerted to the situation months ago he had checked out the airfield's WW2 ammunition store, a massive semi-underground room which he found had three feet of water in. With the Board's approval he'd had that pumped out, the place made waterproof, ostensibly for storage, then declared it could be made into a cinema so put in rows of seats. The over-ground part was reinforced with galvanised corrugated steel and five feet of earth grassed over, 'to stop it being an eyesore'. The ventilation system was in actuality a robust filtration system.

Some had muttered he was 'nuts', but as the international situation had worsened and he sent round a Memo to every employee on the site that it was a 'Shelter if ever things blow and they're on duty here', they changed their minds.

As soon as Anne had alerted Sonia she drove home. The water tanks now needed to be filled.

By evening Sonia and Sarah had arrived, soon followed by Kathleen and Terry. By 11 o'clock Tim and Janice had arrived as the airfield had closed for the night. He went back to the Control Tower at 2.00 pm the next day when due on shift.

Radio and TV reports were that the Soviet ships now escorted by warships, at their present speed were expected to cross the 'Boundary Line' within a matter of hours. If the Americans tried to sink or board the Soviet cargo ships carrying the nuclear missiles the Soviet warships would be bound to resist and fire back.

And those first shots would start the war which was expected to 'go nuclear' in minutes.


Late on the 26th October a letter was handed to the American government saying the Soviets would remove the missiles if the

Americans undertook to never invade Cuba. That was taken as conciliatory and EX-COMM were ready to agree.

But in the very early morning of the 27th October, the Soviets delivered another Note to The White House increasing the pressure by demanding that the US nuclear missiles based in Turkey be withdrawn as well, as a *quid pro quo* in return for removing the Soviet missiles from Cuba.

EX-COMM debated that new demand. One view was to agree to the demand in the letter of the 26th to undertake not to invade Cuba and simply ignore the letter of the the 27th with the new demand.

While debating that, the news came that a Cuban SAM had shot down a U-2 spy 'plane.

The first shot of WW3?

In Europe troops on both sides were poised to attack the other with ground and air weapons including battlefield nuclear weapons as soon as the order was given. Fuelled up Strategic nuclear bombers (American, British and Soviet) were at their Holding Points awaiting the order to attack. At sea Soviet submarines, some with nuclear weapons on board and close to Cuba and the US, had been tracked and were now being blasted with Practice Depth Charges to force them to the surface rather than deadly Charges to sink them. To do that, EX-COMM thought would have then been the 'opening shots'.

EX-COMM argued. The ships were now closing fast and battle would commence in a matter of a few hours, certainly by that evening unless the Soviet ships stopped or the Americans pulled back further. But would pulling back for the second time be seen as a sign of weakness and so encourage the Soviets to keep going? And if they made no response to the shooting down of the U-2, would that be seen as weakness too? So at the very least they should 'Take out' the SAM site that launched the missile.

But Kennedy ordered no response.

Krushchev heard the news of the shooting down of the U-2 and he immediately gave desperate orders and the Soviet ships with the nuclear missiles aboard slowed their speed abruptly to delay the crunch moment.

While the Media didn't know all the details, enough was made known for people to believe nuclear war was both certain and imminent.

Tim was at the Control Tower, the War-time Airfield Alarm Klaxon had been refurbished, tested and was ready. He would be 'phoned if 'DEFCON 1' was notified, for Staff to go to the Airfield Shelter.

On the night of the 27th October the Jackson family were all in the Shelter, including Tim now as the Airfield had closed. Dorothy and her husband, both now elderly, were there. No one slept much with Ron and May 'on watch' and the radio and TV on very low.

In the early hours of the morning of the 28th October the Soviet Ambassador went to The White House with another letter from President Krushchev. In it he said he would order the Soviet ships to return, dismantle all the nuclear launching sites and remove all the bombers now in Cuba but repeated both of his previous demands that the US must undertake never to invade Cuba again and that the US would remove and not replace their missiles based in Turkey that threatened the Soviet Union as closely as missiles based in Cuba would threaten the US.

EX-COMM debated but there was now little or no real argument. They had got what they wanted – the removal of Soviet nuclear missiles from Cuba and they could undertake not to invade Cuba easily enough, there were still other ways of undermining the Communist regime that stopped short of actually 'invading' it, they believed. The removal of the missiles from Turkey would not cause any real reduction to the nuclear deterrent.

Later that day both President Krushchev and President Kennedy announced their agreement, and that the disarmaments would be monitored by U Thant the Secretary-General of the UN. And that a 'Hot Line' for direct communication between the US and Soviet Presidents would be set up..

And the 'DEFCON' level went back to 'DEFCON 4'. Six months later it went down to 'DEFCON 5', Normal State of Readiness.

In the Shelter, listening to the broadcast, May burst into tears burying her face in her hands. Des went over to put his arms around her and hug her tight. Anne grabbed Ron's hand, biting her lip.

This war had stopped short of killing or injuring them.

"What'll you do with this now Dad?" Tim asked, smiling, waving his hand around the Shelter.

"Drain the water tanks and keep it properly maintained, of course," he answered promptly. "The Cold War is still on – for the present anyway. This near war might have scared the politicians on all sides so much that they'll never get this close to nuclear war again. But I wouldn't bet on the common sense of any politician. If I could there'd be no wars anyway let alone nuclear ones. So it still could be needed some time."

# Chapter 19
## Confessions

"Guess what Nanny!" four year old Anne (who refused to be called 'Little' now but accepted 'Annie' when here) burst out as soon as she jumped out of the car, running towards Anne. Terry and Kathleen had brought her to a 'birthday picnic in Nanny's garden' in Anne's honour.

Nearly two years had passed since the Cuban Missile crisis but Cold War confrontations around the world were continuing and tensions were still high in Europe with rumours circulating that both sides now had War Plans in being that involved just the use of 'tactical' nuclear weapons as they were now called, in a 'limited nuclear war' though 'Strategic missiles and bombers were still available as well. So people now worried that the 'Mutual Assured Destruction' policy was no longer the governing strategy, which could make a 'limited nuclear war' more likely.

"I'm never able to 'guess what' with you Annie," Anne laughed catching her up in her arms.

"Mummy's getting a brother or sister for me. She says she doesn't know which it'll be yet but I've told her I want it to be a sister to play with."

"Nothing like making a booking early!" Anne laughed again,

"And we've got a special birthday present for you. I know what it is but I mustn't tell you, Daddy says, or it'll spoil the surprise. And he wants to take a picture on his new camera of you being surprised."

"Then you mustn't say a single word must you! You run on. Janice and Sarah are there."

"We were going to tell you later but she beat me to it," Kathleen laughed, taking Anne's arm while Terry unloaded a large box from the car with Ron's help. Together they walked in the sunshine from the front drive to the picnic laid out on the lawn at the side of the house.

"Mother sent me a long letter and a photo of Frank and Sophie," she said. "It was a really friendly letter too. Mostly about Frank and Sophie getting Engaged."

"Do you feel any closer to her since that time in the Shelter?" Anne asked quietly.

Since then Kathleen and May had started writing to each other and had talked a few times on the 'phone.

"A bit. But to be honest there's still ..." Kathleen stopped, then burst out. "If she'd been like you Mum, this would never have happened." She slapped her artificial leg.

"No."

"I'd never have kept Annie and any others we have at home in London in '39. I'd have gone away with them till the bombing had completely stopped. Even if that had meant leaving Terry at home alone." She paused. "It would have been a struggle to know what to do but the children would have had to come first."

"Yes." Anne knew she'd have made exactly the decision that Kathleen had said she would. "At that time May – your mother – had become extremely jealous of Edith because you had become close. Because she loved you and feared she'd lost you. That Edith had 'stolen' you away from her? Which is why she decided to keep you away from her."

May and Anne had talked while sharing the Shelter.

"She gave me that excuse years later. She didn't say anything about that at the time though. Only that I'd understand when I was older. Then altered that to when I was a mother myself."

"And now that you are?"

"The same situation would never have arisen because I'd have gone with them at their ages. Even if later I had gone back to London leaving them away in a place of safety. Once I was totally satisfied with the foster-parents and become friends with them which I would have done." Kathleen paused. "If mother was that bothered about me – and Tim – in that way why did she send us away in the first place? When she could have come with us? And when she kept Frank back with her in London? It was obvious to Tim and me that she really only cared for him. It's a lovely day for your birthday picnic isn't it, Mum?" she went on immediately, forcibly changing the subject.

"We are lucky," Anne accepted Kathleen's switch. "With the forecast yesterday we wondered how it would turn out."

Anne had just finished opening her presents, including the new state-of-the-art TV set (at which she dutifully registered complete surprise and delight for Annie and Terry's camera) when Ron cocked his head to listen.

"'Phone. Excuse me." He ran into the house. "Hello?"

"Ron? It's Des here. I'm ringing to let you know May has had a stroke. Quite a bad one I'm afraid. We're at the hospital now, Frank and I. There's nothing for you to do but Frank thought that Kathleen and Tim ought to know."

"Right. Thanks." Ron hesitated a bare moment, taking it in. "Look Des, if there is anything you think I need to do, just let me know. Alright?"

"Thanks Ron. But as you said to me some years ago now, May's my responsibility."

"Keep me informed though please."

"I'll do that."

Ron slowly replaced the receiver and made his way back to the group.

"Anything wrong?" Anne asked as he sat down, seeing his expression.

"That was Des phoning. Frank had asked him to let us – Kathleen and Tim - know that May's had a stroke and is in hospital. Not that anything needs to be done necessarily but that you should know."

"But he hasn't said we can't go and see her?" Tim said quickly.

"No. He said he's ringing from the hospital. There's nothing to stop you ringing them to check about going to see your mother Tim. Use the 'phone here right now if you wish. She'd be in Lewisham Hospital I should think. Telephone directories will give you the number."

"Right." Tim got to his feet and hurried into the house.

Anne stole a look at Kathleen. She was staring at the grass, a strained look on her face.

Fifteen minutes later Tim came back.

"She is in Lewisham. She's awake now and the hospital says that they're hoping the stroke won't be too bad in its effects, but they'll have to see. I can ring again tomorrow and then maybe see about going up.

"I was able to speak to father, to Des, and he said she simply keeled over this morning while getting breakfast. He recognised the signs so got an ambulance straight away. The hospital said his prompt action getting medical help had probably saved her life."

"Will she be disabled?" Kathleen asked abruptly.

"No idea. The hospital said it was too early to tell what the longer-term effects might be. Dad, I'm off work tomorrow at the Airfield anyway but could I take some leave for a few days from the day after to go to the hospital?"

"I'm sure that'll be no problem. I'll tell them."

"Mum. What are strokes exactly?" Kathleen asked after the others had gone and Annie was 'helping' Terry and Ron clear up after the picnic.

"Let's go and check the Medical books," Anne replied. They had several in the library.

"So she could end up being crippled. Disabled. Like me to some extent even. Or Tim," Kathleen said finally in an odd voice.

"Could be," Anne said quietly. "But not necessarily."

"I wonder if she'll want to see me."

"You have been writing. And talked on the 'phone." Anne paused. "I'm sure she would like a full reconciliation. If you can find it in you for it to be fully genuine."

Two days later Ron drove Kathleen up to Lewisham hospital leaving Annie with Anne for the day. Tim had been there for those days but had felt that as she had now stabilised there was no point in his staying longer.

Together they made their way to the private room where May was lying in bed, wires leading to machines.

As they went in quietly, Des stood up.

"Thanks very much for coming," he said softly. "Since I told her that you had asked if you could come, she has been asking when you'd be getting here."

Kathleen went and sat by the bed, and took May's hand. She had worked out how she would approach her and how she would respond to any of the myriad of ways her mother might act towards her that she had thought of.

"Hello Mum," she said quietly. "I've come to see you. It's Kitty."

May opened her eyes.

"Kitty?" Kathleen could barely distinguish her slurred words.

"That's right. I didn't bring Annie because she's a bit young and lively and I wasn't too sure how she'd behave. But I'll bring her as soon as you feel up to it."

"I've had a most awful nightmare, Kitty. I dreamed you'd been bombed in a war and been terribly crippled. But somehow we were all together safe in a big Shelter." She frowned. "But if we were all in a Shelter how could you have been bombed?"

"Don't worry about that Mum. I'm here, I'm talking to you aren't I? So how could I have been bombed? You just have a sleep and get better."

"Will you have to go away again Kitty? To Wales?"

"No Mum. I'll be here with you. You just have a sleep now and don't worry about anything."

May's eyes closed and she seemed to relax, still holding Kathleen's hand. Her breathing deepened.

"I'll get you both a cup of tea," Des whispered. And slipped out.

Half-an-hour later Kathleen whispered, "Dad. I'm desperate for a loo!"

"See if I can take your place holding May's hand," Des whispered.

They eased positions and did a changeover with May barely stirring as her loose grip was changed from hand to hand.

Together Ron and Kathleen slipped out.

"When you've been to the loo we'll see if we can have a word with Sister or someone."

"Right Dad."

In Sister's office they explained who they were. Sister spoke only to Kathleen.

"Your mother is making progress Mrs. Murray, but it was quite a severe stroke. You may have found her speech has been affected and at times she can be a little confused."

"So we found," Kathleen said. "She thought my being bombed and injured was a nightmare instead of reality."

"I beg your pardon?" Sister was taken aback.

"I was in Thompson Road School when it was bombed in 1943,

brought to this hospital and needed to have both legs amputated. One above the knee the other below the knee. My brother was also severely injured and treated here for a while."

"I see." Sister paused. "How is your relationship with your mother?"

"'Bad' for many years, you could say. As it was her fault that I was in London and at that school at the time it was bombed when I could have still been in Wales. But more recently we have been writing to each other again. And talked on the 'phone a couple of times. In a more friendly way."

"How are you approaching your mother now? In her fragile state?"

"Carefully. She has always called me 'Kitty', though for many years I have called myself 'Kathleen'. There is history behind that. But here and to her I am referring to myself as 'Kitty'."

"Good."

"Is it possible to give any kind of prognosis yet?" Ron asked.

Kathleen immediately repeated the question as Sister seemed to be ignoring Ron as being a divorced husband with May's present husband being on the premises.

"A matter of concern is that her legs seem to have no movement whatsoever so we fear they may be permanently paralysed. She can move her hands and arms to some degree but we have not attempted yet to get her to move her whole body, like sitting up. But when asked to move her legs or even twitch her toes, she doesn't seem able to."

"Oh."

Kathleen looked at Ron, experiencing mixed feelings.

"I'd better be getting back. Mother – Mum - may be waking up," she said standing up, assisted automatically by Ron.

Sister watched them go. There was obviously an awful lot of history with this family. She wondered if it would be appropriate to ask the present husband some questions. Not out of idle curiosity but because it could be very relevant to assisting the patient's recovery.

An hour later as the room was getting dark May opened her eyes.

"Kitty," she whispered.

"I'm here Mum," Kathleen answered instantly.

"I can't see you. It's so dark. Have I gone blind?" Her speech seemed just a little less slurred.

"I'll put the light on," Des said and switched on the dimmer light of the two in the room.

"Kitty? But – you're so big!" May gasped. "You're a woman! You're not thirteen. You've grown up!"

"That's right Mum. I have grown up a bit." Kathleen tried to treat it lightly.

May looked around the room then focused on Des, frowning. Puzzled.

"You're – you're Des aren't you?" she recognised him.

"That's right May. Your husband."

May looked from Kitty to Des, frowning. Struggling to remember. About Kitty. About Des. Her husband? Kitty was thirteen wasn't she? But she was so big! So she wasn't thirteen any more. She was grown up. And she'd talked of bringing an 'Annie', hadn't she? Who was 'Annie'? And wasn't she (May) married to Ron?

Ron opened the door quietly and walked in.

May looked at him. Then stared, recognising him as more memories began to trickle back.

"You're – you're Ron," she mumbled.

"That's right. How are you feeling May?" he asked gently.

May stared at him frowning. Ron. Wasn't he her husband?

More memories slowly came back. There was that other time when she had been lying out when he came into the room like he had just now.

But she'd been on a settee then. At home. Not in a hospital bed like this. Her mind had been feeling numb then, rather like it felt now. And Ron had come into the room. And he'd stood by that table in the front room. And he'd told her something. Something terrible. Something about the children.

That was when he'd told her – told her ….

"I – I remember you now. It was you who told me about the children." She pointed a shaking finger at him. "You told me about Kitty. And Tim. When they were in that school."

She stared from him to Kathleen, and her face changed as more memories suddenly flooded back overwhelmingly. Awful memories. Memories of the war. The Evacuation. The bombing. That letter from Kitty's foster-parents about adopting Kitty if she and Ron were killed in the bombing. Her keeping Kitty at home because of that.

And then the worst memories of all came. The school!

All the ghastliness she had seen there. The dead and injured children she had seen being brought out of the wreckage of the school just as she got there. And that Kitty and Tim had still been under all that rubble then. And they had been under it for hours and hours more. In agony from their injuries. In terrible fear. And the way, the brutal, terrible way Ron had told her about how horribly crippled they both now were.

AND THEY HAD ONLY THERE IN THE SCHOOL BECAUSE OF HER! IT WAS SHE WHO HAD DECIDED IT. AND HAD THREATENED RON WITH DIVORCE TO MAKE SURE THE CHILDREN STAYED IN LONDON. SO THEIR BEING THERE IN LONDON, IN THAT SCHOOL AT ALL THEIR BEING AS CRIPPLED AS THEY WERE – AS THEY ARE – **IT WAS ALL HER FAULT!**

"It wasn't a nightmare I had!" she shrieked, eyes staring at Kitty. "It was real! It was real! You were in that school. You have lost both your legs! And Tim is crippled! And it was ALL MY FAULT. IT'S BECAUSE OF **ME**."

She screamed, her arms thrashing, head whipping from side to side, eyes rolling as she screamed. And screamed. And screamed.

Ron dashed through the door for help but it was already coming.

"Get out!" the Doctor snapped to all three as he readied a sedative needle and nurses struggled to hold May's thrashing arms.

They scrambled to get out of their way and out into the corridor. To listen to May screaming. That gradually died away as the sedative took hold.

It was half-an-hour before the medical staff came out, silence now in the room.

"Let's go to Sister's office. I want to know exactly what happened, what you did, what you said, to spark that reaction," the Doctor snapped.

Once there and the door closed Des described what had happened in the room.

"Now you need to understand the background, Doctor," said Ron grimly. "Because that is vital to your understanding the reason for May blaming herself for Kathleen – Kitty – and Tim being in the school and so injured."

When he'd finished the Doctor and Sister nodded. They now knew it was not just a stroke patient they had on their hands but one with many deep-rooted psychological, psychiatric, problems too.

The next morning Des 'phoned the hospital about visiting but was advised to wait till the next day and to check again before coming. May was no worse as far as the stroke was concerned but there were 'Specialists' she needed to see today.

They had decided it would be better for Ron to go back to Folkestone because of May's reaction to seeing him, while Kathleen stayed with Des and Frank with a view to them seeing May the next day. If they were allowed to. If she would agree to see Kathleen. So arrangements needed to be made for looking after Annie perhaps for several days, while they saw how May responded to treatment for the stroke – and to Kathleen.

They decided that Anne and Terry's mother would be able to manage that between them as Anne, Ron and Terry all had work commitments they could not altogether miss. Kathleen and Des talked of what had happened in years past and both understood things a lot better at the end

The next morning the hospital said that May had seen the 'Specialist' (without saying what the Specialism was), that she 'had had a quiet night' and agreed that Des and Kathleen should visit but not till the afternoon.

They found May was lying on her back staring at the ceiling when they walked into her private room having spoken to the Doctor again.

"Hello Mum," Kathleen said smiling as soon as she saw May was awake. "How are you feeling?"

May turned her head away from her to stare at the window. Kathleen went to sit on that side of the bed so that May would be looking at her. May turned her head to face the other way to see Des sitting on that side. So she closed her eyes.

As she sat down Kathleen took May's hand that was lying on the coverlet. May did not resist. Nor respond.

"You know Mum, I need to say to you how really and truly sorry I am for the way I've treated you for all these years."

"What!" May's head switched around for her to stare at Kathleen.

"When I look back over all the years, ever since I came back from Wales in fact, I think I've treated you terribly. I realise that now and I'm so, so sorry."

"But Kitty, you so wanted to go back there! To be safe. And I wouldn't let you. And what I said to your father what I'd do if he tried to get you back to Wales. And then that raid at Christmas and I still wouldn't let you go. That should have been a warning to me. And then – and then the school happened." Tears were now running down May's cheeks. "And you were – are – so terribly injured. And I couldn't let you know how totally devastated I was. How guilt-ridden Kitty, because my mother had told me that the right way to bring up children was to never, ever let them see how upset you really were. Not over anything. Because that would only make the children still more upset, she told me.

"But she was wrong! She was **so** wrong Kitty. I should have told you how upset I was. Let you **see** it. I was so upset over everything that had happened. Which was all my fault. Kitty it's not you that should say sorry. It's me. And I am. Kitty, I truly am so sorry. Can you ever forgive me?"

"Of course I do Mum. We'll forgive each other."

Kathleen's tears mingled with May's as they hugged each other.

Much later after Doctors had been in to check May's condition and were pleased, while they were drinking the tea Des had brought them, Kathleen said, "Mum, there's something I'd like to ask you."

"What's that?" a trifle warily.

"I'm pregnant again. If it's another girl, can we name her 'May'? After you?

# When the bombs begin to fall
## The Jackson Story – Part 1

In 1939 like many other families in Britain, the Jacksons in London had to decide whether to evacuate their children to safer areas. It was expected that German saturation bombing would devastate the cities immediately war was declared.

Ron and May decide their two eldest children, Kitty (10 yrs.) and Tim (5 yrs.) would be Evacuated while Frank (3 mos.) and May would stay in London with Ron, a Driver for NAAFI, so is in a Reserved Occupation. May agrees mainly because she has a Premonition that 'something terrible' will happen to Kitty and Tim if they remain in London. Ron becomes a Warden.

Kitty is very happy with the foster-parents she has in both Folkestone and Wales, but Tim is not in Wales. May becomes very jealous of Kitty's close relationships with the Davies's in Wales and after a letter from them regarding Kitty's possible future she determines to bring Kitty home to London at the first opportunity. An upsurge in the bombing of London stops her – temporarily but using an excuse brings Kitty back to London in March 1942, then Tim in the September. Ignoring her Premonition. For many reasons Kitty is extremely resentful, Tim very glad.

Four months later the school they are attending is bombed at lunchtime and both children are severely injured. Kitty blames May totally for her now being injured.

Ron and Kitty's first foster-mother (Miss Carruthers) have become lovers and eventually formulated plans that would have have taken Ron and Kitty to Folkestone but these were abandoned after the school was bombed and May needed Ron.

But totally unexpectedly, some information provokes a crisis and transforms the situation.

# Enemies and Allies
## The Jackson story – Part 2

The saga continues from where 'When the bombs begin to fall' ends with Ron Jackson moving in with Anne Carruthers.

He develops the Transport Section.

Suddenly worried about Kathleen still being in London he finds Anne's contacts most helpful to bring her quickly to a Folkestone Hospital.

Conflict between May and Ron continues as May moves in with Des, officially at first as 'Housekeeper'.

As World War 2 ends Ron sees an opportunity to buy surplus bombers to use as cargo aircraft. This gets a boost as the Berlin Crisis of 1948 begins, culminating in the Berlin Airlift – which could begin war with Russia.

Unexpectedly Tim decides that a job on the airfield is much more interesting than either of the jobs suggested by Des, now his Step-father. Des confronts Ron as Tim is packing to move to Folkestone – and then talking to others as well learns things about May and Ron that he had not known before.